RULES OF DECEPTION

RULES OF DECEPTION

Christopher Reich

RANDOM HOUSE
LARGE PRINT

Copyright © 2008 by Christopher Reich

Published in the United States of America by Random House Large Print in association with Doubleday, New York. Distributed by Random House, Inc., New York.

ISBN 978-0-7393-2794-4

The Library of Congress has cataloged the hardback edition as
Reich, Christopher.
    Rules of deception / Christopher Reich.—1st ed.
        p. cm.
    1. Physicians—Fiction. 2. Wives—Crimes against—Fiction.
    3. Terrorism—Fiction. 4. Switzerland—Fiction. I. Title.
    PS3568.E476284R85 2008
    813'.54—dc22   2007036368

www.randomhouse.com/largeprint

10 9 8 7 6 5 4 3 2

This Large Print edition published in accord with the standards of the N.A.V.H.

Cover design by Will Staehle
Cover Illustration by Peter Crowther Associates /
www.debutart.com

To my daughters, Noelle and Katja, who give me joy

RULES
OF DECEPTION

PROLOGUE

The cold breeze swept across the plain, carrying the butterfly on its drafts. The remarkable insect flitted about, climbing, diving, arcing high and low. It was a beautiful specimen, its wings colored a vivid yellow with a latticework of black, and unlike any in the region. It had an unusual name, too: **Papilio panoptes.**

The butterfly flew over the custodial road, over the electrified security fence, and over the rolls of barbed wire. Beyond the fence lay a field of wildflowers, stunning in their variety and color. There were no structures anywhere to be seen: no houses, no barns, no buildings of any type. Only the mounds of freshly impacted soil, barely distinguishable beneath the flower canopy, gave evidence of the recently completed work.

Despite its long voyage, the butterfly ignored the

flowers. It did not seek their richly scented pollen or feast on their sweet nectar. Instead, it chose to fly higher, seeming to gain its sustenance from the air itself.

And there it stayed, a shimmering yellow flag against the pale winter sky. It did not land on a lavender bush to rest. It did not drink from any of the rushing streams that descended from the harsh, majestic mountains and ran across the fertile grasslands. In fact, never once did it venture outside the fence's precisely established one-square-kilometer perimeter. Content to hover over the colorful fields, it flew back and forth, day after day, night after night, never eating, never drinking, never resting.

After seven days, a fierce wind, the **nashi,** visited from the north. The wind roared down the mountain passes and hurtled across the plains, gathering velocity and force and pummeling everything in its path. The butterfly could not fight the relentless drafts. Its circuits inside the perimeter had left it worn and vulnerable. A swirling gust picked it up, spun it round, and dashed it to the ground, shattering its fragile body.

A guard patrolling the custodial road caught the flash of yellow lying in the dirt and stopped his jeep. He approached cautiously, kneeling in the ankle-deep grass. It was not like any butterfly he had seen before. First of all, it was larger. Its wings were rigid, with jagged bits of a paper-thin metal protruding from the silken skin. The fuzzy thorax was split in two and connected by a green wire. Mystified, he picked it up and examined it. Like all those who worked at the facility, he was first and foremost an engineer, and only reluctantly a soldier. What he saw left him shaken.

Inside the thorax was an aluminum-cased battery no bigger than a grain of rice, and attached to it, a microwave transmitter. Using his thumbnail, he sheared away the antennae's skin to reveal a cluster of fiber-optic cables, thin as human hair.

No, he argued to himself. It could not be. Not so soon.

Suddenly, he was running back to the jeep. Words tore through his mind. Explanations. Theories. None made sense. An exposed stone caught his foot and he crashed to the ground. Clambering to his feet, he hurried toward the jeep. Every minute was vital.

His hand shook as he radioed his superiors.

"They have found us."

1

Jonathan Ransom knocked the ice from his goggles and stared up at the sky. If this gets any worse, he thought to himself, we're going to be in trouble. The snow was falling harder. A snarling wind snapped ice and grit against his cheek. The craggy, familiar peaks that ringed the high alpine valley had disappeared behind an armada of threatening clouds.

He lifted one ski, then the next, leaning forward as he climbed the slope. Nylon sealskins attached to the underside of his skis gripped the snow. Touring bindings granted him a walking stride. He was a tall man, thirty-seven years old, slim at the waist and broad-shouldered. A snug woolen cap hid a thatch of prematurely graying hair. Glacier goggles shielded wine black eyes. Only a determined mouth and cheeks rough with a two-day stubble were visible. He wore his old ski patrolman's jacket. He never climbed without it.

Below him, his wife, Emma, clad in a red parka and black pants, labored up the mountainside. Her pace was erratic. She climbed three steps, then rested. Two steps, then rested. They'd only just passed the halfway point and already she looked done in.

Jonathan turned his skis perpendicular to the hill and rammed his poles into the snow. "Stay put," he shouted through cupped hands. He waited for an acknowledgment, but his wife hadn't heard him over the howling wind. Head lowered, she continued her unsteady ascent.

Jonathan sidestepped his way down the slope. It was steep and narrow, bordered on one side by a sheer rock face and on the other by a plunging ravine. Far below, perched on a sweeping hillside, the village of Arosa in the eastern Swiss canton of Graubünden was intermittently visible, winking from beneath the strata of fast-moving clouds.

"Was it always this hard?" Emma asked when he reached her side.

"Last time you beat me to the top."

"Last time was eight years ago. I'm getting old."

"Yeah, thirty-two. A regular dinosaur. Just wait till you're my age, then it's really all downhill." He dug into his daypack for a bottle of water and handed it to her. "How are you feeling?"

"Half dead," she said, hunching over her poles. "Time to call the Sherpas."

"Wrong country. Here they have gnomes. They're smarter, but not half as strong. We're on our own."

"Sure about that?"

Jonathan nodded. "You're just overheating. Take your cap off for a minute and drink as much as you can."

"Yes, Doctor. Right away." Emma removed her woolen cap and drank thirstily from the bottle.

In his mind, Jonathan had a picture of her on the same mountain eight years earlier. It was their first climb together. He, the newly minted surgeon fresh from his first posting in Africa with Doctors Without Borders; she, the willful English nurse he'd brought back as his bride. Before they started out, he'd asked her if she'd climbed much before. "A little," she'd answered. "Nothing too serious." In short order, she'd clobbered him to the top, showing off the skills of an expert alpinist.

"That's better," said Emma, running a hand through her untamed auburn hair.

"You sure?"

Emma smiled, but her hazel eyes were rimmed with fatigue. "I'm sorry," she said.

"For what?"

"For not being as fit as I should be. For slowing us down. For not coming with you these last few years."

"Don't be silly. I'm just glad you're here."

Emma lifted her face and kissed him. "Me, too."

"Look," he said more seriously. "It's getting ugly out here. I'm thinking maybe we ought to turn back."

Emma tossed the bottle to him. "No way, buster. I beat you up this hill once. Watch me do it again."

"You willing to put money on that?"

"Something better."

"Oh yeah?" Jonathan took a drink, thinking that it was good to hear her talking trash again. How long had it been? Six months? A year even, since the headaches had begun and Emma had taken to disappearing into dark rooms for hours at a time. He wasn't sure of the date. Only that it was before Paris, and Paris had been back in July.

Pulling back his sleeve, he ran through the functions on his Suunto wristwatch. Altitude: 9,200 feet. Temperature: −10° Celsius. Barometer: 900 millibars and falling. He stared at the numbers, not quite believing his eyes. The pressure was dropping through the floor.

"What is it?" Emma asked.

Jonathan stuffed the water bottle into his rucksack. "The storm's going to get worse before it gets better. We need to make tracks. You sure you don't want to go back?"

Emma shook her head. No pride this time. Just resolve.

"Alright then," he said. "You lead. I'll be on your tail. Give me a second to adjust my bindings."

Kneeling, Jonathan watched as a track of snow tumbled over the tips of his skis. In seconds, the skis were covered. The tips began to quiver and he forgot all about the bindings.

Warily, he rose. Above his shoulder, the Furga **Nordwand,** a wall of rock and ice, shot a thousand feet to a craggy limestone summit. Prevailing winds had piled loose snow against the base of the wall, forming a high, broad embankment that appeared choked and unstable. "Loaded," in the mountaineer's parlance.

Jonathan's throat went dry. He was an experienced mountaineer. He'd climbed in the Alps, the Rockies, and even for a season, the Himalayas. He'd had his share of scrapes. He'd come through when others hadn't. He knew when to be worried.

"Do you feel it?" he asked. "It's getting ready to rip."

"Did you hear something?"

"No. Not yet. But . . ."

Somewhere out there . . . somewhere above them . . . the sound of distant thunder rolled across the peaks. The mountain shuddered. He thought of the snow on the Furga. Days of unremitting cold had frozen it into a mammoth slab weighing thousands of tons. It wasn't thunder he heard, but the noise of the slab cracking and breaking free from the older, crustier snow beneath it.

Jonathan stared up at the mountain. He'd been caught in an avalanche once before. For eleven minutes he'd lain beneath the surface, entombed in darkness, unable to move a hand, even a finger, too cold to feel that his leg had been yanked out of its socket and twisted backward so his knee was inches from his ear. In the end, he'd survived because a friend had seen the cross on his patrolman's jacket a moment before he'd been swept under.

Ten seconds passed. The rumbling died. The wind slackened and an eerie quiet reigned. Without a word, he unwound the rope coiled round his midsection and fastened an end around Emma's waist. Retreat was no longer an option. They needed to get out of the path of the coming avalanche. Using hand signals, he motioned that they would be taking a path directly up the face and that she was to follow closely. "Okay?" he signaled.

"Okay," came the reply.

Pointing his skis up the hill, Jonathan set out. The face rose steeply, following the flank of the mountain. He kept a demanding pace. Every few steps he glanced over his shoulder to find Emma where she should be, no more than five paces behind. The wind picked up and shifted to the east. Snow attacked in horizontal slats, clawing at the folds of their clothing. He lost all feeling in his toes. His fingers grew numb and wooden. Visibility dwindled from twenty feet to ten, and then he couldn't see beyond the tip of his nose. Only the burn in his thighs told him that he was moving uphill and away from the ravine.

He crested the ridge an hour later. Exhausted, he anchored his skis and helped pull Emma up the final few feet. Lifting her skis over the edge, she collapsed in his arms. Her gasps came in spasmodic gulps.

He held her close until she found her breath and was able to stand on her own.

Here, in the saddle of two peaks, the wind pummeled them with the fury of a jet engine. The sky, however, had partially cleared, and Jonathan was granted a fleeting view down the valley that led to the village of Frauenkirch, and beyond it, Davos.

He skied to the far side of the ridge and looked over the cornice. Twenty feet below, a chute of snow plummeted like an elevator shaft between outcroppings of rock. "This is Roman's. If we can get down here, we'll be okay."

Roman's was part of the local lore, named for a guide killed by an avalanche while skiing down it. Emma's eyes opened wide. She looked at Jonathan and shook her head. "Too steep."

"We've done harder."

"No, Jonathan . . . look at the drop. Isn't there another way?"

"Not today."

"But . . ."

"Em, we get off this ridge or we freeze to death."

She moved closer to the lip, craning her neck to get a good look at what lay below. She pushed back, her chin resting on her chest. "What the hell?" she said, not half meaning it. "We're here. Let's do it."

"Just a little drop, a quick turn, and it's all cake. Like I said, we've done harder."

Emma nodded, more certainly now. And for a

moment she gave the illusion that nothing was out of order, that they weren't flirting with frostbite, and that she'd been looking forward to testing herself against this near-suicidal chute all along.

"Okay then." Jonathan removed his skis and peeled off the skins. Gripping one ski like an ax, he cut a three-foot-square slab of snow and dropped it over the edge. The slab struck the incline and tumbled down the mountain. Here and there, trails of snow dribbled lazily, but the slope held firm.

"Follow me down," he said. "I'll mark the trail."

Emma came alongside him, the tips of her skis dangling over the cornice.

"Get back," he said, hurrying to put on his skis. She had the look. He didn't even need to see her to know it. He could sense it. "Let me go first."

"Can't let you do all the heavy lifting."

"Don't even think about it!"

"Last one down, remember?"

"Hey . . . no!"

Emma pushed off, hung for a moment, then dropped to the slope, skis striking the ice with a sizzle. She landed awkwardly and traversed the chute at lightning speed, her downhill ski slightly askew, pressed hard against the snow. Her hands were too high; her body too far over her skis. Her entire figure looked ungoverned, out of control. Jonathan's eyes shot to the rocks bordering the chute. **Turn!** a voice shouted inside him.

Ten feet separated her from the rocks. Five. The

next instant, she executed a perfect jump turn and reversed her direction.

Jonathan relaxed.

Emma raced across the chute and made another flawless turn. Her hands dropped to her side. Her knees flexed to absorb any hidden bumps. All signs of fatigue had vanished.

He raised a fist in triumph. She had done it. In thirty minutes, they would be seated in a booth at the Staffelalp restaurant in Frauenkirch, two steaming **cafés Lutz** in front of them, laughing about the day and pretending that they'd never been in any danger. Not really. Later, they would go to the hotel, fall into bed, and . . .

Emma fell making the third turn.

Either she caught an edge or she turned a half second too late and nicked her skis against the rocks. Jonathan's stomach clenched. Horrified, he watched as she carved a scar down the center of the chute. Her hands clawed at the snow, but the incline was too steep. Too icy. Faster she went. And faster still. Striking a bump, her body was flung into the air like a rag doll. She landed with one leg twisted beneath her. There was an explosion of snow. Her skis shot into the air as if launched from a cannon. She began to starfish, arms and legs akimbo, cartwheeling head over heel.

"Emma!" he cried out, launching himself down the chute. He skied with abandon, arms flung wide for balance, his body taut, attacking the hill. A veil of mist crossed the slope, and for a moment, he was lost in white, visibility nil, with no idea which way was up or down. He straightened his skis and shot through the cloud.

Emma lay far down the slope. She had come to rest on her stomach, head below her feet, face dug into the snow. He stopped ten feet away from her. Stepping clear of his skis, he took high, bowlegged strides through the powder, his eyes hunting for a flicker of movement. "Emma," he said firmly. "Can you hear me?"

Slinging off his daypack, he fell to his knees and cleared the snow from her mouth and nose. Placing a hand on her back, he felt her chest rise and fall. Her pulse was strong and steady. Inside his pack was a nylon mesh bag holding a spare cap, mittens, goggles, and a Capilene shirt. He folded the shirt and placed it under her cheek.

Just then, Emma stirred. "Oh, shit," she murmured.

"Stay still," he commanded in his emergency room voice. He ran a hand along her pants, starting at the thigh and working down. Suddenly, her face contorted in agony. "No . . . stop!" she cried.

Jonathan pulled his hands away. A few inches above the knee, something pressed sharply against the fabric of her pants. He stared at the grotesque bulge. There was only one thing that looked like that.

"It's broken, isn't it?" Emma's eyes were wide, blinking rapidly. "I can't wiggle my toes. It feels like a bunch of loose wires down there. It hurts, Jonathan. I mean the real thing."

"Keep calm, and let me take a look."

Using his Swiss Army knife, he cut a slit in her ski pants and gingerly separated the fabric. Splintered bone protruded from her thermal underwear. The material around it was wet with blood. She'd suffered a compound fracture of the femur.

"How bad is it, really?" Emma asked.

"Bad enough," he said, as if it were only a hairline fracture. He shook out five Advil and helped her take a sip of water. Then, using adhesive tape from the first aid kit, he secured the tear in her ski pants. "We need to get you on your back and facing downhill. Okay?"

Emma nodded.

"First, I'm going to splint your leg. I don't want that bone moving anywhere. For now, just stay still."

"Christ, Jonathan, does it look like I'm going to walk anywhere?"

Jonathan walked up the slope to retrieve her skis and ski poles. Placing one pole on either side of the leg, he cut a length of climbing rope, tied off one end, and wrapped it round and round the thigh and calf. Kneeling by her side, he handed her his leather wallet. "Here."

Emma clamped it between her teeth.

Jonathan slowly tightened the rope until the poles embraced the broken limb. Emma sucked in a breath. He tied off the other end of the rope, then turned her on her back and rotated her body so her head lay above her feet. After that, he spent a minute fashioning a hill behind her back so she could sit up. "Better?" he asked.

Emma grimaced as a tear sped down her cheek.

He touched her shoulder. "Alright, let's get some help up here." He took the two-way radio from his jacket. "Davos Rescue," he said, turning out of the wind. "I need to report an emergency. Skier injured on the south side of the Furga at the base of Roman's. Over."

Silence greeted his call.

"Davos Rescue," he repeated. "I have an emergency requiring immediate assistance. Come back."

A blizzard of white noise answered. He tried again. Again, there was no response.

"It's the weather," said Emma. "Go to another channel."

Jonathan flipped to the next channel. Years ago, he'd worked as an instructor and ski patrolman in the Alps, and he'd programmed the radio with the frequencies of every emergency rescue service in the area—Davos, Arosa, and Lenzerheide—as well as the Kantonspolizei, the Swiss Alpine Club, and Rega, the helicopter rescue outfit known to skiers and climbers as the meat wagon.

"Arosa Rescue. Skier injured on the south side of the Furga. Immediate assistance required."

Again, there was no response. He brought the radio closer. The power light flickered weakly. He banged the radio against his leg. The light blinked and went dark. "It's dead."

"Dead? The radio? How's that? I saw you try it last night."

"It was fine then." Jonathan clicked the instrument on and off several times, but it refused to come to life.

"Is it the batteries?"

"I don't see how. I put in a fresh set yesterday." Removing his mittens, he examined the inside of the set. "Not the batteries," he said. "The wiring. The power unit's not attached to the transmitter."

"Attach it."

"I can't. Not here. I'm not sure I could even if I had the tools." He tossed the two-way radio into his bag.

"What about the phone?" Emma asked.

"What about it? It's a big-time dead zone up here."

"Try it," she commanded.

The signal icon on Jonathan's cell phone showed a parabolic antenna cut through with a solid line. He dialed the number for Rega anyway. The call failed. "Nothing. It's a black hole."

Emma stared at him a moment and he could see that she was working hard to keep it together. "But we've **got** to talk to someone."

"There's no one to talk to."

"Try the radio again."

"What for? I told you, it's broken."

"Just do it!"

Jonathan kneeled beside her. "Look, everything's going to be okay," he said in as calm a voice as he could muster. "I'm going to ski down and bring back help. As long as you have your avalanche transmitter, I won't have any problem finding you."

"You can't leave me here. You'll never find your way back, even with the beacon. You can't see twenty feet in any direction. I'll freeze. We can't . . . **I can't** . . ." Her words trailed off. She dropped her head onto the snow and turned her face so he wouldn't see that she was crying. "I almost had it, you know . . . that last turn . . . I just was a little late . . ."

"Listen to me. You're going to be fine."

Emma looked up at him. "Am I?"

Jonathan brushed the tears from her cheek. "I promise," he said.

Reaching into his rucksack, he found a thermos and poured his wife a cup of hot tea. While she drank, he gathered her skis and placed them in the snow behind her, forming an X so he could spot them from a distance. He removed his patrolman's parka and laid it over her chest. He took off his cap and placed it over Emma's, pulling it down so that it covered her neck. Finally, he fished the space blanket from the rucksack and gingerly slid it beneath her back and around her chest. The word "HELP" was spelled across it in large fluorescent orange letters, meant to aid in cases of air evacuation. But there would be no helicopter flying in today.

"Pour yourself some tea every fifteen minutes," he

said, taking her hand. "Keep eating and above all, don't fall asleep."

Emma nodded, her hand gripping his like a vise.

"Remember the tea," he went on. "Every fifteen—"

"Shut up and get out of here," she said. She gave his hand a last squeeze and released it. "Leave before you scare me to death."

"I'll be back as quickly as I can."

Emma held his eyes. "And, Jonathan . . . don't look so unsure of yourself. You've never broken a promise yet."

2

Three hundred kilometers to the west of Davos, at Bern-Belp airport outside the nation's capital, snow had been falling since morning. Menacing Arctic CAT snowplows rumbled up and down the runways, making mountains out of the gathered snow, ugly parodies of the Alps, and depositing them at the head of the taxiway.

At the west end of runway one-four, a cluster of men stood huddled together, eyes trained to the sky. They were policemen waiting for a plane to land. They had come to make an arrest.

One man stood slightly apart from the others. Marcus von Daniken was fifty, a short, hawkish man with black hair shorn to a grenadier's stubble and a grim, downturned mouth. For the past six years, he'd headed up the Service for Analysis and Prevention, better known as SAP. It was SAP's job to safeguard the country's domestic security against extremists, terrorists, and spies. The same role was performed in the United States by the FBI and in the United Kingdom by MI5. At that moment, von Daniken was shivering. He hoped the plane would land soon.

"How are conditions holding?" he asked the man next to him, a major from the Border Guard.

"Another ten minutes and they're closing down the field. Visibility's for shit."

"What's the plane's status?"

"One engine down," the major said. "The other's overheating. The aircraft just turned onto final approach."

Von Daniken searched the sky. Low above the runway a set of yellow landing lights blinked in and out of the mist. Moments later, the plane dropped out of the clouds and into view. The aircraft was a Gulfstream IV flying out of Stockholm, Sweden. Its tail number, N415GB, was known to the intelligence agencies of every Western nation. The same aircraft had transported Abu Omar, the radical Muslim cleric spirited off the streets of Milan, in February 2003, from Italy to Germany, and finally to Egypt, to undergo interrogation at the hands of his countrymen.

It had also carried a German citizen of Lebanese descent, one Khaled El-Masri, arrested in Macedonia, to the "Salt Pit" prison at Bagram Air Force Base, outside Kabul, Afghanistan, where it was eventually discovered that he was not, in fact, the same Khaled El-Masri who was sought in connection with terrorist activities.

One success. One failure. It was the going rate these days, thought von Daniken. The important thing was that you stayed at the table and kept playing.

The aircraft hit the tarmac hard. Ice and water sprayed from its tires. The engine roared as its bafflers moved into place.

"Smug bastards," said a thin, nearly gaunt man with longish red hair and a professor's round spectacles. "I can't wait to see their faces. It's about time that we taught them a lesson." His name was Alphons Marti, and he was Switzerland's minister of justice.

Marti had represented Switzerland as a marathoner in the Seoul Olympics in 1988. He'd come into the stadium dead last, legs rubbery from the heat, bobbing and weaving like a drunk on a three-day bender. The emergency medical personnel had tried to stop him, but somehow he'd pushed them away. One step past the finish line, he collapsed and was immediately transported to the hospital. To this day, there were those who viewed him as a hero. Others had a different view, and whispered about an amateur masquerading as a professional.

"No mistakes now," Marti continued, gripping von Daniken's arm. "Our reputation is on the line. Switzerland does not permit this kind of thing. We are a neutral country. It's time that we take a stand and prove it. Don't you agree?"

Von Daniken was old enough and wise enough not to answer. He brought the radio to his mouth. "No one hit their lights until I give the order," he said.

One hundred feet away, hidden behind a checkered barrier, a minor fleet of police vehicles waited for the signal to move in. Von Daniken glanced to his left. Another barricade concealed an armored personnel carrier holding ten heavily armed border guards. He had argued against a show of force, but Marti would have none of it. The justice minister had waited a long time for this day.

"Pilot has requested to deplane," said the major from the Border Guard. "The tower is directing him to the customs ramp."

Von Daniken and Marti climbed into an unmarked sedan and drove to the designated parking spot. The others followed in a second vehicle. The Gulfstream veered off the runway and approached the customs ramp. Von Daniken waited until the plane had come to a complete halt. "All units. Go."

Blue and white strobes lit the slate sky. The police cruisers sped from their hiding places and surrounded the plane. The personnel carrier lumbered into position, a soldier bringing the .50-caliber turret gun to bear. Commandos in assault gear spilled out of the vehicles and formed a semicircle around the plane, submachine guns raised to their chests and aimed at the doorway.

All this circus because of a simple telefax, thought

von Daniken, as he climbed out of the sedan and checked his pistol to ensure that there was no bullet in the chamber and that the safety was in the on position.

Three hours earlier, Onyx, Switzerland's proprietary satellite eavesdropping system, had intercepted a telefax sent from the Syrian embassy in Stockholm to its counterpart in Damascus giving the passenger manifest of a certain aircraft bound for the Middle East. Four persons were aboard: the pilot, the copilot, and two passengers. One an agent of the United States government, the other a terrorist wanted by the law enforcement authorities of twelve Western nations. The news was passed up the chain of command within minutes of receipt. One copy was e-mailed to von Daniken, another to Marti.

And there it stopped. One more piece of intelligence to be digested and graded "No Further Action." Until, that is, the flight in question radioed Swiss air traffic control reporting an engine malfunction and requesting emergency clearance to land.

The jet's forward door swung outward and a stairwell unbuckled from the fuselage. Marti hurried up the steps, with von Daniken behind him. The pilot appeared in the doorway. The Justizminister produced a warrant and offered it for examination. "We have information indicating that you are transporting a prisoner in contravention of the Geneva Convention on Human Rights."

The pilot barely glanced at the legal document.

"You're mistaken," he said. "We haven't got a soul on board besides my copilot and Mr. Palumbo."

"No mistake," said Marti, shouldering past the pilot and entering the aircraft. "Swiss soil will not be used for the practice of extraordinary rendition. Chief Inspector von Daniken, search the plane."

Von Daniken walked down the aisle of the aircraft. A lone passenger was seated in one of the broad leather seats. A white male, about forty years old, head shaved, with a bull's shoulders and cold gray eyes. At first glance, he looked like an experienced man, someone who could handle himself. From his window, he had a clear view of the storm troopers surrounding the plane. He didn't appear unduly concerned.

"Good afternoon," said von Daniken, in good but accented English. "You are Mr. Palumbo?"

"And you are?"

Von Daniken introduced himself and offered his identification. "We have reason to suspect you are transporting a prisoner named Walid Gassan aboard this flight. Am I correct?"

"No, sir, you are not." Palumbo crossed his legs and von Daniken noted that he was wearing boots with a sturdy toecap.

"You don't mind, then, if we search the aircraft?"

"This is Swiss soil. You can do what you please."

Von Daniken directed the passenger to stay in his seat until the search was completed, then he continued to the rear of the plane. Plates and glasses were stacked in the galley sink. He counted four settings.

Pilot. Copilot. Palumbo. Someone was missing. He checked the lavatory, then opened the aft hatch and inspected the baggage hold.

"No one," he radioed to Marti. "The passenger compartment and cargo area are clear."

"What do you mean 'clear'?" demanded Marti. "That can't be."

"Unless they have him stuffed inside a suitcase, he's not aboard the plane."

"Keep looking."

Von Daniken made a second circuit through the cargo area, testing for hollow compartments. Finding nothing, he closed the aft door and returned to the passenger compartment.

"You've checked the entire plane?" asked Marti, standing with his arms crossed next to the captain.

"Top to bottom. There are no other passengers aboard besides Mr. Palumbo."

"Impossible." Marti shot an accusing glance at von Daniken. "We have proof that the prisoner is on board."

"And what proof is that?" asked Palumbo.

"Don't play games with me," said Marti. "We know who you are, who you work for."

"You do, do you? Then I guess I can go ahead and tell you."

"Tell us what?" demanded Marti.

"The guy you're looking for . . . we let him off thirty minutes back over those big mountains of yours. He said he'd always wanted to see the Alps."

Marti's eyes widened. "You didn't?"

"Might have been what jammed up the engine. Either that or a goose." Palumbo looked out his window, shaking his head in amusement.

Von Daniken pulled Marti aside. "It appears that our information was incorrect, Herr Justizminister. There's no prisoner aboard."

Marti stared back, white with anger. A current passed through him, rattling his shoulders. With a nod to the passenger, he left the aircraft.

A lone commando remained at the door. Von Daniken waved him off. He waited until the soldier had disappeared down the stairs before returning his attention to Palumbo. "I'm sure our mechanics will be able to repair your engine with the shortest possible delay. In case the weather continues and the airport remains closed, you'll find the Hotel Rossli just down the road to be quite comfortable. Please accept our apologies for any inconvenience."

"Apology accepted," said Palumbo.

"Oh, and by the way," said von Daniken. "I happened to find this on the floor." Leaning closer, he dropped something small and hard into the CIA officer's hand. "I trust you'll pass along any information that concerns us."

Palumbo waited until von Daniken had left the aircraft before opening his hand.

In his palm was a man's torn and bloody thumbnail.

3

"She's gone."

Jonathan stood on the crest of a foothill two hundred meters from the foot of Roman's. The wind howled in fits and spurts, blanketing him in white-out one minute and tapering off the next. Holding a pair of binoculars to his eyes, he was able to spot the crossed skis, the letters "H-E" screaming from the survival blanket, and farther to the left, the orange safety shovel. But he did not see Emma.

Jonathan left the three members of the Davos Rescue Squad and skinned up the final hill. Four hours had passed since he'd left to ski down the mountain for help. Snow buried the crisscrossed skis to the top of the bindings, but only a finger's width dusted her rucksack. He opened it and saw that the sandwiches and energy bars were gone. Her thermos was empty. He dropped the bag at his feet. The imprint where Emma had lain remained faintly visible. She hadn't been gone long.

Jonathan activated the avalanche beacon strapped to his chest and turned in a circle searching all points of the compass. The beacon contained a homing device with an effective range of one hundred meters, some three hundred thirty feet. The instrument emitted a long beep—a test function—then was silent. The **whomp whomp** of snow settling, distant as Indian war drums, drifted across the mountainside.

"Do you have a signal?" asked Sepp Steiner, chief of the rescue team, when he reached his side. Steiner was a short, spare man with hollow cheeks and gun slits for eyes.

"Nothing."

It was then that he saw it: a crimson petal lying in the snow. Jonathan bent down to touch the drop of blood. There was another a few inches away, and another farther on. "This way," he said, waving an arm for the others to join him.

"Don't go any farther," cautioned Steiner. "There's a crevasse just ahead a few meters."

"A crevasse?"

"A deep one. It cuts to the bottom of the glacier."

Jonathan squinted, trying to make out the fissure, but saw nothing beyond an impenetrable white wall. "Get me roped up." He removed his skis, then pulled on a seating harness and attached the rope to his waist.

"Be careful," said Steiner, after taking off his skis

and securing Jonathan to his own harness. "We don't want to lose you, too."

Jonathan swung round to face the smaller man. "She isn't lost yet."

At first, the drops were difficult to find, hardly more than pinpricks. Then they grew larger, more closely spaced, until the blood ran in a steady line as if someone had punctured a can of grenadine and poured it into the snow. Except this syrup was colored the oxygen-rich red of arterial blood.

When had Emma passed this way? Jonathan wondered. Five minutes ago. Ten? Bending lower, he discerned where she'd placed her good foot and where she'd dragged the other. Ahead, there was a depression in the snow, and in its center, a gaping hole.

Dropping to his belly, he crawled forward and shined his flashlight into the opening. A gallery of ice and stone beckoned, ten meters across, bottomless. Rolling to one side, he checked the homing beacon. The digital readout flickered and the number 98 appeared. Jonathan's stomach buckled. Ninety-eight meters translated to over three hundred feet.

"Do you have a signal?" asked Steiner. "Is she in there?"

"Yes," said Jonathan, but he refused to elaborate. "I'm going down. On belay."

"Belay on," confirmed Steiner.

Jonathan enlarged the hole with his ax. A chunk of snow fell away and the crevasse yawned beneath him. Dangling his boots into the hole, he shimmied backward until the snow collapsed under his chest. He plunged into darkness, slamming into an ice wall before the rope grew taut and caught him. "I'm in."

Kicking off the wall, he allowed the rope to pay out between his fingers and dropped farther into the chasm. The flashlight revealed a pristine and savage landscape, an ice queen's eternal palace. It was an illusion. The crevasses existed in a state of flux, widening, narrowing, slaves to the constantly churning forces of the underlying rock strata.

Ten meters down, he spotted a patch of black and white on a ledge a stone's throw away. It was Emma's cap. Like a pendulum, he swung back and forth, springing off the ice wall to build his momentum. The third time, he tilted his body perilously close to horizontal, stretched his arm, and grabbed it.

Cap in hand, he steadied himself and directed the flashlight toward the ledge. The snow there was disturbed and violent with blood. Not a trail this time, but a stain as large as a grapefruit. He could no longer lie to himself about what had happened. Emma had tried to walk down the mountain. Her movement had caused the splintered bone to nick the femoral artery. The artery was the principal passageway for blood pumped by the heart to the lower extremities: legs, feet, and toes. As a surgeon, he knew the consequences. Without a tourniquet, she would exsanguinate in minutes. In layman's terms, she'd bleed to death.

He checked the beacon. The readout showed

eighty-nine meters. Just under three hundred feet. The directional indicator pointed down. He shined the beam toward the floor of the crevasse. Oblivion.

"Lower," he said.

"I can give you another twenty-five meters. That's all we've got."

Jonathan glanced up. The gap he'd come through appeared as bright as a tear in the night sky. He waited for the second line to be tied to the first. Steiner gave him a tug and Jonathan recommenced his descent. He paid the line out slowly, stopping every ten feet to swing the light around him, check for obstacles, and search for Emma. The numbers on the beacon grew smaller. Light from the world above disappeared. The ice walls glowed a ghostly blue . . . 70 . . . 68 . . . 64 . . . Suddenly, the rope grew taut.

"That's it," said Steiner.

Jonathan guided the light slowly back and forth, painting the ice below with a pale beam. He caught a flash of red. His patrolman's jacket? He moved the beam a few inches to the left and saw a glint of copper. Emma's hair? His heart jumped. "I need more rope. Another length."

"We have no more."

"Get some," he ordered.

"There's no time. A small avalanche just ripped out the slope behind us. The entire mountain could come down at any moment."

Jonathan directed his gaze along the beam of light.

The patch of red came into focus. He moved the light an inch to the right. It was the cross on his patrolman's jacket. The glint of copper was his wife's hair.

Emma. Her name caught in his throat.

He could see her now, at least her outline. She lay prone on her stomach, one arm extended above her head, as if calling for help. But there was something wrong . . . the ice around her was not white at all, but dark. She was lying in a slick of her own blood.

"She's here," he said stubbornly. "We can reach her."

"She fell one hundred meters," argued Steiner. "She could not have survived. You must come out. I won't risk the lives of four men."

"Emma!" Jonathan shouted. "It's me. It's Jonathan. If you're okay, move your hand."

His wife's form remained still, as his voice echoed inside the chasm.

"Quiet," said Steiner, his anger tight as a fist. "You'll kill us all."

The rope gave a jerk. Jonathan bounced against the wall and rose a few feet. Steiner was hauling him out. Enraged, he dug his toe spikes into the ice, then drew his knife and pressed the blade against the rope, inches from his face. He had crampons. He had an ice ax. He would climb down the wall to her.

He kept his eyes on the body. Already it looked smaller, somehow foreign. He detected no sign of movement. It didn't matter if Steiner was right about the fall, whether it was too far or if there had been any obstructions to slow her descent. There was simply too much blood.

He pulled the knife away from the rope and freed his crampons from the ice. The lifeline jerked again, and he was lifted another meter out of the crevasse. He shone the light at the patch of red he'd seen, but it was no longer visible. He had lost sight of his wife.

"Emma!" he yelled as tears streamed down his cheek.

Only his voice called back, echoing over and over again.

4

The Land Rover hurtled down the Seestrasse on
its way out of Zurich. A lone man sat behind the
wheel. Heavy stubble covered his cheeks. Dark circles cupped his eyes. He had been on the move for
twenty-four hours. He needed a meal, a shower, and
a bed. All that would come. First, he had a job to
complete.

Opening the glove compartment, he withdrew a
silenced pistol and set it on the seat beside him. He
looked out the window at the lake. Whitecaps
flashed in the dark. Far away, the running lights of
a large boat bobbed dangerously. It was not a good
night to be on the water.

At the next signal, he turned and guided the car up
a winding road. Falling snow choked the headlights,
but he did not slow. He knew the route. He had
driven it once already, earlier in the evening. He had

studied maps of the area, committing avenues of access and escape to memory.

A burst of acceleration delivered him to a plateau. Large, well-tended homes lined either side of the street. This eastern side of the Lake of Zurich was known as the Gold Coast, for its dawn-to-dusk sun exposure as well as for its luxurious residences. He cut his speed as soon as he spotted the target's home. Modeled on a French country estate, it was set back from the street on a rise with snow-crusted orchards bordering either side.

Twenty meters farther along, he brought the car to a halt in the shadow of a towering pine. He doused the lights and sat listening to the engine tick down and the wind beat at his windows. From his jacket, he removed a sterling silver case. Four bullets lay inside it. Slender shells with an X carved into the bronze-colored nose. Tapered fingers set them in a row on the center console. Next, he freed the ceramic vial hanging round his neck and unscrewed the cap. He began to chant softly, words from an ancient and forgotten language. By his own tally, he had killed over three hundred men, women, and children. The words formed a prayer to protect his soul against spirits from the next world. Twenty years as an assassin had left him a superstitious man.

One by one, he dipped the bullets into the vial, coating them with a viscous, bitter-scented liquid. It was his ritual. First the prayer, then the liquid. As a professional, he knew there was no such thing as too many precautions. In this world or the next. He blew a single breath on each, then fed them into the clip. *magazine* When he'd finished, he took up the pistol, slid the clip into the butt, and chambered a round. He checked that the safety was on, then removed a sturdy twill bag from his opposite pocket and attached it to a point above the ejection chamber.

He stepped out of the car. Caged eyes darted up and down the street. He saw no one. Tonight the weather was his ally. At nine-thirty, the neighborhood was still.

Buttoning his overcoat, he set off briskly up the road. He was a trim man, no more than average height, with narrow shoulders and lank black hair that fell to his collar. His cheeks were sunken, his nose slender and aristocratic, his complexion so pale as to be cadaverous. From afar, he appeared not to walk so much as to glide above the pavement. It was this combination of his deathly pallor and his ethereal presence that lent him his work name. The Ghost.

Passing the target's home, he was afforded an unobstructed view through a bay window adjacent to the front door. A woman and three children sat side by side on a couch entranced by their evening's television. He slowed long enough to see that the youngest was a boy, dark and pale like himself, arms wrapped around his mother. His heart beat faster. Memories fluttered behind his eyes like a trapped bird beating against a window.

He looked away.

Verifying that no traffic was approaching from either direction, he hopped the single-strand wire fence fronting the meadow and took up position behind a woodpile stacked neatly against the side of the home. There, crouching in the snow, he waited.

At other times, he'd been part of a team, though never its leader. He knew that there should be a rotating two-man squad covering the target at the restaurant; a car to follow him home; and an extraction team waiting to whisk the shooter to the nearest airport or train station and out of the country. All were standard operating procedure.

But he preferred it this way. Alone in the darkness. An agent of death.

From a side pocket he removed a metallic box, activated its toggle switch, then slipped it back again. The box emitted a jamming signal that rendered the garage door opener inactive. The target would be forced to step out of his car to manually open the garage, or perhaps, to enter by a side door and open it from the inside.

In the distance, he made out the velvet growl of a powerful engine. He slipped the silenced pistol from his jacket and focused on the road at the point where the target's car—a late model Audi A8—would crest the hill. Headlights appeared and grew bolder. His thumb nudged the safety downward.

All at once, the car was in view. As it passed under a streetlamp he confirmed the make and license. The car slowed, pulling into the driveway and stopping short of the garage. The driver's door opened. The target stepped out. He was a tall man, solidly built, with ginger hair and well-nourished cheeks. An engineer of some stripe. A family man. A man of rigid discipline.

By now, the Ghost was making his approach. He covered the distance to the target in three effortless strides. The man looked at him, confused. Why wasn't the garage door working? Who was this stranger appearing as if out of thin air? The Ghost saw all this in the man's eyes as he raised his arm and pulled the trigger. Three shots struck the man squarely in the face. The shells flew into the twill bag. The target collapsed to the driveway.

The Ghost leaned over the body. Nuzzling the silencer against the man's chest, he shot him through the heart. The body jumped. It was then that he noticed something peculiar on the man's lapel. A pin of some kind. He bent to take a closer look.

A butterfly.

5

Marcus von Daniken returned to his home a few minutes after eleven o'clock. Beneath his arm, he carried two long-stem roses wrapped in florist's paper. He walked through dark hallways to the kitchen where a single light burned above the table. He set the flowers down, then tossed his gun and his wallet onto the counter. Stifling a yawn, he opened the refrigerator and took out a bottle of beer. There was a ham sandwich on the center island, a plate of potato salad, and a lemon tart. All were neatly wrapped in cellophane. A note from his housekeeper reminded him to put the leftovers back in the refrigerator. Throwing his jacket over the back of a chair, he rolled up his sleeves and washed his hands in the sink. He ate the sandwich, then dutifully returned the potato salad and lemon tart to the fridge, untouched.

Von Daniken lived alone in a hulking chalet in the foothills outside of Bern. The house was too big for a bachelor. It had been his father's and his grandfather's, and so on, all the way back to the nineteenth century. He didn't like living by himself, but he liked the idea of moving less. Over the years, he'd made friends with the echoing corridors, the brooding silences, and the unlit rooms.

Turning back to the table, he unwrapped the florist's paper and removed the roses that lay inside. With care, he trimmed the stems and placed them in a blown glass vase, one of a pair purchased on his honeymoon at the famous factory in Murano. He'd been married once. He'd had a daughter and another on the way. The house wasn't too big then. Still, when he'd first wed, his wife had pleaded with him to sell it. She was an attorney from Geneva, spirited and impetuous, brilliant in her field. She saw the house as a relic, as rigid and hidebound as the society that had built it. He disagreed. They never had a chance to settle the argument.

Von Daniken flipped on the living room light. A photograph of his wife and daughter sat above the fireplace. Two blondes, Marie-France and Stéphanie, taken from him fifteen years ago in an airline disaster. He replaced the day-old roses with fresh ones, then sat down in an old recliner and drank the rest of his beer. He picked up the remote and flicked on the television. Thankfully, there was no mention of the failed arrest that afternoon on the late news. He

changed channels, stopping to watch a French liter-
ary program. He didn't care much for literature,
French or otherwise, but he loved the moderator, a
gorgeous middle-aged brunette. He killed the sound
and stared at her. Perfect. Now he had company.

Television was safer than real life. Over the years,
he'd had plenty of first dates, fewer second ones, and
only two relationships that had lasted longer than six
months. Both women had been attractive, intelli-
gent, and not unaccomplished in bed. Neither, however, had compared to his wife. Once he realized
this, the relationships withered. Phone calls went
unreturned. Dates grew infrequent. More often, they
were canceled at the last minute because of a case. It
didn't take long for either of the women to get the
message. Strangely, the parting had been bitter, and
more painful than he liked to admit.

His cell phone rang. "Yes?"

"Widmer. Zurich Kantonspolizei. We have a situation. A murder in Erlenbach. The Gold Coast. A
professional job."

Von Daniken swung out of the recliner and turned
off the television. "Why me? Sounds like it belongs
to the Criminal Police."

But already he was moving. He walked into the
kitchen and poured the cold beer into the sink. He
attached his holster to his belt, put on his jacket, and
picked up his wallet.

"The victim turned up on ISIS," Widmer explained. "The file was flagged 'Secret' with a note

saying he'd been the subject of an inquiry twenty years back."

"ISIS" stood for the Information System for Internal Security, the Federal Police database that contained files on over fifty thousand individuals suspected of being terrorists, extremists, or members of a foreign intelligence agency, both friendly and not.

"Who's the lucky fellow?" von Daniken asked, scooping up his car keys.

"Name of Lammers. Dutch. Permit C holder. Lived here fifteen years." Widmer paused, and his voice grew taut. "There's something else. Something you might want to see yourself."

"Give me ninety minutes."

Von Daniken needed only eighty-five minutes to make the hundred-ten- kilometer journey. Stepping out of his car, he walked cautiously across the icy sidewalk and ducked beneath the fluttering police tape. An officer from the Kantonspolizei caught a glimpse of von Daniken's face and drew himself to attention. "Good evening, sir."

Von Daniken patted him on the shoulder. "I'm looking for Captain Widmer."

"Up there," said the officer, pointing toward the garage.

Von Daniken made his way up the driveway toward a battery of mobile lights that had been erected around the perimeter of the crime scene. The array of thousand-watt bulbs lit the victim as if he were sunbathing on Plage Tahiti in Saint-Tropez. He looked at the body, then looked away. "Some piece of work," he muttered.

A bald, broad-shouldered man kneeling next to the body glanced up. "Three to the head, one to the chest," said Walter Widmer, head of the Zurich Kantonspolizei capital crimes division. "Small caliber. Dumdums by the mess it made. Whoever did this wasn't taking any chances."

"Still think it was a hit?"

"No shells. No witnesses." Widmer stood, frowning. "We're guessing that the shooter electronically jammed the garage door to make sure Lammers had to get out of the car. You tell me."

Von Daniken hurried back to the street. The sight of the victim's ruined physiognomy would be with him for days.

Marcus von Daniken was not a homicide cop. In fact, he had little experience with violent crime. He had come up the other way. After four years as an infantry officer, he had joined the Federal Police's financial crimes division. It was a slow climb. Years as an investigator in the field looking into fraud, counterfeiting, and money laundering—the holy trinity of Swiss banking. Then, ten years back, he caught his big break: a slot as Fedpol's representative on the Swiss Task Force on Nazi Victims' Assets.

Working alongside directors of his country's

largest banks, diplomats from a dozen nations, and representatives of too many aggrieved organizations to name, he had been instrumental in fashioning a solution that was acceptable to all interested parties: the Swiss government, the Swiss banks, the World Jewish Congress, the White House, the German government, and lastly, the wronged parties themselves. His reward was a posting to the Service for Analysis and Prevention, regarded as the elite division of the Federal Police.

"What about the wife?" he asked, pointing to the picture window that overlooked the garage. "Did she see anything?"

Widmer shook his head. "She's a tough one. Moluccan by birth. She says that she and the kids were watching the television when it happened. She saw the car pull up. When she didn't hear the garage door open, she went to look for him. She swears it was only two minutes. I went through the usual questions. Husband have any enemies? Had he received any threats lately? Anything strange happen the last few days? She claims that everything was fine."

"You believe her?"

"I don't believe anybody," said Widmer.

"Maybe Lammers knew the killer? Could that be why he didn't open the garage? A little rendezvous set up in advance?"

"Doubtful. We found some footprints by the

woodpile. I'd hazard a guess and say that the killer hid there while he was waiting. Were you able to pull up anything on the drive over?"

"Only that the Belgian police had him under weekly surveillance in Brussels in 1987. When Lammers moved to Switzerland, they kicked their files over to us. We added him to ISIS as a matter of course. There's more, but it's archived and I can't access it until morning. What I can tell you is that since he moved to Zurich, he's been a law-abiding resident. Pays his taxes. Stays out of trouble. ISIS is packed with people like him. You know . . . not guilty of anything **yet**."

"He was guilty of something. Come inside."

Widmer led the way up the drive and into the house. Inside the foyer, he made a sharp turn and descended a flight of stairs leading to a suite of rooms off the garage. "One of my officers had to use the WC. The mistress of the house told him to go downstairs so he wouldn't drag any dirt into the place. He got disoriented and went into the workshop by accident."

Von Daniken walked past the bathroom, its door open, lights blazing, and continued down the corridor. "I can see how he might be confused."

Widmer flipped on the light in a room at the end of the hall. The workshop was a stainless steel marvel. Stainless steel workbench, stainless steel tool rack, all as shiny as the day it left the factory. But this was no Sunday tinkerer's room. No saws and hammers here. Instead, there was a collection of high-tech instruments that screamed "professional engineer."

On a nearby table lay a freezer bag stuffed with passports.

"What's this?" asked von Daniken.

"My man found it in the top drawer."

"Looking for some toilet paper, was he?"

Widmer sniffed, and raised an eyebrow. Von Daniken had his answer. The officer had engaged in a quick and dirty search of the premises. The evidence was inadmissible, but so what? Lammers wasn't going to be standing trial anytime soon.

"Holland. Belgium. New Zealand." He flipped through the passports one by one. "A regular world traveler. Did your man **happen** to find anything else?"

"Under the cabinet," said Widmer. "It seems that Mr. Lammers was aware that he had some enemies. Oh, and be careful. It's loaded."

Von Daniken kneeled down and stuffed his head into the space beneath the workbench. Clamped to the back wall was an Uzi submachine gun. He felt his pulse quicken. "Try and find out who sold it to him," he said, getting to his feet and scooping up the passports. "I hope you don't mind if I keep these."

"I need a chit," said Widmer.

Von Daniken wrote out a receipt for the passports and ripped it from his notepad. "All square. Now you have something to question Mrs. Lammers about.

Inform her that we will deport her and her three children in twenty-four hours unless she tells us everything she knows about her husband's need for multiple identities. We'll see how closemouthed she is then."

"That's a bit harsh, isn't it?" asked Widmer. "I mean, her husband was the victim."

Von Daniken buttoned his coat and headed out the door. "A victim?" His expression hardened. "Anyone with three passports and a loaded Uzi isn't a victim. He's either a criminal or a spy."

6

Darkness pressed in from all sides. Jonathan blinked. His eyes were open, but the black remained absolute. He tried to raise his head, but found it locked into place. His legs and arms were likewise pinned down. Snow encased his body as if he lay in a concrete bath. He could not lift a hand, not a finger. All the while, a steady voice told him to remain calm. It mused that it was not as cold as he'd expected. But, yes, it was dark. No one had ever mentioned the dark. His breathing grew labored. The air was going fast. He realized that he was buried deep below the surface, and that no one could possibly find him in time. Fear rose from deep inside him, crawling upward through his stomach, gathering speed and strength, gutting his discipline and strangling the calm, reasonable voice. The dark. The pressure. The failing air. He was overcome by a full-throated terror. He opened his mouth to scream and sucked down a torrent of snow and ice.

He bolted upright in bed.

"Emma," he gasped, his hands searching the mattress beside him.

He'd had the dream again. He needed to hear her voice. To feel her hand on his shoulder. He turned on the light. Emma's side of the bed was unbothered. The crisp white duvet remained neatly folded down. A corner of her nightshirt extended from beneath her pillow.

She's gone.

It came over him slowly, like an approaching storm. His breath quickened. His fingertips began to tingle. Something sharp and cold tore into his stomach and forced him to bend double at the waist. He sobbed.

She's gone.

The words played over in his mind as images of her body lying alone and abandoned in the frozen darkness tormented him.

Finally, a measure of calm returned. His breathing slowed. The terror passed, but he knew it wasn't gone for good. He could feel it lurking nearby, waiting.

He stood and walked to the window. Snow continued to fall heavily, and the faint light of dawn cast the low, stately clouds with a funereal hue. The view gave out over rolling hills dotted with chalets. A half mile farther on, a forest climbed the flank of the imposing peaks that cradled the town.

Opening the balcony door, he stepped outside. Cold scrubbed the air clean of scent, and his first breaths burned his throat and lungs. He stood at the railing, studying yesterday's route. His eyes followed the path deep into the mountains, through cloud and mist to the hooded peak of the Furga. And beyond it, to Roman's.

I know this mountain and I didn't do anything to protect you from it.

I know this mountain and I left you alone on it.

I know this mountain and I let it kill you.

When his shivering grew uncontrollable, Jonathan stepped back inside. He was struck by how neat the room appeared. He knew that it was foolish to think it should look different now that she was gone. Yet he couldn't help feeling betrayed by its normalcy, when nothing was normal at all.

He sat down at the desk and opened the drawer. Sunscreen, pocketknife, maps, lip balm, bandana, beacon, and the two-way radio lay scattered inside. He picked up the radio and flicked it on and off. It was dead.

A wire . . . a detached wire.

After coming off the mountain, Jonathan had been taken to the police station where he'd been examined by a doctor, then made to answer a fusillade of questions. Full name: Jonathan Hobart Ransom. Birthplace: Annapolis, Maryland. Occupation: board certified surgeon. Employer: Doctors Without Borders. Nationality: American. Residence: Geneva.

And then the questions about Emma. Birthplace: Penzance, England. Parents: deceased. Siblings: one sister, Beatrice. Occupation: Nurse. Administrator. Human being with an oversized conscience and a "duty to interfere." Wife. Best friend. Anchor.

There were other questions. About his experience as a mountaineer. About how he'd failed to monitor the weather. About Emma's fall and whether or not she was bleeding when he'd left her, and his failure to spot the radio's defect prior to climbing. And finally, about his decision to continue climbing when he'd realized the storm was intensifying.

It wasn't his decision, he wanted to say. It was hers. Emma never turned back.

Setting the unit on the desk, he let his eyes wander to the mountains. Jonathan could trace the beginning of his love affair with climbing to a trip to California the Ransom family had taken when he was nine years old. Their goal was to ascend Mount Whitney, the highest point in the lower forty-eight states. The plan was for his older brothers to set out from Whitney Portal, altitude 8,500 feet, at five in the morning, and make the twenty-two-mile round trip to Whitney's 14,500-foot summit in one day. Jonathan and his father would accompany them the first few miles, then stop to enjoy a picnic lunch and do some fishing until the boys returned.

But even then Jonathan was showing signs of an independent streak. Like all boys who idolize their older brothers, he had no intention of being left behind. His father, who was forty years old and never missed a chance to have a meal with his cocktail, might stop. But not him. And so, when Ned Ransom pulled up after four miles and suggested they break for an early lunch, Jonathan sprinted ahead, defying all calls for him to come back. He didn't stop until he reached the peak almost eight miles later. One hundred yards ahead of his brothers.

The die was cast.

By the time Jonathan was sixteen, all he cared about was climbing. An equivalency test freed him from high school. College wasn't a consideration. Summers were spent guiding up Mount McKinley, winters combing the slopes as a ski patrolman. Every penny saved was put toward the next expedition. He bagged his share of big names: Eiger Nordwand, Aconcagua, K2 by the Magic Line without a lick of bottled oxygen. It was all about the rush. Hanging it out there as far as you dared, then pulling it back at the last second.

It was at this time that he became aware of a flaw in his character. The flaw derived from his almost unnatural strength and his (all too natural) rebellious spirit, and it involved a growing and pronounced inclination for fistfighting. The bars of mountain resorts were as full of braggarts and louses as any others. He was choosy and made it a point to single out the loudest of the bunch. Someone deserving of comeuppance. Someone who looked like they might make a match of it. He would order a shot of bourbon to get his nerves just right. Then it was just a matter of making the proper comments. With any luck, he'd find himself in a back alley within five minutes.

The fights were brutish and short. He was a canny fighter, quick to pick up on an opponent's weaknesses. He would circle for a minute or two, avoiding the sweaty clenches and ungainly wrestling that were the hallmarks of amateur brawls. Then he would move in. A jab to the jaw, a punch to the gut, and a roundhouse to the side of the head. It rarely lasted longer than that. He prided himself on his economy.

He knew that the trait was dangerous and, worse, self-destructive. He also knew that it involved his addiction to risk. He found himself challenging bigger men, venturing into openly dangerous establishments. He began to lose, but even then he was unable to cure himself of this flaw. During his climbs, he sought out uncharted routes. He hungered for the impossible face. He yearned to go higher, farther, and faster.

Then one day, it went away. The fighting. The desire to master a stretch of vertical granite. The need to endanger his life to feel alive. Gone like that. He hung up his gear and decided that that part of his life was finished.

People whispered that it was because of the avalanche. They said he'd lost his nerve. They were wrong. He hadn't quit. He'd just found a bigger rush. And it was on a concrete highway, not on a vertical face.

He was twenty-one. It was a Sunday night and he

was coming back to Aspen after a weekend doing free ascents up Angels Landing, a two-thousand-foot slab of red rock in Zion National Park. As usual, the traffic through the mountains was a nightmare. A Ford Bronco in front of him tried to pass the eighteen-wheeler a few vehicles up. The Bronco was old and consumptive, hopelessly slow, and it collided with an even bigger juggernaut coming the other way. The driver died instantly. The passenger was alive when Jonathan reached her. She was a girl, fourteen at most. Jonathan got her out of the car and laid her on the ground. The gearshift had pierced her chest and blood was spurting from the wound like a ruptured hydrant. With only his patrolman's training to rely on—knowing only vaguely what to do—he'd rammed his fist into the perforation, keeping pressure on the ruptured artery and arresting the loss of blood. The girl was conscious the entire time. She never said a word. She just stared up at him with his hand buried inside her ribs until the ambulance arrived.

All that time, he could feel her heart beating . . . actually feel the organ itself, pumping against his hand.

The ultimate rush.

He quit his job the next week and enrolled in college to study medicine.

Jonathan's thoughts came back to the here and now. Turning away from the window, his eyes fell on Emma's night table. It stood as she'd left it. An open bottle of mineral water. Reading glasses balanced on a stack of romance novels. "You don't understand," she'd said once, trying to explain why she was so slavishly devoted to stories about strapping Scotsmen and time-traveling buccaneers who rescued damsels in distress and lived in castles on the Firth of Forever. She liked them because they were predictable. Happy ending guaranteed. It was an antidote to her job where hardly anything ended happily, or, at the very least, not predictably.

Finally, his eyes landed back on the corner of angel's-blue fabric extending from the pillow. Sitting down on the bed, he freed Emma's nightshirt and brought it to his face. The wool was worn and soft and smelled of vanilla and sandalwood. A wave of sensations washed over him. The feel of the firm, rounded muscles that ran the length of her spine. The warmth that radiated from the base of her neck. The desire sparked by her coy smile peeking up at him from beneath the spray of hair.

"Yes?" Emma would say, drawing out the word like a dare.

Jonathan lowered the nightshirt to his lap. All that was gone. A current of longing seized him. A current so powerful that it threatened to grow into a panic. Panic at his permanent, inconsolable loss.

He looked at Emma's nightshirt and breathed easier. He was not ready to say goodbye. He folded it up and replaced it under the pillow. For a while yet, he wanted to keep her with him.

7

The headquarters of the Service for Analysis and Prevention was located in a modern steel-and-glass building on the Nussbaumstrasse in Bern. The staff of the Swiss counterespionage service numbered fewer than two hundred souls. Their tasks were geared primarily toward information collection and analysis, and involved keeping tabs on registered agents of foreign governments, most of whom resided in Bern, and monitoring what it regarded as clandestine communications traffic in and out of the country. Only thirty officers were assigned to more active work—that is, the day-to-day investigation and infiltration of extremist groups operating on Swiss soil, including foreign terrorist cells. In every sense it was a small, tightly run operation.

Marcus von Daniken arrived at seven sharp and set

to work. Picking up the phone, he dialed an internal number. A woman answered. "Schmid. ISIS."

Von Daniken identified himself. "I need everything we have on a subject on our watch list named Theo Lammers. It's urgent."

"Yes, sir. I'll send it right away."

A minute later, a chime rang from his computer indicating a newly arrived e-mail. Von Daniken was pleased to see that it was the file from ISIS. The report was a summary of information passed along by the Belgian police.

Theodoor Albrecht Lammers was born in Rotterdam in 1961. After earning a doctorate in mechanical engineering at Utrecht University, he drifted in and out of jobs at several undistinguished firms in Amsterdam and The Hague. He came to the notice of the authorities in 1987 while working in Brussels as an associate of Gerald Bull, the American armaments designer. At the time, Bull was busy creating a "supergun" for Saddam Hussein. Code-named Babylon, the gun was actually a giant artillery piece capable of lobbing a shell hundreds of miles with deadly accuracy. His work for the Middle Eastern potentate was a matter of public record. All the same, Bull and his associates (Theo Lammers included) were considered "persons of interest" by the Belgian police.

Von Daniken knew the rest of the story himself. Gerald Bull was murdered in 1990, shot five times in the back of the head by an assassin waiting in the foyer of his Brussels apartment. At first, speculation had it that it was the Mossad, Israel's intelligence service, which had killed him. The speculation was incorrect. At the time, the Israelis had kept up a distant but cordial relationship with the scientist. As prospective clients, they were eager to know exactly what he was up to. It was for this very reason that the Iraqis had killed him. Once the Babylon gun was built, Saddam Hussein did not want Bull sharing its secrets with anyone, especially the Israelis.

Von Daniken closed the e-mail, then stood and walked to the window. The morning was gray and grim, wet snow dropping from low-lying cloud cover. The view gave onto a parking lot, and farther on, a half-finished office tower, crawling with laborers despite the weather.

And Lammers? he asked himself. What had he been up to that warranted keeping an Uzi in his workshop and a variety of passports in his bathroom? Or to necessitate sending a professional killer to lie in wait behind his woodshed?

Von Daniken returned to his desk. Several dossiers lay on top. They were labeled "Airports and Immigration," "Counterterrorism/Domestic," "Counterterrorism/Foreign," and "Trafficking." He skimmed their contents, saving "Counterterrorism/Foreign" for last.

This dossier contained a summary of wires from foreign security services. In 1971, the chief of the Swiss intelligence service, alarmed by the specter of politically motivated acts of violence, helped establish a confederation of Western European law enforcement professionals charged with ensuring their country's internal security. The group became known as the Club of Bern. After 9/11, the group formalized their relationship and took the name "Counterterror Group," or CTG.

The topmost report was from his counterpart in Sweden and stated that Walid Gassan, a suspected **extremist** (Sweden did not countenance the use of the word "terrorist") had been spotted in Stockholm. It went on to say that Gassan was deemed a priority suspect in the bombing of the Sheraton Hotel in Amman, Jordan, as well as several failed attacks, and requested that any information regarding Gassan or his accomplices be forwarded to the Swedish intelligence service immediately.

The report was accurate, if incomplete.

Walid Gassan had passed through Switzerland in January. Working off a tip from an informant in Geneva's "Big Mosque," von Daniken had sent a team to track him down and arrest him. Though not wanted in Switzerland, the red flag warrant issued by Interpol gave von Daniken the authority to take Gassan into custody. As it turned out, fate had been with Gassan, and the terrorist had slipped across the border before von Daniken could do anything more than issue an alert about his whereabouts. He thought of the fingernail he'd found in the aircraft. Maybe his reports on Gassan's movements had done some good. He did not know, however, whether the terrorist had been kidnapped off the streets of Stockholm or some other European city. He would leave it to Philip Palumbo, head of the CIA's Special Removal Unit, to inform the Swedes of Gassan's current location, if and when he saw fit.

Von Daniken walked downstairs to the second floor, advancing along a cool, gray-carpeted corridor to the last door on the right. "KILA 2.8," read the room placard.

"KILA" stood for the Coordination Unit for Identity Documents. It was KILA's job to maintain a collection of identity documents from every country around the world. Somewhere in its compendious cabinets was at least one example of every passport, driver's license, birth certificate, and any other commonly produced identity document currently in circulation in more than two hundred countries around the world.

Von Daniken stuck his head in the door. "Max, you busy?"

Max Seiler ran KILA. He was a short, barrel-chested man with blue eyes and thinning blond hair. "I thought you'd be in," he said, looking up from his work. "Heard you had quite a night."

Von Daniken filled Seiler in on the details. "These turned up in the victim's house," he said, tossing the three passports onto the desk.

Seiler examined the documents. "An agent?"

"Agent. Trafficker. Crook. One of the above."

Seiler focused on a maroon passport with a royal

coat of arms and the words "Europese Unie Koninkrijk der Nederlanden" emblazoned on the cover. "This the real one?"

"As far as I can tell, Lammers is his real name. He had a C permit giving his nationality as Dutch. ISIS has him tracked back to a university in the Netherlands. I doubt that he went undercover before he was eighteen. Regardless, I want a thorough check. Run all of them through Identigate, then drill down for the breeder docs."

Breeder documents included social security cards and birth certificates: the government-issued paperwork that validated one's identity.

Leaning to his side, Seiler cleared a stack of papers off a nearby chair. A glance revealed Italian driver's licenses, German medical insurance cards, English birth certificates. All fakes.

"Jules Gaye, born 1962, Brussels," he read aloud, after opening the Belgian passport. He flipped through the pages, studying the immigration stamps, then returned to the front page and held it under a goosenecked ultraviolet light. A faint image of Belgium's royal palace came to life.

"Reactive ink looks good," said von Daniken.

"The new Belgian issues are sharp. This one has five security features to put a crimp in counterfeiting. A laser-cut pinhole of the passport holder, a watermark of Albert II, an optically variable image of Belgium that changes from green to blue depending on the viewing angle, and two microtaggants. Off-hand, I'd say it's genuine."

"You mean the blank?"

"Not only the blank. I mean 'genuine' as in official. Issued by the proper passport authority."

"You're sure?" Von Daniken's skepticism was born of experience. Belgian passports were the VWs of the false documents trade. Cheap, reliable, and easy to come by. Since 1990, over nineteen thousand authentic blanks had been stolen from Belgian consulates, embassies, town halls, and diplomatic pouches the world over. The country lost passports the way some people misplaced their keys.

"We can check." Logging onto his computer, Seiler fed the passport number into Identigate, the Swiss police's repository of over two million stolen and fraudulent documents from around the world. "The Belgians are as scrupulous about reporting stolen blanks as they are lax about losing them," he said. "If it's stolen, we'll get a match." After a moment, his broad features creased in dismay. "Nothing. As far as the Belgians are concerned, it's legit."

"You're sure it hasn't been tampered with?"

"Positive. The pictures are burned into the fabric of the passport itself. It's physically impossible for Lammers to have replaced the original holder's photograph with his own."

"Mind if I use your phone?"

"All yours."

Von Daniken placed a call to a contact in the identity documents department of the Belgian Federal Police. "Frank, I have one of your passports on my desk. Belongs to a man who got himself killed last night. If I didn't know better, I'd say it's the real thing." He read off the number and the corresponding name.

"It's genuine," said Frank Vincent after a second or two. "Number's in the system."

"Funny. We have the man down as Theo Lammers, a Dutch citizen. Do me a favor: run a complete check on this Jules Gaye. Go all the way back. Tell me if he's real, or if he's a straw man."

"I'll need some time. End of the day suit you?"

"Before lunch would be better. And one more thing: tell me where you mailed the passport."

Von Daniken hung up. Max Seiler was examining the New Zealand passport. Again, it passed muster. The document had not been doctored and its number did not turn up on any of their databases for stolen papers. Von Daniken checked his watch. It was five-thirty p.m. in Auckland. Past closing time. He decided to contact the embassy in Paris, instead. Due to the ten-hour time difference, the Kiwis maintained a beefed-up embassy in France capable of handling most official inquiries.

Von Daniken placed the call and was informed that the passport was authentic. According to the New Zealand authorities, the passport holder, Michael Carrington of 24 Victoria Lane, Christchurch, was a citizen in good standing. Officially, NRA. Nothing recorded against. He requested a review of the issuing documents and was told an inquiry would be made forthwith.

"What do you make of it?" he asked after he'd hung up.

Seiler shrugged. "Two valid passports with your victim's picture, and differing names. There's only one answer, isn't there? Gaye and Carrington are legends. We can rule out a dirty businessman. Looks like you've got an illegal on your hands."

An "illegal" was a trained government agent operating clandestinely on foreign soil without his country's protection. A deep-cover spy.

Von Daniken nodded. Unsettled, he returned to his office. It had been seven years since anything remotely resembling this case had come across his desk. He had just two questions: Who was Lammers working for? And what had he been doing in Switzerland that had gotten him killed?

It was only at seven a.m. that the port turbine engine belonging to the Gulfstream IV was finally repaired and the jet made ready for takeoff from Bern-Belp airport. Despite Marcus von Daniken's offer of lodging, Philip Palumbo had remained on board, choosing to sleep on a couch at the rear of the passenger compartment.

As the jet pushed back from the terminal, Palumbo left his seat and ducked through the aft hatch that led to the luggage compartment. The cargo area was a tight space with a sloping ceiling, absent windows. Three suitcases were stacked in one corner. Pushing them aside, he kneeled and slid back a panel in the floor that concealed a sturdy stainless steel handle. Giving a yank, he pulled a section of floor clear to reveal a seven-foot by four-foot compartment kitted out with a mattress and belt restraints.

Lying inside the compartment was a slim, olive-skinned man dressed in a white jumpsuit, his hands and feet bound by flexi-cuffs and connected by a perp chain. His beard had been shaved. His black hair cut to a soldier's regulation length. The diaper he wore was also regulation. All were measures designed to depersonalize the prisoner and make him feel powerless and vulnerable.

He looked like a young man. With his wire-rimmed glasses he might have been a university student or a computer programmer. His name was Walid Gassan. He was thirty-one years of age, an avowed terrorist linked at one time or another to Islamic Jihad, Hezbollah, and like every self-respecting Islamic fanatic, Al-Qaeda.

Palumbo hauled the prisoner to his feet and guided him into the passenger compartment, where he pushed him into a seat and attached the seat belt tight around his waist. He spent a moment daubing Mercurochrome on Gassan's ruined fingers. He'd given up three fingernails before Palumbo had quit.

"Where are you taking me?" asked Gassan.

Palumbo didn't answer. Leaning down, he unlocked the man's foot restraints and spent a moment massaging the prisoner's calves to keep his circulation active. He didn't want Gassan to drop dead of deep vein thrombosis before they squeezed some information out of him.

"I am an American citizen," Gassan went on defiantly. "I have rights. Where are you taking me? I demand to be told."

There was a maxim that had sprung up about extraordinary rendition. If the CIA wanted to question someone, they sent him to Jordan. If they wanted to torture him, they sent him to Syria. If they wanted him to disappear off the face of the earth, they sent him to Egypt.

"Think of it as a surprise, Haji."

"My name isn't Haji!"

"You're right," said Palumbo with menace. "You know what? You don't have a name. As far as the world is concerned, you no longer exist." He snapped his fingers an inch from the prisoner's nose. "You just disappeared into thin air."

Palumbo buckled himself in as the jet lifted into the air. A screen at the head of the cabin showed the plane's progress on a world map, along with updates about its speed, the outside temperature, and time to destination. After a few minutes heading north, the Gulfstream banked to the left until its nose pointed south by southeast. Toward the Mediterranean Sea.

"I'll give you one more chance," said Palumbo. "Talk now or later. I can promise you that the first option is the one you want to take."

Gassan's timid brown eyes darted toward him. "I have nothing to say."

Palumbo sighed, shaking his head. Another hardcase. "What about the explosives you picked up in Germany? Let's start there."

"I don't know what you're talking about."

"Of course you don't."

He looked at Gassan, imagining the terrible things that the young man had done, the deaths he had caused, the families he had torn. And then he thought about what the man would face when they landed.

In four hours' time, Mr. Walid Gassan would get his due.

9

A knock came at the door.

"Moment, bitte." Jonathan pulled a worn Basque sweater over his T-shirt and slipped into a pair of moccasins as he walked to the door. "Yes?"

The hotel manager stood in the hallway. "On behalf of all the staff, may I offer our heartfelt condolences," he said. "If there is anything I or any member of my staff can do . . ."

"Thank you," said Jonathan. "But I'm alright for the moment."

The manager nodded, but did not leave. Instead, he drew a buff envelope out of his jacket and extended it toward Jonathan. "Some mail. For your wife."

Jonathan took the envelope and held it under the light. It was addressed to "Emma Ransom, Hotel Bellevue, Poststrasse, Arosa." The script was large, bold, and meticulous. A man's hand, he thought automatically. He turned the letter over. There was no name or return address.

"A day late, I'm afraid," explained the hotelier. "The crew enlarging the railway tunnel near St. Peter-Molinas brought down an avalanche on the tracks. I explained it all to Mrs. Ransom. She was quite upset. I must apologize."

"You talked to Emma about this?"

"Yes. Saturday evening before dinner."

"So she was **expecting** this letter?"

"She whispered something about a birthday. She made me promise to hold it for her."

A birthday? Jonathan's thirty-eighth was March 13, more than a month off. "That must be it. Thank you."

Closing the door, he walked to the bedroom, turning the envelope over in his hands. **Emma Ransom. Hotel Bellevue. Poststrasse, Arosa.** The postmark was smudged. While the date remained legible, the name of the town where the letter had been posted was blurred. The first letter was an "A," unless, of course, it was an "R." The second letter was a "c," or an "o," or maybe an "e." The third an "l" or an "i."

He gave up. It was useless.

Sitting down on the edge of the bed, he slipped a thumb beneath the flap. Taken by the blue express stamp, he paused. It meant the letter had been mailed Friday for next-day delivery.

Again, he turned it over. No return address.

How long had he suspected? Six months? A year? Was it only after Emma's trip to Paris, or had there been intimations before? Hints that he should have picked up on, but had been too busy to notice.

It was no exaggeration to say that he loved her madly. "Madly" was such a frightening word. It suggested carelessness and danger and abandon. Nothing like his feelings for Emma. His love for Emma had been based on an absolute absence of doubt. He saw her and he knew. The crooked grin that said, "Try me. I'm game." The wild mane of auburn hair that she refused to tame. The torn jeans that cried out for mending. "There are more important things, Jonathan, than putting your hair in braids and wearing a clean frock." The challenging gaze that demanded the best of him. It was as if she had been run up and made especially for him. He held nothing back, because she didn't either.

Yes, he loved her madly. But he had not loved her blindly.

Over the past months, she'd shown a growing disinterest in work. Once routine fourteen-hour days were cut to twelve, and then to eight. As a regional director of logistics for Doctors Without Borders, Emma was in charge of coordinating relief operations for the Middle East. This meant she supervised the hiring and training of staff and volunteers, oversaw shipments of supplies, liaised with local government agencies, and kept a handle on finances needed to keep the operation up and running. It was a hectic job, to say the least.

At first, he attributed her slowing down to burnout. Emma had always been one to drive herself too hard. Her flame burned too brightly. "Incandescent" was not too strong a word. It was natural to need a rest.

But there were other signs. Headaches. Solitary walks. Protracted silences. He had felt the distance between them growing day by day.

All of it had begun after Paris.

Jonathan ran the envelope back and forth between his fingers. It weighed nothing. He guessed there was a single sheet of paper inside. He flipped the letter over and stared at the blank expanse where a return address belonged. A Swiss who didn't put his name on an envelope was one step removed from a traitor. It was a national offense right up there with violating bank secrecy and filching the recipe for Lindt's milk chocolate.

If not a traitor, then what?

A succession of four sonorous beeps emanated from the radio. An officious British voice announced: "It is twelve o'clock noon Greenwich Mean Time. This is the World Service of the BBC. The news read by . . ."

But in Jonathan's mind, a different voice was speaking. **Open it,** it urged him. **Open it now and get it over with.**

If only it were that simple, he mused.

The fact was, he wasn't sure whether he wanted to open it at all. Emma was dead. His memories of her were all that remained. He didn't want to taint them. He brought the letter closer and his thoughts traveled to the one place he never wanted them to visit again.

Paris . . . where Emma had gone for a girls' weekend to drown herself in culture and croissants and the new Chagall exhibit.

Paris . . . where Emma had disappeared for two days and two nights and not even his most fevered messages could reach her.

Paris . . .

———

Jonathan is asleep in his tent, lying on top of his cot in boxers and nothing else. At three in the morning, the heat is still oppressive. It has been a hot summer, even by the taxing standards of the Middle East. During the months he has lived and worked in the Bekaa Valley, he has learned to sleep and sweat at the same time.

The cot next to him is empty. Emma has left for a week's visit to Europe. Four days at the agency headquarters in Geneva, then three days in Paris, where she will join her best friend, Simone, for a whirlwind tour of the City of Light. There will be an afternoon at the Jeu de Paume, an evening enjoying the Son et Lumière at Versailles. With her

old exuberance, Emma has blocked out every minute of their days.

The sound of motors awakens him. The night growls with the approach of a mechanized invasion. Jonathan raises his head from his pillow. A gunshot shatters the darkness.

Jonathan scrambles from his bed and rushes outside. Rashid, a young Palestinian, stands in front of the hospital, arms outstretched, blocking entry. Two mud-encrusted pickups are parked nearby. Music blares from their speakers. A minor-key melody with a sledgehammer beat. A squad of armed militiamen encircles the boy, prodding at him with the barrels of their machine guns, shouting at him to unlock the doors. Jonathan forces his way into their midst. "What do you want?" he asks in rudimentary Arabic.

"You are in charge?" says the leader, a sallow youth of twenty with a wispy beard and catlike eyes. "You are the doctor?"

"I'm the doctor," Jonathan answers.

"We need medicine. Tell this boy to get out of the way."

"Never," shouts Rashid. He is an angry youth, fifteen years old and fiercely independent. Since Jonathan and Emma's arrival, he has been at their side constantly. Jonathan is his idol and mentor, his patron saint and most sacred charge. Rashid plans on studying medicine, if only to care for his numerous relatives. The hospital belongs to him as much as the aid workers.

"Please," says Jonathan, with a smile to soothe raw nerves. "Let me help. Are you ill? Is one of your men hurt?"

"It is my father," says the rabble's leader. "His heart. He requires medicine."

"Bring him here," says Jonathan. "We'll be happy to treat him." He notes the boy's glazed eyes, his dreamy smile. Is he drunk? High? On what? Raki? Hash? Meth?

"He doesn't have the time."

"Have you tried the hospital at El Ain? If your father has a heart ailment, I recommend that he go to Beirut."

But Beirut is an eight-hour drive and the road to El Ain is impassable due to flash floods.

"Out of the way," says the leader, pushing past Rashid. Rashid pushes back. Before Jonathan can react, before he can warn the boy to yield, the leader raises his rifle and fires a bullet into Rashid's face.

"My father requires nitroglycerine for his heart," the leader says, stepping over the body. "And we"—he gestures to his men—"We require something for our souls."

One look at Rashid tells Jonathan that there is nothing to be done. He leads the militiamen to the dispensary. It is a raiding party. Greedy hands clear the shelves of morphine, Vicodin, and codeine. In minutes, the dispensary is bare. It is over as quickly as it began. Wishing the Prophet's blessing upon him, the militiamen climb into their trucks and drive away.

A minute later, Jonathan has the phone to his ear, frantically hoping to reach Paris. Emma must fly to Geneva and go directly to DWB headquarters. He will telephone ahead to arrange a money order that she must take with her so he can re-supply the hospital.

It is three-thirty in Lebanon. One hour earlier in Paris. He calls the Hôtel les Trois Couronnes, but she does not answer. Her cell is likewise out of service. He phones the hotel again and requests that a message be delivered to her room. But Emma does not call back. Not that night. Not the next morning. Not even the next afternoon, after Jonathan has driven into Beirut and used the last of his personal savings to purchase the needed medicines from a black market supplier.

His wife is missing.

Every man's patience has its limits. Sadly, he discovers that faith is not an inexhaustible commodity. At six the following morning, he calls the hotel yet again and asks to speak to the manager. "Are you sure you left the messages in the correct room?" he demands.

"I am certain, Monsieur Ransom. I personally delivered the last note."

"Would you mind checking if my wife is in her room?"

"But, of course. I will transfer the call to my cellular. If I find your wife, you may speak with her immediately."

Like a phantom, Jonathan accompanies the manager up to the third floor. Over the line, he hears the gates of the old-fashioned elevator bang closed; the plodding of well-shod feet down the carpeted hallway; the sharp knock on the door. "Bonjour, madame. It is Henri Gauthier. I am the hotel manager. I would like to ask if you are alright."

There is no response. Time passes. Gauthier enters the room.

"Monsieur Ransom?" comes the urbane French voice. "The messages are all here."

"What do you mean?"

"They are lying on the floor. None has been opened. In fact, it does not look like your wife is here at all."

"I'm not sure I understand."

"The bed has not been slept in. I see no suitcases or belongings of any kind." Gauthier paused, and Jonathan envisions the man's defeated shrug as if it were his own. "The room has not been touched."

Open it.

Jonathan slipped a finger beneath the flap and tore open the envelope. There was a single sheet of paper inside. Blank. No name. No heading. Not a mark. He turned the envelope upside down and gave a shake. Two slips of cardboard paper fell into his palm. They were identical in shape and size. One edge was perforated, as if it had been torn from another piece. A six-digit number printed in red ink ran across the middle of each. To look at, it was a receipt. A claim ticket similar to what you received at a coat check. Some letters were printed in a very small font in the bottom right-hand corner.

SBB.

Schweizerische Bundesbahn.

The Swiss Railway.

The tickets were baggage claims.

10

For the second time in twelve hours, Marcus von Daniken was back in Zurich. The sign above the entry read "Robotica AG" in meter-high letters colored a blazing blue. According to his dossier, Theo Lammers had founded the company in 1994 and was its sole owner and CEO. Its activity was referenced obscurely as "machine parts."

A sturdy, officious-looking woman stood in the reception area, hands clasped behind her back as if awaiting a general on the parade ground. "Michaela Menz," she announced, approaching with two soldierly strides. She was dressed in a sober two-piece suit, her brown hair cut short and parted on the side. Her business card noted that her doctorate was in mechanical engineering. With honors.

In return, von Daniken offered her a look at his ID and a hardbitten smile. Now they were equal.

"We're still in a state of shock," said Menz as she led the way to her office. "None of us can think of anyone who would wish to harm Mr. Lammers. He was a wonderful man."

"I have no reason to doubt it," said von Daniken. "In fact, that's why I'm here. We're as anxious as you to find the murderer. Anything you can tell me will be of great help."

Menz's office was small and neatly furnished. There were no pictures of family, lovers, or friends. He spotted her as a work widow and realized she was probably sick with worry. Not for Lammers so much, but for the business and who would run it now that he was dead.

"Do you think it's a colleague who's responsible?" she asked in a tone of enthusiastic mourning. "Someone abroad, perhaps?"

"I really couldn't say at this point. It's our policy not to comment on an investigation. Perhaps we can start with the company. What exactly is it that you do?"

The executive brought her chair closer to her desk. "Navigation systems. Above ground, underwater, mobile terminal positioning." Seeing the confused look in von Daniken's eyes, she added, "We make instruments that plot the exact position of planes and boats and cars."

"Like GPS?"

A frown indicated that he was off base. "We don't like to rely on satellites. We recently patented a new terrain navigation system for aircraft utilizing a technology called sensor fusion. Our device combines measurements from inertial navigation systems, digital maps, and a radar altimeter. By measuring the terrain height variations along the aircraft flight path and comparing these with a digital terrain map, we're able to establish the exact position of the aircraft within millimeters."

"And who buys this type of device?"

"We have many clients. Boeing, General Electric, and Airbus, among others."

Von Daniken raised his eyebrows, impressed. "So I have you to thank when my airliner doesn't fly into a mountain?"

"Not just us . . . but, in a manner of speaking, yes."

He leaned closer, as if eager to share a secret. "I imagine that kind of work has military applications. Do you have clients in the defense industry? Aircraft manufacturers? Laser-guided munitions? That kind of thing?"

"None."

"But some of the companies you mentioned have rather large defense-related businesses, don't they?"

"They may, but they're not clients. There are other companies that manufacture military navigation systems."

To von Daniken's ear, the answers were a shade too brisk. Lammers had, after all, been put on the watch list because of his involvement in the manufacture of large artillery pieces, including the "supergun" being made for Saddam Hussein. "Would it surprise you to learn that Mr. Lammers designed artillery pieces when he was younger?" he asked.

"He was a brilliant man," said Menz. "I imagine he had many interests he didn't share with me. I can only state that as a firm, we've never had any involvement with weapons of any kind." Her brow drew together. "Why? Do you think that it has something to do with his death?"

"At this stage, anything is a possibility."

"I see." Menz looked away and he could see that she was playing with the idea. Her expression softened. Covering her face, she stifled a sob. "Please, excuse me. Theo's death has disturbed me terribly."

Von Daniken busied himself jotting down notes. He was no Inspector Maigret, but it seemed apparent that Michaela Menz was telling the truth. Or, at least, that if Lammers were involved in anything untoward, she didn't know about it. He waited until the woman had calmed down, then asked, "Did Mr. Lammers travel much for his work?"

Menz raised her head. "Travel? Good Lord, yes," she said, wiping her eyes. "He was constantly on the road. Checking installations. Taking orders. Keeping up goodwill."

"And what countries did he visit primarily?"

"Ninety percent of our sales are within Europe. He was always bouncing between Düsseldorf, Paris, Milan, and London. The industrial hubs, mostly."

"Ever get to the Middle East? Syria? Dubai?"

"Never."

"No business with Israel or Egypt?"

"Absolutely not."

"And who was responsible for booking his trips?"

"He did, I imagine."

"Are you saying that Mr. Lammers didn't have a secretary to make his reservations? Planes, hotels, rental cars . . . there's so much that goes into planning a business trip these days."

"He wouldn't hear of it. Theo was a hands-on manager. He booked his travel on the Internet."

Von Daniken scribbled the information on his pad. He didn't buy the bit about his being a hands-on manager. Secretive was more like it. He didn't want anyone looking over his shoulder when he booked his flights in the name of Jules Gaye or any other of his aliases. "Dr. Menz," he asked with the promise of a smile. "Do you think I might see his office? It would help me get a better feel for him."

"I'm not sure that's a good idea."

In fact, von Daniken was already exceeding his brief. There hadn't been time to apply for a warrant. In the eyes of the law, he had no right to snoop around the establishment. "I want to do everything possible to catch the man who killed him," he said, challenging her with his gaze. "Don't you?"

Michaela Menz rose from the desk and beckoned von Daniken to follow her. Lammers's office was next door. The space was the same size as Menz's, the furnishings equally spare. Von Daniken's eye immediately caught on an intriguing object displayed on the credenza. The device was a half meter in height, made of some kind of translucent plastic and shaped like a V. "And this? Is it one of your products?" he asked.

"It is an MAV," said Dr. Menz. "A micro airborne vehicle."

"May I?" he asked, gesturing toward the MAV. Menz nodded and he picked it up. The object weighed less than one kilogram. The wings were at once incredibly firm and strangely flexible. "Does it actually fly?"

"Of course," she responded, bristling as if insulted. "It has a range of fifty kilometers and can reach a top speed of over four hundred kilometers per hour."

"Impossible!" declaimed von Daniken, playing the part of the yokel. "And he built it here?"

Menz nodded approvingly. "With his own hands in our R and D lab. This one's the smallest he's produced. He was quite proud of it."

Von Daniken memorized her every word. **Range: fifty kilometers. Speed: four hundred kilometers an hour. Built with his own hands . . . the smallest he's produced.** Which meant there were others. He studied the odd aircraft.

No doubt it was guided by a navigation system

accurate to within centimeters. "Is it one of your products? Were you thinking of adding it to the line? Branching into toys?"

As hoped, Menz stiffened at the word. Stepping forward, she relieved him of the remote-controlled aircraft. "The MAV is no toy. It's the lightest vehicle of its kind in the world. For your information, we built it for a very important client."

"May I inquire who?"

"I'm afraid that's confidential, but I can promise you that they have nothing to do with the military. Quite the opposite, in fact. You would recognize their name in an instant. We consider it an honor of the highest order."

"It would be a tremendous help if you let me know who that client is."

Menz shook her head. "I don't see how that could be of any help in finding Theo's killer."

Von Daniken retreated gracefully. He thanked her for her time and asked her to call should she have anything else she wished to add. As he returned to his car, he was not thinking about robots. He was thinking about the MAV.

Michaela Menz was right. It was no toy.

It was a weapon in drag.

11

Jonathan marched down the hill, carving his way past slower walkers. He kept his hands in his pockets, his fingers kneading the baggage receipts. Were they for luggage? Skis and boots? Extra winter clothing? Upon finding them, he'd phoned Emma's office, but no one there could recall sending her anything.

If not them, then who? he wondered. And why hadn't there been a note, let alone a return address? The questions needled him mercilessly. Mostly, though, he asked himself why Emma had wanted to hide them from him.

The Poststrasse snaked pleasantly as it descended the mountain. Shops, cafés, and hotels lined either side of the street. Across Switzerland, the first week of February was "ski week," a traditional school vacation. Families from St. Gallen to Geneva fled en masse to the mountains. Today, however, the continued snowfall and gusty winds had shut down all lifts, including the Luftseilbahn. The sidewalks were crowded to bustling. There would be no going up the mountain. Not for Jonathan or anyone else.

Passing Lanz's Uhren und Schmuck Boutique, he stopped abruptly. In the center window, flanked by glimmering wristwatches, stood an out-of-date meteorological station: a thermometer, hygrometer, and barometer all built into one. It had been in the same place eight years ago when he'd come here with Emma on their first trip to the mountains. The setup was the size of an old ham radio and was comprised of three pen-graphs that recorded the atmospheric conditions. In its center, a bulb burned red, indicating that the barometric pressure was falling. Poor weather would prevail. The snow would continue for some time yet.

Jonathan bent toward the glass to study the readings. Over the past thirty-six hours, the temperature had dropped from a high of three degrees Celsius to a low of minus eleven. Relative humidity had skyrocketed, while barometric pressure had plummeted from one thousand millibars to seven hundred, where it now stood.

"Why didn't you check the weather?" the policeman had asked him the night before.

In his mind, Jonathan was back on the mountain with the snow and the wind and the menacing cold.

He felt his arm around Emma's waist as she crested that final ridge and collapsed against him. He remembered the look of accomplishment in her eyes; the swell of pride and the quicksilver certainty that they could do anything together.

"Jonathan!"

Far off, someone was calling his name. A gravelly voice with a French accent. He paid it no heed. He continued to stare at the red light, until it burned a corona into his vision. Emma **had** checked the weather. But she'd been too determined to make the climb to tell him that the forecast wasn't good.

Just then, a hand gripped his shoulder. "What's this?" asked the French-accented voice. "I have to track down my own welcoming committee?"

Jonathan spun and looked into the face of a tall, attractive woman with wavy dark hair. "Simone . . . you made it."

Simone Noiret dropped her overnight bag and hugged him tightly. "I'm sorry."

Jonathan hugged her back, closing his eyes and clamping his jaw. Fight as he might, he was powerless against the emotion that came with seeing a familiar face. After a moment, she eased her grip and held him at arm's length. "And so," she asked. "How are you holding up?"

"Okay," he said. "Not okay. I don't know. More numb than anything else."

"You look like shit. Stopped shaving, showering, and eating? This is not good."

He forced a smile, wiping at his cheek. "Not hungry, I guess."

"We're going to have to do something about that."

"I guess so," he said.

Simone forced him to meet her eye. "You guess so?"

Jonathan pulled himself together. "Yes, Simone, we're going to do something about that."

"That's better." She folded her arms and shook her head as if she were castigating one of her fourth-grade pupils.

Simone Noiret was Egyptian by birth, French by marriage, and a teacher by profession. Recently turned forty, she looked ten years younger, a fact which she attributed to her Arab heritage. Her Levantine blood was evident in her hair, which was black and thick as Nile straw and cascaded elegantly to her shoulders, and her eyes, which were dark and untrusting and made the more imposing by liberal use of mascara. She carried an expensive leather handbag over one shoulder. She dug in it for a cigarette—a Gauloise—one of the sixty or so she smoked each day. So far, the cigarettes had confined their damage to her voice, which was as scratched as one of the old Brel records she carted around with her from one city to the next.

"Thanks for coming," he said. "I needed to have someone around . . . someone who knew Emma."

Simone began to speak, then caught herself, turning away from him and throwing her cigarette to the ground. "All during the train ride, I promised myself

I wouldn't cry," she said. "I told myself that you needed someone strong. Someone to cheer you up. To look after you. But, of course, you're the strong one. Our Jonathan. Look at me. Like a baby."

Tears ran from the corners of her eyes, smearing her cheek with mascara. Jonathan pulled a tissue from his pocket and wiped away the smudges.

"Paul sends his condolences," she managed between sniffles. "He's in Davos for the week. Mr. Bigshot is to deliver a speech on the corruption in Africa. Now there's an original topic. He wanted you to know that he is devastated that he couldn't come."

Simone's husband, Paul, was a French economist, a highly-placed paper pusher at the World Bank.

"It's alright. I know he'd come if he could."

"It's not, and I told him so. These days we are all slaves to our ambition." Simone caught a glimpse of herself in the shop window and winced. "**Mais merde.** Now I look like shit, too. What a pair we are."

The Ransoms and the Noirets had met in Beirut two years before, neighbors in the same apartment building during Jonathan's tour with DWB. At the time, Simone was teaching at the American School in Beirut. Learning that Emma was in the aid game, she'd used her contacts to secure cheap digs for the "mission," which was what aid workers called their operational units. The act of kindness had cemented Emma's loyalty forever.

Jonathan's assignment to DWB headquarters in

Geneva was greeted with joy, at least by the women. (Jonathan had dreaded the move . . . and with good reason, it turned out.) Paul Noiret was due to rotate back to Geneva two weeks earlier. The Noirets had once again come to the rescue, helping Jonathan and Emma find an affordable apartment at their upscale complex in Cologny. The couples dined together whenever their schedules permitted. Burgers at the Ransoms' one month. Coq au vin at the Noirets' the next. It was not, as Emma had liked to point out, exactly a fair trade.

Jonathan picked up Simone's overnight bag. "Come with me," he said, starting off down the hill.

"But I thought the hotel was in the other direction."

"It is. We're going to the train station."

Simone hurried to catch up. "Getting rid of me already?"

"No. There's something I have to check on." He held up the receipts for her inspection.

"What are they?" asked Simone.

"I think they're baggage claims. They came in a letter for Emma yesterday. The only thing inside was a blank piece of paper. No signature. No note. Just these things."

Simone plucked them from his fingers. "SBB. That means the Schweizerische Bundesbahn. Is she missing any luggage?"

"That's what I want to find out."

"Who sent them?"

"No idea. There's no name anywhere." He took back the receipts. "Think it might be from a friend of hers?"

"I wouldn't know."

"You were with her in Paris."

"Yes, I was. And so?"

Jonathan hesitated. "There was this emergency at work while you two were there. I tried to reach her for two days. When I couldn't, I got upset. She said she'd camped out in your room at the hotel and didn't bother going to her own."

There it was then; his suspicions set out plain to see. Naked insecurities. In the light of day, they appeared petty and insubstantial.

"And you didn't believe her?" Simone put her hand on his arm and gave a squeeze. "But it's true. We stayed together the entire time. It was our 'girls' weekend.' We didn't even begin to talk until after midnight. That's when the motors got going. That was our Emma. All or nothing. You know that." She laughed wistfully, not so much recollecting the moment as to dispel his worry. "Emma wasn't cheating on you. She wasn't the type."

"What about these bags? She never mentioned anything to you? A trip she had planned? A surprise of some kind?"

"A 'lightning safari'?"

"Something like that."

A "lightning safari" was the name they'd given Emma's jaunts to secure supplies. At least once a month, she made unannounced dashes to points near and far to obtain type-A blood, penicillin, or even just vitamin C. Everything from the mundane to the miraculous.

Simone shook her head. "It must be something she ordered. Have you called her office?"

Jonathan said he had, and that they were quick to state that they hadn't sent anything to her.

"Well, I wouldn't worry," said Simone, as she slipped her arm into his and they walked to the bottom of the hill.

At the main post office, they turned left, skirting the Obersee, a small lake, now frozen over and cordoned off by ropes to allow the new snow to settle. The Bahnhof was deserted. Two trains serviced Arosa each hour. The first, taking passengers down the mountain to Chur, departed at three minutes after the hour. The second, bringing passengers up, arrived at eight after.

Jonathan headed toward the luggage counter. The attendant took the tickets and returned after a minute, shaking his head. "Not here," he said.

Jonathan stared into the recesses of the storage area where dozens of bags were stacked on a maze of iron shelves. "You're sure you checked everything?"

"Try the ticket office. The station manager can tell you if the bags are in the system."

The ticket office was likewise deserted. Jonathan stepped to the counter and slipped the receipts beneath the window. "Not here," reported the station manager, his eyes locked on the monitor. "The bags are in Landquart. They arrived two days ago."

Landquart was a small town on the Zurich–Chur line, best known as the terminus for Klosters, favored haunt of the British monarchy, and Davos, the fashionable ski resort.

"Do you know where they were sent from?" Jonathan inquired.

"Both items were sent from Ascona. Part of our drop-and-ship program. Put aboard the 13:57 to Zurich. Transferred onward to Landquart."

Ascona was on Switzerland's border with Italy. One of the palm-frocked resorts dotting the shores of Lago Maggiore. He had no friends who lived there. Apparently, Emma did.

Simone leaned her head toward the window. "Can you tell us who exactly sent the bags?"

The station manager shook his head. "I don't have the authority to access that information from this terminal."

"Who does?" she asked.

"Only the issuing station at Ascona."

Jonathan reached for his wallet, but Simone beat him to the punch. She slipped her credit card across the counter. "Two tickets to Landquart," she said. "First class."

12

The compound was called Al-Azabar and it belonged to the Palestine branch of Far Falestin, a division of Syrian military intelligence. Philip Palumbo stepped inside the building and winced at the odor of ammonia permeating the main hall. It was not his first visit, not even his tenth, but the eye-watering smell and barren surroundings still got to him. Concrete floor. Concrete walls. Pictures of President Bashir Al-Assad (referred to by his countrymen as "the doctor" because of his training as an ophthalmologist) and his late father, the strongman Hafez Al-Assad, were the only decorations in sight. A desk manned by a lone officer occupied the center of the room. A German shepherd slept at his feet. Seeing Palumbo, the officer stood from the desk and saluted. "Welcome back, sir."

Palumbo swept past him without answering. For

the record, he was not present. If pressed, evidence could be produced to prove he'd never stepped foot on Syrian soil.

Philip Palumbo headed up the Special Removal Unit of the CIA. On paper, the Special Removal Unit belonged to the Counterterrorist Command Center. In truth, the SRU functioned as an autonomous unit, and Palumbo reported directly to the deputy director of operations, Admiral James Lafever, the second-ranking man in the Agency.

Palumbo's job was simple enough. Locate suspected terrorists and abduct them for interrogation. To this end, he disposed of a fleet of three corporate jets, a team of operatives poised to travel to all four corners of the map with an hour's notice, and the unwritten dispensation of Admiral Lafever, and behind him, the president of the United States, to do whatever needed to be done. There was only one caveat: Don't get caught. It was a double-edged sword, to be sure.

The plane had touched down in Damascus at 1:55 p.m. local time. His first act was to transfer custody of the prisoner to the Syrian authorities. The papers he had signed in triplicate made Prisoner 88891Z a ward of the Syrian penal system. Somewhere over the Mediterranean, Walid Gassan had ceased to exist. He had been officially "disappeared."

A trim, businesslike officer in a starched olive uniform emerged from a brightly lit corridor. His name was Colonel Majid Malouf—or "Colonel Mike," as he insisted on being called—and he would be handling the interrogation. Colonel Mike was an unattractive man, his face haggard, his cheeks and neck violently pockmarked. He greeted the American with a kiss on each cheek, a hug, and a handshake as powerful as a bear trap. The two men retreated to Colonel Mike's office where Palumbo spent an hour going over the details of the case, concentrating on the holes they needed Gassan to fill.

The Syrian lit a cigarette and studied his notes. "What's the time frame?"

"We think the threat is imminent," said Palumbo. "Days maybe. A couple of weeks at the most."

"A rush job, then."

"I'm afraid so."

The Syrian picked a loose shard of tobacco from his tongue. "Will we have time to bring in any relatives?"

A proven interrogation technique involved producing a suspect's mother or sister. The mere threat of physical harm to either was usually sufficient to secure a full confession.

"No way," said Palumbo. "We need something actionable now."

The Syrian shrugged. "Understood, my friend."

Officially, Syria still figured on the United States' list of state sponsors of terrorism. Though it had not been directly linked to any terrorist operations since 1986 and it actively forbade any domestic groups from launching attacks from its own soil or attacks targeting Westerners, it was known to provide "passive support" to various hard-line groups calling for Palestinian independence. Islamic Jihad based their headquarters in Damascus, and both Hamas and the leftist Popular Front for the Liberation of Palestine kept offices in the city.

Despite this, and Syria's abysmal record of human rights, the American government viewed the Syrians as partners in the war on terror. After 9/11, the Syrian president had shared intelligence regarding the whereabouts of certain Al-Qaeda operatives with the United States and had condemned the attacks. During the Iraq war, the Syrian military had worked to staunch the cross-border flow of insurgents into Iraq. A secular dictatorship, Syria wanted no part of the Islamic fundamentalist revolution sweeping the Arab world. Extremism was not tolerated.

The interrogation cell was a narrow, dank room with a barred window high on the wall and a drain in the center of the floor. A guard led the prisoner into the room. A moment later, a second guard dragged in a schoolboy's wooden desk, the kind with the chair and writing table attached to one another. Gassan was made to sit down. One of the guards removed the black hood covering his head.

"So, Mr. Gassan," began Colonel Mike, speaking Arabic. "Welcome to Damascus. If you cooperate and answer our questions, your stay will be brief and we will transfer you back to the custody of our American friends. Do you understand?"

Gassan made no reply.

"Would you like a cigarette? Some water? Anything at all?"

"Go fuck yourself," muttered Gassan, but his bravado was ruined by the nervous glances he threw over his shoulders.

Colonel Mike gave a signal and the guards fell on Gassan. One wrenched his left arm behind his back, while the other extended the right arm, landing a knee on his forearm and flattening his palm on the table. The fingers twitched as if stimulated with an electric current.

"I am an American citizen," shouted Gassan as he writhed and struggled. "I have rights. You are to free me at once. I wish to call a lawyer. I demand to be repatriated."

Colonel Mike took a pearl-handled penknife from his breast pocket and freed the blade. Carefully, he separated Gassan's pinky from the other fingers, slipping a wine cork in the hollow to prevent it from moving.

"I demand to see the ambassador! You have no authority! I am an American citizen. You have no right—"

Colonel Mike laid the blade at the base of the finger and severed the digit as if he were chopping a carrot. Gassan screamed, then screamed louder when Colonel Mike applied a bandage moistened with disinfectant to the stump.

Palumbo looked on, showing no emotion.

"Now then, my friend," said Colonel Mike, lowering himself on his haunches so he was face to face with Gassan. "On January tenth, you were in Leipzig, Germany. You met with Dimitri Shevchenko, an arms dealer who was in possession of fifty kilos of plastic explosives. Ah, you are surprised! Don't be, my friend. We know what we're talking about. Your colleagues in Germany have been most generous with their information. It is pointless to keep your silence. So much aggravation. So much pain. You know what they say. 'In the end, you will talk anyway.' Come, **habibi,** let us be civilized."

Gassan grimaced, his eyes locked on his ruined hand.

Colonel Mike sighed and went on. "You paid Shevchenko ten thousand dollars and transferred three boxes containing the trophies into a white Volkswagen van. This much we know. You will tell us the rest. Namely, to whom you delivered the explosives, and what they plan to do with them. I can promise that you will not leave before giving us this information. And if you think you can lie, I must add that we will wait to learn if it is true. Let us begin. Tell us about the explosives. To whom did you deliver them?"

Palumbo studied his shoes. It was at this point that they discovered a man's mettle.

Gassan spat in his interrogator's face.

A fighter, then.

Palumbo left the room. It was time to get some coffee. It was going to be a long night.

13

Fangs of ice hung from the railway clock at the Landquart station. Jonathan and Simone walked the length of the platform, heads bowed against the gusting wind. A group of skiers were clustered around the baggage depot, glumly checking in their equipment. There would be no skiing today. Jonathan took his place at the rear of the line, patting his leg impatiently, claim checks out and ready.

Simone nudged him with her shoulder. "Have you called Emma's relatives?"

"There's only her sister, Beatrice. She's in Bern."

"The architect? I thought Emma disliked her."

"She did, but Bea's her only family. You know how it is. It was one of the reasons Emma wanted to come to Switzerland. I tried to phone her this morning, but only got the machine. I couldn't leave a message saying that Emma was . . . I just couldn't."

"What about a service?"

"We'll have one when we recover the body."

"When will that be?"

"Hard to tell. A few days, maybe. It all depends when we can go back up the mountain."

"Will you have it here or in England?"

"England, I imagine. It was her home."

The line crept a pace forward.

"And your brothers?" Simone asked.

"I'll call them when I have something to say. I'm not in the mood for sympathy."

The line advanced and Jonathan found himself facing the baggage clerk. He handed over the receipts. The clerk returned carrying a black overnight bag and a medium-sized rectangular package wrapped in plain brown paper.

The black bag was made from supple calfskin and sported a gold zipper secured by a gold lock. It was unquestionably expensive. A bag to take on a weekend trip to your country home. A bag to place on the front seat of your Range Rover. No name tag. Just a receipt attached to the grip.

Jonathan turned his attention to the package. A shirt box, he thought absently. It was tied with twine, but likewise unmarked except for the receipt. He picked it up and was surprised to find it so light. He took out his pocketknife, eager to sever the coarse string.

"Is it what you expected?" Simone asked. "I mean, are they Emma's?"

"They must be," said Jonathan shortly. "Someone sent them to her."

"Next, please," the clerk called over his head.

The line pushed forward. The man behind Jonathan shouldered his way to the counter. So much for Swiss manners. Jonathan put away the knife, hauled the bags off the counter, and headed down the platform, looking left and right for a place where he could open the bags. He was surprised to find the Bahnhof buffet packed and a queue of those waiting for a table curling out the door.

"The next train back to Chur leaves in forty minutes," announced Simone, gazing at the monitors displaying arrival and departure information. "There's a tearoom across the street. Shall we get a coffee?"

"Why not?" said Jonathan. "Maybe we can get a little privacy there."

They waited until there was a break in traffic, then jogged across the street. As they neared the opposite side, a silver sedan rounded the curve driving rapidly.

"Watch out!" Jonathan grabbed Simone and dragged her onto the sidewalk.

The car swung into the slow lane, its tires jumping the curb. With a screech, it came to a halt, its front bumper barely a foot away. The doors opened. From either side, a man emerged and started toward them.

Jonathan looked from one man to the other. The man circling from the driver's side was short and muscular, clad in a leather jacket and wraparound sunglasses, hair shorn to the scalp. The other was taller and heavyset, dressed in jeans and a roll-neck sweater, with ice blond hair and eyes too narrow to betray their color. The men moved nimbly, advancing with obvious aggression. It was equally obvious that he, Jonathan Ransom, was their target. Before he could react—before he could warn Simone or get a hand up to protect himself—the blond in the fisherman's sweater slugged him in the face. Knuckles to the cheek. Jonathan fell to a knee, dropping the box and the bag.

"Jonathan . . . my God!" Simone uttered the words weakly, retreating a step.

The blond man bent over Jonathan and picked up Emma's calfskin bag and the brown-paper-wrapped package. **"Los,"** he said to his partner, with a tilt of the head.

If they had left then, Jonathan would have done nothing. His face throbbed terribly. His vision was blurred; his mouth brassy with the taste of blood. He'd had his share of brawls and dustups. He knew when to push back and when not to.

But then the crewcut man shoved Simone to the ground. She cried out. And something in that cry summoned all the terrors of the past twenty-four hours—the onset of the storm, Emma's fall, the discovery of her body in the crevasse—making them barbed and raw, and somehow more painful than ever.

Before he knew what he was doing, he was on his

feet running toward the blond-haired man. Only one thing mattered: he'd stolen Emma's belongings and Jonathan wanted them back.

With a cry, he hurled himself onto the thief's back. Throwing an arm around his neck, he grabbed him in a headlock and tried to bring him down to the ground. Immediately, an elbow pounded Jonathan's ribs. A roundhouse to the jaw followed a second later. Jonathan collapsed to the ground, winded and shaken.

The blond man tossed the black bag into the car. He regarded Jonathan with a victor's disdain and let go a low sweeping kick aimed for the face.

But this time Jonathan saw it coming. Deflecting the boot with one hand, he grasped the man's foot and wrenched it violently, snapping the ankle and toppling his assailant. The man had hardly hit the ground before Jonathan was on him, pounding him about the eyes and nose with a blunt fist. Cartilage gave way. Blood squirted from his nostrils.

By now, the other thug was halfway round the hood of the car. He was half a foot shorter, with sloping shoulders and a lineman's grotesque neck. He came at Jonathan like a bull across the ring. Dragging himself to his feet, Jonathan raised his hands in a boxer's stance.

The attacker neared and Jonathan threw a jab, then another. The assailant knocked both aside easily. Taking hold of Jonathan's parka, he flung him onto the hood of the sedan, pinning an arm with one hand and seizing his throat with the other. Fingers dug into Jonathan's neck, collapsing his larynx.

With his free hand, Jonathan struck the man repeatedly, but the blows landed weakly and with little effect. Wrapping his fingers around the automobile antenna, he struggled to pull himself clear of the assailant. The antenna snapped, and he held it limply in his hand.

Suddenly, a shadow loomed overhead. Simone raised her hand high in the air and beat the man with a chunk of cobblestone. "Stop!" she cried. "Let him go!"

The attacker loosed a hand and clubbed Simone across the face. She tumbled to the ground, her head striking the pavement with a resonant thud. A second later, the hand was back at Jonathan's throat, the grip stronger than ever.

Jonathan's field of vision shrunk to the face glowering inches from his own. The odor of beer, onions, and cigarettes assaulted his nostrils. The attacker slid him down the hood and brought his other hand to Jonathan's neck, fingers taking hold like steel claws. The pressure increased and Jonathan felt his esophagus giving way.

It came to him that it was no longer just a question of escaping, but of surviving. He would have to kill the man on top of him. His consciousness ebbed and he thought of Emma. He saw her broken form lying in the ice. Alone. Abandoned. He knew that it was his fault and that he couldn't leave her there. Someone had to bring her down from the mountain.

The thought galvanized him.

His fingers tightened around the antenna. He searched the man's face—eyes, nose, mouth—looking for the proper spot. Summoning the last of his strength, he sat up. In the same motion, he brought the antenna to the attacker's head in a vicious, stabbing arc.

Instantly, the hands weakened.

Jonathan rammed the antenna home.

The attacker staggered from the car, sunglasses dangling from one ear. Turning in a circle, he frantically gulped down air. One half of the antenna protruded from the man's ear. Repeatedly, he tried to grasp the rod, but his fingers went wide every time.

Dazed, Jonathan slid off the hood of the car, his eyes never straying from his assailant. A clinical voice informed him that after piercing the eardrum, the antenna had entered the cerebellum, where it had scrambled the motor reflexes, the autonomic nervous system, and God only knew what else.

The attacker sank down to his knees. His chin fell to his chest. Eyes open, he went as still as a toy whose batteries had run out.

Simone pushed herself to her feet. The side of her face was red and swollen. "Is he dead?"

Jonathan placed his fingers on the assailant's neck.

He nodded. He stood, kicked loose a chunk of ice, and pressed it to her cheek.

"Who is he?" Simone asked.

"No idea. I've never seen either of them before in my life."

The attacker's jacket had fallen open. A silver badge was visible on his belt, and next to it, a pistol. Jonathan knelt to examine the badge. Engraved across the top were the words "Graubünden Kantonspolizei." His stomach dropped. He slipped his hand into the man's jacket and came up with an ID case. **Sergeant Oskar Studer.** The photograph matched.

"A cop." Jonathan tossed the ID to Simone.

"Go," she whispered. "Get out of here."

"I can't leave. I have to tell the police what happened."

"They **are** the police."

Jonathan had trouble accepting the notion. "What were they doing? They didn't even say anything."

"I don't know and I don't care," said Simone. "I grew up in a country where you couldn't trust the police. They took my father. They took my uncle. Never an explanation. I know what the authorities are capable of."

"Be serious. This isn't Egypt."

Simone looked at him as if he were a jackass. "And so? Is that badge fake?"

"I don't know . . . I mean, it doesn't matter. It's not right. I can't run away. The guy's dead. I killed him. I just can't do—"

"You! **Amerikaner.** Stay where you are." Ten feet away, the heavyset blond man rose on all fours. If his carriage was unsteady, the voice was anything but. One hand held a pistol and he was pointing it in their direction.

Amerikaner, thought Jonathan, incredulously. He'd never seen this man before. How could he possibly know anything about him?

The blond man leveled his gun and pulled the trigger. Nothing happened. Gazing confusedly at the pistol, he struggled to free the safety.

Jonathan looked from Simone to the corpse in the road to the bloodied man fighting to his feet and pointing a pistol at him. "Get in the car!" he shouted. "Move! Now!"

The driver's door was open. He flung himself into the car and started the engine. Simone landed in the passenger's seat and slammed the door, her eyes wild.

A millisecond later, the rear window exploded, pelting their backs and necks with glass.

Simone screamed.

Jonathan threw the car into reverse and rammed his foot on the accelerator. The automobile struck the gunman and there was a solid thwack as he hit the pavement.

Jonathan braked, and shoved the gearshift into first. He let out the clutch too quickly and the car lurched before accelerating down the street.

In a minute, they were out of town doing a hundred eighty kilometers along the highway.

14

Marcus von Daniken stood beneath the awning of the Sterngold outdoor café at Bellevueplatz, a cell phone pressed to his ear. "Yes, Frank," he said, speaking loudly to drown out the voices of the diners around him. "Did you get anything on the passport?"

It was one o'clock. A malicious wind screamed across the lake, snatching bits of flume off the white-caps, swirling them through the air, and slapping the foam against von Daniken's cheek.

"An interesting question," said Frank Vincent of the Belgian Federal Police. "Tell me, Marcus, is there anything you forgot to mention about Lammers? I mean, any ties to us?"

"What kind of ties?" asked von Daniken.

"With our country. With Belgium."

"No. Lammers worked in Brussels for a year or

two, but that was in 1987, twenty years ago. What have you got?"

Vincent grunted, disappointedly. "You see, we tracked down the original passport holder, Jules Gaye. We located his application and ran through his home address, birth certificate, even checked his tax records. He's an international businessman, if you're interested. Owns a dozen companies all over the world. Clothing was his line. Traveled quite a lot. Dubai. Delhi. Hong Kong."

Von Daniken thought of all the stamps in Lammers's passports. Lammers traveled frequently, too. "So he's a real man?"

"Oh, yeah," said Vincent. "Wife. Kids. House on the Avenue Tervuren. He's real, alright."

"What are you saying? That Lammers was leading a double existence? One family in Zurich, one in Brussels?"

"No. That much we can rule out. Lammers and Gaye are definitely two different people."

Only then did von Daniken catch the noise of a car honking in the background. "Frank, where are you?"

"At a pay phone," said Vincent. "The last one in Brussels."

"A pay phone? What the hell are you doing there?"

"You'll know well enough in a second."

"Frank, did you find Gaye or not?"

"Of course I found him." Vincent paused, and his

voice lost its serrated edge. "Gaye's passport was a replacement job. He lost his old one while he was traveling and needed a new one on the spot. He showed up at our consulate in Amman."

"Amman? What was he doing there?"

"Visiting a textile factory. All strictly legit. I called our boys out there and they remembered the case. In fact, it's safe to say they'll never forget it."

Von Daniken pressed the phone to his ear, straining to hear Vincent over the ambient traffic noise. He was wondering what was so memorable about issuing a new passport to a tourist.

"Happened two years ago, August," Vincent went on. "Gaye showed up with a story that his passport had been stolen from his hotel room, along with his wallet and some other belongings. He offered his driver's license as proof of identity. A nice gentleman, by all accounts. The passport was issued on the spot. About two weeks afterward, the body of a European man and his wife were found in a wadi halfway to nowhere. The local gendarmes said the couple had been killed by bandits, but it was hard to tell. They'd been dead a long time. Weeks. Maybe months. You can imagine the condition of the bodies in that heat, not to mention the desert jackals, the flies. The thieves had made off with their belongings, so identification was impossible. Eventually, the police traced the rental car back to a small hotel. They hauled the manager into the morgue and he was able to confirm that the corpses in the jeep had been his guests. He recognized the man's shirt. According to him, it was Gaye."

"But it was never proved . . ."

"Sure it was. His family asked for a DNA test. It took three months, but the hotel manager was right. It was Gaye sure enough."

"Are you saying that it was Lammers who applied for the replacement passport?"

"You tell me. Was Lammers one meter eighty tall, eighty-five kilos, fair hair going to gray, blue eyes?"

Von Daniken drew up an image of the prostrate corpse lying in the snow. "Close enough."

"You know what I'm thinking, Marcus? That job out there in the desert . . . it was also professional."

One point still bothered von Daniken. "But that was two years ago. Surely you blocked the passport."

"Of course we did. We blocked it immediately."

"So what's the big deal? Why are you calling me from a pay phone?"

"Because a month later, someone unblocked it."

"Who?" demanded von Daniken.

There was a moment of silence. Far away, on a crowded boulevard in Brussels, a truck blared its horn. "Someone high up, Marcus. Very high up."

15

"Bastards! **Espèce de salopards!"** Simone Noiret banged the dashboard with every epithet. "He was trying to kill you! Why?"

"I don't know," replied Jonathan, in a faraway voice. The heater was blasting him with a torrent of warm air, yet he couldn't keep from shivering. The image of the policeman lamely grasping at the antenna protruding from his skull played front and center in his mind.

"But you must," Simone insisted.

"They wanted the bags. That's all I can think of. The guy lost his cool when I fought back."

"The bags? That's all? There must be more to it than that. Surely—"

"What do you want me to say?" Jonathan protested, turning toward her. "I've never seen those men before in my life. I'm just as frightened as you are. Arguing about it won't help. We have to figure out what to do."

Simone recoiled at the outburst. "Pardon me," she said, settling into her seat. "You're right. We're both frightened. I didn't mean to imply . . ."

"I know you didn't. Let's just sit here a few minutes, chill out, and figure out what we're going to do."

They had parked in a pine glade high on the mountain overlooking the city. Below them, no more than two miles' distance, a swarm of flashing lights had converged on the train station. He counted ten police cars and two ambulances.

He poked his index finger into the neat round hole that the bullet had drilled into the dashboard. "Those men back there . . . one of them is dead, the other's gravely injured at the least. I can't just sit here. I've got to explain what happened. I've got to tell them that this whole thing is some kind of mistake. They went after the wrong person . . ."

"Look at the bullet hole, Jon. It's your police who made it. And now you want to turn yourself in?" Simone threw up her hands in exasperation.

"What other choice is there? By now, every cop in this canton, and probably the whole country, has a description of us. Tall American with gray hair accompanied by a dark-haired woman traveling in a silver BMW 5 Series. In an hour, they'll have our names . . . or at least mine. We won't be hard to find."

"And then what are you going to say? Are you

going to tell them it was all in self-defense? They won't believe a word." Simone fished in her bag for a cigarette. "**Pourris,** Jon. You know what that means? Rotten. Bent. These policemen, they were no good." She needed two hands to steady her lighter.

Jonathan opened the ID case. The identification belonged to Oskar Studer. Wachtmeister. Graubünden Kantonspolizei. It was then that he noticed that the car wasn't equipped like other police cars. There was no two-way radio. No inboard computer. No gun rack. It was remarkably clean. Not a speck of dirt on the carpets. No empty coffee cups. The odometer read two thousand kilometers. There were some papers in the side compartment. Car rental documents made out to one Oskar Studer. The car had been taken out that morning at ten and was due back in twenty-four hours.

Pourris. He knew precisely what the word meant.

All thoughts of going to the police vanished.

He put the papers back. "They knew I was an American," he said. "They were waiting for me."

Simone nodded, her eyes meeting his, sharing his distress.

He glanced at the leather bag and the neatly wrapped package.

"Open them," she said. "Let's find out what this is about."

He chose the package first. Using his Swiss Army knife, he sawed through the twine. The paper peeled away easily, revealing a glossy black box. A golden sticker embossed with a designer name decorated the upper right-hand corner.

"Bogner," said Simone. "It must be a present."

"Looks like it," said Jonathan, unconvinced, as he cut the ribbon encircling the box.

Bogner made high-end clothing designed to keep jet-setters warm and chic on their trips to the Alps. On a lark, he and Emma had ducked into one of their shops while on a getaway to Chamonix last October. It was a sunny day, he remembered, a weekend between fall and winter when the nip in the air sharpens to a bite.

"Which one do you fancy?" Emma had asked, under her breath as they prowled the aisles. They were raiders operating behind enemy lines. The "enemy" being the vain and wealthy. Those who ignored their "duty to interfere."

Jonathan pointed to a charcoal crewneck sweater. "I'll take this one."

"Consider it yours."

"Really?" he said, playing along.

"It suits you. We'll take it," she said to the hovering salesgirl.

"We will?" said Jonathan, loud enough to risk blowing their cover.

Emma nodded, threading an arm through his. "I have hidden resources," she whispered in his ear, though not before giving it a nibble.

"Does Madam have some Monopoly money hidden in a shoe box?"

Emma didn't answer. Instead, she continued speaking to the salesgirl as if he weren't there. "An extra large. And wrap it, please. It's a present for my husband." Her tone was no longer subdued or surreptitious. And neither was the look in her eye.

"Emma, come on," he said. "Enough's enough. Let's get out of here."

"No," she insisted. "You've earned it. Back pay."

"For what?"

"I'm not telling."

At which point, Jonathan had seen the price tag, and after practically fainting, yanked her out of the store. Outside, they'd laughed at her impetuous behavior. But even then, she'd shot him a chilly look that said he'd committed a sin and was exiled to her bad graces until further notice.

Jonathan recalled her expression as he removed the box cover. Gauze paper concealed a dark garment. Parting the wrapping, he lifted it partially out of the box. He'd forgotten how soft it was.

"Lovely," said Simone.

It was the sweater from Chamonix. A simple charcoal crewneck. Well made and elegant, but at first sight, nothing out of the ordinary, which was precisely his style. He passed his fingers over the collar. Four-ply cashmere. There was nothing softer on earth. It had cost sixteen hundred dollars. Half a month's salary.

"I have hidden resources."

Was this the birthday present she'd mentioned to the manager of the Bellevue?

Jonathan laid the sweater back in the box. The balance of Dr. and Mrs. Ransom's checking account presently stood at fifteen thousand some-odd Swiss francs. Roughly twelve thousand dollars. And that was before paying the hotel bill.

Setting aside the box, he pulled the calfskin bag onto his lap. He had the unsettling feeling that he was never meant to see its contents, just as he was never supposed to have opened Emma's letter. "Those who listen at closed doors rarely hear good of themselves," his mother had warned him as an adolescent. But to Jonathan, there was no longer good or bad. There was only truth and deception. He could no sooner discard the bag than he could ignore the baggage receipts. He had an image of himself opening a colorful Russian **matryoshka** stacking doll, each shell containing its smaller twin.

A sturdy gold lock held the zipper closed. He looked at Simone. She nodded. With that, he slipped the blade of his knife into the calfskin and guided it the length of the bag.

The first thing he saw was a ziplock bag containing a set of Mercedes-Benz car keys and a hand-drawn map with a square labeled "Bahnhof," and a rectangle next to it labeled "Parking" with an "X" inked at its far end. Was it referring to the Landquart station? There were a lot of Bahnhofs in Switzerland.

A navy crepe blazer lay beneath the keys, along with a pair of matching slacks and an ivory blouse. It was the kind of stylish outfit worn by young executives in Frankfurt and London. Women you saw charging through airports on four-inch heels, cell phone clapped to their ear, and laptop bag over their shoulder. Then came a black lace brassiere and panties. There was nothing businesslike about these, he mused, lifting them by a finger. These were designed to impress an entirely different clientele.

A makeup kit presented itself next. Jonathan dug around inside it. Mascara. Eyeliner. Lipstick. Foundation, blush, moisturizer, and God help him, a set of false eyelashes. There was perfume, too. Tender Poison by Dior.

"And Emma?" he asked himself. She swore by Burberry's Tender Touch. An English Rose by name and virtue.

Beneath the tubes and jars and compacts, he found a satin pouch bound by an elegant golden rope. With an inelegant yank, he unknotted it. A pirate's booty lay inside: a Cartier slave bracelet and an emerald baguette; diamond earrings and a gold mesh necklace. He had no experience with jewelry, but he knew quality, and this was it.

He glanced up to find Simone staring at him. Jonathan felt an eerie communion between them. Their Emma did not wear power suits. Their Emma did not sport flaming red lipstick. She did not put on false eyelashes or dab Tender Poison behind her ear;

and she most certainly did not possess an heiress's jewelry. He had the impression that he was looking through another woman's belongings.

Simone was examining a ring she'd taken from the pouch. "E.A.K.," she said. "Know anyone by those initials?"

"Why do you ask?"

"Take a look on the inside." It was a gold wedding band engraved "E.A.K. 2-8-01." "That's who the bag belongs to," she said. "Mrs. E.A.K., who was married February 8, 2001. It must be one of Emma's friends."

Jonathan ran through the E's he knew. He came up with an Ed, an Ernie, and an Étienne, but he didn't think the thong was their size. The female list was shorter and ran to one name: Evangeline Larsen, a Danish doctor with whom he'd worked four years earlier.

There was a last item in the jewelry pouch. A stainless and gold ladies' Rolex wristwatch with a diamond-crusted bezel. To Jonathan, it was the surest proof yet that his wife had no claim on the bag. A Rolex was the symbol of everything they found wrong with the world. Status for sale at five thousand bucks a shot. And Emma's timepiece of choice? A Casio G-Force favored by hockey players, U.S. Marines, and aid professionals with a duty to interfere.

There was more in the bag. A pair of shoes. Size 5½. Emma's size. He knew because she had small feet and often carped about how hard it was to find anything that fit. Stockings. A box of breath mints. An eyeglass case holding fashionable tortoiseshell spectacles.

Jonathan ran his hands along the inside of the bag. He felt something firm and rectangular tucked inside the wall. A wallet, he guessed. But even as he unzipped the compartment and removed the grosgrain crocodile billfold inside, something was nagging at him. It was the ring. A married woman didn't take off her wedding band unless she was bathing or swimming, and even then, it was questionable. The thought of trusting it to a poorly secured overnight bag that had been placed on a common train was . . . well, it was **unthinkable.**

The billfold held a Eurocard, a Crédit Suisse ATM card, an American Express card, and a Rainbow Card entitling the bearer to use of Zug public transit for a year's time.

"Eva Kruger," he said, reading the cardholder's name. **E.A.K.** "Ever heard of her?"

Simone shook her head. "She must be one of Emma's contacts. I'm glad it will be you telephoning her to tell her what you did to her lovely bag and not me."

But Jonathan didn't respond. Not to the comment or its implicit humor. He had set about making an inventory of the wallet. There was cash in the amount of one thousand Swiss francs and five hundred euros. In the coin purse, he found four francs and fifty rappen.

Abruptly, he sat up. It came to him that there was one thing missing. Something Mrs. Eva Kruger, the law-abiding owner of a Mercedes-Benz, wouldn't be caught dead without. Mind racing, he opened the crocodile wallet. It was a surgeon's shockproof hands that defied his thumping heart and navigated through the credit cards and banknotes, delving into every possible nook and cranny.

He discovered Eva Kruger's driver's license, slipped into the space beneath the credit cards. He unfolded it and studied the color photograph affixed inside. An attractive woman with sleek brown hair pulled severely off her forehead, chic tortoiseshell spectacles hiding large amber eyes, and a full mouth gazed into the camera.

"What is it?" asked Simone. "You look like you've seen a ghost."

But Jonathan couldn't speak. There was a great pressure on his chest, robbing him of air. He looked at the driver's license again. Behind the diva's mascara and the tart's lipstick, Emma stared back at him.

Jonathan threw open the door and stepped outside. Walking a few paces, he stopped to lean against a tree. It was difficult to keep moving, to act as if the world hadn't just shifted beneath his feet. He forced himself to regard the image of the severe woman with the slicked hair and the fashionable spectacles staring brazenly into the camera.

Eva Kruger.

One look at the photo and the idea of Emma having had an affair seemed an annoyance. No worse than a fly on a horse's ass. But this—a false driver's license, a false name, an entire double life—this was a black hole.

Simone came round the front of the car and stood next to him. "I'm sure there's an explanation. Wait until we get back to Geneva. Then we'll find out."

"That watch costs ten thousand francs. And what about the other jewelry? The clothes? The makeup? Tell me, Simone, just what kind of explanation do you have in mind?"

She paused, thinking. "I don't . . . I mean I can't."

He glanced down at his jacket and saw a patch of blood encrusted on it. He didn't know if it was his or one of the policemen's. Either way, the sight revolted him. He struggled out of the jacket and tossed it onto the hood of the car. The cold hit him immediately. "Hand me the sweater, would you?"

Simone retrieved the cashmere sweater from the car. "Here you are . . ."

An envelope dropped from the sweater's folds into the snow. Jonathan traded glances with Simone, then picked it up. The envelope was unmarked, but heavy. He knew its contents immediately. It had the right heft, the right shape. He tore it open. Money. Lots of it. Thousand-franc notes. Newly minted and crisp as tracing paper.

"My God," said Simone, eyes agog. "How much is it?"

"A hundred," he said, after counting the stack.

"A hundred what?"

"One hundred thousand Swiss francs."

I have hidden resources, Emma had said.

"You've got to be kidding." Simone was laughing, a high-pitched, hysterical laugh a hair's breadth from out of control.

"Now we know," said Jonathan, transfixed by the stack of banknotes.

"Know what?" asked Simone.

"Why the police wanted the bag."

He slipped the bills back into the envelope and stuffed it into his pocket. It remained to be seen how they'd known the bags were in Landquart, and more important, at least to Jonathan's mind, why Emma was meant to be the recipient of so much cash.

A breeze rustled the branches, wrestling flocks of snow to the ground. Shivering, he pulled the sweater over his head. The cashmere crewneck clung at his chest and his shoulders. The sleeves stopped three inches short of his wrist.

It was another man's sweater.

16

"*Have you seen these?*" demanded Justice Minister Alphons Marti, as von Daniken entered his office. **"NZZ. Tribune de Genève. Tages-Anzeiger."** He snatched up the phone messages and balled them in his fist. "Every newspaper in the country wants to know what happened at the airport yesterday."

Von Daniken removed his overcoat and folded it over his arm. "What have you told them?"

Marti threw the wadded-up ball into the garbage. " 'No comment.' What do you think I told them?"

The office on the fourth floor of the Bundeshaus was nothing less than palatial. High ceilings decorated with gold leaf and a trompe l'oeil painting of Christ ascending to heaven, Oriental rugs adorning a polished wooden floor, and a mahogany desk as big as the altar at St. Peter's. A battered wooden crucifix hanging on the wall testified that Marti was really just a simple man.

"And so," Marti began, "when did they take off?"

"The plane left as soon as their engine was repaired," said von Daniken. "Sometime after seven this morning. The pilot listed their destination as Athens."

"Another shovelful of shit the Americans expect us to swallow with a smile. I've made stopping rendition on European soil a cornerstone of this office's policy. Sooner or later, someone will talk to the press and I'll have egg all over my face." Marti shook his head ruefully. "The prisoner was on the plane. I'm convinced of it. Onyx doesn't lie."

Utilizing three hundred phased-array antennas positioned high on a mountainside above the town of Leuk in the Rhône valley, Onyx was capable of intercepting all civilian and military communications passing between an equal number of pre-targeted satellites in geosynchronous orbit over the earth. Algorithm-based software parsed the transmissions for key words indicating information of immediate value. Some of those key words were "Federal Bureau of Investigation," "Intelligence," and "prisoner." At 0455 yesterday morning, Onyx had struck pay dirt.

"I reviewed the intercept last night," Marti went on. "Names. Itinerary. It's all there." He pushed a buff folder across the table. Von Daniken picked it up and examined the contents. Inside was a photocopy of a telefax sent from the Syrian consulate in

Stockholm to the Syrian Directorate of Intelligence in Damascus titled, "Passenger Manifest: Prisoner Transport #767." The list gave the pilot and copilot's names, as well as two that were more familiar. Philip Palumbo and Walid Gassan.

"Check the time stamp, Marcus. The manifest was transmitted **after** the plane took off. Gassan was on-board. I don't buy for a second that Palumbo pushed him off. You know what I think. I think someone tipped off Mr. Palumbo that we intended to search the aircraft. I'd like you to start an investigation into the matter."

"Only a few of us had copies of the intercept. You, me, our deputies, and, naturally, the technicians at Leuk."

"Exactly."

"We searched the aircraft top to bottom," said von Daniken as he laid the folder back on the desk. "There was no sign of the prisoner."

"You mean **you** searched it." The hyperthyroid blue eyes peered at him.

"I believe you were present."

"So we can rule ourselves out," said Marti, a smile showing his bad teeth. "It'll make your investigation that much easier. I'll expect a report daily." He tapped the folder twice with his knuckles, indicating the matter was closed. "And so? What is it, then? Your secretary informed me that you have something on the murder in Erlenbach last night. What's this about a search warrant?"

Von Daniken hesitated, waiting for Marti to ask him to be seated. When it became apparent that no such invitation was forthcoming, he launched into a summary of what he'd learned about Lammers, including his past history designing artillery pieces and his recent interest in MAVs. He ended with his suspicion that the Dutchman was part of a larger network and his request for a warrant to search the premises of Robotica AG.

"That's all?" asked Marti. "I can't fill in 'suspicious miniature airplane' on a warrant. This is a legal document. I need a legitimate reason."

"It's my opinion that Lammers posed a threat to national security."

"How? The man's dead. Just because you saw a model airplane . . . not even a model airplane . . . a pair of wings with God knows what."

Von Daniken tried on a smile as a means to camouflage his simmering anger. "It's not just the plane, sir. It's the whole setup. Lammers had been in place a long time. He's got a history of playing with the bad boys, and then one day, out of the blue, he's executed on his own front stoop. I'm certain that something's going on. Either it's coming together or falling apart. The evidence may be inside his office."

"Conjecture," barked Marti.

"The man had an Uzi hidden in his workshop, along with a batch of passports that were stolen from individuals either living in or visiting the Middle East. That much is not conjecture."

The New Zealand embassy in France had called back minutes before von Daniken reached Marti's office, reporting that the passport found in Lammers's car had been stolen from a hospital in Istanbul. The true passport holder was, in fact, a quadriplegic who'd been confined to a nursing facility for three years. He hadn't even known that his passport was missing. Lammers had pulled the same trick as in Jordan, claiming to be a businessman who had lost his passport.

"There's only one reason someone would want to steal a Belgian and New Zealand passport," von Daniken went on. "Ease of passage in and out of the Middle East. Especially to countries with travel restrictions. Yemen. Iran. Iraq. This kind of operation requires not only funding but infrastructure and some damned fancy footwork. Lammers was scared. He saw this coming. The operation was active."

"Conjecture," repeated Marti. " 'Scared' is not grounds for issuing a warrant to search a registered Swiss company. We're talking about a corporation here, not a private citizen."

Von Daniken forced himself to count to five. "By the way, sir, the official name for the device is 'micro airborne vehicle.' It's also called a drone."

"You can call it a mosquito on steroids for all I care," retorted Marti. "I still won't sign the warrant. If you want to search his premises so badly, open a dossier with an investigating judge in Zurich. If he thinks you've got enough evidence to warrant a search, you won't need me."

"That will take a week at the least."

"And so?"

"What if there's an imminent threat to Swiss soil?"

"Oh, Christ, let's not get hysterical."

Behind Marti's desk was a photograph of him entering the Olympic Stadium at the end of his disastrous marathon. Even in a still frame, he looked wobbly. It was apparent that he had vomited on himself earlier in the race. Von Daniken wondered what kind of man displayed an image of himself at the lowest, most humiliating moment in his life.

"If you believe that there's an imminent threat, then give me some substantiation," said Marti. "You said Lammers used to design artillery pieces. Fine. Then show me a big gun. This warrant isn't just going to disappear into a file. It'll be my head if I act as your rubber stamp. I'll be damned if I let you go off half-cocked, mobilizing every resource to check out a wild hunch."

A wild hunch? Is that what thirty years of experience boiled down to? Von Daniken studied Marti. The hollow cheeks. The too-fashionable long hair dyed a too-fashionable henna. The man could make a Dutch pretzel out of the law if he desired. He was purposefully being obdurate as payback for the botched raid on the CIA jet.

"What about the Uzi?" von Daniken asked.

"What about the passports? Don't those count for anything?"

"You said it yourself. He was scared. He was on the run. Those facts alone do not allow us to invade his privacy."

"The man is dead. He doesn't have any privacy anymore."

"Don't play games with me! I will not quibble over semantics."

"God forbid we piss someone off." Von Daniken respected the constitution as much as the next man. Never in his career had he strayed from either its letter or its intent. But a policeman's job had changed radically in the last ten years. As a counterterrorist, he needed to stop a crime **before** it happened. Gone was the luxury of collecting evidence after the act and presenting it to a magistrate. Often, the only evidence was his experience and intuition.

He walked to the window and looked out over the River Aare. Dusk had turned the sky into a palette of warring grays doing battle low over the city's rooftops. The snow, which had tapered off earlier, was falling again in earnest. A gusting wind batted the flakes into an angry maelstrom. "Don't bother with the warrant," he said finally.

Marti stood and rounded the desk, shaking his hand. "I'm glad to see that you're being more reasonable."

Von Daniken turned and headed to the door. "I have to be going."

"Wait a minute . . ."

"Yes?"

"What are you going to do about the little plane? The MAV?"

Von Daniken shrugged as if the matter no longer interested him. "I'm not going to do anything," he said.

It was a lie.

17

Jonathan trained his eyes on the entrance to the Landquart station, and the parking lot directly across the street from it where a late-model Mercedes sedan sat in the center of the third row, precisely where the map in Eva Kruger's bag said it would be. His vantage point was the doorway of a shuttered restaurant fifty meters up the road. For the past ninety minutes, he'd been circling the station. Trains arrived on the half hour from Chur and Zurich. For a few minutes before and after, the sidewalk filled with commuters. Cars entered and left the parking lot. And then activity died until the next train arrived. Not once in that time had he caught sight of a policeman. Still, it was impossible to determine if someone was watching the parking lot. Whatever the case, he'd decided that Simone was right. The cops who'd wanted to steal Emma's bags were crooked.

At five minutes to six, evening traffic was at its height. Headlights passed in a blinding parade. He stamped his boots, working to keep his circulation active. He'd left Simone at the edge of town, against her strident wishes. There was a time for teamwork and a time to go it alone. This was a solo run, no question.

Huddling inside his jacket, he kept his eyes trained on the Mercedes.

Pick up letter.

Show receipts.

Retrieve bags.

Consult map for location of parked car.

Change clothing. Slick back hair. Don't forget wedding ring.

Change lives.

Deliver sweater with envelope containing one hundred thousand francs.

But where? When? To whom? And, most maddening of all: **Why?**

He ran his fingers over the car key, thinking about Emma.

Question: When is your wife, your wife?

And when she isn't your wife, who is she?

———

Dr. Jonathan Ransom, graduate of the University of Colorado at Boulder, Southwestern Medical School, chief surgical resident at New York's Memorial Sloan-Kettering Cancer Center, and Dewes fellowship recipient at Oxford Radcliffe

Hospital with a specialty in reconstructive surgery, stands on the tarmac of Monrovia-Roberts Airport in Liberia, as the last of the passengers deplane and stroll past him. At eight a.m., the sun sits low in an angry, orange sky. Already, the day is hot and humid, the air rank with the scents of jet fuel and sea salt, and cut by shouts coming from the horde of black faces bunched on the far side of the stadium-high fence bordering the runway. From all too near, the rat-a-tat-tat of machine-gun fire punches the air.

Not a thing to worry about, they had promised him during his orientation. The fighting is confined to the countryside.

He walks toward the immigrations building, passing a pair of bloated corpses pushed against the fence. A mother and daughter, to judge by the way they hold each other, though it's hard to tell because of the flies.

"You're Ransom?"

A battered military jeep trawls alongside him. A young, suntanned woman with wild auburn hair pulled into a ponytail grasps the oversized steering wheel. "You?" she shouts to be heard over the roar of a departing transport. "You're Dr. Ransom? Get in. I'll rescue you from this circus."

Jonathan throws his bag into the back of the jeep. "I thought the fighting was out in the country," he says.

"This isn't fighting. This is 'dialogue.' Haven't

you been reading the papers?" She extends a hand. "Emma Rose. Delighted."

"Yeah," says Jonathan. "Back at ya."

They drive through the worst slums he has ever seen, a wall of poverty five miles long and ten stories high. The city stops abruptly. The countryside takes over, as quiet and lush as the city is noisy and barren.

"First posting, is it?" she asks. "They always send the newbies."

"Why's that?"

Emma doesn't respond. A Mona Lisa smile passes for her answer.

The hospital is a converted sumphouse situated on the edge of a mangrove swamp. Dozens of women and children lie idle in the grass and the red, scalloped mud surrounding the drab building. It's apparent that many are injured, some severely. Their silence is an affront.

"We get a group like this every few days," says Emma, stopping the jeep around the back. "Mortar attacks. Thankfully, most of the wounds are superficial."

Jonathan glimpses a boy with a chunk of shrapnel the size of a three iron jutting from his calf. "Superficial," meaning he won't bleed to death.

A short, bearded man with bloodshot eyes greets Ransom warmly. He is Dr. Delacroix from Lyon. "Good thing the plane was on time," he says, wiping his hands on a blood-caked T-shirt.

"The girl in OR two is yours. Chop-chopped her right hand."

"Chop-chopped?"

"You know?" Delacroix makes a gesture like a guillotine falling. "Took a machete to it."

"Where do I scrub?" asks Jonathan.

"Scrub?" Dr. Delacroix exchanges a tired look with Emma. "You can wash your hands in the lavatory. You'll find some gloves in there, too. Save them. We try to use each pair at least three times."

Afterward, Jonathan stands on the patch of alkali dirt outside the field hospital that serves as terrace, reception, and triage area. At midnight, the air is wet with heat, populated with the cries of howler monkeys and the punctuation of small arms fire.

"Coffee?" Emma hands him a cup. She looks different from when he saw her earlier. Thinner, smaller even, no longer so full of piss and vinegar.

"No O positive," says Jonathan. "We lost two patients because we didn't have enough blood."

"You saved a few."

"Yes, but . . ." He shakes his head, overwhelmed. "Is it always like this?"

"Only every other day."

It is Jonathan's turn not to reply.

Emma looks at him thoughtfully. "The older ones won't come," she says after a moment.

"Excuse me?"

"You wanted to know why they only sent the newbies. That's the reason. It's too hard after a while. All this gets to you. It wears you down. The older ones can't handle it. They say you can only look at so many dead people before you start feeling dead yourself."

"I can understand."

"Not like Blighty, is it?" Emma goes on, her tone sympathetic, comrade to comrade. "I saw you were at Oxford. I was at St. Hilda's. Comparative Political Systems."

"You mean you're not a doctor?"

"God no. I've got my practical nursing on the side, but admin's my thing. Logistics and all that. If we ever do have enough O positive, you'll have me to thank."

"I didn't mean to—" Jonathan begins to apologize.

"Of course you didn't."

"I couldn't tell at first whether you were English. Your accent, I mean. I thought either Scottish or London by way of Central Europe. Prague or something."

"Me? I'm from the southwest. Cornwall, that area. We all talk funny down there. Near Land's End. Penzance. You know it?"

"Penzance? In a way." He takes a breath, and though he knows he will look foolish, he puffs up his chest and recites in a sing-song voice:

I'm very well-acquainted, too, with matters
    mathematical,
I understand equations, both the simple and
    quadratical,
About binomial theorem I'm teeming with a lot
    o' news,
With many cheerful facts about the square of
    the hypotenuse.

When she says nothing, he adds, "Gilbert and
Sullivan. Pirates of Penzance. Don't tell me you
don't know the Modern Major-General?"

Suddenly, Emma bursts out laughing. "Of
course I do. One simply isn't used to hearing that
in the wilds of Africa. My God. A fan."

"Not me. My dad. He was a diplomat. We lived
all over the place. Switzerland, Italy, Spain. Wherever we moved, he joined the light opera. He
could sing that song in English, German, and
French."

A driving backbeat lifts to them across the
crowded night sky. The electric thump of a funky
bass. Emma tilts her head in its direction. "The
Muthaiga Club. Great dance spot. They don't do
the Mikado, though, I'm afraid."

"The Muthaiga Club's in Nairobi. I saw Out of
Africa."

"So did I," she whispers, standing on her tiptoes. "Don't tell anybody I pinched the name.
You coming?"

"Dancing?" He shakes his head. "I've been up way too long. I'm fried."

"So?" Emma takes his hand and leads him toward the source of the pulsing music.

Jonathan resists. "Thanks, but really, I've got to rest."

"That's the old you talking."

"The old me?"

"The chief resident. The terrible drudge. The one who wins all those awards and fellowships." She tugs his hand. "Don't look at me like that. I told you I was admin. I read your papers. Want some advice? The old you, the one who works far too hard. Forget about him. He won't last a week out here." Emma's voice drops a notch, and he can't be sure if she's serious or scandalous. "This is Africa. Everyone gets a new life here."

Later, after the dancing and the home brew and the wild, joyous singing, she leads him out of the club, away from the throbbing drums and the swarming bodies, into the bush. They walk through a grove of casuarinas along a footpath, a scratch in the night shadow, until they reach a clearing. Above them a howler monkey lets go with a cry, then bandies from tree to tree. She turns to him, her eyes locked on his, hair askew, falling about her face.

"I've been waiting for you," she says, a hand going to his belt, pulling him toward her.

Jonathan has been waiting for her, too. Not for weeks, or months, but longer. In the space of a day, she has seized him. He is kissing her and she is kissing back. He runs a hand beneath her shirt, feeling the hard, moist skin, sliding it higher, cupping a breast. She bites his lip and presses herself into him. "I'm a good girl, Jonathan. Just so you know going in."

She unbuttons his shirt and smooths it off his shoulders. A palm rubs his chest, then moves lower. Stepping back, she pulls her T-shirt over her head and kicks off her jeans. She devours his hungry regard.

"How do you know?" he asks, as she wraps her body around his.

"The same way you do."

He lies down in the grass and she arranges herself above him. The moonlight dances across her burnt copper hair. The trees sway. Somewhere, a shriek pierces the sky.

The train pulled in from Chur, and a minute later, from the opposite direction, one from Zurich. Passengers crowded the pavement fronting the station. It was now or never. Jonathan left the doorway and hurried across the street. Vaulting the wall bordering the parking lot, he walked down the center aisle. If anyone was watching the station, they had a clear view of him. One six-foot-three-inch Caucasian male clad in a newly purchased navy parka, a matching ski cap pulled low over his brow to hide the thick, slightly curly hair that had started to go gray at the age of twenty-three.

Don't rush, he told himself, straining to keep his muscles in check.

He pulled the keys from his pocket and activated the remote entry. He had the feeling that things were run very tightly around here. Emma had always been a stickler for organization. The car beeped. Don't look around, he told himself. It's Emma's, which means it's yours. An S600. Diamond Black. The car every surgeon's wife was born to drive.

He slid into the driver's seat and closed the door. He touched the gearshift and the engine roared to life. He jumped in his seat, slamming his head against the roof. "Shit," he muttered, before realizing that he'd pressed the ignition button atop the shift lever. It was the latest in automatic functions. He settled down, finding his breath. Soon, he decided, cars would be driving themselves.

It was then that he took in the interior of the automobile. The smell of fresh leather, the pristine condition of the cabin, the air-crackling "newness" of the vehicle. Not just a Mercedes, but a brand-spanking-new, top-of-the-line sedan. Cost: stratospheric. Not so much a car as a temple of luxury; automotive engineering elevated to a higher plane. He got himself settled, adjusting the seat, the mirrors, putting on his seat belt. He slid the transmission into reverse and backed out of the space. The car moved in hushed silence, negotiating the ice-encrusted pavement as if floating on a cloud.

He felt a sudden, irrational streak of hatred for it, not just because it was evidence of Emma's deception, but because it represented the life he'd never wanted. Too many of the surgical residents at Sloan-Kettering had dreamed aloud about their Park Avenue practices and houses in the Hamptons. They could have their baubles and bangles. God knew they'd worked hard enough to get them. It was just that to him, medicine was not a means to an end. Medicine was the end itself. He refused to be defined in any way by his possessions. By cars like this. It was actions that mattered. Dr. Jonathan Ransom took care of others.

He backed out of the parking space and drove to the exit. On the main road, traffic sped past in both directions. Pedestrians took advantage and crossed in front of the Mercedes. A man drew up and stopped in the glare of Jonathan's headlights. Shielding his eyes, he looked through the windscreen at Jonathan. It was a policeman. Jonathan was sure of it. He dropped his hands from the wheel and waited for the man to draw his pistol and shout, "Out of the car! You're under arrest."

But a moment later, the man was gone, another head weaving in and out of the sea of homebound commuters.

Traffic cleared. Jonathan eased the car onto the street, turning left, away from the station. Four blocks down the road, he pulled over and rolled down the window. "Get in."

Simone climbed into the car. Pulling her coat around her, she took in the car's interior. "This is Emma's?" she asked.

"Guess so." Jonathan joined the autobahn, heading east. A roadside sign read, "Chur 25 Km."

A shadow crossed Simone's face. "Where are you going?"

"Back to the hotel. We have to find out who sent those bags."

18

"Hotter."

A guard turned the nozzle regulating the butane burners. Blue flames flared from beneath the enormous copper vat. The temperature gauge showed one hundred forty degrees. The needle inside it began to rise.

It was called the Pot, and it dated to the early seventeenth century. Five feet high and again as wide, it had been a fixture of the public laundry works in Aleppo when Syria had been a province of the Ottoman Empire. The needle touched one hundred fifty degrees. Immersed to his shoulders in the rapidly heating water, Gassan began to kick frantically. He could not allow his feet to touch bottom for fear of being scalded.

The needle passed one hundred sixty degrees.

It had been a long night. Gassan had showed impressive pluck. He had suffered and still not divulged a word about to whom he'd delivered the fifty kilos of plastic explosives. Colonel Mike no longer looked so cleaned and pressed. His mustache drooped with the sweat of his exertions. The evil of the place had sunk into his pores.

"Hotter."

Bubbles formed at the edge of the cauldron. Gassan began to call out. No prayers for him. No pleas to Allah. Just a stream of obscenities cursing the West, cursing the president, cursing the FBI and the CIA. He was no zealot. He was that other thing. The terrorist defined by his actions. The rebel with no cause but to destroy.

Philip Palumbo sat on a chair in the corner. He had grown tired of the pitiable cries long ago. He'd run out of sympathy for dirtbags like Gassan around the time that he'd worked the bombings in Bali. Twenty bodies. Men, women, and children enjoying a seaside jaunt to the tropics. All dead. A hundred more wounded. Lives ended. Lives ruined. And for what? Just the usual tripe about getting at the West. The way Palumbo saw things, we all had a contract with society to treat our fellow man fairly and to obey the laws. Break that contract, go outside the boundaries of fair play, then all bets were off.

Gassan wanted to kill innocent people. Palumbo intended to stop him. Turn up the heat and let's get the party started.

"Let's go back to the beginning," said Colonel

Mike with infuriating calm. "On January tenth, you met Dimitri Shevchenko in Leipzig. You transferred the plastic explosives into a white Volkswagen van. Where did you go after that? You had to give the explosives to someone. I don't imagine you fancied keeping them any longer than necessary. You're a smart boy. Lots of experience. Tell me what happened next. I'll even help you. You delivered the explosives to the end user. I want his name. Talk to me and we'll stop these unpleasantries. To tell you the truth, I don't sleep well after this kind of thing."

The questions hadn't varied in ten hours.

Outside, dogs could be heard baying at the full moon. A large transport rumbled past, shaking the walls.

Gassan began to speak, then pursed his lips and drove his chin into his chest. A guttural scream formed in his throat and erupted into the room.

"Hotter," said Colonel Mike.

The flames grew. The needle touched one hundred eighty degrees.

"What are their plans? Give me the target. I want a place, a date, a time." Colonel Mike was relentless. A man was either made to do this kind of thing or not. Colonel Mike had been born to torture like a jockey to riding.

One hundred ninety.

"The first thing that falls off is your dick. It bursts like an overcooked sausage. Then your stomach will swell inside you and your lungs will begin to boil.

Look at your arms. The flesh is peeling off. The sad thing is that this can go on for a long time."

Gassan's eyes bulged as he continued to hurl imprecations at the unfairness of his predicament.

"What was your contact's name? How will they use the explosives?"

Two hundred degrees.

"Alright," screamed Gassan. "I will tell you. Get me out! Please!"

"Tell me what?"

"Everything. Everything I know. His name. Now, get me out!"

Colonel Mike raised a hand to the guard controlling the gauge. He stepped closer to the vat so that the heat drew sweat on his forehead. "Who is the end user?"

Gassan gave a name Palumbo had never heard before. "I delivered it to him personally. He paid me twenty thousand dollars."

"Where did you deliver the explosives?"

"Geneva. A garage at the airport. The fourth floor."

The dam had broken. Gassan began to talk, spewing information like water from a ruptured main. Names. Aliases. Hideouts. Passwords. He couldn't speak fast enough.

Palumbo got it all on tape. He stepped out of the room to review the information. Five minutes later, he returned. "A few of the names check out, but we've got a lot more to get through."

"And so?" asked Colonel Mike. "Any other questions for our distinguished guest?"

"Oh yeah," said Palumbo. "Mr. Gassan's been in business a long time. We're just getting started."

Colonel Mike nodded at the guard.

"Hotter."

19

Jonathan reached Arosa in ninety minutes. Driving to the top of Poststrasse, he parked across from the Kulm Hotel, three hundred meters up the road from the Bellevue. Simone sat slouched in the passenger seat, smoking.

"There's no reason for you to stay," he said. "It's better if we split up. I can take it from here."

"I want to," she answered, peering out the window.

"Go home. You've done your duty. You held my hand when I needed it. I can't be responsible for you."

It was obvious the suggestion irritated her. "No one's asking you to be," she snapped. "I've made it this far looking after myself, thank you very much."

"What are you going to say to Paul?"

"I'm going to tell him that I helped a friend."

"That'll sound nice when you call him from jail. All you're doing is getting yourself deeper into trouble."

Simone shifted in her seat, swinging her gaze at him. Her cheek was purple where the policeman had struck her. The bruise contrasted violently with her usual immaculate appearance. "And what are you doing? Tell me that, Jon."

Jonathan had told himself that he was going to take things one step at a time. Technically, he knew that he was on the run, but it wasn't the police—either the honest variety or the other kind—that scared him. It was the truth. "I'm not sure yet," he said after a moment.

Simone sat up straighter. "How many brothers do you have?"

The question caught him off guard. "Two. And a sister. Why?"

"If this was happening to one of them, would you go home?"

"No," he said. "I wouldn't."

"I don't have any brothers or sisters," Simone continued. "I'm married to a man who treats his work as his mistress. I have my children at school and I have Emma. I'm every bit as confused as you about what she was up to. If I can help you in any way find out, I want to try. I understand your concern for me and I appreciate it. Tomorrow, I'll go to Davos to see

Paul. I'm sure that by then we'll have this straight-ened out. But if we have to confront the police, I am going to be with you."

Jonathan saw that there was no getting around her. He couldn't deny that her presence would be of help when he was standing in front of a police captain. She was a teacher affiliated with a prestigious school in Geneva; her husband, a respected economist.

He reached over and plucked the cigarette out of her mouth. "Okay, you win. But if you stay, you have to stop smoking these things. You're going to make me puke."

Simone immediately took another cigarette from her purse and screwed it into the corner of her mouth. "**Allez.** I'll wait for you here." She leaned over and kissed him on the cheek. "Be careful."

Head bowed, Jonathan hurried down the road. Wind kicked up snow and flung it at his cheeks so violently that it was necessary to shield his eyes just to see ten feet ahead. He followed a fork that led off the Poststrasse, then veered onto a footpath that cut through the Arlenwald, the forest that carpeted the lower flank of the mountain. The wind was calmer here, and he began to walk faster.

Beyond the spray of the streetlights, the path grew dark, bordered by tall pines and ramrod-stiff birches. To his right, the hillside fell steeply. After a few min-utes, he came upon the rear of the hotel and made his way down the slope through knee-deep snow. He stopped at the edge of the woods, pinpointing his room. Fourth floor. Front corner. A hundred-year-old pine shot from the slope near the building, its upper branches extending tantalizingly close to balconies on the third and fourth floors.

It was then that he felt the hairs on the nape of his neck prickle. He turned sharply, certain that someone was watching him. He scanned the hillside behind him. An owl perched high in a tree hooted. The throaty, low-pitched call made him shiver. He looked a second longer, but didn't see anyone.

Five strides took him to the sturdy pine. Selecting a branch, he pulled himself into the tree, then climbed higher. Ten meters up, he crawled out onto a limb. The balcony was barely an arm's length away, the pitch of the slope so severe that if he fell, he would land in the snow three meters below. He hung from the branch and swung his legs until he caught the retaining wall. Shifting his balance, he hopped onto the balcony.

Lights burned from behind closed curtains. The balcony door was open a crack. He stepped forward, rolling on the balls of his feet. At that moment, the curtains parted. The balcony door swung inward. He had a fleeting image of a man in a suit holding open the door and speaking to a woman. Retreating, Jonathan threw himself over the balcony. Dangling by his fingertips—what climbers called a bat hang—he inched past the divider separating the balconies. The railing was icy and intensely cold. He glanced down. It was sixty feet to the driveway, and if he missed that, another sixty to the street below. His fingers numbed out. He tried to convince himself that this was no different than hanging off a nubbin on a granite face. But he didn't go free-climbing granite faces in the dead of winter. Inch by inch, he crossed the outside of the balcony. With a grunt, he pulled himself over the railing.

Gathering his breath, he tried the door. It was unlocked, just as he'd left it that morning. Inside, the lights were extinguished. He stepped into the room, pausing a moment to allow his eyes to adjust to the darkness. The maid's efforts were plain to see. The bed was made. The pleasing scent of wood polish lingered in the air. Still, he couldn't ignore the feeling that something wasn't as it should be.

He approached the bed. Emma's nightshirt was beneath the pillow. Her paperbacks stacked neatly on the night table. He picked up the one on top. **Prior Bad Acts.** The title was appropriate enough, but he was relatively certain that she hadn't started that book yet. He found the book Emma had been reading at the bottom of the stack.

He walked into the hall and opened the closet. Drawer by drawer, he checked Emma's things. He was supposed to be looking for clues to her activities. But what kind of clues? If he didn't know what she'd been doing, how could he know what to search for?

He closed the closet and checked above it, where he stored their suitcases. Standing on his tiptoes, he pulled down the larger of the two. It was Emma's suitcase, a Samsonite hardshell similar to those favored by stewardesses. He put it on the ground, then froze.

He never put Emma's suitcase on top. That's where he put his own, which was smaller and flimsier.

Somebody had been in the room.

For a minute, he didn't move. Head cocked, he listened. Each beat of his heart hammered a nail into his chest. But apart from his rattled nerves, he didn't hear a thing. Finally, he picked up the suitcase, carried it to the bed, and opened it.

Another surprise. The cover's interior lining had been peeled back along its perimeter, just like the transparent plastic sheets used to hold snapshots in a photo album. It hadn't been cut or damaged in any way. Looking more closely, he discovered a track in place to secure it, no different than a ziplock bag. By the moon's half-light, he discerned a rectangular indentation the size and shape of a wallet or a deck of cards. It was a compartment for concealing papers or documents, something to escape a customs inspector's scrutiny.

He closed the suitcase and returned it to its place. Emma's carry-on bag was sitting below the desk. No black leather calfskin this time, just an all-weather rucksack stained from years of use. He opened the outside compartment and was relieved to find her wallet where she kept it. Her identification was intact; money too, in the amount of eighty-seven francs. Her credit cards were untouched. He opened the coin purse. A few francs. A bobby pin. Tic tacs. He closed the bag, then ran his hand along its bottom. His fingers snagged on a bracelet. He recognized it as one that Emma wore from time to time. It was light blue and fashioned from pressed rubber similar to the Livestrong bracelets popularized by Lance Armstrong, the seven-time winner of the Tour de France.

Three-quarters of the bracelet was thin, but at the point where it rested beneath the wrist, it was noticeably thicker. He ran a finger over the protrusion. There was something hard and rectangular inside it. He played with the bracelet for a moment, before realizing that he could pull it apart. The bracelet split to reveal a USB flash drive. It was a device used to move files from one computer to another. He'd never seen it before. Emma was a demon with her Black-Berry, but she rarely took her laptop out of the office. He reconnected the bracelet and slipped it over his wrist.

Just then, he heard footsteps advancing down the hallway. He put down the rucksack and searched the desk. Maps. Postcards. His compass. Pens. The footsteps came nearer, echoing loudly.

"Right this way, Officer. It's the room at the end of the hall."

Jonathan recognized the hotel manager's voice. The key entered the lock. He opened the center drawer and saw a brown, leather-bound book. Grabbing Emma's rucksack with one hand, he threw the book inside it and bolted for the terrace.

The door opened. Light spilled into the room from the hotel corridor.

"The policeman was dead?" the hotel manager was saying.

Without a backward glance, Jonathan flew from the room and jumped off the balcony onto the hillside.

"They've been there," gasped Jonathan as he flung himself into the Mercedes. "Someone searched the—"

He looked over to the passenger seat. Simone wasn't in the car. He checked the floor for her purse and found that it was gone, too. She's left, he thought. She came to her senses and got the hell out of here while she still could. Jonathan leaned on the dashboard, gathering his breath. His eyes moved to the ignition. The keys were nowhere in sight. With a fright, he spun and checked the backseat. Neither Emma's bag nor the box containing the sweater was there. Simone had left and taken everything with her.

He fell back, confused, tired. He looked at the fat book on his lap. Opening it, he began to skim the names, addresses, and phone numbers. It's a start, he thought.

Just then, the passenger door opened and Simone slid into the car.

"Where were you?" he asked.

Simone shrunk back. "I walked to the top of the

hill and back. If you must know, I wanted to smoke a cigarette."

"Where are Emma's things?"

"I put them in the trunk in case one of us wants to lie down."

Jonathan nodded, calming himself. "I didn't mean to snap at you. It's just that they've been there. I mean in our hotel room. They took the place apart. Top to bottom. But they were good. Very neat. I'll grant them that. They almost got it right. And then I would never have known."

Simone stared at him, his fright mirrored in her eyes. "What are you going on about? Who was there? The police?"

"No. At least, not the real police." He explained about the strange manner in which someone had searched behind the lining of the suitcase and the odd depression the size of a deck of cards.

"Only her suitcase?" Simone asked. "What were they looking for?"

"I don't know."

"Think, Jon. What could have been inside it?"

Jonathan brushed off the question. He had no idea. "Give me the keys. They might be coming."

Simone handed him the car keys. "Slow down. No one's coming. Look."

Jonathan stared out the rear window. The street was deserted. The storm had confined the town to quarters. He leaned back and closed his eyes. "Okay," he murmured. "We're okay."

"Of course we're okay," said Simone.

"I heard voices in the hallway. I think the hotel manager was with the police. They were talking about the policeman in Landquart. They know it's me."

"You're safe for now. That's what matters." Simone gestured toward the book in his lap. "What's that?"

"Emma's address book. We need to find who she knew in Ascona. If one of her friends sent her those bags, their name will be in here."

"May I?"

Jonathan handed her the leather-bound volume. It was as thick as a Bible and twice as heavy. Emma had liked to say that it contained her life, and nothing less. Simone placed it on her lap and opened it solemnly, as if it were a religious text. Emma's name was inscribed on the flyleaf. A succession of addresses had been scratched out below it. The most recent was Rampe de Cologny, Geneva. Before that there was Rue St. Jean in Beirut. U.N. Camp for Refugees, Darfur, Sudan. The list went on, a road map of his once and future life.

"How many names does she have in here anyway?" Simone asked.

"Everyone she ever met. Emma never forgot anyone."

Together, they pored over every page. A to Z. They were looking for an address in the Tessin. Ascona. Locarno. Lugano. Any phone number with the 091 area code. They found names in every corner of the globe. Tasmania, Patagonia, Lapland, Greenland,

Singapore, and Siberia. But nowhere did they find mention of Ascona.

Thirty minutes later, Simone set the address book on the center console.

Emma didn't have a single friend who lived in the southernmost canton of Switzerland. Ascona did not exist.

Rooting in his pockets, he came out with the customer half of Emma's baggage receipts. "We still have these," he said. "The porter said that the name of the sender was recorded at the departure station."

"I don't think the Swiss are so easy to give out information as that. You'll have to show identification."

"You're probably right." Jonathan handed Simone the receipts, then started the engine.

"Where are we going?"

"Where do you think?" he asked, head turned over his shoulder as he backed the car onto the road.

Simone shifted in her seat, pushing her hair behind one ear. "But Emma had no friends there. We have no idea even where to begin to look. What can we hope to accomplish?"

Jonathan pointed the nose of the car downhill and touched the gas. "I know how to find out who sent Emma those bags."

20

At five minutes before midnight, an unmarked van pulled up to the loading dock at the rear of Robotica AG's headquarters in the industrial quarter of Zurich. Four men climbed out. All were dressed in dark clothing and wore watch caps pulled low over their brows, surgeon's gloves, and crepe-soled shoes. Their leader, the shortest by three inches, rapped once on the passenger door and the van drove away.

Clambering onto the dock, he walked past the corrugated steel curtain that secured the delivery bay. He held two keys in his hand. The first disarmed the security system. The second opened the employee entrance. The men filed into the darkened building.

"We have seventeen minutes until the patrolman makes his next rounds," said Chief Inspector Marcus von Daniken as he closed the door behind them. "Move fast, be careful what you touch, and under no circumstances are you to remove anything from the premises. Remember, we are not here."

The men slipped flashlights out of their jackets and headed down the corridor. With von Daniken were Myer from Logistics/Support, Kübler from Special Services, and Krajcek from Kommando. All had been apprised of the circumstance surrounding the operation. All knew that if caught, their careers would be terminated and that each stood a chance of going to jail. Their loyalty to von Daniken superseded the risks.

It was Myer from Logistics who'd contacted the security company to obtain the watchman's schedule, as well as the keys to safely enter the premises. Swiss industry had a long history of cooperating with the Federal Police.

Allowing the others to pass, Kübler removed a rectangular device resembling a large, bulky cell phone from his workbag and held it in front of him. He moved slowly down the corridor, his eyes glued to the histogram pulsing across the backlit screen. Abruptly, he stopped and punched the red button beneath his thumb. The histogram disappeared. In its place appeared "Am-241." He glanced up. Directly over his head was a smoke detector.

The device he was carrying was a handheld explosives and radiation sensor. He was not worried about Am-241—or americium-241—a mineral used in smoke detectors. He was looking for something a little more exciting. He continued down the corridor, waving the radiation sensor in front of him as if it were a divining rod. The space looked clean. So far.

Von Daniken didn't have the key to Theo Lammers's office. Cooperative or not, the security company couldn't provide what it didn't have, and the chief executive's office was strictly out-of-bounds. Myer spread a chamois roll containing his picks and blanks on the floor and set to work. A former instructor at the cantonal police academy, he needed just thirty seconds to open the lock.

Von Daniken swept the beam around the office. The MAV was on the table where he'd last seen it. He picked it up, studying it from varying angles. It was amazing that such a small device could travel at such high speeds. What interested him more was its purpose, peaceful or otherwise.

He put down the MAV and took several photographs of it with his digital camera, then moved on to Lammers's desk. Surprisingly, the drawers were unlocked. One after another, he removed the dead executive's folders, spread the documents on the desk, and photographed them. Most appeared to be customer correspondence and internal memoranda. He saw nothing to indicate why a man might feel it necessary to keep three passports and a loaded Uzi in his home.

This is his public life, von Daniken told himself. The smiling side of the mirror.

"Twelve minutes," whispered Krajcek, sticking his

head into the office. Krajcek was the muscle, and the silenced Heckler & Koch MP-5 he carried in his hands proved it.

The agenda.

Von Daniken spotted it almost by accident on a sideboard next to a photograph of Lammers with his wife and children. He picked up the leather-bound book and skimmed through the pages. The entries were curt to the point of being coded, mostly notations for meetings with the name of a company and its representative. He turned to the last entry, made the day of Lammers's death. Dinner at 1900 hours at Ristorante Emilio with a "G.B." A phone number was listed beside it.

Von Daniken photographed the page.

Finished in the office, he and Myer made their way past the reception area and through a pair of swinging doors onto the factory floor. "Where's his workshop?" Myer asked as the two men snaked between mobile pushcart workstations.

"How should I know? I was only told that Lammers built the MAVs there."

Myer stopped and held him by the arm. "But you're sure it's here?"

"Reasonably." Von Daniken recalled that Lammers's assistant had not specifically indicated that the workshop was on the premises.

" 'Reasonably'?" asked Myer. "I'm risking my pension for 'reasonably'?"

A walled-in enclosure occupied the far corner of

the floor. Entrance was governed by a steel door decorated with a sign that read **"Privat."**

"I'm **reasonably** sure this is it," said von Daniken.

Myer took a knee and brought his flashlight to
bear. "Shut up as tight as the National Bank," he
muttered.

"Can you open it?" von Daniken asked.

Myer shot him a withering glance. "I'm **reasonably** certain I can."

Myer laid out his tools and began fitting one after
another into the keyhole. Von Daniken stood
nearby, his heart pounding loud enough to be heard
in Austria. He wasn't cut out for this kind of thing.
First, breaking and entering without a warrant, and
now, tampering with private property. What had
gotten into him? He'd never been one for the cloak-
and-dagger stuff. The fact was that he was a desk
man and proud of it. Fifty years of age was a little
long in the tooth to be participating in one's first surreptitious operation.

"Nine minutes," said Krajcek, his nerveless voice
funneling through von Daniken's earpiece.

By now, Kübler and his radiation detector had
made their way onto the factory floor. He shunted the
detector to his right and the histogram morphed into
a new signature. The display read "$C_3H_6N_6O_6$," and
next to it the word "Cyclotrimethylenetrinitramine."
He recognized the name, but he was more accus-
tomed to calling it by its trade name. RDX. Maybe
this wasn't a wild-goose chase after all.

"Eight minutes," said Krajcek.

Kneeling on the factory floor, Myer manipulated two picks with a conjurer's touch. "Got it," he said as the tumblers fell into place and the door swung open.

Von Daniken stepped inside. The beam of his flashlight landed on a workbench littered with power tools, pliers, screws, wires, and scrap metal. One look and he knew that they'd found it. Theo Lammers's workshop.

Von Daniken turned on the lights. It was a larger version of the one he'd seen the night before in Erlenbach. Drafting tables stood at either end of the room. Both were covered with mechanical drawings and schematic blueprints. All manner of boxes sat on the floor. He recognized the names printed on them as manufacturers of electrical equipment.

Taped to the nearest wall was a blueprint for some type of aircraft. Standing on his tiptoes, he studied the specifications. Length: two meters. Wingspan: four and a half meters. This was no MAV. This was the real thing. The drawings identified it as a drone, the remote-controlled aircrafts used to overfly enemy territory and, if he wasn't mistaken, on occasion to fire missiles. The thought raised the hackles on his neck. There, pinned to the corner of the blueprints, was a photograph of the finished product. It **was** large. A great condor of an aircraft. A man was standing next to it. Dark hair. Dark complexion. He brought the photo closer. The timestamp showed it was taken one week ago. He turned it over. "T.L. and C.E.," as well as a date, were written on the back. T.L. was Lammers. Who was C.E.?

"Four minutes," said Krajcek.

Von Daniken traded concerned looks with Myer. The men continued with their search. Myer foraged through the boxes while von Daniken rooted around the papers on the drafting desks.

"Two minutes," said Krajcek.

Just then, von Daniken remembered the initials in Lammers's agenda. **G.B.** He looked at the back of the photograph again. The initials weren't "C.E." but "G.B."

He brought up the photo he'd taken and used the in-camera zoom to read the phone number next to G.B.'s name. Area code 078. The Tessin, the country's southernmost canton, where the cities of Lugano, Locarno, and Ascona were located. It was his first real lead.

It was then that he saw Kübler standing in the doorway. The man didn't speak, but walked toward them like an automaton, his eyes fixed to the radiation detector. "RDX," he said. "The place is thick with it."

The initials required no explanation. RDX, short for Royal Demolition Explosive, was well known to any law enforcement official involved in counterterrorism. First developed by the British prior to the

Second World War, RDX was the prime component in many types of plastic explosives, and the inciting charge used in all nuclear weapons.

Von Daniken felt as if he'd had the wind knocked out of him. A drone, a company that manufactured hyperaccurate guidance systems, and now plastic explosives. "But I don't see any in here," he protested. "Where could it be hidden?"

"It's not here now. I'm just detecting traces. But the readings are fresh."

"How fresh?"

Kübler studied the display. "By the rate of decay, I'd say twenty-four hours."

Before Lammers's dinner with G.B.

"Sixty seconds," said Krajcek. "I have the watchman's car three blocks away and closing."

"Out," said von Daniken as he furiously snapped photographs of the blueprints. Kübler hustled out of the workshop. Myer followed. Von Daniken moved to the door. It was as he was going to turn off the lights that he saw it.

A baby brother.

At the far end of the room, pushed back on a shelf beneath the counter, was a smaller version of the MAV in Lammers's office, perhaps half the size—no more than twenty centimeters long, another twenty high. The wings, however, were cut from a different shape, nearly triangular. He observed that they were fixed to a central hinge and flapped up and down, like a bird's wings.

Caught for a moment between staying and going, he rushed over and grabbed the miniature aircraft. The assembly weighed no more than five hundred grams. Not exactly light as a feather, but pretty damn close.

"Does it fly?" he'd asked Michaela Menz earlier that afternoon.

"Of course," was the indignant reply. "We launch it from the loading docks."

Von Daniken noted that the underside of the wings was covered with a light, tensile fabric that was colored a flashy yellow and patterned with a familiar black marking.

Myer pushed his head back into the office. "Goddamn it, man, what are you doing? We have to get out of here!"

Von Daniken held up the MAV. "Look at this."

"Leave it!" Myer fired back. "What the hell do you want with a toy butterfly, anyway?"

21

Outside the city of Vienna, in the wooded hamlet of Sebastiansdorf, lights burned in the windows of Flimelen, a traditional Austrian hunting lodge. Built as a retreat for Emperor Franz Josef, the rambling estate had followed its owner to the grave at the close of the First World War. For forty years, it had sat abandoned and uncared for. Windows broken, doors pried loose for firewood, the stones of its foundation removed to build other, less majestic homes, it seemed to have been swallowed whole by the forest itself.

And then in 1965, it was reborn. From one day to the next, workmen arrived and began to restore the decrepit building. New windows were put in. Sturdy doors installed. Farther down the road a guard post was built. Needing a secluded getaway in which to discuss its most confidential affairs, another organization had claimed Flimelen for its own. Not a government, but the creation of many intent on preventing disaster or war.

Four men and one woman sat around a long table in the Great Hall. At the table's head presided a stiff, unsmiling man of Middle Eastern extraction with a fringe of graying hair and a neatly trimmed mustache. He wore a scholar's narrow spectacles, and indeed, he held degrees in law and diplomacy from universities in Cairo and New York. Though it was close to midnight, and the others had long since taken off their neckties and loosened their collars, he kept his jacket on, his necktie in the finest order. He viewed his position with the utmost gravity. For his efforts, he had been awarded the Nobel Peace Prize. Few people could boast that the fate of the world depended on him and not be branded an arrogant, bald-faced liar. He was one.

His name was Mohamed ElBaradei. He was the chairman of the International Atomic Energy Agency.

"This can't be true," said ElBaradei, running his finger across the report.

"I'm afraid there's no doubting it," said the man next to him, Yuri Kulikov, a poker-faced Russian who headed the IAEA's Department of Nuclear Energy.

"But how?" ElBaradei searched the faces gathered at the table. "If this is so, we've failed in our every duty."

"A program of institutionalized deception," said Kulikov. "A shell game. For years, we've concentrated our inspection efforts in one spot, while they were secretly working in another."

The men and woman seated beside him came from the top ranks of the secretariat, the professional staff that ran the IAEA. There was Oniguchi, a native of Japan, who headed Nuclear Science and Applications; Brandt, an Austrian and the sole woman in the room, who ran Technical Cooperation; Kulikov; and Pekkonen, the stolid Finn who headed up Safeguards and Verification, the IAEA's most well-known department.

"There can be no question as to the data's accuracy," said Pekkonen. "The sensor was equipped with a next-generation chip capable of pinpointing gamma ray emission signatures with ten times the precision of the older model."

ElBaradei was not a trained scientist, but twenty years' work at the IAEA in Vienna had provided a grounding in the principles of nuclear physics. Emissions from radioactive materials like uranium or plutonium give off unique signatures. If accurately measured, those signatures indicate the age and enrichment of the radioactive material, and more importantly, as far as he and the individuals seated around the table were concerned, its intended use.

Uranium in its natural form could not be used to incite a nuclear reaction. It had to be enriched, or pumped up with a particular isotope—uranium-235. The most common means was to process uranium hexafluoride gas through a centrifuge, a rapidly spinning steel drum. Every time the gas was cycled, it became more enriched. To speed up the process, centrifuges were linked one to another so that the gas cascaded from one machine to the next. The path to success was straightforward: the more centrifuges you had, the quicker the uranium could be enriched.

For use in nuclear power plants, the radioactive mineral had to be enriched to thirty percent. For use as a fissile material—that is, to be capable of generating a nuclear reaction—it needed to achieve a level of ninety-three percent. The paper under ElBaradei's eyes reported gamma ray signatures of an astounding ninety-six percent.

"The butterfly was over the target area for seven days," Pekkonen went on. "In that time, it sent back thousands of atmospheric measurements. It's unlikely that they're all wrong."

"But these readings are sky-high," protested ElBaradei. "How could they have hidden it from us for so long?"

"The new facility was built deep beneath the ground and disguised as an underground reservoir."

"If it's so well disguised, how did we find it?"

Pekkonen leaned forward, his blond forelock contrasting with his florid complexion. "A rumor about its location was passed to us by a member of the American delegation to the United Nations. It came from a source high in the Iranian government. The Americans thought we might be able to confirm or disprove it. We had an inspection team in a country a hundred miles to the south. We were able to launch and monitor the butterfly from that site without attracting attention."

"And you did this without my approval and in complete violation of our mandate to inspect facilities with the permission and cooperation of our hosts?"

Pekkonen nodded.

"Well done," said ElBaradei. "Do the Americans know about our findings yet?"

"No, sir."

"Keep it that way." ElBaradei looked at the faces around the table. "A year ago, we came to the consensus that Iran possessed five hundred centrifuges and had been successful in enriching no more than a half kilo of uranium to sixty percent. Nowhere near weapons grade. Now this! Just how many centrifuges are necessary to generate these kinds of readings?"

"Over fifty thousand," said Oniguchi from Nuclear Science.

"And just where are we to assume they obtained these centrifuges? This isn't a crate of counterfeit iPods we're talking about. It's a planeload full of the most highly monitored, closely regulated machinery in the world."

"Clearly, they were smuggled in," said Pekkonen.

"Clearly," ElBaradei repeated. "But by whom?

From where? I have four hundred inspectors whose job it is to keep an eye out for this kind of thing. It was my opinion until five minutes ago that they were competent in the extreme." He removed his eyeglasses and set them on the table. "And so? How much weapons-grade uranium are we to assume they now possess?"

Pekkonen looked nervously at his superior. "Sir, it's our conclusion that the Republic of Iran currently possesses no less than one hundred kilograms of enriched uranium-235."

"One hundred? And how many bombs can they make out of that?"

The Finn swallowed. "Four. Maybe five."

Mohamed ElBaradei replaced his glasses. **Four. Maybe five.** He might as well have said a thousand. "Until we receive an independent evaluation of this data, no one in this room is to repeat a word of these findings."

"But mustn't we share—" began Milli Brandt, the Austrian woman.

"Not a word," hammered ElBaradei. "Not to the Americans. Not to our colleagues in Vienna. I want absolute silence. The last thing we need is an incident before we can confirm these findings."

"But sir, we have a responsibility," she went on.

"I'm fully aware of our responsibility. Do I make myself understood?"

Milli Brandt nodded her head, but her eyes betrayed a different decision.

"The meeting is adjourned."

As ElBaradei waited for the others to leave, he sat listening to the wind rattle the windows, tormented by his thoughts. Finally, the door slammed. The voices died. He was alone.

Cupping his hands, he stared out into the night sky. He was not a religious man, but he found himself lacing his fingers in prayer. If news of the report were to leave this room, the consequences would be immediate and devastating.

"God help us, every man," he whispered. "It will be war."

22

The Pilot ran his hand over the aircraft's wings as he completed his preflight check. The gas tanks were full. The antifreeze topped off. The bird was good to go. He walked down the runway, kicking away loose rocks.

Tonight was the final test flight. It was imperative that everything be rehearsed exactly as the day itself. Repetition brought precision, and precision, success. He had learned these rules the hard way. His body bore the scars of his ignorance. Retracing his steps to the plane, he rapped the wing twice for good luck, then headed indoors.

Many years had passed since he'd last flown a combat mission. Then, he'd been young, reckless, and handsome. A drinker. A womanizer. A man who shunned the Righteous Path. He glimpsed his reflection in the mirror. He was no longer young, no longer reckless. God knew, he was no longer hand-some.

He couldn't look at himself without remembering. The memories of that forsaken spot were never far from the surface, an ever-lurking phantasm cloaked in fear, guilt, and fire. He recalled the night in the desert. The high spirits, the promise of triumph, the certainty that God was fighting on their side. The side of the faithful. He could hear their voices in his ears. Friends. Comrades. Brothers.

And then, suddenly, there was the haboob, a vast cloud of violently swirling sand that rose from the desert floor a mile into the sky, enveloping them all, wreaking chaos and havoc, and worse.

The mission ended in flames. Eight men burned to death. Five more critically injured. He was among them, with third-degree burns covering seventy per-cent of his body.

In the days that followed—long days etched in pain and doubt—it came to him that he had been spared for a purpose. He had been given a second chance. The scars he carried were to remind him of that chance, to forswear his obedience unto Him. If the Almighty had robbed him of his physical endow-ments, He had gifted him with a spiritual awaken-ing. He had drawn him close and spoken unto him. To make him one of His Personal Servants. An anointed one. All was for a purpose and that purpose was nigh.

The Pilot burned for the Righteous One. He lived only for His return.

Inside the ready room, he gathered the members of the crew. All linked hands.

"O mighty Lord, I pray to you to hasten the emergence of your last repository, the Promised One, that perfect and pure human being, the One that will fill this world with justice and peace."

The circle broke up. Each man went to his post.

The Pilot approached the aircraft's controls with trepidation. Much had changed since he'd last flown a combat mission. Instead of an array of dials and instruments, he faced a wall of six flat-screen monitors broadcasting the aircraft's crucial functions. He slid into his seat and oriented himself. His hand took hold of the joystick, and he spent a moment getting a feel for it.

"Systems check complete," said one of the technicians. "Ground link established. Satellite connection established. Video functional."

"Affirmative." The Pilot fired the engine. The lights on the control panel burned green. The single Williams turbofan engine turned over, revving smoothly as he pushed it through its preflight run-up.

The time was two a.m. Outside the cockpit, the night was pitch-black. Not a single light burned in the high Alpine valley where the test was to take place. He kept his eyes focused on the screen positioned in the center of the control panel, where an infrared camera mounted in the plane's nose offered a grainy green-glow picture of the runway. It was like looking at the world through a soda straw.

"Requesting permission to take off."

"Permission granted. Have a safe flight. **Allahu akbar.** God is great."

The Pilot eased the throttle forward. He released the brake and the aircraft began to roll down the tarmac. At one hundred knots, he rotated the front wheel up and the plane rose into the air.

The Pilot studied the ground terrain radar. The valley was ringed by mountains, some as high as four thousand meters. The location was not ideal, but it provided the one essential element: privacy. He increased his speed to two hundred fifty knots and trimmed the ailerons. The aircraft handled deftly, with only a short delay in executing his commands. He banked to the right and found himself leaning with the aircraft.

"Execute Test One," he said, after completing a circuit of the valley.

The Pilot studied his radar. A moment passed and a blip appeared. The target was six kilometers away, gaining in altitude. He hit the contact button and designated the blip as "Alpha 1." The onboard computer charted a direct path to the target.

"Initiating target run. Contact in two minutes ten seconds."

"Two minutes ten and counting," said ground control.

The Pilot brought the aircraft in line behind the target. The blip moved closer to the center of the monitor. It was just a kilometer away and two hundred meters below him. Just then, the plane entered a bank of cloud. His vision disappeared. He checked a second monitor, offering infrared vision. There was no heat signature visible. A violent gust forced the nose down. A buzzer sounded. The stall warning. A bolt of panic ran along his spine. It was like the night in the desert all those years ago. He felt as if he were once again caught in the haboob.

Trust your instruments. It was a pilot's cardinal rule.

He remembered the collision. The jet fuel spraying over his body, incinerating his copilot. The horrid scent of burning flesh. His flesh.

Trust your instruments.

This time it was another voice speaking to him. A calm, unimpeachable voice. **Rely on me,** it said.

He pulled the joystick toward him and eased the throttle forward. Airspeed three hundred knots. The nose rose. Suddenly, he was through the cloud. Stars twinkled above him. His pulse eased, but he could feel the sweat sliding the length of his spine.

Once again, he took up position behind the target. At five hundred meters he armed the nacelle. The target came into view, looming like a great whale. He increased his airspeed and closed for the kill.

Three . . . Two . . . One.

The aircraft struck the target. On the monitor, the blip designated Alpha 1 disappeared.

"Direct hit. Target destroyed," announced ground control. "Test completed."

A cheer went up from the crew. This time the target had been a simulation generated by the computer.

The Pilot circled the valley and brought the aircraft in for a smooth landing. Climbing out of the cockpit, he crossed the control room and pulled back the curtains of a broad picture window. Outside on the road, the drone he had piloted by remote control sat on the tarmac. A team of men surrounded the aircraft and began to disassemble it.

The Pilot lowered his eyes and gave thanks.

Next time, it would be the real thing.

23

The clock read 4:41 a.m. when Jonathan drew the car to the side of the road and killed the motor. Rain pounded the windshield. In front of him, a three-story stone and terra-cotta building sat cloaked in mist.

"But it's not even open," said Simone. "There's no one here."

Jonathan pointed out a pair of laundry lines strung from the second floor window. "The station manager lives above the office." He put out an open palm. "You have it?"

Simone fished Sergeant Oskar Studer's identification out of her purse. "What if he doesn't believe you?"

"It's five in the morning. The last thing in the world he's going to do is question a cop who comes to his door. Besides, I can't go flashing that ID in broad daylight unless I put on forty pounds, shave my head, and break my nose a couple times. Take a look. What do you see?" Jonathan held the ID next to his face. Simone moved her head backward and forward, squinting to focus on the thumbnail-sized picture. He gave her three seconds, then flapped the wallet closed. "So?"

"It's too dark. I couldn't see anything."

"Exactly."

Simone, however, was not so easily convinced. "But how do you know you'll find something?"

Jonathan slipped the receipts from his pocket and tucked them into the ID holder. "No one sends that kind of money without a way of getting it back."

Simone shook her head. Arms crossed, shorn of her earlier bravado, she appeared smaller, older, no longer his willing accomplice. "Really, Jon, I think we should wait."

"Get in the driver's seat. If I'm not back in fifteen minutes, take off."

He opened the door and stepped into the rain.

"Sì?"

An unshaven man dressed in flannel pajamas stared bleary-eyed through a crack in the door. Jonathan held the policeman's badge up so he could see it. "Signor Orsini," he began in workmanlike Italian. "Graubünden Kantonspolizei. We need your help."

Orsini snatched the identification from Jonathan's hand and brought it near his face. His eyes snapped into focus. "What is it that it can't wait until morning?" he asked, his gaze going back and forth between the ID and the man standing in front of him.

"It **is** morning," said Jonathan, grabbing the ID right back. He crowded the doorway, forcing the station superintendent to step back into his home. "A murder. A fellow officer. My partner, in fact. You may have heard about it on the news."

He waited for Orsini to comment on the photograph, but Orsini only looked peeved. "No, I didn't," he said. "No one called me about this."

Jonathan barreled on, as if he couldn't be bothered by who had or hadn't called. "A few hours ago we discovered that bags belonging to the suspect were sent on a train originating from your station. We have the baggage receipts. We need the name of the individual who left them with you."

"You have written authorization?" asked Orsini.

"Of course not. There wasn't time. The murderer is headed in this direction."

The news didn't affect Orsini one way or the other. "Where's Mario? Lieutenant Conti?"

"He asked that I come directly to the station."

Orsini considered this, as he sniffed and hitched up his pajama bottoms. "Give me a minute." The door closed.

Orsini emerged five minutes later, hair neatly combed, face washed, dressed for the day in gray trousers and a porter's sturdy blue jacket. Jonathan followed him around the outside of the building to the ticket office.

A minute later, Orsini was seated at his desk, tapping the numbers of the baggage receipts into his computer. "Let's see . . . sent to Landquart . . . bags picked up yesterday afternoon. **Basta!** Too late. Once the bags are picked up, the file is automatically deleted. I can't help you."

Orsini's look of resignation infuriated Jonathan. "Is there another record of the transaction?" he demanded. "Maybe when the customer purchased the ticket? This is a murder we're talking about. Not a stolen purse. Get me that name!" He slammed his palm against the table.

Orsini recoiled, but a moment later he was banging at the keyboard like a madman. "Tickets were paid in cash . . . had to fill out a receipt . . . hold on. . . ." Standing, he pushed past Jonathan to a row of filing cabinets. Humming nervously, he pulled out sheaf after sheaf of bundled receipts, examining each in turn before tossing them onto the table next to him. Suddenly, he slapped his fingers against a chosen receipt. "Got him!"

Jonathan stood at his shoulder. "Who is it?"

"Blitz. Gottfried Blitz. Villa Principessa. Via della Nonna." Orsini's voice was plumped with victory as he studied the receipts. "So, are you happy now, Officer?"

But when he turned around, he found his office empty.

Jonathan had already left.

24

Marcus von Daniken paced inside the passenger terminal at Bern-Belp airport. A Sikorsky helicopter sat on the tarmac as a crew completed de-icing the rotors. Word had come from the tower that the weather was clearing over the Alps and that they had a window of sixty minutes to get over the mountains to the Tessin before the next front arrived and effectively partitioned the country once again between north and south. Flying was not von Daniken's cup of tea, but this morning there was no other choice. An eighteen-wheeler had overturned at the northern entrance to the Gotthard Tunnel and traffic was backed up twenty-five kilometers.

An announcement was made to board the helicopter. Reluctantly, he left the warm confines of the terminal, followed by Myer and Krajcek. "How long?" he asked the pilot as he climbed aboard.

"Ninety minutes . . . if the weather holds." The response was accompanied by the offer of an air-sickness bag.

Von Daniken strapped himself in tightly. He looked at the white paper bag on his lap and muttered a short prayer.

The helicopter landed at an airfield on the outskirts of Ascona at 9:06. Throughout the flight, violent headwinds had buffeted the chopper like a ping-pong ball in a lottery machine. Twice the pilot had asked if von Daniken wished to turn back. Each time, von Daniken merely shook his head. Worse than his nausea was the suspicion that Blitz was at that very moment packing his bags and hightailing it across the Italian border.

The phone number listed on Lammers's agenda had come back as belonging to one Gottfried Blitz, resident of the Villa Principessa in Ascona. A call had alerted the local police to von Daniken's imminent arrival. Instructions were given that under no circumstances should anyone attempt to contact or arrest the suspect.

The engine moaned, then died altogether. The rotor blades slowed and bent under their weight. As von Daniken placed his foot onto solid ground, it was all he could do to keep from falling to his knees and kissing the tarmac. Come hell or high water, he was driving home in an automobile.

Lieutenant Mario Conti, chief of the Tessin police,

stood at the edge of the helipad. "You will ride with me to Blitz's house," he said. "I believe your assistant is already there."

Von Daniken made a beeline for the waiting automobile. The engine noise was still rife in his ears, and he wasn't sure if he'd heard the lieutenant correctly. "My assistant? These are my men: Mr. Myer and Mr. Krajcek. No one else from my office is working this case."

"But I received a call from Signor Orsini, the manager of the railway station, earlier this morning saying that he had been visited by an officer who had come to inquire about the bags. I assumed he was working on the same case as you."

"Exactly what bags are you talking about?" asked von Daniken, pulling up sharply.

"The bags that were sent to Landquart," Conti explained. "The officer informed Signor Orsini that they belonged to the suspect in the killing of the policeman yesterday."

"I'm not investigating the killing of the policeman in Landquart. I didn't send anyone to speak with the station manager."

Conti shook his head, his cheeks losing their pallor. "But this policeman . . . he showed his identification. You're certain you are not working together?"

Von Daniken ignored the question, driving to the heart of the matter. "What exactly did this man want?"

"The name and address of the man who had originally sent the bags."

Von Daniken started walking toward the car. His pace quickened as it came to him. "And that man's name was—"

"Blitz," said the police chief, almost jogging to keep up. "The man you are looking for, of course. He lives in Ascona. Is something wrong?"

Von Daniken opened the passenger door. "How far is it to his home?"

"Twenty minutes."

"Get us there in ten."

25

Mist tumbled from the hillside, curling around the centuries-old buildings and winding its way through narrow cobblestone alleys. The man known within his profession as the Ghost drove through the quiet resort town of Ascona. Several times he was forced to slow the car to a crawl as the mist thickened to fog and drowned the road.

Fog . . . it followed him everywhere . . .

It had been foggy when the squads had come, he reminisced, as he continued into the surrounding hills, passing down country lanes lined with rustic villas and tended gardens. Not a fog like this. But a night fog from the high mountain valley where his family grew coffee, the mist sly and meandering as a deadly snake. He had been made to watch as the soldiers pulled his parents from their bed, dragged them outside, stripped them, and forced them to lie naked in the mud. They took his sisters next, even Teresa who was not yet five. He closed his eyes, but he could not block out their screams, the lament of their spirits fighting until there was no fight left. When the soldiers had finished, they shot the girls in the stomach. Some went inside and found his father's prized Scotch whisky. They stood on the terrace, drinking and making jokes as his sisters passed into the next world.

He was a boy, just seven and terrified. The **commandante** thrust a pistol into his hand and marched him to his parents, who were made to rise to their knees. The **commandante** took his hand in his own, raised it, and guided his finger to the trigger. Then he whispered in his ear that if the boy wished to live he must shoot his parents. Two shots rang out in quick succession. His father and mother fell sidelong into the mud. It was the boy who had pulled the trigger.

Then, showing neither fear nor hesitation, he turned the gun on himself.

Miraculously, he did not die.

Impressed by this show of unflinching courage, the **commandante** made a decision. Instead of leaving him with his father and mother, his four sisters, and his dog, as examples to the peasantry about the wisdom of exercising their right to vote, the **commandante** spirited the boy out of the mountains. Surgeons removed the bullet that had obliterated his jaw. Dentists repaired his broken teeth. After the operations, he was taken to a private school where he proved a devoted student. All this the government paid for. It was an investment in a very special "project."

As a student, the boy excelled in all subjects. He learned to speak French, English, and German, as well as his own native tongue. In athletic endeavors, he proved to be fleet of foot and graceful. He shied away from team sports and concentrated on solitary competitions: swimming, tennis, and track.

Every week, the **commandante** looked in on him. The two enjoyed tea and pastries at a local café. At first, the boy would complain about his nightmares. Each night in his sleep he would meet his mother and father, who would plead with him for their lives. The images were so haunting, so real, that they followed him into the waking world. The **commandante** told him not to worry. All soldiers had these nightmares. Over time, a bond developed between them. The boy took to referring to the older man as his father. He grew to have affection for the man. But the nightmares did not go away.

He began to have problems at school.

The first involved his social disposition. Either unable or unwilling, he refused to interact in a normal manner with his fellow students. He was courteous. He was cooperative . . . to a point. But never did he let down his veneer of arctic aloofness. He had no friends, nor any desire to make any. He took meals alone. After practice on the athletic fields, he returned to his room where he dutifully completed his homework. On weekends, he would either play tennis with one of several acquaintances (refusing any invitations to join them afterward) or stay in his room and study his languages.

This was all the more strange because the boy was growing into a handsome young man. His features were thin, well-defined, and wholly aristocratic, betraying barely a drop of his mother's Indian blood. Further, he had about him a charisma as was found in natural leaders. His company was sought after by the more popular boys. Always he refused. The spurned invitations quickly turned into taunts. He was labeled a queer, a bastard, and a freak. He responded with a savagery uncommon in a boy so young. He discovered that he was good with his fists and that he enjoyed bloodying his opponent. Before long, the word went out. He was a loner and not to be bothered.

The second sin, and in the school's eyes, by far the graver, was the boy's unwillingness to participate in worship. The school was of Roman Catholic denomination and demanded that its students attend daily mass. While he would take his place in the pews, he would neither pray nor join in hymns. When kneeling at the altar, he refused the body and the blood of his Lord Jesus Christ. Once, when the father tried to force the sacrament into his mouth, he bit the priest's fingers hard enough to draw blood. Even worse, the school's chieftains observed that he was teaching himself his mother's ancestors' language and had taken to uttering prayers to a pagan deity in the forgotten words.

Of all this, the **commandante** was apprised. Instead of being disheartened with the way his "project" had turned out, he was pleased. He had uses for individuals whose conscience had been scrubbed clean of artifice. Especially a man who by appearance and education possessed all the qualities of a gentleman. Such a man would be able to move in the highest circles of society. He would be granted access to the most rarefied gatherings.

In short, he was a perfect assassin.

In a minute, "the perfect assassin" was through the town and into the surrounding hills. He turned onto the Via della Nonna and found the Villa Principessa easily enough. He continued on a kilometer and parked his car at the top of a shaded dead-end street. There he followed his ritual. He freed the vial from around his neck and dipped the bullets into the amber liquid, blowing lightly on each. All the while, he offered his prayer.

When he finished, he stepped out of the car and opened the trunk. He donned a fleece pullover, a rain slicker, and a flaming red Ferrari cap. People saw the cap, never the face. Off came the loafers. In their place, he donned a pair of hiking boots. As a final touch, he threw a rucksack over his shoulder. The

Swiss were crazy for walking. Closing the trunk, he tucked the weapon into his belt and set off down the street.

He had walked a hundred meters when he saw a dark-haired man led by three dachshunds emerge from the front door of Villa Principessa and start toward him up the street. The man was in his mid-fifties. He had blue eyes and wore a navy sweater. It was him.

The Ghost approached with a welcoming smile. "Good morning," he said amicably. It was not often he had the chance to speak to those he was assigned to kill. He enjoyed the opportunity. Over the years, he had developed certain beliefs about mortality and fate, and was curious to see if this man had any notion that his time on earth was at an end.

"Morning," Gottfried Blitz replied.

"May I?" The Ghost bent to pet the dogs, who eagerly licked his hands.

Blitz crouched and scratched the dogs about the head and neck. "My children," he said. "Grete, Isolde, and Eloise."

"Three daughters. Do they take good care of their father?"

"Very good care. They keep me in good health."

"What else is a child's job?"

Inches separated the men. The Ghost gazed into Blitz's eyes. He sensed a current of disquiet within the man. Not fear, but caution. He held the man's gaze long enough to convince him that he was not a threat. He does not see it, mused the Ghost. He is oblivious to his fate.

Giving a casual **"salud,"** the assassin rose and walked on to the bottom of the street. A glance over his shoulder told him that Blitz had continued in the opposite direction.

The encounter left him shaken. The man might be nervous, but he did not suspect that his life was at its end. His soul had not considered the idea.

The Ghost pressed down a bolt of fear. Nothing terrified him more than the prospect of dying suddenly and without warning.

Turning the corner, he jogged up a short hill. Fifty meters along, a dirt road ran into the street from the right. He headed down the track, counting the houses as he went. Coming to the fourth in line, he hopped the low fence and walked unhurriedly to the villa's back door. He looked to his left and right, scanning for inquisitive eyes. Satisfied that he couldn't be seen, he knocked twice loudly. The gun rested in his palm, one bullet chambered, three more to make sure the first did the job. He noted that the house wasn't wired with an alarm system. Arrogant, but a nice touch all the same. He pressed his fingertips to the door, feeling for any vibrations. The house was quiet. Blitz had not returned from his walk.

Seconds later, the Ghost was inside.

26

Milli Brandt couldn't sleep. Tossing in her bed in her home in Josefstadt, a fashionable district of Vienna, she was unable to think of anything but the damning verdict delivered by Mohamed ElBaradei at the emergency meeting six hours earlier. **"Ninety-six percent concentration . . . one hundred kilos . . . enough for four or five bombs."** The words haunted her like the memory of a bad accident. But the look on ElBaradei's face was worse. Anguish and anger and frustration, all covering what she read as surrender. The future was a foregone conclusion. The world was going to war again.

Suddenly, she sat up. Her breath came fast, and she had to pause as she gulped down the glass of water next to her bed. Quietly, she rose, and with a glance at her husband, padded down the hallway to her study. Inside, she locked the door behind her, then moved to her desk. A sense of resolve stirred within her. She was no longer thinking, but doing. This is duty, she told herself.

It was with a steady hand that she lifted the receiver. Amazingly, she recalled the number she'd been told to memorize all those years ago for use in emergencies only. The phone rang once, twice. Waiting, she realized that her life had changed drastically from what it had been only a minute ago. She was no longer the deputy director for Technical Cooperation at the International Atomic Energy Agency. As of this moment, she was a patriot, and a little bit of a spy. She had never felt so sure of herself in her life.

"Yes," a voice answered, brusque, demanding.

"This is Millicent Brandt. I need to speak with Hans about the Royal Lipizzaners."

"Stay on the line." She could practically hear the man on the other end of the line consulting his files or logs, or whatever it was that intelligence professionals look at when an agent calls in.

"Agent," of course, was not the right word. Then again, Millicent Brandt was not her real name. Born Ludmilla Nilskova in Kiev, she was the third daughter of an outspoken Jewish chemist, a refusenik, who had immigrated to Jerusalem, and then to Austria, some thirty-odd years earlier. Though brought up speaking German, attending Austrian schools, and holding an Austrian passport, she had never forgotten the country that had secured her family's release from the Soviet Union. Not long after beginning at the IAEA, she received a phone call from a man claiming to be an old family acquaintance. She recognized the accent, if not the name.

They met at a discreet restaurant near the Belvedere, across the city from her workplace. It was a friendly dinner, the conversation never lingering on any one subject. A little politics, a little culture. Interestingly, the acquaintance (whom she had never, in fact, met) knew all about her passion for riding, her love of Mozart, and even her attendance of a monthly Bible study group.

As the dinner concluded, he asked if she might consider doing him a favor. Immediately, her alarm bells went off. He touched her arm lightly to soothe her worries. She had the wrong idea. He wanted nothing immediate. Nothing improper. Certainly, nothing that would risk her losing her job. On the contrary, it was vital that she keep her position. All he asked was that she look out for their best interests. A promise to let him know if she learned of anything that might put into question the security of her adopted homeland.

He gave her a phone number and a sentence she was to repeat if ever she felt the necessity to call him. He asked that she memorize both, and insisted on quizzing her until she could repeat the ten-digit phone number and the sentence flawlessly. Finished with this piece of business, he regained his light manner. He hugged her and offered his sincerest thanks.

As she climbed into a taxi for the ride home, Millicent Brandt, née Ludmilla Nilskova, felt an unfamiliar stirring in her breast. Part fear, part apprehension, part thrill. She had joined the ranks of countless others—executives, officials, bureaucrats, and professionals from every walk of life—who had sworn an oath to the state of Israel, and had promised to help the country in any way it saw fit.

On the telephone, the sharp voice returned. "Hans will meet you at the Gloriette at Schönbrunn Palace at ten a.m. Bring a copy of the **Wiener Tagblatt** and make sure the masthead is visible."

"Yes," she said. "Of course." But the phone was already dead.

Milli Brandt hung up. She had done it. She had kept her promise. She was officially a **sayyan.**

A friend.

27

Gottfried Blitz shooed the three dachshunds inside the house. Closing the door behind him, he stood stock-still, listening for a cry of alarm. The dogs' trained noses were more effective than any electronic security system. The house remained quiet. He walked into the living room. The hounds lay camped out on the marble floor, panting after their morning's exertion.

Stepping to the window, he peeled back the curtain and glanced down the road. The street was empty. There was no sign of the hiker he'd spoken with earlier. Blitz made it a habit to memorize faces, and he knew that the pale, slim man was not a neighbor. His Italian was fluent, but not that of a native. Who then? A tourist eager to explore the surrounding hills? But in this weather? And why hadn't he been headed toward the paths that began just past the end of the road?

Blitz peered at the darkening sky. It was not yet nine o'clock and the day was already done. Rain began to fall. He listened as the drops grew heavier and began to strike the windowpane. Shivering, he dropped the lace curtain into place.

Lammers's death had him spooked. The papers indicated that the killer had been waiting for him at his home. There were suggestions that it had been a professional job, and that Lammers may have been involved with organized crime. Blitz knew better. He also knew that if Lammers had been compromised, it wouldn't be long until he was, too. At any other time, he would break camp and call it a day. Gottfried Blitz was in grave danger.

But this was not any other time.

The end game had begun. The Pilot was in the country. The final test of the drone had been a resounding success. Operational status had been elevated to red. It was a go. For all intents and purposes, the attack had already been launched.

And now, the mess in Landquart. One man dead, the other injured.

Blitz chewed on his lip. He'd questioned sending the bags by train, but in the end, there had been no other way. It was not just a question of manpower (Division had only seven operatives in the country) but risk. At this stage, it was too dangerous to hand off the bags personally. Using the Swiss mail system hadn't troubled him, though he could see now that putting his name to the receipts had been a mistake. It was Finance that had insisted. They didn't want the money left unclaimed should something go wrong. Operations had signed off on it, too. The money was key, they'd said. It's the first thing they'll look for. Crumbs for the trail, went their logic. You had to lead the police by the nose if you wanted them to find anything. And all trails led to him. To Gottfried Blitz.

Still, he couldn't get Theo Lammers out of his mind. A professional job. Someone waiting for him at his home. He shuddered. It could mean only one thing. The network had been penetrated.

In the living room, he turned on the stereo. Wagner, as always. Just loud enough to let his neighbors know that he was at home, and that today was a day like any other.

Friends and neighbors knew Gottfried Blitz as a wealthy German businessman, one of thousands who had fled to southern Switzerland to enjoy the milder clime and the Mediterranean atmosphere. He drove the newest Mercedes sedan. He made annual pilgrimages to Bayreuth for the **Ring** cycle. Sunday mornings, the good Herr Blitz attended Lutheran services like any other good Christian. As a cover, it was complete.

Blitz walked to the study, sat down at his desk, and removed the pistol he kept in his waistband. Slipping the gun into the top drawer, he turned on his laptop and went over his checklist. **New Bogner sweater for P.J. WEF creds for H.H. 100k cash wire.** He whistled softly. Another hundred thousand francs. That one was not going to fly with the boys in Finance. On the other hand, it paled beside what had already been spent. Two hundred million francs to buy control of the company in Zug. Another sixty million to finance the shipments of equipment. The payoffs to P.J. alone amounted to twenty million francs, and that didn't include the Mercedes and all its special equipment.

He finished typing the request for the monetary transfer and e-mailed it to Finance. Just then, Blitz cocked his head toward the door. The hairs on his forearm were standing on end.

"Hello?" he called. "Someone there?"

There was no reply. The house was too quiet. And where was the barking that accompanied the arrival of a guest?

"Gretel, Isolde," he called to his dogs.

He sat up, straining for the scrabble of their paws across the marble floor. Wagner drifted in from the living room. The rumble of timpani like distant thunder. The lament of a Teutonic maiden mourning her vanquished prince.

Where were the dogs?

Something shifted in the air behind him. A presence, dark and cold.

A klaxon sounded deep inside him.

Blitz looked at the drawer holding his gun, then at the computer.

Choose one.

Thirty years of training took over. The mission came first. He positioned his fingers above the keyboard and typed in the "destroy" command, obliterating the laptop's hard drive.

He felt the air rustle behind him. Something cold and hard pressed against his temple.

And then there was light. A thunderclap of hellish color that lasted an instant, and then was no more.

28

The Villa Principessa sat at the end of a gravel drive, a renovated eighteenth-century cottage with ivy creeping up pitted walls and geranium-filled window boxes decorating its upstairs bedrooms. A low stone-and-mortar wall surrounded the dormant rose garden that fronted the house. At nine a.m., the rain fell in a steady curtain, as pounding and relentless as a waterfall.

Simone buttoned up her coat and tucked her hair behind her ears. "So we're just going to confront him? What if he says he didn't send the bags? Then what are we going to do?"

"Why would he deny it?" said Jonathan. "Once he knows Emma's dead, he'll be happy to get his car back."

"And his money?"

"And his money." Jonathan opened the glove

compartment and took out the cash-filled envelope. "I've been thinking about this all night . . . I mean about what Emma was up to."

Simone's eyes ordered him to go on.

"Medicine," said Jonathan. "Emma was always talking about how aid never reached its intended destination. It drove her crazy. You know how it is where we operate. Half the time cargos are impounded by the government or stolen by customs officials who then try to sell it back to us at twice the price. If we get seventy percent of what's meant for us, that's considered good. I think it had something to do with that. I mean, look at this house. It had to cost a bundle. My guess is that Blitz is an executive at one of the big pharmaceutical companies. Together they were up to something. Bribing someone. A payoff. Emma always thought she wasn't doing enough to make a difference."

"And you expect Blitz to tell you about it?"

"A hundred thousand francs buys a lot of cooperation."

"Or a lot of silence. It seems to me that you're overlooking something. Have you considered that Blitz might have been the one who sent the policemen?"

"It doesn't compute. First off, he'd have had to know about Emma's accident, and that's impossible. How do you see it? That he sent Emma the bags, then stuck some crooked cops on her to take the bags back as soon as she picked them up? No way. It wasn't Blitz. It was someone else."

"Someone who knew about Emma's accident?"

"Or someone who was waiting for the bags all along."

Jonathan left the car and passed through the wrought-iron gate. Simone caught up a moment later. "Gottfried Blitz" read the nameplate below the doorbell. Jonathan pushed the button and the bell chimed like the tolling of a campus carillon. No one answered. Digging in his pocket, he found the breath mints he'd taken from Eva Kruger's overnight bag and popped one into his mouth. "Want one?"

Simone shook her head.

Jonathan pressed his ear to the door. Strains of classical music came from within. He rang the door-bell again. When no one answered, he threw a leg over the railing and craned his neck to look through the front window. Three dachshunds lay sleeping on the marble floor. He caught a shadow flitting at the periphery of his vision.

"Mr. Blitz," he called. "I need to speak with you. Open up, please."

He looked back at the dogs. His vision felt sharper than normal. He observed how still the animals were lying. Unnaturally still, to a doctor's eye. He studied their torsos. It didn't appear as if any of them were breathing. One, in particular, lay with its head cocked at a severe angle, its tongue lolling from the corner of its mouth.

Jonathan tried the door, but found it locked.

"What are you doing?" Simone asked. "You can't just go inside."

Jonathan banged on the door. "Mr. Blitz! My name's Ransom. I think you know my wife, Emma. Please open up. It's about the bags. I've got them. And the money."

Just then, a door slammed inside the house.

"Keep knocking," he said, turning and running down the stairs.

"Where are you going?" Simone called.

"Around back. Something's wrong here."

"But . . . wait!"

He ran around the side of the house and came up the rear path through the garden. Somewhere behind him, Simone was calling for him to stop, but her words registered as a distraction. The back door was open. Music played from the stereo. "Ride of the Valkyries." He stepped inside the house, finding himself in a narrow kitchen. He advanced across the floor, grimacing with every squeak of the parquet. He sensed an imbalance in the atmosphere, but instead of being frightened, he felt alert and exhilarated. Battle bright.

He left the kitchen and crossed the living room to where the dogs lay near the front door. None lifted a head as he approached. He bent to examine them. The dachshunds were dead, their necks broken. He stood, aware of his sharp breathing and his heart's pistonlike contractions. Directly ahead, a flight of stairs led to the second floor. He heard something . . . something just ahead . . . and he continued down the hall. He threw open the door to his left. Guest bathroom: empty. The sound grew more distinct. A labored, arrhythmic wheezing.

It was then that he smelled the cordite and his eyes began to water.

He came to the study.

"Oh, God," he said as he rushed into the room.

A man sat slumped over his desk. His mouth hung open, his chest heaving as he fought for breath. Blitz? He assumed so. There was an entry wound at the temple, a neat hole ringed by gunpowder. Was it a suicide? Jonathan stepped back, searching for a pistol, but he didn't see one anywhere. He recalled the shadow flitting at the far corner of the living room. Not suicide. Murder.

Jonathan glanced toward the door, wondering if the killer might still be in the house, and if he himself might be in danger. He dismissed the thought and began talking to Blitz, telling him his name and that he was Emma's husband. He instructed him to hang on, and stated that he was going to do everything he could to keep him alive.

As gently as possible, he lifted Blitz off of the desk and laid him on the floor, taking care to keep his air passage open and unobstructed. He turned Blitz's head and studied the exit wound. He'd seen too many like it before. Large caliber. Hollow point. He was not optimistic about Blitz's chances. Still, at that moment, the man was alive. Nothing else mattered.

Running into the living room, he snatched the phone and dialed 144 for Emergency Services. When the operator asked what had happened, he said, "Life-threatening head injury with a large loss of blood." When he realized that he was speaking English, he repeated the words in Italian.

"Jon, what is it? What happened?" Simone stood at the entry to the living room, concern etched across her forehead. "You have blood on your hands."

"There's a bathroom down the hall. Soak some towels in hot water and bring them to me."

"Towels? What happened? Why—"

"Do it!"

Jonathan returned to the study and knelt down beside Blitz. There was little he could do until the paramedics arrived except make sure that the man's heart continued beating. Blitz's pupils were dilated and his respiration was shallow. Jonathan took the man's wrist, but was unable to find a pulse. He commenced CPR. Three plunges, then two breaths. Simone barreled into the room. Seeing Blitz, she let out a cry and dropped the towels onto the floor.

"I called EMT," he said. "They should be here any minute. Put the towels beside his head."

"But why?" Reluctantly, she picked up the towels and deposited them on the floor next to Jonathan. She stood quickly, teetering as she viewed the blood spreading across the carpet. "He's dead."

"Not yet, he's not. If I can keep his heart beating until the paramedics arrive, he'll have a chance."

"He's been shot in the head. Just leave him."

Jonathan put his head to Blitz's chest. There was no heartbeat. Respiration had ceased. He looked up at Simone and shook his head.

"Who did this?" she asked.

"I thought I saw something . . . a shadow . . . I heard a door slam. He must have run away."

"The police will be here any minute. We have to go."

Jonathan stood. Suddenly, the light seemed to be exceedingly bright and he had to blink. He took a breath, waiting for the remorse that inevitably accompanied death. But it didn't come. If anything he felt fresh, almost happy, and much too energetic for someone who hadn't slept a wink the night before. He ran a hand through his hair. His fingertips bristled at the touch. All his senses were enhanced. Sight. Touch. Sound. His mouth, though, was dry and pasty. He checked his image in the mirror hanging on the wall. His eyes stared back, wild and accusing, the pupils almost fully dilated.

The buzz was coming on stronger now, and he recognized what it was: high-octane, clean-burning amphetamine, with a little something special thrown in to heighten the senses.

He dug the package of mints from his pocket. How many had he consumed in the last hour? Two? Three?

"Come, Jonathan. Right now." Simone grabbed his arm and tried to guide him toward the door, but

Jonathan shook himself free. "Give me a minute," he said, taking stock of the situation. "I'm not leaving until I find out something about this guy."

"But, Jonathan . . ."

"Did you hear me?" he snapped. "Do you think we're supposed to just keep running?" He took a breath, calming himself, fighting the manic voice in his head. "Blitz knew Emma," he said. "They were working together. This is our one chance to discover what it was."

A laptop sat opened on the desk, the screen a blizzard of warring pixels. He hit a few keys, but the image failed to clear up. He turned his attention to the desk and its contents. He opened the top drawer and came eye to eye with a semiautomatic pistol. He was well enough acquainted with handguns to recognize it as a SIG-Sauer, the sidearm favored by military officers across the Third World. The rest of the drawer held a mess of papers, pens, and pencils. He spilled the contents on the desktop and rummaged through it. Notes with names and telephone numbers. Assorted bills. Matchbooks.

The filing drawer was locked. He snapped a letter opener in two trying to pry it open, before giving up. He turned his attention to the "in" and "out" trays on the credenza behind the desk. He flipped through the papers. "ZIAG" read the header on an office memorandum, and beneath it the company's full name: Zug Industriewerk AG. It was from a Hannes

Hoffmann to Eva Kruger, and cc'd to Gottfried Blitz. Subject: Project Thor.

Eva Kruger.

There it was: his proof in black and white. As if the corpse with a bullet in his brain wasn't enough.

The memo read, "Completion is foreseen for late first quarter 200–. Final shipment to client will be made on 10.2. Disassembly of all manufacturing apparatus to be completed by 13.2."

"I hear a siren," pleaded Simone. "Please, Jonathan. Let's get out of here."

"In a second."

Several buff envelopes lay beneath the memo. Inside the first, he found three passport-sized photographs of Emma, similar to the one on the fake driver's license. A second envelope held more photographs, this time of a wan blond man more or less Jonathan's age. "Hoffmann" was printed on the back in the same masculine block letters used to address the letter to Emma. He stared at the photograph. **Hannes Hoffmann.** Issuer of the memo to Eva Kruger.

"Cover," Jonathan murmured, remembering a word he'd picked up from one of the spy novels he'd devoured as a teenager. Everything is cover. Emma who isn't Emma. Amphetamines made to look like breath mints. To everything and everyone, a disguise. He looked at the body sprawled on the floor. And Blitz? Who was he when he wasn't Blitz?

Jonathan shuddered as the scale of the deception grew clearer. This was no one-time subterfuge. Emma was not bribing African health ministers or buying pharmaceuticals on the gray market. This was something bigger. Something on an entirely different scale. This was the world of "Go" pills and false identities and perfectly doctored driver's licenses.

"Jonathan, please!" Simone clutched the chair back, as if to keep herself from running away.

Sirens. At least two of them. He lifted his head, and in that second, he could tell that they were getting closer, not farther away, and that they were approaching at warp speed. Sweeping his arm across the desk, he gathered all the papers and stuffed them into a leather briefcase next to the credenza. "Go," he said. "I'm right behind you."

"Hurry!"

"I'll be right there," he said, pushing her out of the room. "Go out the back!"

Simone ran from the room.

Jonathan stood in the doorway. The sirens were just outside. Agitated voices punched through the relentless patter of rain. Instead of leaving, he ran to Blitz's desk and opened the top drawer. He stared at the pistol, then picked it up and slipped it into his waistband.

In the hall, he slowed long enough to see the police cars next to the curb, officers with guns drawn rushing the house. A short, determined man in a black overcoat was leading them up the gravel path.

Police? Where was the ambulance he'd phoned?

Questions. Too many questions.

Jonathan ran through the house, catching up to Simone at the back door. Grabbing her hand, he pulled her through the garden.

"Where are we going?" she asked, struggling to keep up with him. "The car's the other way."

"Forget the car. We can come back for it."

They didn't stop at the dirt road, but continued up the hillside. Ignoring the wind and the rain and the chest-high brush, Jonathan carved a path to the crest. Simone huffed and wheezed and swore, but somehow she stayed with him. When he finally looked back, they'd gained four hundred feet in altitude and the villa was a half mile away.

"I can't go on," said Simone, clamoring for breath. "I need to rest."

But it was Emma's voice he heard, and for a moment, he swore he saw her, dressed in red and black, standing on the slope beneath them. He grabbed Simone's hand. "Come on," he said. "There's only one way."

And clutching the briefcase to his chest, he turned and headed higher into the mountains.

29

Milli Brandt walked briskly down the snowy path, surrounded on both sides by tall, manicured hedges. In better times, she had enjoyed visiting the gardens of Schönbrunn Palace. Stretching more than a mile in each direction, the immaculately groomed grounds spoke of an earlier era when royalty meant unbridled power. For good and evil.

It was shortly after her arrival from Israel that she had first visited the palace gardens. Along with her parents and her sister, she had spent the day walking from one end of the grounds to the other, climbing the hill to the Gloriette, the immense colonnade built in 1775 by the Emperor Joseph and his wife, Maria Theresa. Even then, the two girls had been ambitious. Milli dreamed of being a prominent judge. Tovah had planned a career as a diplomat. Of the two, Tovah was quicker to achieve her goals. By the age of twenty-five, she had moved back to Jerusalem and earned a position as a spokeswoman for the Israeli Foreign Ministry. Married and the mother of a baby girl, she was a regular fixture on the nightly news.

One evening, Tovah and her husband drove to Tel Aviv to enjoy a seafood dinner at one of the fine restaurants that lined the coast. She was in a celebratory mood. Earlier that week, her doctor had informed them that she was pregnant with a second child.

Realizing that it might be their last chance in a long while, they decided to go dancing at Teddy'Z, an outdoor discotheque. Sometime near midnight, a tanned, handsome youth named Nasser Brimm entered the disco and pushed his way to the center of the dance floor. By the time anyone noticed that his formal attire and woolen blazer were out of place for a sultry spring evening, it was too late.

Afterward, the police figured that Tovah had been standing next to the bomber when he had detonated his belt charge of C-4 **plastique** layered with thousands of nails, nuts, and bolts. Her head, strangely unscathed, was the only part of her body ever found.

The death toll for the attack counted sixteen young men and women. Two others were blinded. A third lost both his arms. A fourth was paralyzed from the neck down. In fact, the final toll was higher. No one had counted the new life growing in Tovah's womb.

"Miss Brandt."

Milli spun at the sound of the deep, accented voice. A slim, academic-looking man stood a few feet behind her, smiling. She had not heard him approach. "Mr. Katz?"

"I see you have the paper. I appreciate your following our directions."

The man linked arms with her, and in the manner of husband and wife, they strolled through the deserted gardens. As they walked, Milli informed him about the emergency meeting held in the Viennese woods the night before and the findings delivered by Mohamed ElBaradei.

"Enriched to ninety-six percent. You're certain about that?"

Milli said that she was.

"And what chance is there of an error in measurement?"

"It would be the first time. I'm sorry to bring such news. I thought it was my duty."

" 'Every subject's duty is the king's; but every subject's soul is his own.' I'm alone on this, but I'm convinced Shakespeare was a Jew." A timid smile as he stopped and turned to her. "No one likes to betray a trust."

Milli watched the tall, thin figure disappear among the snowcapped topiaries. A sharp wind stirred, filling her ears with the rush of desolation. She'd expected him to say that she'd done the right thing. She wanted a speech about how he would take immediate action and that she had saved thousands of lives, but he'd said none of those things.

In parting, he simply requested that she call the number she'd been given should she learn anything of further importance. Not even a thank-you.

30

"Is it him?"

Von Daniken compared the snapshot of Gottfried Blitz standing next to the drone with the ruined face lying at his feet. "You tell me," he said, handing the photo to Kurt Myer and turning away before the bile rose any farther in his throat.

"Same sweater. Same eyes. It's him." Squatting on his haunches, Myer studied the corpse with an expert's keen eye. "He was killed while seated in the chair, then moved to the floor. The shot had to be taken at waist level with the muzzle aimed downward to have expelled Blitz's brains all over the desk and wall."

Using a fountain pen, he pointed to the rash of gunpowder tattooed into the skin. "Look at the abrasion collar and the stippling. The shooter was a foot away when he pulled the trigger. Blitz didn't even know he was there. He was working on his laptop until the moment he was shot."

But von Daniken was interested in something else Myer had said. "Back up a second, Kurt. What do you mean 'moved to the floor'? Are you saying the killer shot him, then laid him on the carpet? Did he bring him the towels, too?"

"Someone did. It certainly wasn't Mr. Blitz." Myer tested the pile of towels heaped near the body. "Still warm."

The men shared an uncomfortable glance.

From the street came the sound of another siren approaching. Doors slammed. There was a commotion in the hall. Two paramedics entered the study.

"That was quick," said von Daniken, referring to the near instantaneous arrival of the medical technicians.

"Did you call?" one of the paramedics asked. "Dispatch said it was an American."

"An American?" Von Daniken traded looks with Myer. "How long ago did the American call?" he asked the paramedic.

"Twelve minutes ago. Nine-oh-six."

"It's him," said Myer. "Ransom."

Von Daniken nodded, then glanced at his watch. During the drive from the airfield, he'd called Signor Orsini, the station manager, for a description of the man who'd shown up at his door early that morning impersonating a police officer and asking about who had sent a certain pair of bags to Landquart. After-

ward, he'd phoned the Graubünden police for details about the murder of one of its officers the day
before, also in Landquart. Orsini's description perfectly matched that given by a witness to the crime.
The police in Landquart even had a name: Dr.
Jonathan Ransom. An American. There was more.
Ransom's wife had perished two days earlier in a
climbing mishap in the mountains near Davos.

"If it was Ransom who called," he said to Myer,
"that explains the towels. He's a doctor."

Lieutenant Conti, who had been listening in on
the exchange, tucked his chin into his neck and lifted
his hands in a quintessentially Italian gesture. "But
why would Ransom shoot Blitz and then call the ambulance to save his life?"

Von Daniken exchanged looks with Myer. Neither
man wanted to answer the question for the time
being.

Von Daniken walked over to the desk and tapped
a few keys on the laptop. The screen displayed a
hodgepodge of fractured colors. Here was something
else that bothered him. Was Blitz working on a broken computer when he'd been shot? Or had he purposefully ruined it to prevent anyone from finding
out what was on its hard drive?

One by one, he opened the desk drawers. The top
two were empty, except for a few scraps of paper,
rubber bands, and pens. The bottom drawer was
locked, but appeared to have been tampered with.
He glanced up and noticed a few moving boxes

placed against the wall. He rushed to see what was inside and was disappointed to find them empty as well.

Just then, the crime scene technicians arrived. All unnecessary personnel were ordered out of the room. Myer slipped past von Daniken in the corridor, whispering that he was going to get the daisy sniffer, which was what he called the explosives and radiation detector.

As the technicians filed into the house, von Daniken went upstairs and made his way to Gottfried Blitz's bedroom. He wasn't thinking about the victim so much as the man who might have killed him. He was looking for a clue as to why a cop killer whose wife had died in a mountaineering accident was in such a hurry to visit Blitz.

The search of Blitz's bedroom turned up nothing. The night table was stacked with German celebrity glossies; the dresser filled with neatly folded clothing; the bathroom stuffed to bursting with cologne, hair products, and a variety of prescription drugs. But nowhere did he find anything that would tie Blitz to the drone, or indicate how he planned to use it.

Von Daniken sat down on the bed and stared out the window. It came to him that there were two groups and that they were somehow battling one another. There was Lammers and Blitz on the one side, and those who wanted them dead on the other. The quality of the killings combined with the discovery of the drone and the RDX marked it as an intelligence operation.

The prospect angered him. If an intelligence agency knew enough about a plot involving RDX and a drone to take decisive measures to stop it, why hadn't they contacted him with the information?

He turned his mind to Dr. Jonathan Ransom, who apparently had phoned the paramedics. According to the station manager, Ransom had been hellbent on discovering who had sent the bags to Landquart earlier in the week. The logical assumption was that he didn't know Blitz. How, then, had Ransom come to be in possession of the baggage claims?

If, however, von Daniken were to assume that Ransom and Blitz were working together—that they did know each other—the pieces fell into place. Stopped by the police after picking up the bags, Ransom had panicked, killed the arresting officer, then run down his partner in his hurry to flee the scene. Cover compromised, Ransom fled to Ascona to seek instructions from his controller. His ignorance of Blitz's address could be put off to a cardinal rule of espionage: Compartmentalize information, or in the vernacular, keep it need-to-know. Hence, his need to speak to Orsini.

And the wife? The Englishwoman who had perished in a freak mountaineering accident? Might Ransom have killed her when she'd discovered that he was an agent?

Von Daniken scowled. He was grasping. Spinning fantasies out of thin air. Rising, he made his way to the stairs. He wanted to know what was in the bags that had made Ransom deem them worth killing for. There was little prospect of finding out, at least in the short term. The officer Ransom had struck with the car lay in a coma. His prognosis was not optimistic.

Von Daniken's phone rang, interrupting his thoughts.

It was Myer, and he sounded worried. "In the garage. Come quickly."

31

The garage was detached from the main house and accessible by a side entry. A late-model Mercedes sedan occupied one space. The other was empty, but a fresh oil stain and a set of muddy tire tracks testified to the fact that a vehicle—either a truck or a van by the width of its axle—had recently been parked there.

Myer skirted the Mercedes and made his way to a storage closet built into the rear wall. He opened the doors and stood back so von Daniken could have a clear view. Stacked on the shelves were bricks wrapped in white plastic and bound in groups of five by duct tape.

"Is it what I think it is?" said von Daniken.

"Thirty kilos of Semtex still in its factory wrapping," said Myer. "Won't be hard to find out where this came from."

Plastic explosives were tagged with a special reactive chemical that identified not only the manufacturer, but the lot number. The practice allowed the explosives to be tracked, and in theory, at least, to defend against illegal sale and trafficking.

"Take one," said von Daniken.

Myer didn't hesitate before removing a brick and tossing it to Krajcek, who slipped it into his overcoat. As material evidence, the explosives officially belonged to the Tessin police, but von Daniken didn't feel like filing a request and waiting a week for the evidence to be catalogued and then released. Plastic explosives were not passports.

"Check the car?" von Daniken asked.

"Just the trunk. It's clean."

Von Daniken climbed into the Mercedes and rummaged through its contents. The vehicle was registered to Blitz. His driver's license was tucked into the flap alongside the door. As he removed it, a piece of blue paper fell into his lap.

An envelope. One of the flimsy old-fashioned ones marked "Air Mail." He saw the writing and his heart skipped a beat. It was Arabic written in a fountain pen's faded blue ink. The postmark read, "Dubai, U.A.E. 10.12.85."

Von Daniken opened it. The letter itself was written in Arabic, too. One page, the script neat and precise. A laser printer could hardly do better. He couldn't read a word of it, but that didn't matter. The faded photograph tucked inside told him all he needed to know.

Staring into the camera was a strapping young soldier dressed in a green uniform complete with a Sam
Browne belt and an officer's oversized cap. Flanking
him were his mother and father. Proud grins were the
same the world over. Von Daniken had never been to
Iran, but he recognized a picture of the Ayatollah
Ruhollah Khomenei when he saw it, and he knew
that the giant, four-story painted portrait of the religious figure that dominated the photograph's background could only have been taken in Teheran. Even
so, his attention kept returning to the military man's
face and his strange blue eyes. A zealot's eyes, he
thought.

Just then, his cell phone rang. He checked the
screen. A restricted number. "Von Daniken."

"Marcus, it's your American cousin."

Von Daniken handed the letter to Myer and told
him to find someone who spoke Arabic. Then he
stepped outside the garage and resumed his conversation. "No more engine problems, I trust."

"All taken care of."

"I'm glad."

"We talked to Walid Gassan."

"I figured." Von Daniken wondered where they'd
hidden him on the plane. "When did you take him
down?"

"Five days ago in Stockholm. One of our informants received word that Gassan had taken delivery of
some plastic explosives up in Leipzig. We brought in a

jump team to nab him, but he'd gotten rid of the stuff before we could arrest him."

"Semtex?"

"How'd you know? He got it from that Ukrainian scumbag Shevchenko."

"You're certain?"

"Let's just say that we had a heart-to-heart with him and he decided to come to Jesus."

Von Daniken didn't require any further details.

"Gassan was acting as a facilitator," Palumbo continued. "He handed over the explosives to someone named Mahmoud Quitab. We ran the name through Langley and Interpol but didn't get anything. Anyway, this Quitab character took delivery in a white Volkswagen work van with Swiss plates. We don't have a number."

Von Daniken had rounded the corner of the garage. As he listened, he noticed that a small chunk of concrete was chipped from the pillar separating the two bays. Visible to the naked eye was a streak of white paint. "A white van? You're sure of the color?"

"The guy said white. The name Quitab mean anything to you?"

"Not a thing." Von Daniken fought to keep the anxiety from his voice. "Anything else on this Quitab . . . phone, address, description?"

"His phone number belonged to a SIM card with a French prefix. We've got a request into France Telecom to run its numbers. We're doing the same with all incoming and outgoing calls registered on Gassan's phone. Nothing on Quitab's address or his whereabouts so far, but we did get a description of him. Maybe fifty. Dark hair. Trim. Medium height. Sophisticated. Well dressed. One of them, but with blue eyes."

One of them, meaning an Arab.

Von Daniken looked at the photo of Blitz. Dark hair. Medium height. A look of sophistication. And, of course, the diamond blue eyes.

Just then, Myer came back with a police officer in tow. Von Daniken asked Palumbo to hold a moment, then addressed the policeman. "Did you read the letter?" he asked.

The officer nodded and explained that it was a note to his parents about daily life. He added that there was no mention of any illegal activities.

Von Daniken took it all in. "And the name? Can you tell me who it was addressed to?"

"Why yes, of course." The policeman told him the name.

It had to be, thought von Daniken. There was no such thing as coincidence in this game.

"Are you there, Marcus?" asked Palumbo.

"I'm here. Go on."

"Apparently, this guy Quitab has a setup in your neck of the woods," said Palumbo. "I called to give you a heads-up."

"Yes, I know."

"What do you mean you know?" Palumbo

sounded annoyed. "I thought you'd never heard of him."

"As a matter of fact, I'm at his home right now."

"You mean you know about this operation?"

"It's more complicated than that. Quitab is dead."

"He's dead? Quitab? How? I mean . . . great! Jesus Christ, that's good news. I was worried for a minute. Thought you had a real white-knuckler on your hands. Did you find the explosives, too?"

"Yes, we did."

"All fifty kilos? Thank God. You guys dodged a major bullet."

Von Daniken hurried into the garage. He counted the bricks of explosive. Six bundles of five bricks. Thirty kilos at most. "What do you mean that we dodged a bullet, Phil? Do you have a line on what Quitab was planning?"

"I thought you did . . ." Reception weakened and Palumbo's voice disappeared in a thicket of crackles. ". . . fuckin' crazy bastard."

"I'm losing you. Can I call you back on a land line?"

"No go. I'm in transit."

Hoping for a better signal, von Daniken moved out of the garage and stood in the rain. "What did you mean when you said we dodged a bullet?"

"I said that Gassan told us that that fuckin' crazy Iranian Quitab was going to Switzerland to take down a plane."

32

The time in Israel was three hours ahead of Switzerland. Instead of rain and snow, a blistering sun ruled the sky. The mercury nudged the century mark as the shores of the Eastern Mediterranean sweltered beneath an early spring heat wave.

Ten miles north of Tel Aviv, in the rocky coastal hillside town of Herzliya, an emergency meeting was under way on the second floor of the Institute for Intelligence and Special Operations, better known as the Mossad, Israel's foreign intelligence service. Present were the heads of the organization's most important divisions. Collections, which handled intelligence gathering. Political Action and Liaison, which was responsible for dealing with foreign intelligence services, and Special Operations, or Metsada, which supervised the dark side of the business:

targeted assassination, sabotage, and kidnapping, among other activities.

"Since when do they have a facility in Chalus?" demanded the fat, proudly unattractive man pacing back and forth at the head of the room. "Last I heard, they'd concentrated their enrichment efforts at Natanz and Esfahan." Dressed in short sleeves, with thinning black hair, an unlined face, and a reptile's bulging eyes, he might have been forty or seventy. What was unmistakable, however, was his air of seething resolve. His name was Zvi Hirsch and for the past seven years, he'd been chief of the Mossad.

"We can't find anything on the maps. No satellite imagery. Nothing," said Collections. "They've been very clever. They managed to keep its construction secret."

"Secret, indeed!" said Zvi Hirsch. "How many centrifuges do they need to process that much uranium? We're talking one hundred kilos in less than two years."

"In so short a time? At least fifty thousand."

"And how many companies manufacture the equipment needed to do that kind of job?"

"Less than a hundred," said Collections. "Exports are strictly controlled and monitored."

"I can see that," Hirsch replied dryly.

"Clearly, they received their technology from outside the usual channels," said Metsada. He was dark and rail thin and spoke in a gentle voice that sounded as if he wouldn't hurt a fly. "Most probably from manufacturers of dual-use goods."

"In Hebrew, please."

"Products made for civilian purposes that can be used by the defense industry. In this case, it would be equipment to assist in the fuel enrichment cycle. High-speed centrifuges sold to dairies to make yogurt cultures that can also be used to separate uranium hexafluoride gas. Heat exchangers designed for steel mills that can be used to cool reactors. Those products aren't subject to export licenses or end-user certificates. Think of it as a false flag operation."

"False flag? I thought we'd cornered the market on that game." Hirsch crossed his arms over his barrel chest. "Okay, so they have the stuff. Can they get it here?"

"They successfully test-fired the Shahab-4 long-range missile sixty days ago," said Collections.

"How long from launch until it hits us?"

"An hour at the outside."

"Can we shoot it down?" Hirsch asked.

"Theoretically, we're as safe as a baby in her mother's arms."

Israel relied on a two-tier air defense structure to destroy incoming long-range missiles. The first was the Arrow II ground-to-air missile, and the second, the next-generation Patriot missile system. Each suffered from the same problems. They could only be launched once the incoming missile was within one hundred kilometers of the target—that is to say, within minutes of striking. And neither had ever been tested in combat.

"What about something that gets in under the radar? Do they have any cruise missiles?"

"Rumors, but that's it."

"Let's hope so," said Hirsch. "What about the Shahab's accuracy?"

The man from Political Action and Liaison spoke up. "Accuracy is something that Germany and France and the U.S. have to worry about. In our case, it's beside the point. Any hit within fifty miles of the target is a fatal blow. If they can smuggle fifty thousand centrifuges into the country under our eyes and build a state-of-the-art enrichment facility without anyone hearing about it, I wouldn't be surprised if they've made advancements in that area as well."

"And so," said Hirsch, rubbing his thick, hairless forearms. "Are we supposed to put our hands up and surrender? Is that what our Persian friends desire? Do they expect us to stand still while they arm their rockets with warheads that can destroy our cities?"

A former major general in the Israeli Defense Force, he knew all too well the scenarios involving a nuclear strike on Israeli soil. Israel occupied a land mass three hundred miles long and one hundred fifty miles wide. However, ninety percent of the population was clustered around Jerusalem and Tel Aviv, cities just thirty miles apart. A nuclear strike on either would not only kill a significant percentage of the population, but would wipe out the country's industrial infrastructure. The radioactive fallout would render the landscape uninhabitable for years to come. Simply put, there would be nowhere for the population to go, save out of the country. A new diaspora.

None of his section chiefs answered.

"I have a meeting with the prime minister in an hour," Hirsch went on. "I'd like to be able to show that we haven't been caught with our peckers in our hands. I imagine he'll be interested in one question and one question only. Will they launch on us?"

Collections pursed his lips. "The president of Iran is a believer in the apocalyptic end times as stated in the Koran. He sees it as his personal mission to hasten the return of the twelfth Imam, known as the Mahdi, the rightful descendant of the Prophet Mohammed. It's written that his return will be preceded by a confrontation between the forces of good and evil that will see a period of prolonged warfare, political upheaval, and bloodshed. At the end of the period, the Mahdi will lead the world to an era of universal peace. First, though, he has to destroy Israel."

"Great," said Hirsch. "Remind me not to come to you for good news next time."

"There's more. The president's drive to gain control of the levers of power has been incredibly successful. He's dismissed hundreds of the country's leaders in education, medicine, and diplomacy who don't share his beliefs, and replaced them with his cronies from the Republican Guard. Worse yet, he's got his own man elected as the country's supreme religious leader. Six months ago, the president's ambitions might have been held in check by the top clerics. Not anymore. This new guy, Ayatollah Razdi, is certifiable. He's on the horn to Mohammed on a regular basis. He is definitely not a rational actor."

"You want to know if he'll pull the trigger," Metsada asked. "I think we have the answer already."

Collections nodded. "The president is taking Iran back to the Age of Mohammed. On numerous occasions, he's said publicly that the Prophet Himself has spoken to him and informed him that His return is only two years away. He's got one hand on the Koran and the other on the trigger."

"He can't keep the program a secret forever." Metsada's voice had acquired a venomous edge. "When word gets out, he knows we'll act."

"Unless he acts first." Hirsch dropped into his chair with a grunt. "It's like March of 1936 all over again."

"What do you mean?"

"When Hitler ordered his troops into the Rhineland to take back the territory annexed to France after the First World War. His soldiers were poorly trained and pathetically armed. Some didn't even have bullets for their rifles. The commander carried two sets of orders in his pocket. One to open if the French fought back, the other if they didn't.

"The French let the Boches walk right in, and

even treated them like liberators. The commander opened the first set of orders. He was told to occupy the territory and hand out German flags to the citizens. The event was a watershed. Until that day, Hitler had been all bluster and hot air. After he took back the Rhineland, he began to take himself more seriously. And so did the rest of the world."

"Excuse me, Zvi," interrupted Collections. "What did the second set of orders say?"

"The second set?" Zvi Hirsch smiled sadly. "If fired upon, the commander was to immediately retreat and return the soldiers to the barracks. Essentially, it told him to cut and run at the first sign of conflict. The shame would have been too great for the country to endure. The government would have fallen. One shot and Hitler would have been forced out of office."

"Are you saying we have to confront him?"

Hirsch turned and stared out the window. "I don't think it will be that easy this time."

33

Jonathan sat with knees drawn to his chest, his back against the wall. A nook in the corner opposite held a vase of fresh flowers. A crude iron crucifix hung above it. The shelter had been built into the hillside by the Swiss Alpine Club and resembled a grotto, its floor and walls fashioned from stone and mortar. From where he sat, he had a clear view of all paths converging to his position. One led from the east, a level track tracing the hillside's contour. Another climbed from the lake, zigging and zagging in a series of switchbacks. A third track approached from the west. Beyond the hillocks that fell steeply away, through the torrential rain, the whipped gray crescent of Lago Maggiore filled the horizon.

Simone lay on her back on the rough flooring, her clothing drenched, her chest heaving. "Do you see anyone?" she asked, panting. "Anyone at all? Are they following us?"

"No," said Jonathan. "There's nobody out there."

"You're certain?"

"Yes."

"Thank God." With a grunt, she pushed herself to a sitting position. "This is too much," she said, cradling her head in her hands. "I'm terrified. That man . . . Blitz . . . I've never seen a man shot like that. What are we going to do?"

"I'm not sure yet."

Abruptly, Simone lifted her head, as if seized by an idea. "I'll tell you what we're going to do," she said. "We're going to get off this mountain. We're going to take a bus into Lugano and find a place to dry off. Then we'll buy you new clothes. A suit. Something professional. Then we'll cut and dye your hair and put you on a train to Milan. That's what we're going to do."

"I need a passport first," said Jonathan. "Preferably one without my name or picture inside it."

Simone waved off her initial plan. "Okay, forget the train. We'll wait for a while, then go back and get the car. We'll drive across the border. They wave everyone through. They won't stop a banker in a Mercedes. I'll come with you."

As she spoke, her eyes bore into him. Christ, thought Jonathan, if I look as scared as she does, we're in trouble.

"And then what?" he said. "Keep running?" Hauling himself to his feet, he pointed across the mountainside in the direction of Blitz's villa. "Look back there. The police know all about the stunt I pulled at the railway station. My fingerprints are all over Blitz's office. I'm the killer, Simone. I'm the guy who blew Blitz's brains out. Whatever chance I had of convincing them that what happened yesterday was self-defense is gone."

"That's why you need to leave the country."

"That won't solve anything."

"But you'd be alive. You'd be safe."

"For how long? They won't stop looking for me just because I crossed the border. They'll send my picture to every country in Europe."

Jonathan crossed his arms, trying to imagine how it would play out if he left the country. Time and again, he came to a dead end. He couldn't see it, partly because his mind wasn't conditioned to cut and run. He'd spent years battling up impossible slopes in impossible conditions. After a while, he'd gotten to thinking that you could do anything if only you didn't quit. You didn't have to be great. You just had to keep going.

When he was young and brash and a little too cocksure, he used to say that he was against retreating on general principle. It was that tenacity that had gotten him through college and medical school in seven years, and had led him to stay in field medicine when, one by one, his colleagues had fallen away.

"They plumb broke and ran," Emma used to say, after a shot or two of Jack Daniel's. "Cowards, the lot of 'em. Hearts the size of mice, and their John Henry Thomas not much bigger."

He heard her voice speaking the words as clearly as if she were sitting next to him. Suddenly, his eyes felt hot, irritated. He wanted to hold her hand. He yearned for her strength.

Simone looked at Jonathan from beneath a tangle of wet hair. "What the hell is going on?" she asked.

"What do you mean?"

"What was our girl involved in?"

"I don't know."

"She never told you? How could she keep something like this a secret? You must have had an idea. It's why you keep going on with this . . . why you keep chasing her ghost. Tell me the truth, Jonathan. Were you in it with her? A team? I've heard of couples doing this type of thing together."

"What type of thing is that?"

"I don't know what to call it. Spying. Being an agent. I mean, that's what this is, isn't it? The fake driver's license. The men after the bags. All that money. One hundred thousand francs. It wasn't a thief who shot Blitz, was it?"

"No," he said. "It wasn't."

The answer seemed to confirm her worst suspicions. Her shoulders slumped, as if weighed down by the sum of her accusations.

Jonathan slid across the floor and sat next to her.

"I don't know what Emma was involved in," he said. "I wish to God I did."

Simone held his gaze a moment too long. "I don't know if I believe you."

Jonathan looked away, running his hands over his face, struggling for a clue as to what he should do next. "And so," he said finally. "What are you going to do?"

"I told you. **We** are going to find our way into Lugano and get you some new clothes. Then we're going to change how you look. And afterward, we're—"

"Simone, stop right there. You can't stay with me. This whole thing is out of control."

"You expect me to leave?"

"When we get down the mountain, we're going to split up. You're going to Davos to see Paul, and you're going to forget that this ever happened."

"And you?"

Jonathan made a decision. "I'm going to find out what she was doing."

"Why? What good can it bring? You've got to look after yourself."

"I am. Don't you see?"

Nodding, Simone clawed in her bag for a cigarette. She lit it and blew out a cloud of smoke. He noticed that her hands weren't shaking anymore. "At least let me help you with some clothes," she said. "Before I go . . ."

Jonathan put his arm around Simone and hugged

her. "That much you can do. Now, let's see if we can make any sense out of this stuff I took from the office."

He opened Blitz's briefcase and began to rummage through the papers he'd grabbed from the desk. Most were bills, miscellaneous housekeeping items. He handed them to Simone, who cast a quick glance at each, then tossed them back into the briefcase. Neither of them found anything to shed light on who Blitz was or who he worked for.

In a side pocket, Jonathan discovered a Palm PDA: a phone, word processor, e-mail, and web browser all in one. He hit the on button. The unit lit up, activated to the phone function. In the upper corner, an asterisk appeared and began to blink, indicating an incoming message. He clicked on the asterisk. The unit demanded a password. He punched in 1-1-1-1, then 7-7-7-7. Access denied. He swore under his breath.

"What's that?" asked Simone, sliding closer to him, her eyes focused on the screen.

"Blitz's PDA. Everything's password protected. I can't access the software. Not e-mail, not Word, not the browser. What do you use for a password?"

"It depends. I've got a different password for each account. I used to use my mother's birthday, and then the street address of my home in Alexandria where I grew up. These days, I've been sticking with 1-2-3-4. It's easier that way."

And Jonathan? He had only one password. Emma's birthday. 11-12-77.

Suddenly, he remembered the bracelet containing the flash drive he'd found in Emma's overnight bag. He slipped it off his wrist, pried it open, and plugged the flash drive into the Palm's USB port. An icon titled "Thor" appeared on the screen. He double-clicked on it, and a screen appeared, asking for his password. "Damn it all."

"Is that yours?" Simone inquired, reaching out to touch the flash drive.

"Emma's. I found it in her bags when I went back to the hotel. It wants a password, too." He tried Emma's birthday, then his own. He tried their newest ATM PIN, then the one before that. He tried their anniversary. All failed.

Plowing through the papers, he located the memo addressed to Eva Kruger on ZIAG stationery concerning Project Thor. "I'm going to call and ask them about it."

"Who?"

"ZIAG, or whatever the name is of the company Blitz worked for."

Simone made a halfhearted attempt to pry the Palm out of his hands. "No, Jonathan, don't. It will only get you into more trouble."

"More trouble?" Jonathan stood and walked to the far side of the grotto.

He activated the phone and heard a dial tone in

his ear. At least that worked without a password. Memo in hand, he punched in the number listed at the top of the page. The phone rang twice before being answered. "Good afternoon, Zug Industriewerk. How may I direct your call?"

The voice was young, female, and eminently professional.

"Eva Kruger, please."

"Whom may I announce?"

Her husband, actually, Jonathan responded silently. He hadn't prepared an answer because he hadn't expected the company to exist. "A friend," he said after a moment.

"Your name, sir?"

"Schmid," said Jonathan. It was the closest thing to Smith he could think of.

"One moment." A neutered beep sounded as the call was transferred. A voice mail message responded. "This is Eva. I'm away from my desk. If you leave your name and number, I'll return your call promptly. For further assistance, dial the star key to speak with my assistant, Barbara Hug."

The language was Swiss German spoken fluently and with a Bernese twang. There was no question but that Eva Kruger was a native Swiss. The problem was that it was Emma's voice. Emma who stumbled over **"grüezi,"** and couldn't pronounce **"chuechikaestli"** if her life depended on it. Emma who, besides a decent grasp of what she called her "schoolgirl's French," was a self-admitted imbecile when it came to languages other than the Queen's English.

Jonathan punched the star key. He wanted to speak with Barbara Hug. He wanted to ask if that was her real name, or if she took it only for liaisons involving false eyelashes and skimpy lingerie, not to mention envelopes packed to bursting with cold, hard cash.

But a moment later, Fräulein Hug's voice mail offered a curt message and he hung up.

Immediately, he redialed the number. When the receptionist answered, he gave the name "Schmid" again. Now he had an alias, too.

"I'd like to speak with **Mrs.** Kruger's superior," he said, remembering the wedding ring with the engraved anniversary. "It's an emergency."

"I'm afraid he's busy at the moment."

"Of course he is," railed Jonathan.

"Excuse me, sir?"

Jonathan had found the envelope containing the passport-sized photos of Emma and a man named Hoffmann. "Give me Mr. Hoffmann."

"One moment, please."

A male voice picked up the line. "Mr. Schmid? This is Hannes Hoffmann. Mrs. Kruger is out of the country. What did you wish to speak with her about?"

"About Thor."

Silence. Clearly, Jonathan didn't have the password to get past Hoffmann either. Then, surprisingly: "Yes, what about Thor?"

"I think you may have a problem getting it wrapped up as soon as you'd like."

"Mr. Schmid, I'm afraid we don't discuss business with strangers."

"I'm not a stranger. I told you I'm a friend of Eva's. It's just that you shouldn't be relying on Gottfried Blitz, either." Jonathan waited for another rejoinder about not discussing business with strangers, but all he got was dead air. "You know him, don't you? I mean his name is on a memo you sent out."

"Yes." The response was tentative. "What about Mr. Blitz?"

"He's dead."

"What are you talking about?"

"They got him this morning. Snuck into his house and shot him in the head."

"Who is this?" asked Hoffmann.

"I already told you. My name is Schmid."

"How do you know about Mr. Blitz?"

"I was there. I saw him."

"Impossible." Hoffmann said it dismissively, as if Jonathan was referring to a practical joke that couldn't be pulled off.

"Send someone to his house if you don't believe me. The police are already there. Give him a call and you'll find out."

"I will. Immediately. Now, tell me who this really is?"

"Check the phone number."

There was a pause, followed by the sound of a sharp intake of breath. "Who is this? What did you do to Blitz?"

Jonathan hung up. From now on, he was going to be the one asking the questions.

34

In accordance with the rules that applied to all homicides, the body of Theodoor A. Lammers, chief executive of Robotica AG, Dutch citizen, suspected agent provocateur for an unknown country, and victim of a professional assassin, was transferred to the University Hospital morgue and given a complete autopsy. The procedure was performed by Dr. Erwin Rohde, chief medical examiner for the canton of Zurich.

Rohde was sixty years old, an elfish man with watery blue eyes and a cap of gray hair. There was no question about the cause of death on this one, he thought, as he stood over the body and examined the wounds to the face and chest. If the shots to the head hadn't killed the victim, the shot to the chest had. The round black bullet hole was positioned directly above the heart.

Murder was relatively uncommon in Zurich, and in Switzerland on the whole. The country had recorded a total of sixty-seven homicides the previous year. Less than the American city of San Diego, which at just over one million inhabitants had one-seventh the population of Switzerland. Of those sixty-seven, twenty died at the hands of organized crime, the victims primarily criminals themselves. But he had seen nothing like this in years.

Selecting a scalpel, Rohde made an incision across the top of the forehead and continued along the circumference of the head. After peeling back the skin (half over the face, half to the nape of the neck), he used an electric saw to cut off the top of Lammers's skull. It was messy work. The gunshots had more or less eviscerated the brain.

Rohde dug out several misshapen pieces of lead and dropped them into the basin to his right. The bullets were dumdums, or hollow points, that mushroomed on impact. He freed another piece of metal and paused. **Isn't that odd?** he thought to himself. Instead of a normal healthy pink, the area around the bullet fragment was colored a brackish brown. Normally, such coloring was indicative of necrosis, the unprogrammed killing of cellular matter by an outside source, either an infection, inflammation, or poisoning.

Rohde excised a chunk of the cerebellum and deposited it in a specimen bag. Leaving the closing to his assistant, he set to work examining the chest wound. The bullet had pancaked upon striking the heart, but was otherwise intact. It was a quick business to remove it. Adjusting the overhead lamps, he bent to study the organ. The heart was colored a rich, healthy maroon. All except the tissue surrounding the wound. There, the muscle was the same fecal brown he'd observed in the brain.

Rohde excised a nub of tissue and held it to the light. There could be no doubt that what he was observing was an advanced case of necrosis. This specimen, too, he preserved.

Scooping up the plastic bags, he took off his robe and hurried from the operating theater.

Two minutes later, he arrived in the forensics lab. "I need to use the GC-MS," he said, referring to the gas chromatograph–mass spectro-meter.

Something on the bullet was killing the flesh.

C31-H42-N2-06.

Erwin Rohde stared at the formula displayed in the mass spectrometer's readout, waiting for the machine to translate it into a known substance. Ten seconds passed without any words appearing. The spectrometer, capable of identifying over 64,000 substances, was stumped. A second request to analyze the tissue offered the same result. Rohde shook his head. It was the first time in twenty years that the machine had failed him.

Writing down the formula, he hurried back to his office. That it was a toxin or poison, he was certain.

The question was what kind of toxin. Rohde tried running the molecular signature through his own computer. Again he came up with a blank. Perplexed, he slid his chair back. There was one man he could count on to provide him the answer.

Consulting his address book, Rohde dialed an overseas number: 44 for England, 20 for London. The four-digit prefix belonged to New Scotland Yard.

"Wickes," answered a dry English voice.

Rohde introduced himself, stating that he had attended Wickes's seminar the past summer titled "New Forensic Technologies." Wickes was a busy man who gave short shrift to social niceties. "What is it, then?"

Rohde offered a summary of Lammers's postmortem and the mass spectrometer's failure to identify the compound causing necrosis of the brain tissue and heart muscle.

"Just the composition," Wickes cut in. "Leave the rest to me."

Rohde read off the list of components. When Wickes returned to the phone, his tone was a good deal less imperious. "Where did you say you found that tissue?"

"Around gunshot wounds to the head and chest."

"Interesting," said Wickes.

"Do you mean you've found the substance?"

"Of course I found it. The compound you gave me is that of a batrachotoxin."

Rohde admitted to having never heard of such a toxin.

"No reason for you to have," said Wickes. "Not in your neck of the woods, is it? From the Greek **batrachos**, meaning frog."

"Frog poison?"

"Genus **Dendrobates.** Poison dart frogs, to be exact. Little devils size of your thumb. Found in rainforests in Central America and western Colombia. Nicaragua, El Salvador, Costa Rica. Batrachotoxin is one of the most lethal in the world. One hundred micrograms—about the weight of two grains of salt—is sufficient to kill a one-hundred-fifty-pound man. The poison's only recorded use, other than by frogs to protect themselves, of course, is by indigenous Indians who coat their darts with the stuff when they go hunting for monkeys and the like."

"So the bullets were coated? But why?"

Instead of answering the question, Wickes posed one of his own. "Do your men have a line on the killer? Don't have him in custody, do they?"

"No."

"Didn't expect so. I'm certain that he's a professional."

Rohde told him that the police did believe that the murder had, in fact, been committed by a trained killer.

Wickes cleared his throat, and when he spoke his voice had assumed a conspiratorial edge. "Reminds me of something I saw when I was with the Royal Marines. This was in El Salvador a while back, 1981 or '82. We were over from Belize, engaging in joint exercises with the Yanks. Back then, the country was on fire. Everyone jockeying for power. Communists, fascists, even a few democrats. The government was running death squads in the countryside, killing off all opposition. Nothing more than cold-blooded murder, really. A few of the soldiers were Indians and none too happy about what they were being asked to do. They're a superstitious bunch. Believe in ghosts and the spirit world. Shamans. Shape-shifters. You name it. They'd a ritual to protect themselves against the ghosts of the men and women they killed. To stop the victims' spirits from haunting them, they'd dip their bullets into poison. Kind of kill the soul before it left the body."

"That's terrible," said Rohde.

"You know who trained those squads, don't you?" asked Wickes.

"What do you mean, 'trained them'?"

"Taught them their craft. Put them into the field. Made them do what they do."

"I have no idea," said Rohde.

"It was the Yanks. The Company. That's what they called themselves back then. You want to find your killer, that's where you better start looking."

"With 'the Company'? Do you mean the CIA?"

"That's right. Bunch of bloody bastards."

Wickes hung up without a goodbye.

Erwin Rohde sat down. He needed a moment to

digest what he had just learned. Poisoned bullets. Assassins. Things like this simply didn't happen in Switzerland.

Almost reluctantly, he picked up the phone and dialed the personal number of Chief Inspector Marcus von Daniken.

"You'll never shoot it down," said Brigadier General Claude Chabert, commander of the Swiss Air Force's 3rd Fighter Wing. "Turboprops are hard enough. They only fly at two hundred kilometers per hour, but this little number has a jet in its tail. Forget it."

"Can't you fire a missile?" groused Alphons Marti, bullying his way closer to the center of the table so he could better survey the blueprints of the drone, or "unmanned aerial vehicle," according to Chabert. "What about a Stinger? Like you say, it's a jet. It has to have a heat signature."

Chabert, Marti, and von Daniken were standing alongside a table in von Daniken's office on Nussbaumstrasse. It was nearly five o'clock in the afternoon. Chabert, a trained electrical engineer and F/A-18 Hornet pilot with six thousand hours of flight time, had been rushed from his base in Payerne to provide an instant education in the destruction of unmanned aerial vehicles. Lean and blond with a shepherd's wizened blue eyes, and still dressed in his flight suit, he was the picture of an accomplished aviator.

"A heat signature isn't enough," said Chabert patiently. "You must keep in mind that it is a small jet. The wingspan measures four meters. The fuselage runs barely two and a half by fifty centimeters. That's not much of a target when it's moving at five hundred kilometers an hour. Conventional radar arrays used by air traffic control are purposefully tuned down to avoid picking up small objects like birds and geese. And this one is stealthy. It has very few straight edges. The exhaust ducts are mounted by the tail fins. If I had to wager, I'd say that silver coating on the body was RAM."

"What's RAM?" asked Marti, as if it were something dredged up solely to annoy him.

"Radar absorbent material. The metallic color serves to make it more difficult to see with the human eye." Chabert finished examining the plans, turning to face von Daniken. "I'm sorry, Marcus, but civilian radar would never see it. You're out of luck."

Von Daniken sat down in a chair and ran a hand over his scalp. The last hour had given him a devil's education in the development and usage of drones as military weapons. In the 1990s, the Israeli Air Force had pioneered the use of unmanned aerial vehicles to overfly their northern border with Lebanon. Back then, a drone was no more than a radio-controlled toy with a camera strapped to its underside that took snapshots of the enemy. The latest models boasted wingspans of fifteen meters, carried Hellfire air-to-ground missiles under their wings, and were piloted via satellite by operators in secure bunkers thousands of miles away.

"Have any idea about the target?" asked Chabert.

"An aircraft," said von Daniken. "Most probably here in Switzerland."

"Any word as to where? Zurich, Geneva, Basel-Mulhouse?"

"None." Von Daniken cleared his throat. The wear and tear of the last few days was taking its toll. Dogged circles ringed his eyes, and even seated, his posture was slumped. "Tell me, General, what kind of runway does this thing need to take off?"

"Two hundred meters of open road," said Chabert. "A drone this size can be out of its transport packaging and up in the air in five minutes."

Von Daniken recalled his meeting at Robotica AG, Lammers's company, and the prideful description of sensor fusion technology that melded input from a variety of sources. For all he knew, the pilot—or "operator"—could be all the way in Brazil, or anywhere else in the world for that matter. "Any chance of jamming the signal?"

"You're better off locating the ground station. The drone works on a three-legged principle. The ground station, the satellite, and the drone itself, with signals constantly passing back and forth between them."

"How big is the ground station?"

"It depends. But if the pilot is flying it out of line of sight—that is, if he's relying on the drone's on-board cameras—he'll require video monitors, radar, a stable power source, and uninterrupted satellite reception."

"Could it be mobile?" von Daniken asked. "Something, say, he could stick in the back of a van?"

"Definitely not," declared Chabert. "The operator will have to be in some kind of fixed installation. Otherwise, he won't have enough power to boost the signal a long distance. You said they intend on taking down a plane. This UAV doesn't have the size to carry air-to-air missiles. Is it your belief that whoever is behind this intends on flying the drone into another aircraft? If that's the case, they'll want to be in visual range of the target. It's a damned tricky business to fly these things by camera and radar."

"I can't say with any certainty," responded von Daniken. "But it's probable that plastic explosives will be used."

"Well," said Chabert, brightening. "Then at least we know what the nacelle is for. I'd assumed it was for more avionics."

"What nacelle are you talking about?"

Using a ballpoint pen, Chabert tapped at a teardrop-shaped canister that appeared to hang from the nose of the drone. "The maximum weight allowance is thirty kilos."

Von Daniken groaned inwardly. Some twenty kilos of Semtex was missing from Blitz's garage.

"Is that enough to bring down a plane?" asked Marti.

"More than enough," said Chabert. "The bomb that brought down Pan Am 103 over Lockerbie fit inside a cassette recorder. It needed less than a half kilo of C-4 to tear a hole two meters by four out of the side of a Boeing 747. At ten thousand meters altitude, the plane didn't stand a chance. Imagine a drone traveling at five hundred kilometers an hour delivering a charge fifty times as big."

Marti backed away from the table, his complexion the color of curdled milk.

"But that's only half your problem," said Brigadier General Claude Chabert.

Von Daniken narrowed his eyes. "How's that?"

"With a charge of that size, the drone itself is, in effect, a missile. It wouldn't necessarily have to wait for a plane to become airborne to kill everyone aboard. It could just as easily destroy the target on the ground. The detonation would ignite the fuel in the wing tanks. The fireball and the shrapnel it would provoke would initiate a chain reaction. Any plane parked within twenty meters would cook off like overheated ammunition."

Grimacing, Chabert ran a hand across the back of

his neck. "Gentlemen, you may very well lose the entire airport."

Chabert had left five minutes earlier. Von Daniken sat on the edge of the conference table, arms crossed over his chest, as Alphons Marti paced the floor. Only the two of them were left in the room.

"We need to alert the proper authorities," said von Daniken. "I think the call should come from your office."

The list was long and ran to the Federal Office of Civil Aviation, the Federal Security Service, the police departments of Zurich, Bern, Basel, and Lugano, as well as their brother agencies in France, Germany, and Italy, over whose airspace the drone could intrude. It would be up to them to contact the airlines.

"I agree, but I think it's too early in the game. I mean, exactly what kind of attack are we talking about?"

"I thought we just went over that."

"Yes, yes, but what about the specifics? Do we have a date, a time, or even a place? Everything we know so far is based on the ravings of a terrorist who gave up the information under what I can only imagine as the utmost duress."

Marti's tone was reasonable, a patient parent upbraiding a rowdy child. Von Daniken matched it note perfect. "Gassan may have been under duress, but what he said has proven accurate. He wasn't lying when he said he delivered fifty kilos of Semtex to Gottfried Blitz, a.k.a. Mahmoud Quitab. We also have a photo showing that Blitz either is, or was, an Iranian military officer. I feel comfortable assuming that Lammers built a drone and delivered it to Blitz. I'd say that, coupled with Gassan's confession that Blitz's target was a plane in Switzerland, is more than enough for us to go to the authorities."

"Granted, but both Lammers and Blitz are dead. Would it be unreasonable to assume that the other members of their group—oh, what do you call it—their cell, might also be dead? If you ask me, I'd say someone's doing our work for us."

Von Daniken thought of the flecks of white paint found on the corner of Blitz's garage, the twenty kilos of missing plastic explosives, the tire tracks that matched those of the Volkswagen van reported to have been used to transport the explosives. "There are more of them out there. The operation's bigger than two men."

"Maybe there are, Marcus. I won't dispute that something's going on. But you're not giving me much ammunition. Tell the civil aviation chieftains, and then what? Do you expect them to cancel their flights? Are they going to reroute all planes headed our way to Munich and Stuttgart and Milan and ship everyone here by rail and bus? What if we had a threat against a tunnel? Should we shut down the San Bernardino and the Gotthard? Of course not."

Von Daniken stared hard at Marti. "We'll need the close support of the local police," he said after a moment, pretending that he hadn't heard a word that Marti had said. "We'll go house to house in a radius of ten kilometers from the airport. Then we'll—"

"Didn't you hear the general?" Marti interrupted in the same maddeningly reasonable tone. "The drone could be launched from anywhere. It could take out a plane in France or Germany, or . . . or, in Africa, for all we know. Please, Marcus."

Von Daniken dug a fingernail into his palm. This wasn't happening, he told himself. Marti was not making light of the threat. "As I was saying, we'll begin with a house-to-house search. I promise you it will be conducted quietly. We'll start in Zurich and Geneva."

"And how many policemen do you expect this will involve?"

"Several hundred."

"Ah? Several hundred quiet policemen who'll walk on their tiptoes and not breathe a word of why they had to leave their wives and children in the dead of night to go knocking door-to-door with instructions to look for an armed missile."

"Not to look for a missile. To speak with residents and inquire if they've noticed any suspicious activity. We'll run the operation under the guise of a search for a missing child."

" 'Quiet policemen.' 'A friendly inquiry.' By to-morrow morning half the country will know what we're up to, and by tomorrow evening, I'll be on the evening news explaining to the other half that we believe that there's a terrorist cell operating within our borders with the intention of shooting down a passenger airliner, and that there isn't a damned thing we can do to stop them."

"Exactly," said von Daniken. "We do believe that there's a terrorist cell operating within our borders with precisely that intention."

He was losing. He could feel the argument slipping from his grasp as if it were sand slipping through his fingers.

Marti shot him a look of damning appraisal. "Do you have any idea of the panic you'll sow?" he asked. "You may very well shut down the entire air transport grid for central Europe. This isn't a bomb in someone's luggage. The economic cost alone . . . not to mention to our country's reputation . . ."

"We'll need to station Stinger teams on airport roofs and move some antiaircraft batteries around the perimeter of the runways."

Von Daniken waited for Marti to protest, but the justice minister remained quiet. He sat down and locked his hands behind his head, staring into space. After a moment, he shook his head and von Daniken knew that it was over. He'd lost. Worse, he knew that Marti wasn't entirely mistaken to preach calm.

"I'm sorry, Marcus," said Marti. "Before we do any of those things, we need to corroborate this plot. If this Blitz, or Quitab . . . or whatever his name is . . . had cohorts, you'll find them, along with the twenty kilos of missing plastic explosives and the white van.

If you want me to shut down our entire country, you must give me concrete evidence of a plot to shoot down an airliner on Swiss soil. I won't paralyze the country based on a confession extracted by your buddies at the CIA."

"And Ransom?"

"What about him?" Marti asked offhandedly as he stood and made his way to the door. "He's a murder suspect. Leave him to the cantonal authorities."

"I'm waiting to learn if the detective who was injured has come out of a coma. I'm hoping he might be able to shed some light on what Ransom might have wanted with those bags."

"You needn't bother. I was told that the detective succumbed to his injuries an hour ago. Now Ransom's wanted for two murders."

Von Daniken felt as if he'd been stabbed in the back. "But he's the key—"

Marti's eye twitched and a hint of color fired in his cheeks. The anger had been there all along. It had just been kept well hidden. "No, Chief Inspector, the key to this investigation is finding that van and the men who want to shoot down a jet over Swiss soil. Forget about Ransom. That's an order."

36

The van trawled the streets of the sleeping neighborhood. It was no longer white. Days earlier it had been repainted a flat black, its side panels stenciled with the name of a fictitious catering company. The phone number advertised was active and would be answered professionally. The Swiss license plates had likewise been replaced by German ones, beginning with the letters "ST," for Stuttgart, a large industrial city close to the border.

The Pilot sat behind the wheel. He was careful to keep his speed under the legal limit. At every stop sign, he brought the van to a full halt. He had checked that all of the vehicle's running lights were in working order. Confronted with a yellow traffic signal, he slowed and was content to wait. Under no circumstance could he risk police attention. Examination of the stainless steel crates in the cargo bay would prove disastrous. If the plan had any weakness, it was this: the necessity to transport the drone on public streets without safeguard.

The van slid through Oerlikon, Glattbrugg, and Opfikon, on the outskirts of Zurich. Soon, it left behind the lanes crowded with apartments and homes, and entered a sparse pine forest. The road climbed steeply through the trees. After a few minutes, the forest fell away and the van crested the foothill, coming upon a broad snow-crusted park. Here the street dead-ended and the Pilot guided the van onto a macadam road that ran the length of the park, approximately one kilometer in length. Black ice layered the asphalt. He could feel the tires losing their grip even at this slow speed. He was not unduly concerned. The location met his demanding specifications. The road—or runway, as he preferred to think of it—was as straight as a ruler. There were no trees nearby to interfere with the takeoff. In a few days, the ice would be gone, anyway. The forecast called for a front of high pressure moving over the area by Friday, bringing sunshine and a sharp increase in temperature.

Continuing to the end of the road, he swung the van into a private drive. The garage door was open and the pavement cleared of snow and ice. Seconds after he pulled into the shelter, the door closed behind him.

He left the garage by a side door and walked outside, eager to stretch his legs after the long drive. As he headed toward the park, a roar built in the air, a shrill, ear-piercing whistle that assaulted his ears. The noise grew louder. He gazed into the night sky as the belly of an airliner passed overhead, no more than a thousand feet above him. The plane was an Airbus A380, the new double-deck jumbo jet designed to carry up to six hundred passengers. The engines whined magnificently as the plane climbed higher into the sky. It was close enough for him to read the insignia on the tail. A purple orchid with the word "Thai" beneath it. The 21:30 flight to Bangkok.

The Pilot watched the plane disappear into the clouds, then turned and looked behind him. Sprawled on the plain below was a city within a city. A multitude of lights illuminating long strips of concrete, steel, and glass passenger terminals, and capacious hangars, surrounded by fields of snow.

Zurich Airport.

The view couldn't have been better.

37

"*Lay your head back,*" said Simone, massaging the dye into his clean wet hair. "First, we let it sink in, then we wash it out, then we cut it. Sicilian Black. You won't recognize yourself."

"It's not me I'm worried about."

Seated on a stool, Jonathan lowered his head into the washbasin and closed his eyes. Simone's strong fingers worked the dye to all parts of his scalp, massaging the temples, the crown, working down the nape of his neck. The amphetamines had long since worn off. The fuel-injected madness that had led him to storm Blitz's house and had scripted his fiery exchange with Hannes Hoffmann, the executive at ZIAG, belonged to some foggy, distant past. He felt bone tired, his skin still tingling from the hot shower. Simone's hands worked the cords at the base of his skull. He exhaled, and for the first time in twenty-four hours, allowed himself to relax.

They had stayed in the hills until early afternoon, when they'd descended to the highway and taken a bus to Lugano, a city of one hundred thousand inhabitants spread along the shores of its eponymous lake, thirty kilometers to the east. While Jonathan hid in a movie theater, Simone had gone store to store, purchasing new outfits for both of them. Afterward, they'd walked to the outskirts of town, looking for a place to spend the night.

The hotel was called the Albergo del Lago. It was a small, family-run establishment situated on the outskirts of Lugano. A terra-cotta palace with twenty rooms all overlooking the lake, and a pizzeria downstairs to justify its two stars. Using Simone's passport and credit card, they had checked in as Mr. and Mrs. Paul Noiret. In place of suitcases, they carried shopping bags filled with clothing, toiletries, and a dinner of roast chicken and **pommes frites** purchased from a Provençal delicatessen. To inquiring eyes, they were lovers repairing to their hotel after a day in the city.

"All done," said Simone, peeling off the latex gloves. "In fifteen minutes, your hair will be as black as Elizabeth Taylor's."

"I didn't know she was Sicilian."

Simone slapped his shoulder. "Smart-ass. Now stay where you are and let the color settle."

She folded a towel and laid it across his eyes to

make sure that no dye seeped down. The next thing he knew, she was shaking his shoulder, telling him to wake up. "Time for your rinse."

The towel came off his eyes. He blinked at the bright overhead lamps. "I fell asleep for a minute."

"More like twenty." Simone turned on the faucet, and when the water was warm, she washed out the dye. Using newly purchased scissors, she trimmed his hair until the curls were gone, and it stayed straight when she combed it. "Stand up. Let me have a look."

Jonathan stood.

"Just a little more work." Laying her fingers along his jaw, she held his head in place while she styled his hair to her satisfaction. Finally, she put her hands on his shoulders and spun him around so he could see the completed picture in the mirror. "Done," she said. "Recognize that guy?"

"That's frightening."

"Not quite the response I was looking for."

The man staring back looked ten years younger. He was the diplomat his father had always wanted, ready and willing to steal away mineral rights from a third world country. The Park Avenue surgeon with an advanced degree in phony compliments. He had to fight from mussing the part in his hair. He smiled and his teeth fairly blazed beneath the bright lights. Not a man you'd want to buy a used car from, he thought.

In short, it was perfect.

"Not Liz Taylor," he said, slipping out of the bathroom. "But I'll settle for Vince Vaughn."

"You're at least Brad Pitt."

"He's blond."

"Who cares? I'll take him any color he wants."

Jonathan walked into the bedroom and picked out the bag holding his new clothing. He put it on the bed and set out the navy suit and overcoat. The television was on. The commentator was speaking Italian, saying that a second policeman attacked the day before in Landquart had died, and that the manhunt for the American doctor wanted in connection with the crime had been extended to the Tessin, where the body of a German businessman had been found early this morning. Jonathan sat down and listened. Twice he heard his name enunciated. **Dottore Jonathan Ransom.** Thankfully, there was no picture.

The commentator moved on to the weather, but Jonathan was no longer paying attention. He was thinking of the television in the lobby that had been blaring the evening headlines when they'd checked in, and the concierge, whose narrow black eyes didn't miss a trick. If the manhunt had been extended to the Tessin, the police would have contacted every hotel in the area. Faxes would have been sent with his name and description. They might even know that he was traveling with a woman.

He walked to the balcony, opened the door, and stepped into the rain. Far along the lake, he caught sight of a flashing blue-and-white strobe approaching. A hundred meters behind it was another.

For a moment, he stared at the oncoming lights.

They could be going anywhere. The concierge downstairs had no reason to suspect him. The lights flickered in the rain and he knew that they weren't going "anywhere." They were headed to the Albergo del Lago. They were coming for him.

"Simone, we have to go," he called. "The police are coming."

Simone poked her head out of the bathroom. "What did you say about police?"

"There was a report on the news . . . the concierge downstairs, he called the police."

"Jonathan, slow down, what is it?"

"They know about us, that we're traveling together. The police will be here in a few minutes. We've got to leave."

He threw on the clothes that she'd purchased for him that afternoon. White dress shirt, navy suit, cashmere overcoat, and a pair of lace-ups. He caught a glimpse of himself in the mirror. The suit. The midnight-black hair cut above the ears and parted with a razor. And Emma? What would she think? He was the enemy. The devil in his deep blue suit. He hated himself on sight.

He returned to the balcony. The lights were definitely coming his way. No more than a kilometer now. He could hear the siren's atonal whine getting louder.

"Come on." He strode across the room, opening the door to the hall.

Behind him, Simone was putting on her shoes.

Grabbing her overcoat, she stumbled against him. "Okay, then," she said. "I'm ready."

They avoided the elevator and the main stairs, proceeding instead to the end of the hall where, behind French doors and lace curtains, a balcony overlooked a parking lot at the rear of the hotel. The French doors were unlocked. Stepping onto the balcony, Jonathan dropped Blitz's briefcase onto the ground below, then shimmied down a drainpipe.

"I can't," called Simone from above.

"It's only the first floor. I'll be right under you."

"What if I fall?"

"You can do it. Come on. We can't wait!"

"Mais merde." Simone climbed over the balcony, and without further prodding, took hold of the drainpipe and slid to the ground. It was over in three seconds.

"Was that so bad?" he asked.

"Yes," she said.

Taking her hand, Jonathan led her down the main road. Instinct told him that couples were less suspicious than loners. The lights of Italy flickered far across the lake. Small sailboats and motor launches bobbed at anchor. Sanctuary, he thought, gazing across the water.

The first police car passed them ten seconds later.

In town, they flagged a taxi and asked the driver to take them to the Via della Nonna in Ascona. Once there, Jonathan instructed the driver to stop two blocks from Blitz's home. The rain had momentarily let up and the neighborhood was tranquil. Soft lights burned behind lace curtains. The scent of pine drifted off the hillside. A dog barked nearby.

"Let me get the car," Simone said, extending an outstretched palm.

"Too risky," he said. "As far as the police know, you don't exist. Better to keep it that way. Wait down the street. I'll be by in ten minutes."

Jonathan walked up the road toward the Mercedes. A band of yellow tape had been placed across the gates leading to the Villa Principessa and another across the front door. A lone police car sat parked in the gravel drive. The calm and security he'd enjoyed in the hotel were gone. His body was tense with worry. He was on the run again. He kept waiting for the moment when his nerves would calm down, when he would adjust to his new status as a fugitive. If anything, he was growing increasingly unsettled. It was as if he could feel the noose being lowered over his head, the sturdy, coarse rope scratching his neck, the slipknot hard against the back of his skull.

Had Emma felt this way? he wondered as he stared at the villa's forlorn facade and the neatly tended rose garden. Had she lived with the constant fear of discovery? The worry that at any moment a trapdoor might drop from beneath her?

The Mercedes was parked where he'd left it, thirty meters down the street from Blitz's home. Jonathan stepped off the sidewalk and crossed the street. From the corner of his eye, he saw the policeman get out of the cruiser. In his new suit and overcoat, Jonathan stopped and forced himself to acknowledge the officer. With a smile and a raised hand, he called out a greeting. The policeman stared at him long and hard before answering, then got back into his car.

Jonathan continued with his business. The remote entry sounded with a beep. He slid behind the wheel and the engine rumbled to life. Gliding from the curb, he drove past the police officer and turned right at the next street. He stopped two blocks farther on to pick up his passenger.

"And?" Simone asked, slipping into the car.

"One cop was parked in front of the house. I waved to him."

"You what? My God, I think you were born to this."

"You're wrong there."

They drove down the winding road, entering town and taking the fork toward the railway station. Twice, he noticed dimmed Xenon headlights trailing at a distance. He asked Simone to check if they were being followed. She stared out the back window and said that she didn't see a soul. He checked again as he neared the station, but the lights were no longer there.

He pulled to a halt in the shadows at the back of the parking lot.

"We've got to split up," he said. "They're looking for a couple."

"You're overreacting. You can't be sure that they know about me."

"Simone." He sighed, and lowered his voice. "I can't do what I need to if you're with me."

She looked into her lap. "What can you hope to gain from our splitting up?" When he didn't answer, she raised her head and stared at him. "At least take my advice and get out of the country while you can. Find yourself a lawyer. Then come back, if you must."

He took her hand. "Tell Paul I send my best. I'll catch up with you both when I get back to Geneva."

"I'm worried about you."

"Say a prayer."

"I don't know if that will be enough."

"Then wish me luck."

"Fool." Simone shook her head in exasperation, then leaned closer and wrapped her arms around him and hugged him tightly. "Take this. It will keep you safe." From around her neck, she took a medallion hanging from a leather lanyard and pressed it into his hand. "Saint Christopher. The patron saint of travelers."

"But he's not a saint anymore."

"That makes two of us," said Simone.

Jonathan looked at the medallion, then put it around his neck. "Goodbye."

"**Adieu.**"

He watched her make her way across the parking lot. When she reached the station, he thought he saw her raise a hand to her face and wipe away a tear.

38

Simone Noiret tugged her purse onto her shoulder and walked into the train station. Strewn from one end of the platform to the other, a dozen people stood waiting for the train. A shrill wind whistled through the rafters, chilling her to the bone. Shoving her hands into her pockets, she made her way to the monitors announcing arrivals and departures.

She'd tried, she told herself. She had done everything humanly possible to warn him. Regardless, she'd failed to sway him from his course. He was a good man. He didn't merit the consequences of his wife's behavior. Simone wondered if her husband would do as much for her. She doubted it. Paul was not a good man. That was why she had married him.

With a gust, the 8:06 pulled into the station. It was a Regional Express with two engines and twenty-odd cars en route from Locarno to Regensburg on the border of Germany. Brakes squealed as the train ground to a halt. Passengers alighted. Simone looked up and down the platform as her fellow travelers climbed aboard. Finally, she stepped onto the train. The smoking compartment was half full. She chose, however, to continue through the partition into the non-smoking car. Again, there were plenty of free seats. She ignored them. Her eyes were on the platform. She saw no sign of Jonathan. Reaching the end of the car, she passed into the causeway, threw open the outside door, and hopped onto the platform.

Alone, she watched the train exit the station.

When the taillights had faded into the darkness, she strode down the platform to the buffet. Decorated in brasserie style, the restaurant was doing a lively trade, mostly businessmen enjoying a beer or **ristretto** on their way home from work. She took a table by the window and lit a cigarette.

The waiter arrived and she ordered a whiskey. **Uno doppelte, per favore.** The drink came shortly and she drank it in a single gulp. She called her husband and chatted with him about the goings-on at the World Economic Forum, then informed him that she would arrive in Davos sometime after one a.m. "Jonathan's fine," she added. "Very upset, naturally, the poor lamb, and keeping it all inside. Just like him. No, he hasn't scheduled a date for the service."

Just then, the table rattled and a pale, compact man sat down across from her. Simone looked up sharply. "I'm afraid this table's reserved," she said, lowering the phone. "There are plenty of other places free."

"I enjoy sitting by the window."

She bit back the comment on the tip of her tongue.

"Paul, I have to go. Train's here. Bye, love." Simone dropped the phone into her purse. For the first time, she looked directly at the man seated across the table. He had sad eyes and skin so pale as to be translucent. She couldn't bring herself to meet his gaze for more than a few seconds. "Yes, the view can be nice," she responded. "But I prefer it in summer."

"I'm in Zurich during the summer."

Simone slipped a piece of paper across the table. "He's in a black Mercedes," she said. "Temporary plates. He's headed to Goppenstein. The car ferry through the mountain. He told me that he's trying to make the 10:21 to Kandersteg."

The Ghost studied the paper for a moment, then tore it in half and dropped it in the ashtray. "And from there?"

"To Zug. You should have no problem following him. He's wearing a tracking device around his neck."

"That will make things easier." The Ghost lit a match and set fire to the scraps of paper.

"What are you going to do?" she asked.

He didn't answer and she felt foolish and angry for having betrayed her concern.

"He has a briefcase with him," Simone continued,

in a harder voice. "Get it. And make sure you find the flash drive. It's concealed in a wristband he's wearing on his right hand. And watch the tailgating," she added. "I had you the whole way from Blitz's house."

"It wasn't me. I was waiting in the parking lot."

"You're sure?"

The black eyes met her own. "I followed your instructions," he said, his voice quieter.

"Good." Simone nodded. "Oh, and one more thing . . . he's armed."

The Ghost rose from his chair. "It doesn't matter."

Simone slid lower into her chair and lit another cigarette. She stared out the window into the darkness.

Leaving Ascona, Jonathan did not follow the signs north, toward Lugano, Airolo, and the St. Gotthard Tunnel that could guide him under the pass and deliver him safely to his destination in three hours. As he had the night before, he took to the mountains. Using the car's onboard navigation system, he punched in the name of the town where he was headed. The route appeared on the screen. A voice told him to turn left in five hundred meters and after five hundred meters he turned left. The road narrowed from four lanes to two and drifted away from the water, moving up the Versazca valley and beginning a series of lazy switchbacks into the mountains. Banks of silvery clouds tumbled down the hillsides. It began to rain in earnest, and soon the rain turned to sleet, striking the windshield like a fistful of nails.

Blitz's briefcase sat on the floor next to him. He thought of the memorandum to Eva Kruger concerning the termination of Project Thor. The memo was innocuous enough, but for the mention of Thor on Emma's flash drive. **"Who is this?"** Hoffmann had demanded, not with anger so much, but with palpable fear.

It was a question Jonathan wanted to ask for himself. It was the subterfuge that gnawed at him worst. The planning. The falsehoods. The deception. How long had it been going on? he wanted to ask Emma. When did it all start? How many times did you lie to me? And, finally, how could I not have known?

He turned on the heater. Warm air swirled inside the car, bringing with it a familiar scent. Vanilla and sandalwood. Reflexively, he looked to the passenger seat. Expectation crowded every corner of his being. It was empty, of course, but for a second, he had been certain of Emma's presence. He had smelled her hair.

———

"I have a confession to make," says Emma. "I've been reading your mail."

It is August. A Sunday morning. They have journeyed to Sanaya, a skeletal town on Jordan's eastern border with Iraq. It is a temporary assignment. Three days filling in for one of Emma's colleagues who has been stricken with appendicitis. The work is pleasant, if undemanding. Colds. Infections. Minor cuts and bruises.

It is early and they lie side by side atop a flurry of tangled sheets. An open window brings a warm, fitful breeze and the chant of the muezzin calling the faithful to prayer. Alone and undisturbed, they have rediscovered the habits of courtship, making love each morning, drifting back to sleep afterward, making love again.

Paris is forgotten. There are no headaches. No empty stares.

"Reading my mail?" Jonathan asks. "Find anything exciting?"

"You tell me."

"A letter from my girlfriend in Finland?"

"You've never been to Finland."

"A copy of Playboy?"

"Nope," she says, sliding on top of him and sitting up. "You don't need a girlie mag."

"I give up," says Jonathan, running his hands over her hips, her breasts, feeling himself stir. "What was it?"

"I'll give you a hint: Voulez-vous coucher avec moi?" Her accent is atrocious. Paris by way of Penzance.

"We just did. At least, I think that qualifies."

Emma shakes her head in exasperation. "Ah, oui, oui," she continues. "Uh, je t'aime. Pepé le pew. Magnifique . . ."

"You love Pepé Le Pew? Now I know I married a nutcase."

"Non, non. Fromage. Duck à l'orange. Pâtisserie."

"Something French? You read my copy of the Guide Michelin?"

Emma claps her hands, her eyes bright. He is getting warmer. "Um . . . Croix-Rouge . . . Jean Calvin . . . Fondue," she goes on, rambling merrily.

The lightbulb goes on inside Jonathan's head. She's talking about the letter from Doctors Without Borders. A curt note from his boss asking if he'll accept a post at headquarters in Geneva. "Oh that."

" 'Oh that'? Come on," she says, falling onto the bed by his side. "You weren't going to tell me? That's great news."

"Is it?"

"Let's go. We've done our bit."

"Geneva? It's admin. I'd be stuck behind a desk."

"It's a promotion. You'd be in charge of organizing all missions going into Africa and the Middle East."

"I'm a doctor. I'm supposed to be with patients."

"It's not like it's forever. Besides, it will do you good to have a change of pace."

"Geneva isn't a change of pace. It's a change of profession."

"You'll be seeing your work from a different side, that's all. Think how much you'll learn. Besides, you'll look cute in a suit. Ever so handsome, I daresay."

"Yeah, that's me. Next thing I know, you'll have me joining a country club and playing golf."

"Aren't doctors supposed to love golf?"

Jonathan fixes her with his serious gaze. He knows there's something else.

Emma props herself up on an elbow. "There's another reason."

"What's that?"

"I want to go. I've had enough of all this for a while. I want to eat at a restaurant with white tablecloths. I want to drink wine from clean glasses. Wine glasses. I want to put on makeup and wear a dress. Does that sound so odd?"

"You? A dress? Not possible." Jonathan throws back the top sheet and climbs out of bed. This is not a discussion he wants to have. Now or ever. "Sorry, I don't do admin."

"Please," says Emma. "Just consider it."

Turning, he looks at his wife draped in the white cotton bedding. Her cheeks are raw and sunburned, strafed by constant exposure to sun and wind. Her auburn hair has gone from teased to tangled to just plain tortured. The cut on her chin is taking too long to heal.

Just consider it . . .

In Geneva, they'd have plenty of mornings like this. Time to lounge. Time not only to talk about starting a family, but to do something about it. And, of course, there's the climbing. Chamonix, two hours' drive to the north. The Berner Oberland, two hours to the east. The Dolomites to the south.

"Maybe," he says, pulling back a curtain and staring across the hard, arid landscape. "But don't get your hopes up."

A loose assembly has gathered in front of the mosque for morning prayer. The men greet each other in the Arab fashion, a kiss to each cheek.

"You getting up?" he asks over his shoulder. "If you want, I can go out and get you some breakfast . . ."

It is then that he sees the car. A white sedan driving madly across the dirt. A car where no car should be. Plumes of dust spray from its tires as it rocks and rattles on the hardscrabble surface. Behind the windscreen, two silhouettes.

"Move," he calls to the crowd, though his voice is only a whisper. Then louder. "Get out of the way! Move! Hurry!"

Helpless, he watches the car plow into the crowd, sending bodies flying. Screams. Gunshots. The car slams into a wall of the mosque, bricks and mortar toppling onto the hood. For a moment, silence. In his mind, he is counting . . .

A flash of light.

A garish pulse that sears his retina.

A quarter of a second later, the noise comes. A thunderclap that strikes his eardrums hard enough to make him wince. Not one explosion, but three in succession.

Jonathan hurls himself onto the bed, covering Emma's body with his own as the shockwave blows out the windows, spraying the room with glass, launching the curtain rod like a Crusader's spear, and shaking loose a veil of dust and mortar.

"A car bomb," he says as the noise dies. "It drove into the mosque."

Dazed, he stands and brushes the debris from his hair. Emma pushes herself off the bed and dances across the broken glass to the dresser, where she throws on her clothes. Jonathan searches for his medical kit, but Emma already has it and is stuffing it with gauze, bandages, and antiseptic wipes taken from their portable supply locker. He comes to her side and begins calling out the medicines he needs. In ninety seconds, his bag is full.

Black smoke curls into the sky. The mosque is gone. The blast has obliterated the structure. Only the base of the building remains, shorn walls resembling broken teeth. Paper and debris rain from above.

Jonathan slows as he approaches the ruined vehicle. He gazes down at a pair of smoking boots. Nearby, an arm reaches to the heavens, its hand clutching a Koran. Somewhere else lies the upper half of a human being. Everything is charred black and daubed with blood. Around him survivors are getting to their feet, staggering aimlessly. Others rush toward them, heeding the piti-ful calls of the wounded. The smell of burning oil and cauterized flesh is overpowering.

"Over here," says Emma. Her voice is rock solid. She stands next to a young man lying on his back. The man's face is a bloody mess, the flesh of his chest flayed and badly burned. But it is his leg that draws Jonathan's attention. Shattered bone protrudes from his pant leg. A compound fracture of the femur.

"Don't move," Jonathan instructs the man in Arabic. "Keep still." To Emma: "I'm getting a splint. It's crucial that he stay just as he is or he'll nick his femoral artery."

Emma grasps the man's shoulders and com-bats his thrashing as Jonathan splints the leg.

Jonathan raises his head and counts a dozen more who need urgent treatment. His decision whom to treat will determine who lives and who dies.

"Okay," he says, meeting Emma's eye.

"Okay what?"

"Geneva. Let's go."

"Really?"

"Those white tablecloths are looking pretty good right about now."

———

Jonathan began the curving descent to Brig. The time was 21:45. The outside temperature a chill −3° Celsius, or 27° Fahrenheit. Negotiating a hairpin turn, he felt the rear tires slip, only to regain their traction a second later. The road was icing up.

Despite the inclement weather, he had made good time. As expected, there had been little traffic on the alpine road. He'd counted six cars passing him from the opposite direction. None of them police. On several occasions, he'd glimpsed the flare of headlights behind him, but the driver had either pulled off the road a while back or hadn't kept up. The navigation unit clicked down another notch. Thirty-eight kilometers remained to his destination. To his right, he observed a sign with the name "Lötschberg" and a symbol of a car piggybacking on a flatbed train next to it.

Emma had arranged the promotion. Not Emma herself, of course, but the people she worked for. Her higher-ups. The implication was clear. They had a person inside DWB.

Who was it, then? Someone in personnel? One of the vice-directors? The director herself? Between them, he counted one Somali, two Brits, and a Swiss.

Would it have been easier if one were American? Jonathan wondered. Would he have considered the problem of Emma's allegiance solved? Stirring America into the mix would only add to the confusion. Emma was a vocal critic of the "world's greatest democracy." She did not believe in nation building and spheres of influence, doctrines going by any name, and realpolitik.

But if she wasn't working for America, then who?

The Brits? The Israelis? What did the French call their espionage unit . . . the wingnuts who had tried to sink the **Rainbow Warrior** in Auckland Harbor way back when? With a fright, he realized that she could be working for anyone. The country didn't matter. Only the ideals did.

Emma and her duty to interfere.

As the windscreen filled with white and the frozen night closed around him, Jonathan's mind was fixated on the fireball that had engulfed the mosque. The blinding burst that erupted a millisecond before the explosion assaulted his ears.

Was the car bomb part of it, too? The final straw needed to convince him to go? He begged Emma for the answer. But he'd lost touch with her.

Disillusioned, he heard only silence.

40

Marcus von Daniken tossed a dossier onto the desk. "Not exactly the manpower I was hoping for," he said. "But you'll do."

He looked at the four men seated around the table. None had slept a wink in the last thirty-six hours. A welter of empty coffee mugs attested to their hypercaffeinated state. The glaring overhead lights didn't help much either.

To his usual crew of Myer, Krajcek, and Seiler, he'd added Klaus Hardenberg, an investigator from the financial crimes division. After a few minutes of bantering, they'd decided to call themselves a task force, in spite of their limited numbers. It would make it easier to explain the long hours to their wives, even if they were forbidden from discussing the focus of their work.

Von Daniken didn't bother to flatter them that they were the best men in his department.

"Let's start with questions," he said, sliding into a chair. "Anything that's bothering you, let's hear it."

The voices came at him fast and furious. Who did he think killed Lammers? What was the connection between him and Blitz/Quitab? If Quitab was an Iranian officer, shouldn't they forward his name to all friendly agencies to check for any background information? Had any evidence beyond the terrorist's confession been found linking Walid Gassan with Blitz/Quitab and Lammers? Did they have any idea of Gassan's activities during his passage through Switzerland a month earlier? Which airport was the most likely target? And what about the American, Ransom? Where did he fit in? What should they make of his killing the two police officers in Landquart? Might he have had time to kill Lammers the same day his wife died?

Finally, there was a question posed in various forms by all the men present: Why did Marti have his head stuck so far up his ass?

Von Daniken was unable to answer any of the questions, and his ignorance highlighted the fault that ran through the center of the investigation. Essentially, they knew nothing about the conspirators or the plot.

It came down to one thing: there was too much to do and too little time to do it.

Von Daniken divided the inquiries into four areas. Finance. Communications. Field investigation. And transportation. He would take finance. His experience as a member of the Holocaust Commission had left him with a raft of acquaintances and contacts, as well as a few friends in the banking establishment.

"We'll start with the Villa Principessa," he said. "That's no squatter's hovel in Hamburg. It takes real money to set up digs there."

It would be his job to find out who had leased it, for how long, and where the payments had come from. The key would be to discover where Blitz did his banking. Of all the threads, this one carried the potential for the greatest yield. Once it was discovered where he conducted his daily business, von Daniken could backtrack and trace the origin of funds transferred into the account. As importantly, he could see where monies were channeled afterward. In one direction the money trail would lead to Blitz's paymasters—the organization or government underwriting his adventures. In the other, it would lead to his co-conspirators.

Klaus Hardenberg would cover the second line of inquiry, focusing on credit. Von Daniken said he wanted all records for Blitz, Lammers, and Ransom over the past twelve months. Tracking their expenditures would yield invaluable information about their daily activities and provide a road map as to their whereabouts during the past twelve months.

Lammers would be the easiest of the three. Five

charge cards had been found in his wallet. In order to avoid deportation, his wife was cooperating with their inquiries.

Blitz was another story. No wallet or identification had been found in his home. However, by a stroke of luck, one page of his December Eurocard statement had slipped beneath the credenza in his home office. The charge card would yield a credit history, along with banking references and some form of national identification number.

The jury was still out on Ransom. Immigration had only just come back with his details. As of this moment, Ransom's passport number and Social Security number were being run through Interpol and forwarded to the Federal Bureau of Investigation's National Crime Information Center.

Kurt Myer was in charge of communications. He'd begun work upon returning from Ascona. "Swisscom is sending over a list of all calls made from Blitz's home in the last six months," he reported. "We've already got Lammers's list for the same period. First, we'll cross the two and see if they have any friends in common. Then we'll go back a level and take a look at all calls made to and from their correspondents. We should have the first reports by seven in the morning."

"Good," said von Daniken. Five years earlier, he'd been instrumental in passing into law a requirement that telecommunications companies keep a six-month call log for every registered number. "After you run the two lists, isolate all cellular numbers and see if we can find some similar names. If they're using SIM cards, trace the numbers back to their point of sale."

"I can guarantee we'll find some similar names," said Myer. "It's just a question of how careful they were. Everybody makes mistakes."

"Let's keep our fingers crossed that they're not registered to foreign telecoms," said von Daniken.

Krajcek rolled his eyes. "Pray not the Germans."

No one protected their citizens' privacy more ferociously than the Federal Republic of Germany.

Finance and communication worked collaboratively. Once von Daniken's inquiries into the suspects' finances began to pay off, all related phone numbers would be passed along to Myer. Each and every hit would be fed into a predictive software program that used the data to map a "web of relationships" neatly illustrating Blitz's and Lammers's socioeconomic lives.

Von Daniken grabbed a cup of espresso in the break area—two sugars, twist of lemon—and downed it in two swallows. It was ten p.m. and he'd been awake for thirty-eight hours. His fatigue, however, had been replaced with a quiet optimism. In the beginning, everything was possible.

He looked at the empty coffee cup. Then again, maybe it was the caffeine boosting his spirits.

He slapped his hand on the desk to get their attention. "Mr. Krajcek will be visiting with our field agents in Geneva, Basel, and Zurich tomorrow, won't you?"

"First thing."

For the past three years, the Service for Analysis and Prevention had been running agents inside the country's most important mosques. Most were volunteers, Muslims angered by the way their religion had been hijacked by fundamentalists. Others were more reluctant and had to be pressed into service by threats of deportation to their home country. The take had yielded critical intelligence about smuggled RPGs, AK-47's, and a network of hawala—or money transfer—agents used by an Algerian terror cell operating out of France, Switzerland, and northern Italy.

"Concentrate on finding someone who visited with Gassan during his recent transit through Geneva," von Daniken said. "I want contacts, places visited, where he holed up, and any mentions of his intent."

All this Krajcek wrote furiously in his notepad.

Von Daniken turned to the next in line. "And now, Mr. Hardenberg . . ."

Hardenberg tried to smile, but succeeded only in looking like he was passing a kidney stone. He was fat, middle-aged, and pudding-faced with heavy tortoiseshell glasses that shielded shy brown eyes and a head as bald as an ice cube. And he was, bar none, the meanest, most dogged investigator von Daniken had ever come across. His nickname was the "Rottweiler."

"You're going to find the Volkswagen van that Gassan used to take delivery of the plastic explosives in Leipzig. My money says that it's being used to transport the drone as well. Find the van and we find our men."

It was a brief instruction masking a gargantuan task. Hardenberg cleared his throat and nodded. Without another word, he stood and left the room. No one believed for a second that he was going home. Every rental car company, automobile sales lot, and government agency was closed for the night, but Hardenberg would be at his desk until morning figuring the best way to begin his attack when they opened for business tomorrow.

Last, but not least, came Max Seiler. His mandate was twofold. First, using Lammers's passports as a starting point, he was to note all entry and exit stamps found inside and reconstruct Lammers's frequent trips. At the same time, they would ask all major airlines to run a passenger flight manifest check for Lammers, Blitz, and Ransom, and all known aliases of the above, during the last year. Seiler's discoveries might not help find the drone, but they would go a long way toward establishing a case against the pay-masters behind the planned attack.

Von Daniken pushed his chair back from the table. "Time to get to work."

41

Goppenstein, altitude fifteen hundred meters, population three thousand, sat nestled in the craw of the Lötsch Valley. The town had no historic or scenic claims. If it was known at all, it was as the southern terminus of a 12.5-kilometer railway tunnel that passed through the Lötschberg and linked the canton of Bern and, as such, northern Switzerland, with the canton of Valais to the south.

Built in 1911, the tunnel was a relic. Only one train at a time could traverse its length. There was no escape or "carcass" tunnel, as was customary in modern construction. Only at either end did it widen enough to accommodate two sets of tracks, and that for just a thousand meters. But it was a crucial relic. Each day the train ferried more than two thousand cars, trucks, and motorcycles through the mountain.

After paying the fare of twenty-six francs, the Ghost guided his automobile into the holding area. Lane markers had been painted onto the asphalt and numbered one through six. The first two lanes were full, a mix of cars and eighteen-wheel international transports. A man in a fluorescent orange vest motioned for him to pull into lane three.

The train lay beyond the parking lot. Instead of passenger cars, there were flatbeds with a spindly steel awning providing protection against the elements. An endless succession stretched past the station and into the darkness beyond. It reminded him of a snake poking its head out of a cave. A great, rusty, reticulated snake.

He checked the clock. Nine minutes remained until the train was due to depart.

The Ghost watched in his rearview mirror as Ransom pulled into the lane three cars behind him. He tapped the steering wheel with his palm. Everything was in order.

He opened the glove compartment, took out his pistol, attached a silencer and muzzle suppressor, then set it on the seat beside him. From around his neck, he freed the vial. He recited the prayer slowly and with passion, hearing the sound of far-off drums beating in the rain forest. One after another, he anointed the bullets in the poison. Certain that the soul of his victim could not follow him into this world, the Ghost finished loading his gun.

He waited.

A green light flashed. Engines turned over. Brake lights blinked. A procession of vehicles began loading onto the train. The lanes to his right cleared. The car directly ahead jerked forward. Jonathan drove up a brief grade, then onto the flatbed. He advanced down the narrow platform, passing from one car to the next farther toward the head of the train. A low barrier was erected on either side of the carriage, and above it a railing flagged with signs instructing drivers to employ the emergency brake and stating that it was forbidden to leave the automobile. Headlights illuminated a confined space, and he had the impression of plunging through a rifle barrel.

He brought the Mercedes to a halt at the head of his carriage, five or six feet behind the car ahead of him. Up and down the train, drivers killed their engines. Minutes passed. Finally the train lurched and began to move, shuddering to life like a sleepy animal. The rhythmic stamping of the ties increased in tempo. The mountains drew closer, hemming in the tracks. He heard the hush of the approaching tunnel. His ears popped from the change in air pressure. The train seemed to rush forward as it entered the pitch darkness.

Jonathan's eyes were open, but he couldn't see a

thing. He rode this way for a while, and in the dark he saw Emma's face. She was looking at him over her shoulder. "Follow me," she said, and her voice echoed inside him. His chin bounced off his chest and he woke with a start. He looked at the analog clock. The tritium hands showed that he'd dozed for five minutes. He snapped to attention and flipped on the overhead light.

He removed the documentation about Zug Industriewerk from the briefcase. First, he reread the memo from Hoffmann to Eva Kruger about Thor. "**. . . final shipment to client will be made on 10.2.**" Something about the date bothered him. The tenth was in three days. Then it hit him. Emma had been due to go to Copenhagen for two days for a regional DWB meeting. For the first time, he was forced to evaluate her actions through a warped lens. Had she really planned on going to Denmark? Or did she have something else in mind? Something arranged by Blitz or Hoffmann or some other unknown character from her double life.

He turned his attention to the glossy company brochure. A photograph inside the front cover depicted a prim three-story headquarters building and a sprawling factory attached to it. He flipped past photos of impressive silver machines and colleagues engaged in oppressively earnest conversation. "**Zug Industriewerk was founded in 1911 by Werner Stutz as a manufacturer of precision gun barrels,**" read a brief history of the firm. "**By the** early 1930s, Mr. Stutz had expanded the firm's product line to include light and heavy armament, as well as the first mass-produced steel aircraft wings." Good timing, commented Jonathan. Half the world was about to need as many gun barrels as they could get their hands on. It was a success story that had been repeated countless times during the bloody twentieth century. So far, things were on track for a repeat performance in the twenty-first.

He turned to the back of the brochure and perused the accounts. Revenues: 55 million. Profit: 6 million. Employees: 478. The numbers had a weight to them that the words couldn't match. Money was real. It was substantial. Money did not lie.

The more Jonathan read, the angrier he became. There was no doubting that ZIAG was a legitimate firm. So how was it that a woman who did not exist had come to be an employee?

It was then that he heard the tapping on his window. Something hard.

He jumped in his seat and turned toward the noise.

All he needed was a towel. The Ghost hadn't counted on the darkness being so complete. The flames from a silencer would be visible ten cars back. He dug around in his overnight bag and came up with a black T-shirt. He tore off a strip of fabric and wrapped it around the silencer. His last act before leaving the car was to attach the twill bag that would catch his spent shells.

The Ghost opened the door with care, leaving it ajar for his return. Precious little space separated the car and the safety railing. Keeping low, he slid alongside the chassis. The air inside the tunnel was clammy and frigid. The pocked stone wall rushed past, barely an arm's length away. He spotted Ransom's car, three back. The interior lights of the vehicles in between were extinguished, the drivers most probably resting. Ransom's dome light, however, was illuminated. He sat reading some papers, lit as if he were on a stage.

Keeping to a crouch, the Ghost moved toward him. He passed one car, then another. He stopped to check his watch. It was nine minutes since the train had entered the tunnel. The clerk at the ticket window had informed him that transit time was fifteen minutes end to end. His eyes focused on Ransom. The interior cabin light posed a problem. He didn't want anyone to see Ransom's body before they reached Kandersteg. Cell phones operated in the tunnel. It wasn't beyond reason that someone might call the police.

He settled back on his haunches.

A minute passed. Then another. Finally, he moved.

Sliding from the rear of the car, he crossed from one flatbed to the next. The Mercedes was parked at the head of its carriage. There were no railings here, and the Ghost had to be careful not to put a foot over the side. He took another step forward, putting his hand out to touch the Mercedes' fender. He drew up to the driver's door. Thumbing the safety to the off position, he stood and tapped the pistol against the window.

Jonathan Ransom looked directly at him.

The Ghost pulled the trigger.

Jonathan stared out the window. Something was there. A shadow. A form. He looked more closely. His eyes widened. A gun was pointed at his forehead.

Suddenly, a flame erupted, blinding him.

He flinched, turning his head away. There was the sound of crunching sand. Again, the same noise. He looked back as a spit of fire smeared the glass. The window bulged inward. He saw the starlike fractures where bullets had struck the glass but hadn't passed through.

The glass was bulletproof.

He had no time to react. Just then, the car door opened and an arm pushed through the gap. All Jonathan saw was the pistol aimed at his cheek. Instinctively, he threw his head back and grabbed the wrist, forcing it up and away from his face before it spat something that tore into the roof. He grasped the wrist with both hands and wrenched it downward. He glanced toward the door and caught a glimpse of a face. Hooded eyes. An expression of cold concentration.

At that moment, the train passed into the wider section of the tunnel. The wall to his right disappeared and he had the impression of gazing into a subterranean cavern. Directly ahead, he saw a flickering light. The station at Kandersteg.

The killer yanked his arm free. Jonathan pulled the door closed and locked it. The shadow melted into the dark. Jonathan started the engine. But where to go? He couldn't go forward or backward, and he couldn't sit there waiting to be shot. He rammed a palm into the horn, then turned on the lights and hit the brights. The Xenon beams illuminated the cars in front of him with a diamond blue light. He noted for the first time that the safety railing didn't extend between the railway cars. A sturdy chain two meters in length spanned the gap.

Just then, the train emerged from the tunnel. The tracks veered left, slotting beside the loading platform. Throwing the car into drive, he turned the wheel and pressed his foot on the accelerator. The Mercedes' V-12 engine propelled the car forward, snapping the safety chain and carrying him onto the platform. Sleet spattered the windshield. He fumbled for the wipers as he pressed his face nearer the glass. Something squat and dark loomed in front of him. Finally, he found the proper control and the blades cleared the windscreen. A kiosk stood only ten meters ahead. Jonathan jerked the wheel and the car dodged the obstacle with only inches to spare.

He continued down the loading ramp and across the parking lot, coming to a stop at the red light that governed access to the highway. Behind him, the train was pulling to a halt, its iron wheels screeching and moaning. No cars had begun to disembark.

The traffic light turned green.

Jonathan turned onto the highway and drove at the speed limit for ten minutes before taking the nearest exit and guiding the car down a series of narrower roads that led as far from the highway as possible. Content that he hadn't been followed, he pulled the car to the side of the road and killed the engine. He met his eyes in the rearview mirror. They were the eyes of a fugitive. His breath came in shallow gulps that left him light-headed and just this side of nauseous.

It wasn't the first time that he'd been shot at. He'd come under gunfire in a general, "duck, you sucker" way. Working in a field hospital in Liberia, he'd found himself in a no-man's-land caught between two warring factions. He was operating when the firing began. It was an amputation, a machete wound gone gangrenous. Even now, after seven years, he could see himself holding the saw as bullets suddenly began to tear into the whitewashed cement walls. Outside, there came the usual cries and whimpers. He remembered one man's voice in particular calling out, **"Cachez-vous vite. Ils vont nous tous tuer." Hide quickly. They're going to kill us all.** But no one in the operating room budged. Not even after a round exploded an IV drip.

Turning, he stared at the driver's side window.

There was no spidering. No fractures. Just three star-shaped scratches in the glass. He ran his fingers over the surface. Not even an indentation. Amazing, he thought, wondering how a piece of glass could fend off a bullet fired at point-blank range. He figured that it wasn't glass at all, but some kind of plastic. Whatever it was, he liked it. He liked it a helluva lot. He poked his finger into the rent in the ceiling fabric, seeking out the bullet, but found nothing.

He sat back in the seat, burdened by his predicament. Somewhere back there he'd crossed a line. He wasn't sure whether it had been when he'd run from the police in Landquart or when he'd decided to track down Gottfried Blitz. It didn't matter. He was no longer looking in, the grieving spouse seeking closure about his wife's double life. **Her clandestine activities.** He was a part of it now, whatever **it** was.

Braving the rain, he got out of the car and examined the Mercedes for damage. The front fender was scraped and dented on the right underside, but otherwise the car was fine.

A tank, he thought with a burst of misplaced pride.

He hurried back inside and cranked up the heat. He wondered about the man who'd tried to kill him. He was certain that it was the same man who'd killed Blitz. He must have been following Jonathan all day, biding his time, waiting for the right moment. But why had he waited so long? There had been plenty of moments, both on the mountain and in the city, when

Jonathan had been vulnerable. He didn't have an answer.

One thing was for sure: the killer must have been surprised about the armored car.

That's right, buddy. A fuckin' tank!

Jonathan touched his neck, feeling the Saint Christopher that lay against his skin. Patron saint of travelers. He had a desire to kiss the medal. The smile wilted after a few seconds, forced aside by a creeping sense of dread. He didn't believe for a second that the killer was going to cut and run. He was back there somewhere, and he was coming, just like the relentless one-armed man in the old ghost stories.

Jonathan put the car in drive. Making a three-point turn, he headed back along the side roads until he reached the highway. He pointed the car north in the direction of Bern. Other automobiles passed him regularly. His eyes checked the rearview mirror frequently, but he saw nothing that caused him concern.

The mountains fell away, and the horizon glowed a dull orange. City lights.

An armored car, a hundred thousand francs, and a cashmere sweater . . . but who were they for?

42

Midnight in Jerusalem.

Heat hung over the ancient city like a worn blanket. The unexpected temperatures had brought the people onto the street. Voices rang from cobblestone alleys. Drivers honked impatiently. The streets buzzed with a boisterous, defiant energy that was Israel itself.

In the prime minister's residence on Balfour Street, four men sat at a long, battered table. Barely twelve feet by fifteen, the office would be considered small for a head of state. Though recently painted, it still retained a scent of mildew and age.

The "red line" had been crossed. The Iranians not only possessed the means to manufacture weapons-grade uranium, they already had one hundred kilos of the stuff. It was no longer a question of preemption, but of self-defense.

Zvi Hirsch stood next to a map of Iran, the harsh overhead lights casting his skin with a greenish pallor, making him look more lizardlike than ever. Overlaid on the map were thirty distinctive yellow and black emblems denoting radioactive materials placed at locations of known nuclear facilities.

"The Iranians have ten plants capable of manufacturing weapons-grade uranium," he said, using a laser pointer to indicate the various sites. "And an additional four where the uranium can be fitted to a warhead. The sites most crucial to their efforts are at Natanz, Esfahan, and Bushehr. And, of course, the newly discovered facility at Chalus. For a first strike to succeed, we must destroy all of them."

"Four isn't enough," said a quiet voice.

"Excuse me, Danny," said Hirsch. "You'll have to speak louder."

"Four isn't enough." General Danny Ganz, Air Force Chief of Staff and leader of the newly created Iran Command, charged with all planning and operations involving an attack on the Islamic Republic, stood from his chair. Ganz was a wiry man and restless, with a hawk's nose and hooded brown eyes. Years of combat and conflict had etched deep wrinkles around his eyes and into his forehead.

He approached the map. "If we want to lock down Iran's nuclear efforts, we have to take out at least twenty, including the facility at Chalus. It won't be easy. The targets are spread out all over the country. We're not talking about single buildings, either.

These are massive complexes. Take Natanz here in the center of the country." Ganz rapped his knuckles against the map. "The complex is spread out over ten square kilometers. Dozens of buildings, factories, and warehouses. But size is only half the problem. Most of the crucial production facilities have been built at least twenty-five feet underground beneath layers of hardened concrete."

"But can you do it?" demanded the prime minister.

Ganz fought to conceal his contempt. It wasn't so long ago that the prime minister had been a vocal peacenik calling for the halt of all new settlements on the West Bank. To his mind, the PM was a turncoat, and just shy of a traitor. But then, he had the same opinion about most politicians. "Before we talk about striking the target, we have to figure out how we're going to get there," he went on. "From our southernmost airfields, it's eight hundred miles to Natanz and a thousand miles to Chalus. To reach both sites, we have to overfly Jordan, Saudi Arabia, or Iraq. I don't think we can count on the first two countries granting us permission to violate their airspace . . . which leaves Iraq."

Ganz looked to the prime minister for comment.

"I'll talk to the Americans at the appropriate moment," said the PM.

"That moment passed a few hours ago," commented Zvi Hirsch out of the corner of his mouth.

The prime minister ignored the jibe. He directed

his question at Ganz. "What about our planes? Are they up to the task?"

"Our F-15I's can make the return trip, but our F-16's are another question," said Ganz. "They'll need refueling en route. Iran has no air force to speak of, but they do have radar. Over the past few years, they've made big purchases of Russian-made ground-to-air missile systems. At Natanz, for example, the missile sites are to the north, east, and south of the complex. We'll have to accept a high casualty rate going in."

"How high?" asked Zvi Hirsch.

"Forty percent." Ganz crossed his arms as a rustle of outrage and disappointment rose from the others. He wanted to make sure everyone present knew the price asked of his men.

"My God," said the prime minister.

"It's hard to dodge missiles when you're delivering a bomb to target," said Ganz.

"What about a preemptive strike to soften up the air defenses?" asked Hirsch.

"Not enough planes." Ganz cleared his voice and went on. "If we want to sufficiently degrade the targets, we'll have to strike repeatedly. And I mean right on top of their heads. I'll need precise GPS coordinates of the production facilities. I know what you're all thinking. We did it before. We can do it again. I'm sorry, gentlemen. But this will not be a repeat of Opera."

Ganz was referring to Operation Opera, the surprise airborne strike launched against the Osirak nuclear plant near Baghdad on June 7, 1981. On that day, fifteen Israeli aircraft flew from Etzion Air Base across Jordan and Saudi Arabia and destroyed Saddam Hussein's maiden nuclear effort. All returned home safely. The planes had enjoyed help from an American agent who had placed transmitters along the route, allowing the Israeli planes to fly via instruments beneath Jordanian and Saudi radar. The same agent had been at the site, painting the target with a laser for the bombs to home in on.

"Which brings up our last issue," the general continued. "Ordnance. Assuming that we do manage to fly twenty jets a thousand miles to each target, and that at least twelve of them make it through the air defenses, what are we going to hit them with? The best we can manage is the Paveway III. The bunker buster. Two thousand pounds of explosive with a warhead that can penetrate eight feet of concrete. Granted, that's a helluva wallop, but what if the plant's twenty-five feet down? Or fifty? Or a hundred, even? Then what? The Paveways will cause some dust to fall from the ceiling, and that's it."

"There are better weapons," suggested Hirsch with a glance at the prime minister. "Something with more bang."

"Paveway-N's with a B61 warhead," said Ganz. "A nuclear-tipped bunker buster carrying a throw weight of a few kilotons. Something a tenth the size of Hiroshima. The Americans conducted a sled test last

year." A "sled test" referred to the process whereby a
missile is fired into concrete to measure its destruc-
tive force. "They achieved penetration to one hundred feet. The crater was five hundred yards in
circumference."

"Just enough muscle to take out the factory,"
added Hirsch, the voice of caution. "We're not bar-
barians, after all."

All eyes fell on the prime minister. He was an
older man, nearly seventy, at the end of a turbulent
political career. His reputation had him as a deal
maker, a negotiator. His enemies questioned his
principles. His friends called him an opportunist.

The PM shook his head with disgust. "It's always
been our philosophy that we cannot allow the Iranians the means to produce weapons-grade uranium.
Unfortunately, they've passed that barrier. It's too late
to go back. I'm of two minds about a strike. My first
responsibility is the people's welfare. But I can't risk
anything that might provoke a nuclear attack on our
soil. I just wish we knew their capabilities better."

"You're forgetting something," said Hirsch. "We
do know their capabilities. They have a bomb and
they're going to launch it."

The PM leaned back in his chair, his hands tented
over his nose and mouth. Finally, he exhaled loudly
and stood. "Once in our history we gave the enemy
the benefit of the doubt. We cannot afford to do so
again. I want a plan of attack on my desk in twenty-
four hours. I'll call the Americans and see what I can

do about securing permission to use Iraqi airspace." He looked at Ganz. "And about the other, God help me."

Slowly, the men in the room rose. Zvi Hirsch was the first to clap. The others joined in. One by one, they pressed to shake the prime minister's hand. All said the same words.

"Long live Israel."

At his home, Marcus von Daniken could not sleep. Lying in bed, he stared at the ceiling, listening as the habitual sounds of the night tolled the passing hours. At midnight, he heard the radiator click off. The old wooden house began to shudder, surrendering its stored heat in groans and cracks and faint, pining voices that seemed to wail forever. At two, the nightly freight passed over the Rumweg Bridge. The tracks were five kilometers away, but the air was so still that he could count the cars as they rumbled over the trestles.

A drone.

He knew that this would be the case that defined his career. He knew it because things like this did not happen often in small, cozy Switzerland, and he was proud of the fact. He imagined the unmanned aircraft cutting across the sky, bearing its nacelle of plastic explosives. He pondered the possible targets. The terrorist, Gassan, had said that Quitab wanted to take down a plane, but here in his bed, in the dark of the night, von Daniken conjured up a dozen other possibilities, ranging from a dam in the Alps to the nuclear power plant at Gösgen. A drone like that could fly anywhere.

In his mind's eye, the white unmanned aircraft grew larger in size and changed shape, until it was no longer a drone packed with twenty kilos of plastic explosives, but an Alitalia DC-9 carrying forty passengers and a crew of six en route from Milan to Zurich, among them his wife, his unborn child, and his three-year-old daughter. He was dreaming and he knew it, but the knowledge did nothing to lessen the impending horror. He saw the plane nosing through clouds, its landing gear hanging clear of the fuselage in preparation for arrival. It was not February, but November. A night much like this. Freezing temperatures. Sleet. Ground fog.

In his dream, he was standing inside the cockpit, lecturing the captain that he had no business flying in such conditions. The captain, however, was busy talking to a stewardess, more concerned about getting her phone number than paying attention to the faulty altimeter that had him flying three hundred meters too low.

And then, with the merciless acuity of all dreams, von Daniken saw his wife and daughter seated in the rear of the plane as it hurtled toward the mountainside. As was his custom, he took the seat next to them and gently laid his fingers over their eyes, closing their eyelids and shepherding them to a deep, painless sleep. He was certain that little Stéphanie's head had been touching his wife's shoulder.

At 19:11:18 hours November 14, 1990, Alitalia Flight 404 struck the Stadelberg, altitude four hundred meters above sea level, head-on, just fifteen kilometers from Zurich Flughafen. The speed at the moment of collision was four hundred knots. According to the accident reports, when the ground collision alarm sounded, the captain had less than ten seconds to avoid hitting the mountain.

Von Daniken shot upright in his bed before he was forced to watch it explode.

"Not again," he said to himself, his breath coming fast and shallow.

No more planes would go down on his watch.

He would not allow it.

44

Sixty kilometers to the south, in the mountain hamlet of Kandersteg, the lights blazed in a small hotel room where a slim, muscular man stood naked in front of the mirror, shuddering violently. He was a sight from a grotesquerie. Great daubs of blood painted his cadaverous flesh. Feverish black eyes peered from sunken hollows. Strands of lank hair were pasted across his damp forehead.

The Ghost was dying.

The poison was killing him.

One of his own bullets had ricocheted off the bullet-resistant glass, entering his abdomen above the liver. The wound was barely the size of a sunflower seed, but the skin surrounding it had colored a sour yellowish brown, like a week-old bruise. With each heartbeat, rivulets of blood slid down his flat, hairless belly. He could feel the lead lodged close to the surface. The impact of the bullet against the glass had shattered the hollow-point jacket. It was only a sliver, and coated with bare micrograms of the poison. Otherwise, he would already be dead.

A spasm wracked his body. He closed his eyes, willing it to pass. Already, his breathing was growing labored and his sight dimming. His fingertips tingled as if being pricked by needles. In the recesses of his mind, he looked across the abyss. He saw shapes there, beasts writhing in torment. He saw faces, too. His victims cried out his name. They were keen for his arrival.

He drew back from the precipice and opened his eyes. Not yet, he told himself. He wasn't ready to pass over.

In one hand he held his knife. In the other a gauze bandage, dampened with rubbing alcohol. With his fingertips, he located the sliver of lead and positioned the blade above it. He stilled his shuddering, then cut deftly and quickly, freeing the sliver. The bandage burned terribly.

Afterward, he forced himself to drink tea while he sat on his bed. He remained there for three hours, doing battle with the poison. Finally, the spasms ceased. His perspiration lessened, and his breathing returned to normal. He had won the battle. He would live, but the victory had left him weak, both mentally and physically.

Though exhausted, he could not permit himself to sleep. He showered to cleanse the blood from his body. He dried himself, and then set up his shrine on the windowsill. The shrine was composed of sticks from a banyan tree, a pinch of soil from the farmland near his home, and drops of water from the sacred headwaters of the Lempa River. He prayed to Hanhau, the god of the underworld, and Cacoch the creator. He asked that he be allowed to find and kill the man who had escaped death earlier that night. When he was finished, he dashed the water around the foot of his bed to guard him against malicious spirits.

Only then did the Ghost crawl between the sheets.

And as he slept, a voice warned that he would never see his home again. It said that he would not kill the American, but that Ransom would kill him. It begged him to take his own life now. It was Hanhau, trying to lure him to the shadow world. In his dreams, he laughed to show Hanhau that he paid him no mind.

He woke at dawn with only one intention.

Kill Ransom.

45

By ten o'clock that morning, the task force had scored its first easy victories.

Von Daniken had pinned down the Banca Popolare del Ticino as the institution where Blitz conducted his banking. Copies of all account transactions—deposits, withdrawals, payments, wire transfers to and from—were due within the hour. Additionally, he'd learned that the Villa Principessa had not been rented or leased, as suspected, but had been purchased twenty-four months earlier for three million francs by a shadowy investment trust domiciled in the Netherlands Antilles. All paperwork had been handled by a fiduciary agent in Liechtenstein. Von Daniken had dispatched emissaries to Vaduz, the capital of the tiny mountain principality, to interrogate the executives who had handled the transaction.

Myer had likewise struck gold, establishing a list of twelve phone numbers called by both Blitz and Lammers on a regular basis. Several belonged to manufacturing concerns with whom Robotica did business. Subpoenas were being issued to force the companies to divulge the names of those who were recipients of the calls. The other numbers were mobile designations belonging to foreign telecoms. It would be necessary to work through the embassies in France, Spain, and Holland to obtain subpoenas granting them access to the records.

Krajcek was in Zurich, debriefing several informants and had not yet reported back.

Only Hardenberg was frustrated. As for locating the van, he'd so far managed to narrow the list to 18,654 owners of Volkswagen vans in the country. He was waiting on word from rental car companies and from the cantonal police authorities regarding stolen vans that fit the description.

"What about ISIS?" von Daniken asked, taking a seat on the edge of his desk.

"I've put in my request," said Hardenberg. "White Volkswagen van with Swiss plates. We'll see what comes back."

"Try centering the search on Germany first."

"Already did. I set Leipzig as a primary target, and all cities in a fifty-kilometer radius as a secondary. We should get some hits."

Cataloguing warrants and maintaining a database on individuals deemed of interest to the government formed only one part of the ISIS system. Another tied into the hundreds of thousands of surveillance cameras located across Europe. Every minute of every day, these cameras snapped photographs of whatever vehicles (and people) happened to cross their lens. The license numbers of every car photographed automatically fed into a system linking the databases of intelligence agencies of over thirty countries. It was a kind of "criminal Internet." Each database would then run the license numbers against any stolen or otherwise suspected vehicles in that country. All over Europe, warnings were continually dispatched that a car stolen in Spain had been seen in Paris. Or a truck used in a jewel robbery in Nice had been spotted in Rome. It was policing without policemen, and it resulted in thousands of arrests each year.

The downside was that the process was painstakingly slow. With the sheer volume of photographs—millions per day—there was nothing like real-time results.

"Keep at it," said von Daniken. "Let me know the moment anything turns up. You have my number."

Hardenberg nodded and set to work.

Satisfied that things were starting off on the right foot, von Daniken took the elevator to the ground floor and left the building. Once in his car, he drove directly to the autobahn, where he joined the A1 in the direction of Geneva. He'd have to hurry if he intended on being at the headquarters of Doctors Without Borders by noon.

The Gasthof Rössli was situated across the street from the factory gates of Zug Industriewerk. It was an old-style **beiz,** or family-owned establishment, with arolla pine walls, a parquet wood floor, and an army of bleached Steinbock antlers mounted on the wall. At noon, the main dining room was warm and stuffy and packed to bursting.

Jonathan walked among the tables, noting the profusion of blue work jackets with the company's name embroidered in gothic script above the left breast pocket. The same name with the same script was also visible on the identification cards worn around the necks of nearly every other diner. ZIAG. Plainly, the Gasthof Rössli was a favored alternative to the company cafeteria.

At the bar, customers sat nursing steins of beer and eating lunch. There were several stools open, and he settled on one next to a burly, bearded man whose ample belly and vein-tipped nose made no secret of his affection for alcohol. Like most of the others, he sported a white identification card dangling on a blue lanyard around his neck. Jonathan had thirty minutes to get his hands on it.

Sliding onto the stool, he took a look at the menu. He was aware of the man observing him. High in one corner a television broadcast the news mutely. It was difficult to keep from looking up at it. He ordered soup and a beer, and waited for his moment.

Jonathan had arrived in Zug at eleven o'clock after spending the night on the backseat of his car in the parking lot of a Mercedes-Benz dealership outside Bern. It was his first rest in thirty-six hours, and though he'd slept longer than he would have liked, at least he was approaching the day somewhat refreshed.

He'd spent the morning circling the factory, first by car, and later on foot. His visit was not unexpected. Hoffmann had taken his call to heart. Jonathan needed no further proof than the compact car marked **"Securitas"** parked near the headquarters' entry. Securitas was a well-known security firm. A similar vehicle had taken up position at a discreet location near the factory entrance. The uniformed guards were content to linger in their automobiles and eye the workers entering the plant from a distance. It was all very low-key. Very discreet. Their presence designed not to disturb, just to be noticed.

The problem was that it was **too** low-key, reasoned Jonathan. If a friend of mine had been killed the day before, and my name might figure next on the list, I'd hire the entire security company to sit out in front of my place of business, he thought. There would be nothing low-key about it.

Then it struck him why . . .

There was no other way.

ZIAG was a legitimate company. It had been in business for over a hundred years. It had revenues of ninety million francs. It employed five hundred people. Hannes Hoffmann, Gottfried Blitz, and Eva Kruger were intruders. They weren't part of the core organization. **The real company.** They made up the shadow company. The company inside the company. With the collusion of someone high up, they'd burrowed into ZIAG the way a tick burrows under the skin. A parasite nourishing itself on its host's lifeblood.

Cover.

But why had they chosen ZIAG?

Jonathan's soup arrived. The bearded man seated alongside him threw him a glance and wished him a perfunctory, **"En guete."** Jonathan thanked him and concentrated on his soup. He didn't want to appear to be too anxious. He finished the soup, then caught the man's eye. "Excuse me," he said with proper deference. "Do you know if the company is hiring?"

The worker took in Jonathan's formal attire. "Always looking for somebody, though I don't know about the director's office."

"Funeral," said Jonathan, offering an excuse for his dark suit and tie. "I'm a machinist by trade. What about you?"

"Electrical engineer."

The man was better trained than he looked. Electrical engineering was strictly for quant jocks, the poindexters at ease solving differential equations.

"I thought ZIAG was in the guns business."

"Long time ago. Now it's custom order stuff. Precision machinery. Extruders. Heat exchangers. Proximity systems."

"Sounds like guns to me."

"All strictly civilian."

"I was wondering if you knew a woman named Eva Kruger?"

"What department is she in?"

"I'm guessing sales or marketing. She's not an engineer. I know that much. Auburn hair. Green eyes. Very attractive."

The man shook his head. "Sorry."

"She worked with Hannes Hoffmann."

"Him I know. New man down from Germany. Came with the new owners. He's running his own project on the factory floor. Word is that it's something cutting-edge. They say he knows what he's doing. Very sharp, but you don't see him much. If your friend's working with him, she's connected, alright. That's all I know. Me, I've got ten little morons to supervise. They're more than enough. If this Kruger woman is in sales or marketing, she'd be in the main building. Look for her there."

A waitress arrived, placing a plate of Wiener schnitzel and **pommes frites** on the bar. The engineer tucked a napkin into his shirt collar, ordered another beer, then attacked his food ravenously.

Jonathan eyed the identification hanging from the man's collar. He knew how to get the ID, but he wasn't sure if he had the guts to go for it. He thought of the assassin who'd pressed his gun to the car window the night before. A man like that would have no compunction about doing what needed to be done in this kind of situation.

The engineer cut another piece of veal, speared several fries and a crown of broccoli, and stuffed all of it into his mouth.

"Would you mind holding my spot for a couple of minutes?" Jonathan said to him. The words came out sounding more confident than he'd expected. "I have to check my meter. I'm parked around the corner. Be right back."

"Of course." The engineer didn't bother looking up.

Outside, Jonathan turned up his collar against the snow and hurried down the block to a pharmacy. The blinking green cross displayed outside its doors was a common sight. From his apartment in Geneva, he would pass no less than four pharmacies on his way to the tram stop, a walk of just five city blocks. He stepped inside and walked directly to the counter. Without hesitation, he passed his international physician's identification over the counter and requested ten five-milligram capsules of triazolam, better known by its trade name of Halcion.

Though aware that he was the subject of a nationwide manhunt, he didn't rate his risk of discovery as high. First of all, Halcion was a frequently prescribed sedative used to treat insomnolence. A prescription for ten capsules wouldn't raise any flags. Second, unlike the States, pharmacies in Switzerland were independently owned mom-and-pop establishments. There was neither a nationwide database monitoring prescriptions, nor a computer system linking them by which the authorities could alert pharmacists to be on the lookout for him. Unless the police had faxed or e-mailed his name and description to each and every pharmacy in the country—a possibility he discounted, due to both the short time passed since the incident in Landquart and the inertia inherent to any large governmental organization—he was safe.

The pharmacist handed him the bottle of sleeping pills. Jonathan walked outside, then paused in a doorway long enough to empty half of them into a neatly folded ten-franc note. He palmed the note in his left hand and hurried back to the restaurant.

He was back at the bar in nine minutes.

"One more for you?" he asked the man seated next to him.

The man smiled at his good fortune. "Why not?"

Jonathan ordered up a beer—a stein this time—and a schnapps for himself. "Prosit," he said when the drinks arrived. The fiery spirits rollicked his stomach. He smacked his lips and drew a pen from his pocket. "You've been a real help. Could I bother you for the name of the personnel director?"

"We're a public company. They call it human resources here." The engineer gave him the name and Jonathan made a show of clicking the pen, giving it a real flick of the wrist. In the same elaborate hoax, he dropped the pen so that it fell on the other side of the man's feet. As expected, the engineer stepped off his stool to search for the pen. As soon as his head dropped below the bar, Jonathan passed his left hand over the beer and dumped the contents of five Halcion capsules into the stein. A moment later, the man reappeared, pen in hand. Jonathan raised his glass. **"Danke."**

Another toast.

Ten minutes after that, the stein was dry as the Gobi and the man's plate as clean as holiday china. The engineer snapped up the last piece of bread from the basket and devoured it in two bites. Jonathan worried that the sheer amount of food in his stomach might delay the onset of the drug.

By now, the engineer was talking nonstop about

his business, going on about exports to Africa and the Middle East, all the paperwork it required, permits, licenses. Jonathan slipped a look at his watch. The drug should have kicked in. Alcohol multiplied the effect of Halcion. Five milligrams was enough to knock an elephant on its ass. The man's pupils were dilated, but his diction showed no signs of impairment. He glanced at the man's gut. It was big enough to hold a medicine ball. Maybe five capsules weren't enough.

"So? You do a lot of business with South Africa?" Jonathan said, struggling to keep up his end of the conversation to prevent the engineer from leaving.

"They're the worssss. You wouldn't believe the red tape."

"Really?" The drugs were finally beginning to kick in.

"Jess one of the quirks of the business. Nothin' to concer yourself with . . ." The man's eyelids fell and didn't open for an uncommonly long moment. Then he shuddered, and his eyes opened wide. "Unless, of course, you stake a thob with usss . . ." His eyes closed again and his head teetered like a bobblehead doll in the backseat of an old clunker.

" 'scuse me. Need to use the bathroom. Then I 'ave to get back to uh floor." He put both hands on the bar in an effort to steady himself as he stood. One knee buckled. Jonathan caught him as he went down. "Whoa, there, my man. Let me give you a hand."

As gently as possible, he guided the engineer to the rear of the restaurant and down the stairs to the men's room. When he bounded back up a minute later, he had a white ZIAG identification card in his pocket. Mr. Walter Keller would be spending his afternoon sleeping inside the far stall of the men's WC.

47

Wait and watch.

The Ghost eyed the restaurant from across the street. His point of vantage was a kiosk selling the usual newspapers and magazines. He passed the time browsing through a number of soccer reviews. When he caught the proprietor giving him a nasty look, he bought some chewing gum, a pack of cigarettes (though he didn't smoke), and a copy of the **Corriere della Sera,** the Italian daily paper.

Tucking the newspaper under one arm, he strolled to the end of the block. The long night's struggle had left him haggard, and he needed all his strength just to cover the short distance. He did it all the same, making sure that no one could spot his frailty.

He was dressed in a trench coat, collar turned up at the neck, a gray wool suit he'd had tailored in Naples, and a pair of hand-cobbled shoes the color of whiskey. Today he was an Italian businessman. Yesterday, he'd been a Swiss hiker. The day before, a German tourist. The only person he wasn't allowed to be was himself. He didn't mind. After twenty years in his line of work, the less time spent in one's own company, the better.

He'd found Ransom at dawn, pulling out of a car dealership's parking lot where he'd spent the night. The American was clumsy and amateurish in his efforts to spot a tail. He drove too slowly when he should have floored it. He stopped regularly to look over his shoulder. He parked too close to his destination. His actions were futile. Any attempt to hide was undermined by the homing beacon implanted in the religious medallion that hung from his neck.

The Ghost was content to wait and watch. The close-in kill was his domain. He'd built his career on caution and planning, making it a rule never to attempt the casual hit. It was his policy to reconnoiter the site, prepare a trap, and then lie in wait. The Lammers case was a model of planning and execution. Blitz, less so, as there had been so little time to prepare. Ransom's sudden arrival was testament to the risks inherent in hurried work.

And then, of course, there was the dream.

Ransom would kill him.

The Ghost tried not to be superstitious. Dreams were the province of the Indians who'd worked his family's coffee plantation. Not that of an educated man. And yet . . .

Just then, he spotted Ransom emerge from the restaurant.

He watched the American cross the street and disappear into a crowd near the factory gates.

For now, he was happy to keep his distance.

He would know the chance when he saw it.

Until then, he would watch and wait.

And he would pray.

48

Jonathan waited for the one o'clock rush, then joined a group of twelve or so blue-jacketed workers as they congregated at the factory gates, walking past the lone guard in the **Securitas** car. He'd taken off his necktie and turned up the collar of his jacket. Around his neck hung the purloined identification card, the photograph deliberately turned toward his chest.

There were no guards inside the building, just an electronic turnstile that governed passage beyond the foyer. He ran the ID over the electric eye and was in. Men went in one direction. Women the other. He entered a locker room. A time clock was attached to the closest wall. He waited in line with the others, his eyes drilled to the patch of ground in front of him, lest someone pay him any notice. When it was his turn to punch in, he picked a card at random. Luckily, it didn't belong to any of the six or seven men behind him. Next to the washroom was a closet full of freshly pressed work jackets. He selected one that fit, then passed through a set of swinging doors that led onto the factory floor.

The floor had the wide-open, airy feel of an indoor stadium, right down to the exposed aluminum rafters that supported the roof. A small army of workers moved about, some on foot, others on forklifts, and still others driving electric carts. The vast floor was partitioned at uneven intervals by stacks of inventory rising ten meters above the ground. Oddly, the sheer size of the space conspired to muffle the sound, giving the factory an otherworldly atmosphere.

Closest to him, several rows of pressurized stainless-steel tanks awaited inspection. Jonathan circled them and proceeded across the floor, stopping where he saw something of interest to ask what was being manufactured. The workers were, for the most part, polite, courteous, and professional. He learned, for example, that the pressurized tanks were in fact blenders being made for a large Swiss pharmaceutical company.

Elsewhere on the floor, teams of laborers fussed over autoclaves, heat exchangers, extruders. It seemed a wide gamut for a single firm to manufacture. As the man in the restaurant had said, Zug Industriewerk was no longer in the arms business at all.

Reaching the far side of the factory, he observed an

attached hall where few people entered and exited. He noted that the entry was governed by a biometric eye scan. A sign posted next to the door read, "THOR. Thermal Heating and Operations Research. Authorized Personnel Only."

Thor. It was the name from Emma's flash drive. The name on the memo he'd found on Blitz's desk. **Completion is foreseen for late first quarter 200–. Final shipment to client will be made on 10.2. Disassembly of all manufacturing apparatus to be completed by 13.2.**

Jonathan knew better than to try to get inside the restricted area. He turned and walked in the other direction. He would have to find the answers to his questions elsewhere. In the main building.

Hanging from the wall was a QC clipboard, and near it, a box containing a half-dozen gleaming valves. He helped himself to both. Following signs posted on interior walls, he guided himself to the main administration building. A polite nod took him past the receptionist and into the elevator beyond.

The floors were marked according to function. First floor: Reception. Second floor: Accounting. Third floor: Sales and Marketing. Fourth floor: Direction. He hit "3."

Once on the third floor, he noted that rooms were numbered sequentially: 3.1, 3.2. Beneath each number was the name or names of the executive who occupied the office. Hannes Hoffmann's was the last office on the left. A well-coiffed secretary sat in the anteroom.

"For Mr. Hoffmann," he said, lifting the box as if it were a Christmas gift.

"Whom may I announce?"

Jonathan gave the name of the man whose identification he'd stolen. "Samples for inspection."

The receptionist didn't glance at his ID.

She's not in on it, Jonathan realized. She's not part of Thor.

"I'll buzz him," the woman said.

"Don't bother," said Jonathan. "He's expecting me."

No longer thinking about consequences, propelled only by a desire to know—about Emma, about Thor, about everything—he threw open the door and entered Hannes Hoffmann's office.

49

Hannes Hoffmann, vice president of engineering according to the nameplate outside his office, sat behind a pale wood desk, a phone to his ear, batting his agenda with a pencil as if it were a snare drum. He was stocky and bland-looking, with thinning blond hair combed straight back from a pudgy, satisfied face, his blue eyes spaced a bit too far apart. It was the face from the photograph in Blitz's desk. It was a face Jonathan had seen a hundred times before . . . familiar, yet not familiar at all.

Seeing Jonathan, he stiffened. His eyes homed in like lasers. **Is it him?** The question was practically broadcast in neon letters across his forehead. Jonathan didn't flinch. Foisting an underling's smile, he asked where to set the box of valves. Hoffmann looked him up and down a moment longer, then pointed to the edge of his desk and went back to his conversation.

"The shipment has to be at the customs warehouse by ten o'clock tomorrow morning," he was saying. "The inspectors won't extend the deadline again. Call me if you run into any problems." Hoffmann hung up the phone and shot an annoyed glance at his visitor. "And you are?"

"We talked yesterday on the phone."

Hoffmann tensed. "Mr. Schmid?"

"That's right." Jonathan set the box on the desk. "Shout," he said. "Now's your chance. Go ahead. Yell for your secretary."

Hoffmann remained immobile as a rock. He said nothing.

"You can't, can you?" Jonathan went on. "You can't risk having the police come running and having me tell them everything I know about the operation you had going with Eva Kruger."

"You're right about that," Hoffmann said evenly. "But it cuts both ways. I can't shout, and you can do nothing to force me to talk."

"All I want to know is what she was involved in."

Hoffmann crossed his arms over his chest. "Sit down, Dr. Ransom. I suggest we dispense with the game playing."

Jonathan approached the desk with caution. He sat down on the edge of the chair, wincing slightly as the SIG-Sauer tucked into his waistband dug into his spine. "How does this setup run? A company within a company? A secret in-house project? Is that it?"

Hoffmann shrugged, a gesture of futility. "Stop this guessing."

"I figure you're manufacturing something you shouldn't and giving it to someone who shouldn't have it. What is it? Guns? Missiles? Rockets? I mean, why else set up shop in a place like this? I saw the area on the factory floor blocked off for Thor. What does 'thermal heating operations research' mean, anyway?"

Hoffmann leaned forward, his cordial demeanor gone. "You have no idea what you've stumbled into."

"I've got some idea. I know that you got your hooks into Emma last year when we were in Lebanon. I figure you have someone over at Doctors Without Borders, too, who helped move me over here."

"It goes back further than Lebanon," said Hoffmann.

"No," retorted Jonathan. "It all started in Beirut. I was there when she made her decision." It had to be then, he told himself. That's why she had the headaches, the depression. She was deciding. "Did she go to Paris to meet with you?"

"Ah, yes, Paris. I remember. All those calls you made, not reaching her at the hotel. We were supposed to forward them, but there was a glitch in technical services. Regrettable. She told me she had a friend cover for her. She said you believed her. I guess not."

Jonathan ignored the barb. "Who do you work for?"

"Suffice it to say we're a powerful group. Look around you. You have the Mercedes. The cash, too, I presume. You saw Blitz's home, and something of what we've set up here." Hoffmann folded his hands and placed them on the desk. He looked as benign as an insurance agent trying to sell him a whole-life policy. "I'm afraid that will have to do."

"Not today, it won't."

"Turn around, Dr. Ransom," said Hoffmann sternly. "Leave this office. Leave the country. I can make sure the police drop the warrants for your arrest. Whatever you do, don't look back. There's still time for you to get out of this predicament."

"Does that also mean you're going to call off that guy who took a shot at me last night?"

"I don't know anything about that."

"And what about the cops who tried to steal Emma's bags? Or don't you know anything about that either?"

"The policemen were contracted out. They got overzealous. I apologize. However, I'd say that you ended up with the better end of the stick."

"Then who killed Blitz?"

Hoffmann considered this for a moment. "People with a different agenda than our own."

"People who don't think Thor's such a good idea?

What if they don't see fit to let me walk off into the sunset?"

"I can't speak for them. If they made an attempt on your life, I imagine it was because they believe you're working with your wife."

"You mean they think I'm working with you?"

Hoffmann kneaded his brow. It was apparent he didn't relish the idea of anyone thinking that Jonathan worked with him. "Either way, I can't help you there."

"I appreciate the honesty," said Jonathan. "Unfortunately, it doesn't do much to solve my problem."

Hoffmann slid his chair away from his desk. He put his hands behind his head and leaned back, as if to indicate that the formal part of the meeting was over. They could talk as friends now. "I feel for you, Dr. Ransom. The not knowing is the hardest part. My marriage didn't last three years. You made it eight. I'd say you did better than most."

As he spoke, his eyes blinked rapidly again. An ocular stutter. It was an odd tic, and something about it reminded Jonathan of someone he'd known a long time ago.

"I reiterate my suggestion," Hoffmann continued. "Leave this office. Get out of the country as quickly as you possibly can. We have no desire to see any harm come to you. In our books, you're one of the good guys. You've been an enormous help to us, whether you knew it or not. Give me your word that you won't look into our activities and I'll call off the hounds."

"And I have your word on that?"

"Yes."

Hoffmann blinked as he said the words, his eyes fluttering for nearly two seconds. In that instant, Jonathan put a name to the face. It had been five years, maybe more, but he was sure of it.

It goes back further than Lebanon.

"I know you."

Hoffmann said nothing, but his cheeks were suddenly pierced by sharp points of red.

Jonathan went on. "You're McKenna. Queen's Household Division seconded to the U.N. peace-keeping force in Kosovo. A major, right?"

Hoffmann chuckled as if he'd been called out on a prank. He sat forward, the look of bemusement plain on his face, and when he spoke, the Berliner's strict German was gone, abandoned in favor of a plummy Belgravia slur. "Took you long enough, Jonny. You're right. It was Kosovo. New Year's Eve, if I'm not mistaken. We tossed back a few that night. You, me, and Em. Put on a bit of weight since then, but who hasn't? Present company excepted, I suppose. You look damn fit, all things considered."

It was him. It was McKenna. Forty pounds heavier, minus some hair and a whisk-broom mustache, but him all the same. The same blinking eyes. The maddening habit of calling him "Jonny."

Jonathan felt a terrible pounding pressing in at his temples. Kosovo. The New Year's Eve shindig at the British barracks. Major Jock McKenna in his highlands kilt, marching in at the stroke of midnight with his bagpipes playing "Auld Lang Syne." And then he remembered the last part. The reason why he'd been so slow to recognize McKenna.

"But you're dead. You were killed in a car accident two days before we left the country."

Hoffmann shrugged, as if to say another artifice disposed of. "As you can see, I wasn't."

"Who the hell are you?" Jonathan asked.

"Whoever I need to be."

Hoffmann sprang from behind the desk. Jonathan struggled to free his pistol, but he was too slow. Inexpert. An arm flashed, knocking the pistol from his hand. A short double-edged blade protruded from between the middle and ring finger of Hoffmann's other hand. He slashed at Jonathan. The blade narrowly missed his neck, slicing through the jacket's lapels. Jonathan jumped back, knocking over a chair.

"Your turn," said Hoffmann as he rounded the desk. "Go ahead. Shout. You want the police. Fine. Call them. I'm protecting myself against a murderer."

Jonathan scooped up the chair and thrust it in front of him, fending off the larger man. Hoffmann darted forward, the blade nothing but a blur. Jonathan raised the chair, deflecting the blow.

He looked toward the desk. The box of stainless steel valves he'd hauled upstairs rested on the corner. Each valve was the size of a drinking glass and weighed nearly a kilo. He stepped forward, forcing

Hoffmann back, and snatched a valve. With only one hand to hold the chair, he was vulnerable. Hoffmann saw this at once. He grasped a chair leg and yanked it to one side. At the same time, he transferred his weight to the opposite foot and attacked. Jonathan was too slow to retreat. A whiz of silver cut the air. This time the blade pierced the jacket and lacerated his chest. At the same moment, Jonathan brought the valve down. The blow glanced across Hoffmann's brow, opening a gash above his eye. Hoffmann grunted, shook it off, and charged, pressing his bulk against the chair like a lineman driving a blocking sled. Jonathan dropped the valve and clutched the chair with both hands. Hoffmann pressed in closer. He was the heavier man and despite his bland appearance, immensely strong. The blade slashed and Jonathan felt a stinging sensation on the side of his throat.

Just then there was a knock at the door.

"Is everything alright, Mr. Hoffmann?"

"Perfect," said Hoffmann in a ridiculously enthusiastic voice. He leaned into the chair, his face a brilliant red, perspiration beading his forehead. Less than a meter separated the men. He raised his hand, preparing to strike.

All at once, Jonathan dropped to a knee and forced the chair to his left. Caught unawares, Hoffmann's momentum carried him in the same direction. He fell forward and dropped to a knee. Jonathan circled behind him, grabbing another valve from the box and slamming it against the back of Hoffmann's head. He began to get up, and Jonathan struck him again.

Hoffmann collapsed to the floor.

"Mr. Hoffmann!" called the secretary, banging on the door now. "Please! What's that noise? May I come in?"

Dazed, Jonathan stumbled backward, seeking the desk for balance. He caught his reflection in a framed photograph. He was a mess. The cut on his throat was leaking blood. It had missed the carotid artery by less than an inch. He pulled a handkerchief from his pocket and pressed it to the wound.

"One second," he said, smiling grotesquely to imitate Hoffmann's jolly voice.

He looked around the office. A window behind the desk opened onto a four-story drop. There were no drainpipes to slide down this time. He hurried to the door, picked up his pistol, and slipped it into his waistband.

"Come in," he said.

The secretary entered in a rush. Before she could take in the scene, Jonathan closed the door behind her.

"My goodness, what happened?" she asked, the disparate elements slowly adding up.

Jonathan forced her against the door, bracing the woman with his forearm. "If you're quiet, I won't hurt you. Do you understand?"

The secretary nodded vigorously. "But . . ."

"Sshhh," he said. "You'll be alright. I promise you. It's better to relax."

The woman's eyes widened in terror.

He pressed his fingers against her carotid artery, cutting off the flow of blood to her brain. She jerked once in his arms, and five seconds later, she passed out. He lowered her to the carpet. He estimated she would regain consciousness in anywhere from two to ten minutes. Hoffmann would be a little longer in coming around.

Jonathan surveyed the office. He could not leave looking as he did. He took off the blue work jacket, then found Hoffmann's overcoat and put it on, sure to button it to the neck. He walked slowly down the corridor, head bowed, hand keeping his handkerchief to his neck. He took the stairs to the ground floor and exited the main entrance. After a block, his stiff gait turned into a jog, and soon after that, a headlong run.

He found the Mercedes parked in the garage on the Zentralstrasse across from the train station. He yanked the first aid kit from beneath the front seat and fumbled for some gauze and tape. It did little good. He needed stitches.

One hand applying pressure to his neck, he drove the car slowly out of town, joining the autobahn and pointing the nose in the direction of Bern.

There was only one place he knew to go.

50

Von Daniken kept his car in the passing lane, the speedometer pushing one-eighty. The highway cut through terraced vineyards high on the slopes of Lake Geneva. The lake's broad blue canvas filled the windscreen. Beyond it, wreathed in cloud, rose the snow-covered peaks of the French Haute-Savoie.

As he neared Nyon, on the outskirts of Geneva, his cell phone rang. He thumbed the answer button on the steering wheel.

"Rohde, Zurich medical examiner's office."

"Yes, Doctor . . ." Von Daniken remembered that he'd moved Rohde's call last night to the delete file.

"It's about the Lammers postmortem. We discovered something odd." Rohde spent several minutes summarizing his findings about the batrachotoxin, or frog poison, coating the bullets. "My colleague,

Dr. Wickes, at New Scotland Yard, is convinced that whoever killed Theo Lammers worked with the Central Intelligence Agency at one time."

Von Daniken didn't answer. The CIA. It figured. When it became clear that Blitz wasn't a German but an Iranian, and a former military officer to boot, he'd suspected the killings to be the work of a professional intelligence organization. He thought of Philip Palumbo. Either the American agent wasn't in on the operation or he had purposely kept the information from him.

Offering his thanks, von Daniken terminated the call. The highway narrowed as he entered the city. The road dipped and followed the borders of the lake. A great rolling park extended to his left, snowy meadows sloping to the shore. He passed a succession of stately institutional compounds built on these grounds. The United Nations. The General Agreement on Tariffs and Trade. The World Health Organization.

The address he was seeking was located in a less stately part of town. He parked on the Rue de Lausanne in front of a Chinese restaurant and a Turkish tailor. It was five past twelve. He was late. The person he was due to meet would have to wait a few more minutes.

He scrolled through his phone's list of contacts to the letter "P." A faraway buzzing filled his ear as the signal bounced between transmission towers connecting him to God only knew what corner of the world.

"Hello, Marcus," answered a hardscrabble American voice.

Von Daniken knew better than to ask where Philip Palumbo was. "I'm afraid this call falls outside the boundaries of our formal relationship," he began, eschewing any preamble as meaningless bullshit.

"This about the news I gave you yesterday?"

"It is. I need to know if there's any more information about Quitab—the man we know as Gottfried Blitz—that you're not telling me."

"That's it, my friend. First I heard of him was two days ago, straight from Gassan's lips."

"And that goes for the plan, too? No prior indications that there was a cell in Switzerland planning an attack? Nothing about his associates? A man named Lammers, for example?"

"You're making me nervous, Marcus. What is it you want to know?"

"I need to know if you have a team working on my soil."

"What kind of team?"

"I don't know what you call it. Wet work. Liquidation. Sanctions."

"That's a helluva question."

"Yes, it is, and I think I'm owed an answer."

"I'd say I paid off that debt yesterday."

"Yesterday was by the books. It's as much in your interest to stop Gassan and his pals as ours. It'll count as your victory, too."

"Maybe," Palumbo admitted. "Either way, I need something more to work with."

Von Daniken sighed, pondering how much information he should divulge. He didn't really have much choice. Such was the price of working with a superpower. Or these days, rather, **the** superpower. He couldn't ask for Palumbo's confidence without showing his own.

"We were working on Blitz, too, but from a different angle. This man I asked you about, Theo Lammers, was an associate of his. The two of them met four nights ago. We believe that Lammers gave Blitz a state-of-the-art drone capable of flying five hundred kilometers per hour and carrying a nacelle packed with twenty kilos of plastic explosives. Lammers was killed the night after they met. It was a professional job. We're guessing that it was the same man who killed Blitz. We have evidence suggesting that the shooter is one of yours."

"What evidence is that?"

Von Daniken told him about the bullets dipped in frog poison and the practice's roots with Indians taking part in the Salvadoran squads run by the CIA.

"Sounds like you might be stretching things," Palumbo responded. "Superstitious Indians, death squads, poison . . . you're talking almost thirty years back. That's ancient history."

"I don't think either of us believe in coincidence."

"You got me there," said Palumbo, but he offered no further assistance.

"Phil, I'm asking you straight-out: Is this guy on the Agency payroll or is he freelancing out to someone else?"

"I can't tell you. You're talking about something that would be run out of Operations. That's the sixth floor. Way above my pay grade. I don't think the deputy director would take kindly to me butting in where I don't belong."

"I realize that," said von Daniken. "But someone's paying this man. Someone's pointing him in the right direction. It seems to me that he knows more about what's going on than you or me. I, for one, find that frightening. I thought that you could ask around. Perhaps . . . unofficially."

"Unofficially?"

"Whatever you can find . . ."

"Frog poison, eh? Then we're even?"

"All square," said von Daniken with the kind of enthusiasm the Americans thought denoted honesty.

Palumbo chewed on this awhile, leaving von Daniken to listen to the sandpaper scrabble of wireless communications. "Alright then," he said finally.

"Alright what?"

"I'll be back at you," said Palumbo without elaboration.

The line went dead.

51

Waldhoheweg 30 was a stark five-story building
situated in a quiet residential quarter of Bern, not far
from the city center. Spindly, denuded birch trees
grew from plots on the sidewalk every twenty meters
or so, looking like skeletal sentries. Jonathan drove
slowly past the building, checking for any signs that
it was being watched. At four o'clock the neighborhood was quiet to the point of being deserted. Seeing nothing out of place, he parked three blocks up
the street.

Emma's real because Bea's real, he reminded himself as he stepped out of the car. During the drive
from Zug, he'd rehearsed everything he knew about
Bea. Thirty-five years of age, she was an architect
by trade, though she'd never gotten a foothold in
the profession. At times, she'd been a frustrated
artist, a frustrated photographer, and a frustrated

glassblower. She was a wanderer. A free spirit and a bit of a lost soul, but she was real. Flesh and blood in loose jeans and a ripped-up motorcycle jacket with an attitude to match.

Over the years, he'd met her only twice, maybe three times. The last time was eighteen months ago, a lunch in London when they were on home leave from the Middle East. Since they'd moved to Switzerland, Emma had made the trip to Bern several times to visit, but he'd never been able to find the time to join her.

Jonathan approached her apartment from the opposite side of the street. There was still no sign of anyone loitering. He ran an eye over the parked cars. No one sitting behind the wheels, either. He jogged across the road, one hand pressed to the bandage. Residents' names were listed outside the entry. Strasser. Rutli. Kruger. Zehnder. He stopped and went back one. A bolt of ice rattled inside his stomach. No Beatrice Rose anywhere to be found, but an E.A. Kruger in apartment 4A.

He began to shiver. What was he waiting for, then? He rang the buzzer. A minute passed. He stepped back and gazed up at the building. The movement caused the gash in his neck to tear anew. Just then, a woman approached and used her key to enter the building.

"I'm here to visit Miss Kruger," he said. "She's my sister-in-law. Do you mind if I wait in the entry?"

The woman's eyes fixed with alarm on his neck.

Glancing at his reflection in the plate glass, he saw that the gauze was soaked red.

"Are you alright?" she asked, not quite kindly.

"An accident. It's not as bad as it looks."

"You should see a doctor."

"I am a doctor," he said, pasting on a smile, trying to make light of the situation. "I can treat myself once I'm inside. I'm sure you know Eva. About yay high. Auburn hair. Hazel eyes. Wears glasses."

The woman shook her head, considering all this. "I'm sorry," she said after a moment. "I don't know Miss Kruger. I think it would be better if you waited outside."

"Of course." Keeping his smile firmly in place, Jonathan turned away and counted to five. When he looked over his shoulder, the foyer was empty. The front door was closing in slow motion. It had an inch to go before it locked. Rushing forward, he rammed his toe into the doorjamb. It was too late. The bolt had struck home.

He turned in a circle, cursing his bad luck. He thought about ringing all the buzzers to see if someone would pass him through, but that was too risky. He'd already been spotted by one resident. He didn't want to be reported to the police.

He dug his hands into his pockets. His fingers touched Emma's key chain. Maybe he did have a key . . .

He produced Eva Kruger's key chain. Besides the car key, there were three others, each marked by a color-coded rubber ring. He tried one at a time in the door. The black one didn't fit. Neither did the red. The green key slid home. With a flick of the wrist, he freed the bolt. He was inside a moment later.

A well-lit staircase wound up and around the elevator shaft. There were three apartments on each floor clustered around an art deco landing with a plant, a side table, and a mirror. As was Swiss custom, the resident's name was engraved below the buzzer. He found Eva Kruger's flat on the fourth floor. He rang the doorbell, but no one answered.

It goes back further than Lebanon.

Hoffmann was McKenna from Kosovo. And Kosovo was five years prior to Lebanon. It might go back further than Lebanon, but Lebanon was as far back as Jonathan could go. Somehow, he couldn't get his mind around the bigger implications. Maybe he didn't want to.

The fact was that he no longer had any choice.

Jonathan slipped the key into the lock and opened the door to Eva Kruger's apartment.

Across the hall, the woman watched through her peephole as the injured man entered the apartment. Of course she knew Eva Kruger. Not well, mind you. It was impossible to have more than a passing acquaintance with a woman who traveled so frequently. Still, on several occasions, the two had spoken and she'd found her nice enough. She knew better, however, than to trumpet the fact to a stranger. Certainly not to a man who was bleeding all over himself.

It was not the first time this week that unknown people had been looking for Fräulein Kruger. Two nights earlier, she'd seen a pair of men acting strangely outside the building. She'd entered without speaking to them, and later, she'd heard noises on the landing and looked out her peephole in time to see them entering Eva's apartment. She still felt bad for not having alerted the police.

And now a man with a neck wound who was practically bleeding on the ground!

She would not make the same mistake twice.

Returning to her living room, she picked up the phone and called the police. "Yes, Officer," she said. "I'd like to report a . . ." She wasn't sure what it was. The man did, after all, have a key. She brushed off her worries. He was an intruder. "I'd like to report an intruder at Waldhoheweg 30. Please come right away. He's inside now."

They had been there. This time they hadn't taken care to conceal their presence, Jonathan observed. What he saw before him was evidence of a painstaking and methodical search conducted without fear of discovery.

The living room was large and sparsely furnished, lit by track lights. Directly in front of him was a black leather couch, its cushions removed, lined up beside it as if it were to be cleaned. Books had been pulled from the shelves and stacked on the floor. Magazines likewise. A Persian carpet had been rolled up and not quite rolled back. There was an Eames chair. A sleek coffee table with too much chrome and polished metal. A tortured sliver of steel that passed as a sculpture. Someone had lived here . . . but it wasn't Emma.

He slid the driver's license from his pocket and stared at the picture of his wife. The furniture matched the chic glasses, the severe hair, the glaring lipstick. It was Eva Kruger's furniture.

He forced himself to make a tour. The kitchen was clean to the point of being antiseptic. Cupboards open. Plates removed, stacked on the counter. Glasses likewise. He opened the refrigerator. Orange juice. White wine. Champagne. A tin of beluga caviar. An onion. A loaf of packaged black bread. A jar of pickles. It was an apartment in which to entertain during her "lightning safaris."

In the freezer, there was a bottle of Polish vodka in an ice ring. He checked the brand. Zubrowka. Made from buffalo grass. Two frosted shot glasses sat on the rack above it.

Opening the bottle, he poured himself a shot. The vodka was colored a pale yellow and had the consistency of syrup. He put it to his lips and knocked his head back. "To Emma," he said aloud. "Whoever you really were."

The liquid slid down like silk on fire.

A fulsome sadness settled on him. The weight pressed on his shoulders and made the ten steps to the study an epic journey. It was another small room. Immaculate. A metal desk and the Aeron chair that Emma coveted but could never afford. The computer had been removed, but the power cords lay on the floor next to a laser printer. No papers. No notes.

He walked into the bedroom. The sheets had been removed and thrown into the corner. The pillows cut open. The closets held a few outfits. A symphony of black. Armani. Dior. Gucci. Shoes to match. Five and a halfs. Emma's size. (Why must he constantly check when he already knew?) And one cocktail dress, also black, cut to elicit gasps from the most jaded guest.

Against his will, he imagined Emma walking into the room wearing it. His eyes traveled up her long legs, stopping to admire her cleavage, then taking in the auburn hair that fell in waves to her shoulders. Yes, he decided, it would fulfill its purpose. She'd chosen the perfect attire to serve vodka and caviar for two.

Emma Ransom and Eva Kruger. Two people. Two personalities. But which one was real? How was he supposed to tell the difference between truth and fiction? And if he couldn't, how had Emma?

It dawned on him that he was a part of it, too. Dr. Jonathan Ransom, globe-trotting physician conveniently stationed in all the world's hot spots. After all, he'd been moved to Geneva for Emma to be involved in this . . . **in Thor** . . . whatever it was. Why shouldn't it have happened before?

Jonathan as pawn.

No, not as pawn. As cover.

He sat down on the edge of the bed and picked up the phone. The dial tone purred in his ear. He called the international operator and asked for the number of St. Mary's Hospital, Penzance, England.

"How far back did it go?" he asked himself. Before Beirut, there was Darfur. And before Darfur, Indonesia, Kosovo, and Liberia, where Emma had greeted him in a battered jeep on the airport tarmac.

Where had Emma drawn the line? Or more importantly, when?

Jonathan took down the hospital's number and dialed it. A pleasant English voice answered and he asked to be transferred to Records. A woman came on the line. "Records."

"I'm calling from Switzerland. My wife recently died and I need to obtain a copy of her birth certificate for the authorities. She was born in your hospital."

"I'll be happy to fax a copy once we receive an official inquiry."

"I'm sure that won't be a problem, but right now, I just need to confirm that you have the original document. Her name was Emma Rose. Born November 12, 1975."

"Give me a minute," said the woman.

Jonathan tucked the phone under his ear. He was holding Eva Kruger's wedding ring. It came to him that there was no sign of a Mr. Kruger in the apartment. **Why did she have the ring?** he wondered. Everything else was so meticulous. An entire double life right down to the false eyelashes.

"Sir, this is Nurse Poole. We found a record of Emma Rose."

"Good. I mean, thank you." The news interrupted his musings. It was difficult to speak. He was on the verge of either breaking down or beginning to heal. He didn't know which.

In his mind, he had a picture of him and Emma driving past the hospital in Penzance, a squat red-brick building in the center of town. It was their only visit to her hometown, made a year after their marriage. "And that's where it all began," Emma was saying proudly. "I came into the world at seven sharp, crying like a banshee. I haven't shut up since. It's where Mum died. Circle of life and all that, I guess."

The nurse went on. "There is one problem. You're certain that she was born in 1975?"

"Absolutely."

"It is rather strange, you see. Was her middle name by chance 'Everett'?"

"Yes."

More proof that it was her. She wasn't Eva Kruger. She was Emma. **His Emma.**

"I did, in fact, manage to find an Emma Everett

Rose in our records," the nurse said, her voice harder now. "She was also born on November twelfth . . . but a year earlier. That's the problem."

"There must be some kind of typo on the document. It has to be her."

"I'm afraid not," stated the nurse. "I don't know quite how to say this."

Jonathan moved to the edge of the bed. "Say **what**?"

"I'm sorry, sir, but Emma Everett Rose, born November twelfth, 1974, in St. Mary's Hospital, is dead. She was killed in a car accident two weeks after her birth, on November the twenty-sixth."

52

"Is this a complete list of his postings?" Marcus von Daniken was seated in a cramped windowless office deep in the corridors of DWB headquarters. The heat was roaring, and every minute that he sat there he felt another grain of his patience slip away.

The medical organization's director faced him across the desk. She was a fifty-year-old Somali woman who had immigrated to Switzerland twenty years ago. She had a shaved head and gold hoop earrings, and she made no effort to hide her hostility as she leaned over the shantytown of papers littering her desk and lectured him at the point of a very long, elaborately painted fingernail.

"Why shouldn't it be a complete list?" the woman asked as she handed him Jonathan Ransom's file. "Do I look as if I have something to hide? Ridiculous, I tell you. The whole thing. Jonathan Ransom, a murderer! It is crazy."

Von Daniken didn't bother to answer. The Graubünden police had preceded him by a day, and it was obvious that they'd ruffled some feathers. He'd be better off having a word with them than trying to argue with her. He accepted Ransom's file and took his time leafing through the papers. Beirut, Lebanon. Team leader for an immunization-vaccination program. Darfur, Sudan. Director, Refugee Operations. Kosovo, Serbia. Chief medical officer leading an initiative to construct local trauma units. Sulawesi Island, Indonesia; Monrovia, Liberia. It was a list of all the world's political hellholes.

"Is it normal for your physicians to spend so much time abroad?" he asked, glancing up from the folder. "I see here that Dr. Ransom spent two years in some of these places."

"That's what we do." A disdainful sigh. Eyes to the ceiling. "Jonathan prefers the more challenging assignments. He's one of our most committed physicians."

"How do you mean?"

"Often the conditions are arduous. The doctor tends to lose sight of the bigger picture and gets caught up in the suffering. The futility of it can be overwhelming. We have quite a few cases of post-traumatic stress, similar to battle fatigue. But Jonathan never shied from the rougher assignments. Some of us think that it was because of Emma."

"Emma? You mean his wife?"

"We took the view that she tended to sympathize a bit too closely with the population. 'Going native,' as it were."

"Is it common for husband and wife teams to work together?"

"No one wants to get married only to leave their spouse thousands of miles behind."

Von Daniken considered this for a moment. He was beginning to see how it might work. The postings to foreign countries. The constant travel. "And how is it decided where the doctors are sent?"

"We match their strengths to our needs. We've tried to lure Dr. Ransom to our Swiss headquarters for a long time. His experience in the field would inject a much-needed dose of common sense into our project evaluations."

"I see, but who **exactly** decides where Dr. Ransom is assigned?"

"We do it together. The three of us. Jonathan, Emma, and I. We look at the list of openings and decide where they will be of most help."

Von Daniken hadn't known that Ransom's wife was so intimately involved in aid work. He asked about her position on these assignments.

"Emma did everything. Her title was logistician. She set up the mission, made sure that the medicine got there on time, coordinated the local help, and paid off the bully boys so they'd leave us in peace. She ran the place so Jonathan could save lives. One of her was worth five ordinary mortals. What happened to the woman is a tragedy. We already miss her."

A wife who involved herself in her husband's work. A competent woman. A woman who asked questions. Von Daniken wondered if she'd asked one too many. "And what is Dr. Ransom working on at the moment?" he inquired.

"You mean before he started murdering policemen?" The Somali woman gave him another smirk to show what she thought of his investigation. "He's supervising an anti-malaria campaign we're mounting in coordination with the Bates Foundation. I don't think he's terribly happy. It's an administrative job, and he prefers to be in the field."

"And how long is the posting to last?"

"Normally, this kind of thing is open-ended. He would remain in his position until the program was implemented, at which time he'd brief his successor and turn over the reins. Unfortunately, I recently received a complaint about his comportment. Apparently, he's been a bit brusque with the American side of this . . . the money side," she whispered. "Mrs. Bates doesn't like him. A decision has been taken to remove him from his post."

Von Daniken nodded, but inside him, a bell sounded and he was aware that he'd located the unseen hand that guided Ransom's moves from country to country. It started with a complaint voiced to the personnel director. A suggestion. Maybe something stronger, but the woman would get the idea. **Jonathan Ransom needs to go to Beirut. He must be sent to Darfur.**

"Any ideas where he'll be going next?"

"I was hoping Pakistan. We have an immediate opening at a new mission in Lahore. The director dropped dead of a heart attack. Only fifty, the dear man. He'd scheduled an important meeting with the minister of Health and Welfare for Tuesday. I'd rather hoped that I could convince Jonathan to fly out on Sunday in time to make it."

"This Sunday?"

"Yes. On the evening flight. I know it's asking rather a lot of a man who just lost his wife, but knowing Jonathan, I think it would do him good."

"Sunday," von Daniken repeated, as it all began to sink in.

Seventy-two hours.

Von Daniken's theory was simple. Ransom was a trained agent in the pay of a foreign government. His position as a physician working for Doctors Without Borders offered ideal cover to move from country to country without attracting undue attention. The way to figure out who Ransom worked for was to discover what he'd done in the past. That was why von Daniken was seated at a computer in the watch room of the Geneva police on Rue Gauthier, staring at a picture of a gravely wounded woman being freed from a pile of rubble inside a bombed-out hospital. The picture came from the front page of the **Daily Star,** Lebanon's English-language newspaper, and was dated July 31 the past year.

The article was titled "Blast Kills Police Investigator," and it concerned an explosion that had killed seventeen persons, including a prominent policeman who had been leading the investigation into the assassination of the former Lebanese prime minister. At the time of the explosion, the investigator was undergoing weekly dialysis to treat a failing kidney. A detective at the scene revealed that he suspected that the bomb had been planted in the floor of the clinic during a renovation completed three months earlier. He estimated that the blast was equivalent to one hundred pounds of TNT.

The article went on to say that no responsibility had been claimed for the attack and that the police were following up reports that Syrian agents had been seen at the hospital prior to the blast.

Von Daniken looked up from the computer. A bomb planted during renovation three months prior to the attack. One hundred pounds of TNT. The scope of the attack sent a chill down his spine. The people involved had to number in the dozens. Builders, contractors, city officials who'd granted permits, someone in the doctor's office to pass on details of the victim's appointments. As a policeman, he was impressed. As a human being, he was horrified.

Before Lebanon, Darfur . . .

A United Nations C-141 transport carrying leaders of the Muslim Janjaweed and the indigenous Sudanese en route to Khartoum to discuss a government-sponsored cease-fire explodes in midair. There are no survivors. Evidence is discovered showing that a bomb had been planted in one of the engines. Both sides claimed that the other was responsible for the calamity. Civil war intensifies.

And before Darfur, Kosovo. Page two of the **National Gazette:** "An explosion has claimed the life of retired General Vladimir Drakic, known familiarly as 'Drako,' and twenty-eight others. At the time, Drakic, 55, was attending a secret meeting of the outlawed right-wing Patriots Party, of which he was rumored to be a top leader. The subject of an international manhunt for over ten years, Drakic was wanted by the United Nations War Crimes Commission in connection with the massacre of two thousand men, women, and children near the town of Srebrenica in July 1995. Evidence at the scene pointed to a ruptured gas main as the cause of the blast. Police are investigating claims that a rival Albanian organization was involved. Two men have been taken into custody."

The three attacks bore similar hallmarks. All involved targeting a highly placed, well-protected individual. All were the product of meticulous planning, extraordinary intelligence, and long-term engagement. And in each case, evidence was found pointing to a third party.

But what finally convinced von Daniken of Ransom's participation was the timing of the three incidents. The bombing in Beirut took place four days before Ransom left Lebanon for Jordan. The downing of the Sudanese jet occurred two days before Ransom left the country. And the attack in Kosovo just one day before Ransom returned to Geneva.

Still, he was at a loss as to who would gain most from the attacks. **Cui bono?** Who would benefit? Motive was the investigator's touchstone, and none was readily apparent.

Von Daniken pushed his chair away from the computer, the words of the director ringing in his ears.

"We have an immediate opening in Lahore. I was hoping he could fly out this Sunday."

53

A two-man patrol responded to the report of an intruder at Waldhoheweg 30. The officers rang the caller's bell and were admitted to the building. They were not unduly concerned. A CrimeStat analysis ranked the street and neighborhood as one of the safest in the city. Only two burglaries had been reported in the last ninety days. There had been no reported instances of armed robbery, rape, or murder in the past year.

"He's inside," said the aggrieved tenant, after shepherding the policemen into her apartment. "I've been watching since I called. He hasn't gone anywhere."

"And what makes you think he's a burglar?"

"I didn't say he was a burglar. I said he was an intruder. He shouldn't be in the building. First he said he was waiting for Eva Kruger. He wanted to come inside. But he was bleeding here . . ." She pointed at her neck. "I told him that since I didn't know him it would be better if he waited outside for his sister-in-law. A minute later, I heard him on the landing. He had a key to her apartment. I watched him enter."

"His sister-in-law is Miss Kruger?"

"That's what he said. He could be lying. I've never seen him here before."

The police took turns asking her questions. "Did you see the woman who normally lives there . . . this Miss Kruger?"

"No."

"Did you ask him about his injury?"

"He said it was an accident. He said he was a doctor and would take care of it once he was inside the apartment."

Exasperation was writ clear on the policemen's faces. "Did this doctor threaten you in any way?"

"No. He was polite . . . but he shouldn't be here if Miss Kruger isn't here. I've never seen him before. He frightened me."

The policemen exchanged glances. Another snoop with too much time on her hands. "We'll have a word with the gentleman. Did he, by any chance, give you his name?"

The woman frowned.

"Stay here, ma'am."

Jonathan stood in the bathroom, chin raised high, studying his neck. The gash had begun to congeal, the torn flesh slowly hardening into place. In the field, he saw injuries like this on a daily basis. The only way to repair it without permanent scarring was to reopen the wound and stitch it closed when the hurt was fresh, but that wasn't an option today.

He poured himself a shot of the buffalo grass vodka and drank it for courage.

"Keep still," he whispered to himself, bringing needle and thread to his throat.

Drawing a breath, he set to work. The needle wasn't bad for something he'd found in a sewing kit. Reasonably sharp. Reasonably sterile. He'd worked with worse. Using the fingers of his left hand to hold the folds of the cut close together, he drew the stitch.

It had been a lie from the very beginning. Emma wasn't Emma. To some degree, his life had been a charade. A play directed by some unseen director. Surprisingly, he felt more liberated than disappointed. The blinders had been removed from his eyes, and for the first time he could see things as they really were. Not just what lay in front of him, but what existed on the periphery. It was a damning vista. Jonathan as pawn. Jonathan as puppet. Jonathan as a government's ignorant, enthusiastic marionette.

Who was it? he wondered. Who put her up to this?

He drew the third stitch. The thread chafed, making his eyes water. He tugged the needle and drew the suture clear.

Angry. That's what he was. Angry at Emma. Angry at Hoffmann. Angry at whoever had had a hand in stealing his life from him and fashioning it to achieve their ends. It was theft of an unforgivable order.

And the rest of it? The part of his life that was just the two of them. Was that an act, too? He was tempted to anoint their private moments as special, divorced from Emma's higher duty. Their lovemaking. The secret glances. The touch of her hand and the moments of unspoken connection.

Eight years . . . how was it possible?

He lowered the needle, throwing a hand onto the sink for support.

He lifted his eyes to the mirror. **You just don't get it. She never told you her real name.** She saw to it that they moved around Africa, Europe, and the Middle East, so she could do her job. She had an entire secret life. Look at this apartment. Look at that itty-bitty dress. She brought men here. She drank vodka with them. She seduced them.

He looked deep into his own eyes and faced the truth.

Numb to the pain, he completed his work quickly and diligently, tying off the thread and cutting it with the vanity scissors he'd found in the sewing kit. It was a good job, all things considered. He dabbed the sutures with alcohol, then put a Band-Aid over the wound. Picking up his shirt, he walked into the kitchen and poured himself another shot of vodka.

He made a mental note to look for the brand in the future. **Zubrowka.** Polish for "dumb trusting asshole."

He threw on his overcoat and dropped his hands into the pockets of his trousers. His right hand came up with the wedding ring. He made a promise to carry it at all times as a reminder. He turned off the kitchen lights and strolled into the living room. He turned a circle, surveying the apartment. All of it was an illusion. No more than a stage.

Just then, a fist pounded on the door. "Police. We'd like to speak with you."

Jonathan froze. It was the woman from downstairs. She must have raised the alarm. He imagined how events would unfold. A request for identification. A routine check for outstanding warrants. The response would be immediate: Dr. Jonathan Ransom wanted for the murder of two police officers. Suspect to be considered armed and dangerous. They'd have him cuffed and spread-eagled on the ground in the blink of an eye.

More pounding on the door.

"Police. Please, Herr Doktor, we know you are inside. We'd like to speak with you about your sister-in-law, Miss Kruger."

Jonathan had come too far to give up. If he was in it, he might as well be in it all the way.

Running into the bedroom, he pried open the French doors onto the balcony. He looked from side to side, up and down. The closest balcony was two floors down. The wall was flat and featureless. There was no way he could lower himself.

The pounding on the door grew angrier.

He returned to the living room, then ran to the office, the bedroom again, and then the kitchen. He stopped, angered by the futility of his efforts. There was nothing to find. The only way out was through the front door.

If he couldn't get out, he had to force them in . . .

He walked to the kitchen. He was no longer hurrying. Never once did he look behind him or consider responding to the increasingly violent knocks. He went directly to the oven. It was a modern convection unit, with stainless-steel frontage and touch-pad controls. No use there. The range, however, was a gas appliance. He pulled off the burner rings. Taking a knife from a drawer, he bashed in the pilot light. Then he turned the knobs on all five burners to high. Gas hissed from the main, a faint, sickly sweet scent filling the room.

The pounding had stopped. Heated voices drifted from the corridor. The doorknob jiggled. A moment later, there came the scribbling of metal on metal. The police were trying to pick the lock.

"I'm coming," called Jonathan. "Give me a moment."

"Please hurry," came the response. "Or we'll enter by force."

"One minute," he yelled. He closed the pocket

door to the kitchen and hustled to the office. He found some paper on the desk and rolled it into the shape of a cone. In the bathroom, he stuffed toilet paper into the cone. Setting the cone to one side, he took a large bath towel and ran cold water over it. He wrung the water from the towel, folded it, and carried it over one arm. He found a book of matches in an ashtray in the living room.

The pounding started up again. Through the door, he heard the squawk of the policemen's two-way radio.

By now, gas was seeping from under the kitchen door. One sniff forced him to recoil. Taking up position with his back pressed to the wall outside the kitchen, he draped the towel over his head and shoulders, struck a match and lit the paper cone. He waited, holding it away from his body until it blazed like a torch.

Now! he told himself.

Opening the pocket door, he tossed the torch into the kitchen and threw himself to the floor.

A billowing fireball exploded inside the confined area, blowing the stacked china off the counters, shattering glasses, breaking windows and roaring like an express train through the doorway into the living room, before being sucked right back into the kitchen.

Jonathan crawled across the floor to the entry and hid in a closet next to the front door. Barely a second later, a gunshot sounded. The door was flung inward on its hinges. Two policemen entered the apartment, guns drawn, rushing the source of the conflagration. All this Jonathan watched through the crack of the closet door.

One of the policemen ventured near the flames. "He went through the window."

The other stepped over the ruined furniture and ducked his head into the kitchen. "He's gone."

Jonathan crept from the closet, slid out the front door, and ran down the stairs.

In a minute, he was clear of the building.

Five minutes after that, he was in the Mercedes, gunning the engine, and heading for the autobahn.

54

Philip Palumbo followed a specific routine upon returning to the United States of America after a
"hunting" trip abroad. Leaving the airport, he
drove to his gym in Alexandria, Virginia. For two
hours, he would ride a stationary bike, lift weights,
and swim. Finally, when he'd sweated all the crappy
food and dirt and noxious air out of his system, he
would repair to the steam room where he'd get rid
of the corruption. The lingering guilt that grew like
a tumor in the dark of a man's soul. He called it
"going to confession." Only then would he drive
home and greet his wife and three children.

Today, however, he forgot all about purging his
sins and pointed his car toward Langley, where he
quickly found his way to the Central Intelligence
Agency's archives. Once there, he accessed a digitized

file from the Latin America section detailing the company's activities in El Salvador during the 1980s.

Inside it, he found a mission statement discussing the need to build democracy in the region as a bulwark against the communist Sandinista regime that had taken root in neighboring Nicaragua and was threatening the governments of Guatemala and El Salvador. Farther along, he found a mention of an Operation Mourning Dove, run out of the embassy in San Salvador beginning in the spring of 1984. The file listed the minutes on Mourning Dove as "Eyes Only," and required a deputy director's signature to access it. This was it. No other operation listed in the file was above Secret classification.

Palumbo flipped back to a list of agency personnel attached to the embassy at the time. He recognized the name of a colleague he worked with at the Counterterrorism Command Center: a lean, outgoing Irishman named Joe Leahy.

Palumbo found Leahy in a glassed-in office overlooking a cubicle farm on the operations deck of the CTCC. "Joe, got a sec?"

As usual, Leahy was dressed to the nines in a navy suit and polished brogues, hair slicked back like a Wall Street banker. Less could be done to disguise his nasal Philly twang. "What's up?" he asked.

"I need to pick your brain about something that went on a long time ago. Got time for a cup of coffee?"

Palumbo led the way to the cafeteria and picked

up the tab for two double lattes. They sat at a table in a back corner. "You were in El Salvador, right?"

"Back in the day," said Leahy. "You were still banging freshmen at Yale."

"Trying and failing was more like it," said Palumbo. "What can you tell me about Mourning Dove."

"There's a name from the past. Why do you ask? You running an audit on that thing?"

Palumbo shook his head. "Nothing like that. Just background."

"It was a long time ago. I was junior. GS-7. A punk."

"It's nothing like that, Joe. You've got my word. This stays between you and me."

"Like Vegas. Right?"

"Yeah, like Vegas. Mourning Dove, Joe. Tell me about it."

Leahy leaned forward and said, "It started as a training gig. A way to knock some of the recruits into shape. These were complete yokels. Half of 'em barely out of loincloths. We brought some Berets down from Bragg. Some firepower, too. The idea was to teach them basic soldiering. Help bolster democracy in the region. The usual bullshit."

"I thought we had the School of the Americas at Benning for that?"

"Sure we do. But that's official. This was sub rosa. Anyway, **el presidente** liked what we were doing, so he conscripted some of these units into his own private force. We did the dirty work. You've got to remember how it was back then, with Danny Ortega porkin' Bianca Jagger, the Sandinistas firing up the region. **No más communista.** At least, that was the idea. It got out of hand almost from the beginning. There was nothing targeted about it. But it worked. Scared the shit out of everyone. By eighty-four, it was all done. The president won reelection. We packed up the bus and came home."

"And what about the guys you trained? Any of them come home with you?"

"What do you mean, 'come home'?"

"I don't know. Maybe you found some men with skills and asked them back to work with the Company."

Leahy's easygoing tone vanished. "Now you're getting out of your depth. These are dark waters you're navigating."

"Between you and me, Joe, a mick from Philly and a goombah from the south side of Beantown."

Leahy laughed at this, but he didn't say anything.

Palumbo went on. "The thing is, I think I came across one of them on my turf. Knocking out a couple of big-time operators, leaving all kinds of voodoo bullshit behind. Word is he coated his bullets in frog poison because he thought it prevented his victims' souls from chasing him into the human world. You ever hear of that cockamamie shit?"

Leahy was shaking his head, the memories practically flashing in his eye.

"You wouldn't know anything about that, would you, Joe?"

"That's Black Bag stuff you're talking about," said Leahy. "If you know what's good for that lovely wife and those brats you got at home, you'll drop it."

Palumbo was as arrogant as the next agent. The warning only served to spur him on. "The guys he killed were involved in the plot with Walid Gassan. They were going to take down an airliner. It was a sophisticated job. We're talking about a drone that does four hundred miles per hour loaded with twenty keys of Semtex. That's a cruise missile, the way I see it. No way some Bojinka motherfucker's able to pull this one off."

"Sounds like the guy's doing the right thing."

"No doubt about it."

"So if it isn't the ragheads, who exactly do you think is behind it?" asked Leahy.

"I'm not saying. But I have an idea. I mean, how many people are there at the end of the day with those kind of resources?"

"You think it's state sponsored."

"Oh, yeah." Palumbo tapped the table with his knuckles. "But this info stays between you and me."

Leahy flicked his hands above his chest, a pantomime of making the holy cross.

"There was something strange about those files," Palumbo continued. "It's what I needed to talk to you about. You see, the name of the agent in charge of the operation was missing. It looked like it had been cut out before they digitized it. Tell me, Joe, which one of our guys was calling the shots for Mourning Dove?"

Leahy stared at Palumbo for a moment, then stood from the table. As he passed, he bent and whispered two words in his ear. "The Admiral."

Palumbo remained in his chair until Leahy had left the cafeteria.

"The Admiral" was James Lafever. The deputy director of operations.

55

"*Seventy-two hours,*" said von Daniken, taking off his coat and throwing it over the back of his chair. "That's how long we've got. Ransom's our man. There's no doubt about it. He's done this kind of thing before. He blows things up. He did it in Beirut and Kosovo and Darfur. He kills people and he's good at it."

The task force had taken up residence in the "morgue," a soulless conference room located in the basement of Fedpol headquarters. Five desks had been arranged in a semicircle. Computers, telephones, and copy machines had been brought down. It was a nerve center in search of a body. At the moment, only Seiler and Hardenberg were present. The sight of the unmanned desks in the cavernous room did not lift his spirits.

"Slow down, Marcus," said Max Seiler. "What do you mean, 'seventy-two hours'?"

Von Daniken took a chair and related his findings to the two men. "He gets the hell out of the country immediately following the act," he said after detailing Ransom's crimes. "Apparently, our Dr. Ransom is all set to head off to Pakistan Sunday evening. He may pretend he doesn't know the transfer is coming, but he knows alright. His men probably killed the poor bastard over there whose place he's supposed to take. We need to locate Ransom and we need to do it now. What do we have on the van, anyway? Someone must have seen it."

"Someone," meaning a surveillance camera somewhere in Europe between Dublin and Dubrovnik.

"Not a trace," said Hardenberg. "Myer's over at ISIS seeing if he can blow some fire up their asses."

"Two million cameras and all of them are blind. What are the odds on that?" Disgusted, von Daniken shook his head.

Just then, the door opened and Kurt Myer shambled in, pulling the belt of his trousers over his ample belly.

"There you are," said von Daniken. "We've just been talking about you. What did you find?"

Myer looked around at the anxious faces. He could tell that something had changed, but he wasn't sure what. He held up a sheaf of photographs. "Leipzig, ten days ago. It was taken near Bayerischer Platz adjacent to the train station. We've got the van."

"Thank God!" said von Daniken as he stood and examined the photo.

With remarkable clarity, the picture showed a white VW van with Swiss plates driven by a bearded man with wire rim glasses. "Gassan's at the wheel. Once I had the plate numbers, I was able to run an advanced search. I got a hit in Zurich seven days ago." Another picture handed round. "This time Blitz is at the wheel."

"Where exactly was the camera located?" asked von Daniken.

"On the corner of Badenerstrasse and Hardplatz."

"That's near where Lammers's company is located, isn't it?"

"Not far," said Myer. "A couple kilometers away. Look at the rear window. There's something very big inside the van. We analyzed the photos and came to the conclusion they're large steel boxes."

"The drone?"

"No idea. But whatever it is, it's big and it's heavy. Look at how low the chassis is riding on the suspension. Compare this picture to the others. We're estimating that in the second photo the van's carrying a load of at least six hundred kilos." Myer chose another photograph from his pile and handed it around. "The last one we got was in Lugano on Saturday."

Lugano, just thirty kilometers away from Ascona, where Blitz lived. Von Daniken had been right about the paint chips he'd found at Blitz's house. The van had been parked in the garage. "So Gassan picks up the explosives in Leipzig, turns them over to Blitz along with the van, then he hightails it to Sweden. Blitz takes the van to Zurich and picks up the drone from Lammers's factory." He studied the pictures a moment longer. "Is that it?"

"That's all we've got on the white van."

Von Daniken shot Myer a glance. "What do you mean on the **white** van? Is there another one you haven't told me about?"

"He's driving a black van now. He painted it."

"How do you know?"

"We don't know where he got the white van originally, but we do know that the plates it carried were stolen from an identical van in Schaffhausen. Most people don't bother reporting this kind of thing to the police. They think it's a prank and report the loss to the motor vehicles department. Gassan and his buddies think they're smart doing this. But we're smarter. I guessed if they stole one set of license plates, they might have stolen another. I drilled down and checked for any reports of missing or stolen license plates. The owner of a black VW van in Lausanne reported his plates were missing two weeks ago. Not the van, mind you, just the plates. I ran the numbers through ISIS. Look what I found."

Myer passed around the last photograph. An 8 x 10

of a black Volkswagen van moving at speed through an intersection. In the background were a billboard advertising Lindt chocolate and the sign of a well-known furniture retailer.

"The photo was taken yesterday at five p.m. on the outskirts of Zurich."

"But how can we be certain it's the same van?"

"Compare the front bumpers of the two vans. Both have a noticeable dent beneath the headlight. And both have a pine-tree-shaped air freshener hanging from the rearview mirror. One might be a coincidence. But both? Never."

"Call the city police," said von Daniken. "Have them put out a warrant for the van. Run a check on every picture of every vehicle taken in the eastern half of the country over the last twenty-four hours."

"You got it."

Von Daniken brought the picture closer. "Who's that driving? It couldn't be Blitz. He was dead by then." He showed the photograph to Myer, who frowned and put on a pair of bifocals. "Something's off here. He doesn't look normal."

"Let's get the photo to the crime lab. They can blow up the picture and send it to Interpol to run through their facial recognition software."

Myer shambled out of the room.

Von Daniken spun in his chair and directed his attention toward the two men still in the room. "So much for the eastern front. Any progress in the west?"

It was Klaus Hardenberg's turn to talk. Hardenberg, the pudgy, whey-faced investigator who'd abandoned a lucrative career with an international accounting firm in Zurich for the rough-and-tumble pastures of law enforcement.

"Blitz did his banking at the Banca Popolare del Ticino. We got the bank's name from Eurocard, which identified it as the bank of record for Blitz's account. The average monthly balance on the account was twelve thousand francs. As for payments, it's mostly the usual. Household items. Credit card bills. Gas. Electric. The man took a weekly cash withdrawal of five hundred francs, always from the same automatic teller in Ascona. All in all, a modest lifestyle for a man driving a luxury automobile and living in a multimillion-franc villa."

"Unless the villa isn't his," said von Daniken.

"My thoughts exactly." Hardenberg smiled thinly. "The first thing that caught my eye was a wire transfer that hit the account a week ago for exactly one hundred thousand francs. The note on the payment instructions read, 'Gift to P.J.' The next day, Blitz withdrew the entire amount in cash over the counter at his branch in Lugano. All on the up-and-up. He called ahead, spoke personally with the bank manager and explained that it was the down payment for a boat he was building in Antibes."

"Did anyone find the money at his home?"

"I checked with Lieutenant Conti. Nothing turned up."

"Who transferred the hundred k to Blitz?"

"Ah," said Hardenberg. "Here's where things get interesting. The money came from a numbered account at the Royal Trust and Credit Bank of the Bahamas. Freetown branch."

"Never heard of it," said von Daniken, whose experience had brought him into contact with most meaningful financial institutions under the sun.

"It's a small bank with just under a billion in assets. It doesn't keep a brick-and-mortar space. It's a paper entity. If you'll permit me, though, I'd like to stop with Blitz for a moment and move on to Lammers."

There were nods all around. Hardenberg fortified himself by guzzling a half a can of Red Bull and lighting a Gauloise.

"As I was saying, our attention now falls on Theo Lammers," Hardenberg went on. "His business was on the up-and-up. All accounts are at USB, which is a first-rate shop. I ran his numbers. Nine months ago, he received a two-million-franc wire transfer from none other than the Royal Trust and Credit of the Bahamas."

"Two million from the same bank?" Von Daniken slid to the edge of his seat. "If it came from the same people who wired Blitz the hundred thousand francs, we'll know precisely who's financing this racket. What was the money for?"

"I took the liberty of calling Michaela Menz at Robotica. The funds hit the receivables account. That meant the two million francs was for work completed. The problem was that there was no invoice number attached to the transfer. She doesn't know what the money was for."

Myer looked at von Daniken. "It was for the drone."

Von Daniken nodded. Now they were getting somewhere. "Did the money come from the same account number at the Royal Trust and Credit?"

Hardenberg shook his head. "That would've made our lives too simple. It came from an unrelated numbered account. At least, unrelated on the surface. The chance that Blitz and Lammers are doing business with the same hole-in-the-wall in the Bahamas is a million to one. I relayed these feelings to Mr. Davis Brunswick, the bank's chief executive. He was not forthcoming. At first, I tried charm. Then I told him that unless he gave me some information on who the accounts belong to, he would find his bank on the weekly black list circulated to over three thousand institutions across Switzerland and shared with every law enforcement agency in the Western world."

"Did it work?"

Hardenberg shrugged. "Of course not," he admitted. "Everyone's a tough guy these days. I had to revert to plan B. Happily, I'd done a little homework on Mr. Brunswick before our conversation. I'd discovered that he maintained several personal accounts in our country to the tune of some twenty-six million francs. I gave him my word that unless he coughed up information on who was behind these accounts—and any others that might be related to them—I would personally see to it that every last franc of his money would be frozen for the rest of his natural life."

"And?"

"Mr. Brunswick sang like a baby. Both numbered accounts were set up by a fiduciary firm that's a subsidiary of the Tingeli Bank. It's the same firm that executed the purchase of the Villa Principessa on behalf of the Netherlands Antilles holding company."

"How did you discover that Brunswick had accounts in our country?" asked von Daniken.

Hardenberg grimaced and shook his very large, very round, and very bald head. "Trust me. You don't want to know."

The men allowed themselves a brief laugh.

Seiler cleared his throat. "As I recall, Marcus, you know Tobi Tingeli personally."

It was von Daniken's turn to grimace. "Tobi and I served together on the Holocaust Commission."

"Do you think he might be amenable to doing you a favor?"

"Tobi? He doesn't know the meaning of the word."

"But you are going to ask him?" Seiler persisted.

Von Daniken thought of Tobias "Tobi" Tingeli IV and the skeletons hanging in the man's closet. Tingeli was rich, vain, pompous, and worse. In a sense, Marcus von Daniken had been waiting for this day for ten long years.

The thought of exacting his revenge gave him no pleasure. "Yes, Max," he said softly. "I'm going to ask him."

56

The headlights were murder. There was an accident on the opposite side of the autobahn. A stream of cars was backed up to the horizon. Squinting, Jonathan veered his eyes to the shoulder in an effort to lessen the glare. Somewhere deep inside his skull a drum beat mercilessly. Get out, it told him. You're in over your head. You're an amateur up against professionals.

The Rhine was one hundred kilometers to the north. Germany lay beyond. There were any number of paths across the border. France was almost as close. He could pass through Geneva, then cross over at Annecy. In three hours he could be having fondue in Chamonix. He knew the town well. He drew up a mental list of pensions and sport hotels where he could hole up for a few days. But the thought of refuge held no allure. Refuge was temporary. He needed a way out.

He pulled off the autobahn at Egerkingen, where the highway split. North to Basel. East to Zurich. There was a Mövenpick restaurant, a motel, and a shopping gallery catering to tourists. He parked and entered the restaurant. He ordered quickly. **"Schnipo und ein cola, bitte."** Wiener schnitzel, **pommes frites**, and a Coke. Every Swiss schoolboy's favorite.

Waiting, he was assaulted by images of the apartment in Bern. **Eva Kruger's apartment.** He thought of the care taken to furnish it according to her persona; the time and effort involved to construct such an elaborate artifice. Once past the deception, it was the discipline that awed him. Never once had he suspected that she was an agent of some kind. An operative in the employ of a nation's intelligence apparatus. Foolishly, he'd imagined that she was having an affair. He pondered the training required to deceive a spouse for eight years.

Digging into his pocket, he fingered the wedding ring. After a moment, he took it out and examined it. Something about it bothered him. He guessed that it was because it didn't fit. It broke cover, therefore it had to mean something. A message. A reminder to herself. Eva Kruger wasn't married, so why the ring?

The food arrived. Ten minutes ago, he was famished. Suddenly, his appetite had left him. He sipped at his drink, then pushed the plate away.

The ring.

He studied the numbers engraved inside: 2-8-01. February 8, 2001. Where had he been? The Sudan. It was during the dry season when the flies were unmanageable. But the date held no special significance for him, and as far as he knew, it hadn't meant anything to Emma either.

And then it hit him.

It wasn't Emma's wedding ring. It was Eva Kruger's. He'd been reading the date incorrectly. Americans list the date as month-day-year. But Eva Kruger was Swiss. She would engrave her anniversary in the European format. Day-month-year.

2-8-01.

As he stared at the numbers, an uncomfortable cold burrowed into his stomach.

On August 2, 2001, he and Emma Everett Rose had wed in a simple private ceremony in Cortina, Italy. No relatives. She'd insisted. Not from his family and not from hers. No one from work, either. "This is our day, Jonathan," she'd said. "The day I give my true self to you."

In his outer pocket, he carried the Palm PDA he'd found at Blitz's. Emma's flash drive was still plugged into it. With deliberate calm, he powered up the handheld computer. The icon bearing the name "Thor" popped into view. He clicked on it, and a request for a password filled the screen. He entered the numbers from the ring.

The screen blinked and the word "Accepted" appeared.

He was in.

The screen glowed blue. A single tab appeared at the top center marked "Intelink." The word flashed from bright to brighter like a neon sign advertising a vacancy. He clicked on it. For a moment, nothing happened. His stomach dipped. Another dead end. Then the screen went white and line after line of text scrolled across the display. The text was written in a kind of shorthand, each entry preceded by a date, time, and code name that identified the sender.

The most recent entry read: **8-2; 15:16 CET. Cormorant.**

Today's date. Sent at 3:16 in the afternoon from someone calling themselves "Cormorant."

Rook penetrated Thor. Attempt at termination failed. Rook injured and fleeing. Request meet to brief on details.

The posting before it was time-stamped three hours earlier at 12:10 CET; sent from Hawk.

Subject: availability new Mercedes armored sedan. Spoke with Daimler-Benz HQ. No new vehicles available through end March. One used: Color: black. Leather: grey. 100k km. Price: E275,000. Await yr. confirmation.

A web log, thought Jonathan as his eyes scanned

the display. A live site where operatives logged on to offer details about their mission. Real-time spying.

He scoured the screen for a web address, but none was listed. He accessed the file directory, then checked the browser software. The default address was at http://international.resources.net. The name meant nothing to him.

He returned to Intelink's main page. More entries:

7-2; 13:11 CET. Falcon. A message sent the day before from Falcon.

Confirm Robin compromised. Cease all communication. Await instructions HQ.

7-2; 10:55 CET. Cormorant. Rook contacted self. Referenced Thor. Rook in possession of Robin's PDA. Stated Robin killed. Confirm.

7-2; 09:55 CET. Falcon. Transfer approved.

7-2; 08:45 CET. Robin. Request transfer Sfr. 100,000 to account at BPT. Replacement lost funds.

Jonathan reviewed the text. "Cormorant" was Hoffmann. "Hawk" was unknown. "Falcon," the individual who approved funding and who confirmed to his agents that Robin was dead, looked to be in charge. "Robin" being Gottfried Blitz. And Emma? Where was she?

He scrolled back through the numerous posts, searching for a specific time, a date. He saw it. Tuesday. The day after Emma's accident.

5-2; 07:45 CET. Falcon. Nightingale lost in climbing mishap. Rook alive.

There it was. Emma was "Nightingale." Jonathan was "Rook," as in chess piece. The castle. Or was it "Rook" as in con, to deceive? That made more sense, he thought angrily. And then he realized that he was wrong on both accounts. If all the agents had been given avian code names, then so had he.

Rook. The British cousin of the crow, but a larger, more aggressive bird altogether.

Devouring line after line of text, he retraced the events of the past few days as viewed from the other side. Here was Blitz stating that the car was in place in Landquart and that the baggage claims had been sent to Emma's hotel. Then came Emma's reply that the mail had been delayed due to an avalanche on the train tracks and that she would pick up the bags the next day. The postings were sent at six-thirty in the evening the night before their climb.

Jonathan looked up. The busy restaurant was swirling around him. The lights were too bright. The voices too loud.

Emma had been in contact with her network all along.

Just then, a new line appeared on the display. The letters blinked to make sure they caught the reader's attention.

A live posting.

8-2; 21:56 CET. Falcon. PJ landed 20:16 ZRH. En route to hotel. Meeting confirmed

9-2; 14:00 Belvedere. Bring shipment advice. Trade for Gold.

Tomorrow, February 9, at two p.m. He knew of the Belvedere Hotel in Davos. A five-star palace for the rich and famous. But who was P.J.? And what was the "Gold" he planned to trade for the shipment advice?

And then, almost instantaneously, a response from Cormorant. **Confirmation copied.** Hoffmann was headed to Davos.

The letters blinked for five seconds, then assumed their normal amplification.

For the first time, Jonathan noted a tab at the bottom of the page marked "Reference." Clicking on the word, he was rewarded with a list of hyperlinks. More code. The date, followed by a name he'd come to know well. ZIAG. Zug Industriewerk.

He opened the first link.

It was a bill of lading detailing the contents of a shipment from ZIAG to Xanthus Medical Instruments in Athens. Two hundred advanced global positioning handheld navigation systems. Technical specifications as noted. Price: twenty-thousand Swiss francs per unit. To ship Friday, February 9, from Zurich to Athens aboard Swissair at seven in the evening.

Was this the shipment advice mentioned in Falcon's earlier instruction to Cormorant?

He clicked on the other hyperlinks. More of the same. Detailed invoices. Not GPS navigation systems but insulin pumps, vacuum tubes, carbon extruders. Shipped December 10, Zurich to Cairo via Nice. Shipped November 20, Zurich to Dubai. Shipped October 21, Geneva to Amman via Rome. The final destination always in the Middle East.

The shipments dated back several months. The first had been made on October 12, a little more than six weeks after he and Emma returned from the Middle East.

As Jonathan reread the list of goods, he realized that he'd been right when he'd told Hoffmann his suspicions. **You're making things you shouldn't and sending them to people who shouldn't have them.**

But who was P.J.? And what was he doing coming to the World Economic Forum in Davos?

Jonathan finished his meal and paid the bill in cash. Leaving the restaurant, he stopped in an adjoining kiosk and looked over the selection of newspapers. Nearly every one featured a headline related to the World Economic Forum. He purchased two Swiss newspapers, as well as the **Herald Tribune** and the **Financial Times**. Folding them under one arm, he crossed the parking lot to the Mercedes.

Turning into his aisle, he found himself staring into the beams of a slow-moving car. It took him a moment to make out the sirens on top. He kept his pace steady, walking directly toward the police car. The cruiser advanced at a crawl. A two-man patrol. A handheld spotlight illuminated one license plate, then the next. He reached his car and got inside. A moment later, the cabin was flooded with light. He waited, breath tight in his chest. The illumination made it easy to see the newspaper on the seat beside him. A photograph on the front page of the **Neue Zürcher Zeitung** showed a Middle Eastern man delivering a fiery oration. The caption identified him as Parvez Jinn, Iranian Minister of Technology, and stated that he was due to give an address to the WEF in Davos Friday evening in which he would detail his country's nuclear aspirations.

Parvez Jinn. The initials were not lost on Jonathan. He'd found P.J.

And then the cabin was dark again. The spotlight moved on to the next vehicle. He wondered if this had been a routine check or if he had been the target?

He started the engine and pulled out of the space.

He was going back to the mountains.

He was going to Davos.

57

Tobias Tingeli lived in an imposing Victorian mansion high on the Zürichberg near the Dolder Grand Hotel. The four-story stone structure had been his father's and, before that, his father's father's, all the way back to 1870 when the first Tobias Tingeli made his fortune bankrolling Kaiser Wilhelm I in his war against Napoleon III.

Relations between Germany and the private bank had remained close over the years. During the Second World War, the Tingeli Bank had been a haven not only for the National Socialists, who transacted a majority of their gold sales through its offices, but also for the Americans, the British, and the Russians, whose spy services all found it to be equally accommodating. Since then, the bank had been content to concentrate on a private clientele, but rumors of questionable activity never quite faded away.

"Marcus, come in," boomed Tobias Tingeli. "I was surprised to hear from you."

Von Daniken smiled. Very surprised, no doubt, he thought to himself. "Hello, Tobi. Things are well? I hope I'm not disturbing you."

"Not at all. Don't just stand there freezing. Let me take your jacket."

Tobias Tingeli IV, "Tobi" to his friends, was the new breed of banker. He was a young man, ten years von Daniken's junior. Answering the door in faded jeans, a black turtleneck, his abundant black hair combed into a fashionable mess, he looked more like an artist than a businessman.

Von Daniken handed over his coat. When he'd visited ten years ago, there had been a legion of uniformed maids and butlers on hand to fetch coats and serve cocktails. He wondered if Tingeli had forgone the luxury, or if he'd dismissed them in advance of his visit. The two men had what would be called a history. A very secret one: and Tobi Tingeli's effervescent manner did little to the fact that he didn't like having von Daniken in his house.

"Follow me, Marcus. You remember your way around, don't you?" Tingeli led the way into his living room, where a floor-to-ceiling window seemed to devour the Lake of Zurich. "Drink?" he asked, pulling the stopper off a cut-glass decanter.

Von Daniken refused. "As I mentioned, it's a matter of some urgency," he began. "I'll have to ask that everything we discuss tonight remains for your ears only. I know that I can count on you to be discreet."

Tingeli nodded gravely. The two sat facing one another in matching leather chairs. Von Daniken explained the rudiments of his investigation into Lammers and Blitz—their murders, the plastic explosives found in Blitz's garage, and their ties to the terrorist Walid Gassan. He was careful not to mention the threat against air travel. "We tracked their finances to a company set up by your subsidiary in Liechtenstein. An entity called Excelsior Trust."

"Do you have any idea how many laws I'd be breaking if I divulge my clients' information?"

"If you'd like, I can have Alphons Marti issue a warrant."

A wave dismissed the suggestion. "Forget about the rules. I'm willing to bet that the names on the trust belong to lawyers. They're the ones who know everything. Go after them."

"Give me their names and I will. As I recall, a trust must have a certain number of directors. Their names will be on the paperwork."

Tingeli flashed his blinding smile. "I'd like to cooperate, but if word gets around that we're working with the government, it will be the end of our business."

Von Daniken surveyed the room's decor. The furniture was minimalist and spare. All attention was meant to be focused on the walls. A giant oil hung to his right, some abstract psychological nightmare worth ten or twenty million francs no doubt. It was cheap in comparison to the Paul Klee facing it. Last year, a Klee had fetched the highest price ever at an auction. Some 130 million dollars. Tingeli could stand to lose one or two clients and he'd still be among the richest men in Europe.

"I'm afraid that I'm not asking for your help. I'm ordering it. First thing in the morning, I want to see all the paperwork you have on the trust holding those Curaçao companies. Lawyers' names, directors, everything."

"The government has no right to order me to do anything."

"Who mentioned the government?"

"Come now, Marcus, no one cares about all that old business anymore. The war's been over seventy years. People barely remember Hitler, let alone the Nazis. Besides, we paid our debt. A billion dollars buys a lot of understanding."

As part of his work on the Holocaust Commission, von Daniken had been detailed to look into the degree of collaboration between Swiss banks and the Economic and Administrative Main Office of the SS, the agency charged with handling the Third Reich's financial dealings. If the Swiss banks had been remiss in their conduct toward survivors after the war, the vast majority could claim in good conscience that they had only been following long-established rules to guarantee the privacy and safety of their clients' deposits. The same rules that denied their deceased clients' heirs access to their money had also denied access to less scrupulous forces, namely a constant parade of German officers sent to Zurich, Basel, and Geneva with orders to pry imprisoned, and soon to be dead, Jews' money out of the bankers' greedy little fingers.

One bank, though, had not been as stringent in the enforcement of these rules as the others. Not only had the Tingeli Bank cooperated with the Germans and transferred millions of francs from their rightful (Jewish) owners to the Third Reich, it had actually set up an office in-house for officers of the SS to systematically loot these accounts.

Von Daniken had discovered all of this and more in his research, including a photograph of Tobi Tingeli's grandfather, Tobias II, in the company of Hermann Goering, Joseph Goebbels, and Reichsführer Adolf Hitler. In the photograph, Tingeli was wearing an SS officer's black uniform with the rank of Standartenführer, or colonel.

News of the discovery was vehemently hushed up. In exchange for the Commission's silence, the Tingeli Bank had donated one hundred million dollars to the survivors' fund. Case closed.

"You're right," said von Daniken. "The war is old hat. I'm talking about something more recent." He slid an envelope from his pocket and handed it to the banker. Tobi Tingeli opened it. Several photographs were inside. Not photos of old Nazis from a bygone era. But something equally shocking.

"Where did you get this?" Tingeli's face drained of color.

"My mandate is to cover extremists. I'd say the activity in those pictures qualifies. Not political extremism, but some rather embarrassing behavior all the same. You see, I don't like you, Tobi. I don't like your father, either. For far too long you've been allowed to buy yourself a clean conscience. I've been keeping an eye on you. I always knew that you were a strange one. I just didn't know how strange."

There were only two pictures, but two were enough. The first showed Tobi Tingeli standing at a bar in a dark room, dressed in his grandfather's SS tunic, the death's-head cap cocked rakishly on his head. He wore nothing else. No pants. No socks. No shoes. He stood with an erection in one hand and a quirt in the other, whipping the hairy white ass of a man bent over beside him.

The second picture was, if possible, more bizarre. In it, Tingeli was on his knees, dressed head to toe in a black latex suit with slits cut out for the eyes, nose, and mouth. Hands cuffed behind his back, his head was buried in a woman's crotch. True, his face wasn't visible, but the large gold signet ring engraved with his family crest that he wore on his right hand was. The cops in the undercover unit had gotten laughs out of it for months.

"Not exactly something to inspire the shareholders, are they? I'd imagine the scandal sheets would love to get their hands on them. If I wanted, I could feather my retirement nest very nicely. What do you think they'd pay? A hundred thousand? Two?"

Tingeli tossed the photographs onto a coffee table. "Bastard."

"Count on it."

Tingeli stood. "You'll have the names in the morning. But I want those pictures."

"Deal." Von Daniken walked himself to the front door. "Just remember that I can always get more."

58

Alphons Marti popped his head into Marcus von Daniken's unoccupied office. The overhead lights were extinguished. A sole desktop lamp burned, casting a halo on the papers covering the desk. It was eight o'clock in the evening, and he'd come for a briefing on the day's progress. He wandered down the hall until he found an office still occupied. "Excuse me," he said with a knock on the door. "I'm looking for Mr. von Daniken."

A stocky bald man shot from his desk. "Hardenberg, sir. I'm afraid Chief Inspector von Daniken isn't here at the moment."

"I can see that. He was due to update me on today's activity."

"It's not like him to miss a meeting. Was it scheduled?"

Marti avoided the question. The visit was unannounced. He hadn't wanted to give von Daniken time to doctor his findings. "Where is he?"

"In Zurich. Looking into a lead regarding the financing of the operation."

"Really? Aren't the banks closed at this hour?"

"He's not at a bank. He's visiting Tobias Tingeli. They know each other from the Holocaust Commission. You can reach him on his cell phone."

Marti considered this. "Not necessary," he said after a moment. "I'm sure you can fill me in. You said that you've discovered a lead on the financing of this operation. Do you have any idea which group is behind the plot? Is it the Revolutionary Guard? Al-Qaeda? Islamic Jihad? Or is it some organization we haven't heard of?"

"We're not certain yet," replied Hardenberg. "All we know is that Blitz's house was purchased by an offshore company based in Curaçao. Once we find out who paid his bills, we'll be a lot closer to knowing who's behind this attack."

"What's standing in your way?"

"The law, sir. The existing bank secrecy requirements make it difficult for us to obtain the information we need. Still, Mr. von Daniken is confident he'll be able to get around them. He has close ties with a number of bankers."

"Yes, yes, of course," said Marti, laboring to sound pleased. "Keep up the good work."

Hardenberg accompanied him to the door. "I'll

tell Mr. von Daniken that you came by. I'm sure he didn't mean to miss the meeting."

Marti hurried down the stairs, a man with a mission.

Back in his office at the Bundeshaus, Marti rooted around in the files until he found the paperwork relating to the government's request to Swisscom, the national telecommunications authority, for a record of all of Blitz's, Lammers's, and Ransom's phone calls. Papers in hand, he phoned the Swisscom executive in charge of judicial relations.

"I need a complete record of all calls made to and from these numbers," he said, after introducing himself. He provided Marcus von Daniken's business, home, and cellular numbers.

"Certainly. Is there any time period you're interested in?"

"Last Monday from eight a.m. to four p.m."

"Just last Monday?"

"That's all," said Marti. "How soon can you have it?"

"Tomorrow at noon."

"I need it by eight a.m."

"You'll have it."

Marti hung up. In less than twelve hours, he would have his proof.

59

Jonathan drove until he was exhausted. He pulled off the highway in Rapperswil at the south end of the Lake of Zurich and maneuvered through the town and into the hills beyond. When he hadn't seen a home or the light of another car for ten minutes, he pulled to the side of the road and killed the engine. Davos was another hundred kilometers ahead.

Using the emergency flashlight clipped to the interior wall of the glove compartment, he pored over the newspapers he'd bought. He knew little about the World Economic Forum other than what he'd glimpsed on the television news.

The WEF was an annual conference that brought together approximately one thousand political and business leaders from around the globe to share information about a subject deemed crucial to the world's welfare. This year's topic was the proliferation of nuclear weapons. An article stated that "eighteen heads of state, two hundred cabinet-level ministers, and forty-seven of the Fortune 100 CEOs" will be in attendance. This year's guests included two former U.S. presidents, the British prime minister, the sultan of Brunei, the king of Jordan, and the chairmen of Shell Oil, Intel, and Deutsche Bank, to name a few.

An article in the **Financial Times** discussed security for the event. Some three thousand soldiers would assist a battery of two hundred local police officers in guarding the World Economic Forum. No one was permitted entry without prior vetting. There were photos of large fences cutting through snow-covered fields, imposing floodlights, armed sentries with German shepherds. Based on the photographs, Davos looked more like a concentration camp than a ski resort.

In the **Tages-Anzeiger,** he found a boxed feature discussing a Swiss firm that manufactured the identification card readers utilized by the law enforcement authorities to govern access to the event. The company's chief executive boasted that no one could get past his card readers. He noted that there were three levels of security. The green zone was free to residents and visitors, who nonetheless had to present a form of identification at one of three security checkpoints before being issued an official Forum identification that they must wear around their necks at all times. The yellow zone encompassed that part of the town nearer the Kongresshaus where the Forum would actually take place, as well as common areas in proximity to hotels putting up the event's VIPs. To gain access to the yellow zone required an official invitation to the event and prior vetting by the Swiss Federal Police.

The red zone included the Kongresshaus, where all speeches were delivered and breakout sessions held, as well as the Hotel Belvedere, where many of the VIPs boarded. Identification badges permitting visitors access to these areas carried not only photographs but also memory chips loaded with pertinent information about the individual. Those individuals granted access to the red zone received their own personalized card readers. These readers scanned a ten-meter-square footprint around them to pick up signals from their fellow attendees, flashing that person's name, photograph, and bio on the reader's display. While no one would fail to recognize Bill Gates or Tony Blair, the oil minister of Saudi Arabia was a different story.

Jonathan dumped everything from the glove compartment onto the seat next to him. He reasoned that if Emma were to deliver the car to P.J. in Davos, she had to have been given an ID allowing her into the red zone. He sorted through the automobile's user's guide, a service book, and customs papers, then leaned over and ran a hand over the glove compartment's surface. Nothing there.

He sat back, thinking. If the ID wasn't in the

bags Blitz sent to Landquart, it had to be in the car. But where? The user's manual explained that armor wasn't the vehicle's only unique feature. The car also boasted run-flat tires, antiskid brakes, and automated parking.

He found what he was looking for listed under "Custom Specifications": a strongbox hidden beneath the rear passenger seat. He got out of the car and opened the rear door. Leaning into the cabin, he muscled a tab in the center of the banquette. The seat rose. In the space beneath it was a dull black steel box. He popped the catch. A manila envelope lay inside with the name "Eva Kruger" typed on it. He ripped it open. A plastic identification card strung with a cloth lanyard fell into his hand. The ID was issued by the World Economic Forum and bore the same photo that adorned her driver's license. There was more: a French passport with Parvez Jinn's photograph inside and a cell phone.

A passport to go with the one hundred thousand Swiss francs and the armored Mercedes sedan. All, Jonathan surmised, in return for "Gold" to be provided by Parvez Jinn, Minister of Technology of the Fundamentalist Islamic Republic of Iran.

He picked up the phone. It was one of the cheapest models. He turned it on and saw that it had been charged with fifty Swiss francs. Why leave Emma a phone unless she had to call someone . . . someone who only wanted to be called on a certain number. Parvez Jinn? He checked the directory, but found no numbers listed. He wondered if Jinn was supposed to call her? That made more sense. The minister of technology would have to find a suitable moment when he was free of his guards.

Jonathan began to gain a sense of what was taking place. He didn't fathom all of it, just the bare bones. Shipments in exchange for information. "Gold," they called it. There was only one type of product that he imagined the Iranians desired. Products the Western world had forbade them.

Heart pounding, he sat up straighter. He logged on to the Intelink website and began reviewing the shipping lists. Centrifuges, navigation units, vacuum tubes. He worked backward through the months: December, November, October. Carbon extruders. Maraging steel. Coolant systems. And further back still. September, August. Ring magnets. Heat exchangers. He had no doubt but that the items were falsely labeled. It made no difference whether or not he knew their exact functions. He knew their purpose and that was enough.

Suddenly, he was overcome with a need to be free of the car. Stumbling outside, he set off up the road. His stride lengthened and he began to jog up the incline, pushing himself, reveling in the burn in his legs, the pounding of his heart, the scuff of his breath.

His mind took flight and he imagined himself in the mountains, deep in the wilderness, at the moment a few days out on an expedition when it finally hit that, at least for now—for a sharp, glinting moment—you'd left everything behind: your past, your present, your future. It was a new world, separate from everything that had come before, with no ties to bind you and no expectations to draw you forward. You were just a solitary man, alone with rocks and trees and fast-running streams. One beating heart surrounded by a world that had been there long before mankind had begun to despoil it. For that moment, you were boldly and gloriously alive.

After ten minutes, he reached the crest of the hill. A cairn had been erected on the summit. He circled the stones, his lungs burning, his eyes stinging from the cold. To the north the long, curving shadow of the Lake of Zurich fell away like a scythe bordered by sparkling jewels. To the south the valley was long and dark, lit at varying distances by clusters of light. Hardly a kilometer away, the foothills of the Alps pushed against the plain, erupting from the flat, fertile land as towering granite escarpments that rose in vertical plains a thousand meters or more, capped by jagged summits.

Why, Emma? he demanded silently. How could she send these materials to the most dangerous country in the world? It's to make bombs. And not just any bombs. **The bomb.**

After a while, he headed down the hill. In ten minutes, he regained the Mercedes. He climbed inside and turned on the heat. One question stayed with him above all.

Who was she working for?

He laid his head back and closed his eyes, but his mind was racing. He didn't fall asleep until much later, when the first light of dawn crept above the horizon and lit the sky a dead, ashen gray.

60

It's none of your business. **Leave it. It can only go badly for you.**

Philip Palumbo mulled over the words, then leaned across the front seat of his car and removed his service sidearm from the glove compartment. It was because nobody took a stand that the world was in such sorry shape.

The pistol was a Beretta 9mm, left over from his days as an officer with the 82nd Airborne. He'd given fourteen years to the military, including his time as a cadet at West Point, and advanced as high as major before getting out. There were plenty of opportunities in private enterprise for a man with his background, but he'd never had much of an interest in making money. Seven weeks after signing his separation papers, he put his name on a contract with the Central Intelligence Agency. And despite all that he'd seen and all that he'd done, he still considered it the best decision he'd ever made. He did not relish giving it all up.

He checked that the magazine was full, chambered a round, and clicked down the safety.

The house was a two-story colonial with forest-green shutters and a shake roof. He took the stairs two at a time and rang the bell. A slim, unprepossessing man wearing a gray cardigan, bifocals hanging from a chain around his neck, opened the door. "There you are, Phil," said Admiral James Lafever, Deputy Director of Operations of the Central Intelligence Agency. "A matter of some urgency, I take it."

Palumbo entered the home. "I appreciate you seeing me at such short notice."

"No problem at all." Lafever led the way into a spacious foyer. He was a workaholic and lived alone. "Can I get you some coffee?"

Palumbo declined.

Lafever walked into the kitchen and poured himself a mug of steaming coffee. "I understand that you got solid information out of Walid Gassan that helped prevent an attack."

He knows, thought Palumbo. **Someone's tipped him off.**

"Actually, that's why I've come."

Lafever added some sugar to his coffee, then signaled for Palumbo to go ahead.

"On my way back from Syria, I got a call from Marcus von Daniken, who heads up the Swiss counterintelligence service. He was investigating the murder in Zurich of a man named Theo Lammers, a Dutch national who was shot outside his house. It was a professional job. Clean. No witnesses. Lammers owned a business that designed and manufactured sophisticated guidance systems. On the side, he built drones. Unmanned aerial vehicles. Small ones, big ones, you name it. Von Daniken was looking into it when a colleague of Lammers also got killed: an Iranian by the name of Mahmoud Quitab who was residing in Switzerland under the work name of Gottfried Blitz. Any of this sound familiar?"

"Should it?"

"With all due respect, sir, I think it might ring a few bells."

Lafever added some milk to his coffee. When he returned his attention to Palumbo, his expression had changed. The social portion of the visit had officially concluded. "Go on, Phil. Let's save my part for the end."

Palumbo knew an order when he heard it. "I called Marcus to fill him in on the details of Gassan's interrogation."

"You mean regarding Gassan's involvement in a plot to shoot down an airliner?"

"That's correct. Von Daniken was surprised, to say the least. It turns out that the two deceased gentlemen he was looking into were Gassan's co-conspirators."

"Quite a coincidence." Lafever's voice made clear that he knew it was anything but.

Palumbo went on. "The next day, von Daniken received a report from the coroner that both victims were killed by someone who liked to dip his bullets in poison. This coroner had asked around if anyone had ever come across a similar case. One of his colleagues at Scotland Yard knew exactly what he was talking about. The man was a former British Marine, and had seen that same poison used in El Salvador back in the early eighties. I guess it was a common practice among the Indians down there. Some kind of local voodoo to ward off evil spirits. The Englishman shared his belief that it was **us** that trained them. According to him, whoever killed Lammers and his partner had at one time or another been working with the CIA. Von Daniken wants to know if we have an op running on his turf. Sir, if we have credible information about a cell looking to take down an airliner in Swiss airspace, it's our duty to keep them in the loop."

"And what did you tell him?" asked Lafever.

"I said I'd look into it."

"So you haven't spoken to him since?"

Palumbo shook his head. "You were running the station in San Salvador back then. Wasn't Mourning Dove one of your operations?"

"That's classified information."

"I have classified clearance. One of the locals was recommended for recruitment. His name was Ricardo Reyes. His mother was half Indian. He did some training up at the Farm, then was sent overseas. He's still on payroll."

"Been digging, eh?"

"I'm guessing he's the one who pulled the trigger."

Admiral Lafever stepped closer and Palumbo could smell the coffee on his breath. "What concern of yours is one of my ops?"

Palumbo shifted his weight and felt the pistol digging into his back. "None. I'm out of my depth here. It's just that I was able to track down some info on Lammers, the man who was shot and killed in Zurich."

"And so?"

"Sir, we've got a file ten inches thick on the man. He was on our payroll for ten years. He worked in industrial espionage and was run out of our London substation. He fell off the books in 2003. I asked myself why in the world was Walid Gassan delivering explosives to men even remotely affiliated with the U.S. government. Something didn't feel right to me about the whole thing. I made some calls around town to ask if Lammers had gone over to the other side."

"What did you find out?"

"Oh, he'd gone over to the other side, alright. Lammers was picked up by the Defense Department two years back. At the time of his death, he was working as a consultant to the Defense Intelligence Agency. Admiral, can you tell me what in God's name we're doing taking out American agents?"

"I thought you'd be more concerned about why the Pentagon is trying to take down an airliner."

"That's my next question."

Palumbo had been expecting a tirade. Instead, Lafever put down his coffee cup and smiled bleakly. "Are you familiar with a unit called Division?"

"Division? No, sir, I'm not."

"Didn't think so." Lafever led him by the elbow toward a sliding door in the kitchen. "Let's go outside. I need a smoke."

Palumbo followed Lafever onto the back patio and down a flight of stairs into his backyard. It was a cold evening, the sky grim and forlorn. Their feet crunched in the snow as they ambled through a thicket of barren trees.

"It's that Austen. He's the problem," said Lafever, shaking loose a cigarette from a pack of Marlboros. "Crazy Christian sonuvabitch will have me yet. Between all his prayer meetings and fundamentalist mojo, he can't keep his fingers out of the other guy's pie."

"Do you mean Major General John Austen of the Air Force?"

"The one and only. It started eight years back, even before 9/11. The boys at the Pentagon wanted to start mounting clandestine operations on foreign soil. They were pissed off at how terrorists were nailing our overseas installations and had taken to going around town saying that we at CIA couldn't do squat to stop them. The Khobar Towers in Saudi Arabia, the bombings of our embassies in Nairobi and Dar es Salaam, the numerous attacks against U.S. multinationals operating abroad. Austen went to the president and asked if he could put together a team of operators and give it a shot. The president didn't need much convincing. He'd been riding us hard to find out who was behind the attack on the USS **Cole** and we weren't able to help him. Austen's team found the culprits lickety-split. Thirty days later, the president signed a National Security Presidential Directive authorizing the Defense Department to run units overseas.

"They called it Division. Austen ran it out of a little-known office called the Defense Human Intelligence Service, whose official job is to manage military attachés assigned to our foreign embassies. He moved fast. Within a year, he had five teams in the field. We're talking the blackest of black ops. Clandestine. Deniable. Operating without any oversight from Congress, or even the president. The kind of blanket authorization any intelligence officer would kill for. Me included. They did some good work. I won't deny it. Took out that murderous lunatic in Bosnia, Drako, and a couple of warlords in the Sudan. The successes went to Austen's head. He started overstepping his bounds. Got his fingers dirty in that affair with the Lebanese prime minister. Got mixed up in the insurgency in Iraq. We are intelligence officers. It's our job to gather information and pass it on. It's not our job to be judge, jury, and executioner. That's policy, and the last I looked, it was run out of the White House. Anyway, by God, Phil, after a while I'd had enough."

"But, sir, they're American agents."

"They're not American. Quitab's an Iranian. Lammers is Dutch. Foreign born and foreign bred."

"Even so, sir, why didn't you go to the president?"

"And say what? I'd only look like a jealous suitor. It was the president who authorized all this. Only he can pull the plug."

"I don't think he would authorize U.S. agents working in concert with an Iranian illegal to take down an airliner."

"I agree, but he wouldn't authorize me running a mole in Austen's network either. What with his beliefs pinned on his sleeve and all those shiny medals on his chest, John Austen is what passes for a saint on Pennsylvania Avenue. He was in the fight since the beginning. By that I mean our holy war against Jihad, Incorporated. Austen set up the plan to rescue our hostages in Iran back in 1980. He organized the first Special Ops teams. And like our commander-in-chief, he burns for Christ. What's a whiskey-drinking pagan like me to do?"

"But that rescue attempt in Iran was a fiasco," said Palumbo. "We crashed and burned. We lost eight men."

"It doesn't matter, Phil. John Austen is a hero. Like being on the hill at Calvary way back when. Whatever he says, goes . . . until proven otherwise."

"With due respect, Admiral, I can't just stand by and let him take down a plane."

"There's no other way, Phil. This country can't have two separate espionage services conducting operations without one talking to the other. For too long now, the boys at Defense have been out of control. Once this thing blows up in their face, it will be over. John Austen will never be allowed to put a team in the field again. The Pentagon will be permanently out of the espionage business."

"So you sent over Reyes to put a stop to it?"

"I sent Ricardo Reyes to show that we weren't just sitting around with a thumb up our ass while this was going down. If we get caught flatfooted on something this big, it will just go to prove that everything Austen's been saying to the president about the CIA is true. But if we can get within a hair's breadth of knocking down that drone . . . if we can take out members of the plot . . . we will look like the heroes." Lafever crushed his cigarette beneath his shoe. "Mr. Reyes won't be able to stop the attack, and frankly, I don't want him to. Once that plane goes down, I can go to the president with proof of who did this and show him just how badly things got out of hand. I can also show that I tried to stop it. The president will have no choice but to back me to the hilt. Division will be shut down in a second. At the end of the day, those pricks at Defense will have their asses handed to them, and the Agency will be back on top."

Palumbo had nothing to say. He stood rooted to the spot, stunned and saddened.

Lafever stepped closer. "I can't have any flag-waving officer of mine running off at the mouth about what he thinks he's discovered. I need your word that you're going to keep quiet."

"But, sir, the plane . . . all the passengers . . ."

"I need your word."

"But, Admiral . . ."

"But nothing!" said Lafever. "It's a small price to pay to make sure that Austen doesn't do anything else even more foolish."

Palumbo sighed. He knew then how it was going to turn out. "I'm sorry. I just can't allow it."

Lafever looked at him like he was a poor, dumb rube just off the farm. "Neither can I."

When he raised his hand again, he was pointing a compact, nickel-plated revolver at Palumbo's heart. It was a throwaway piece with its registration filed off, loaded with standard ammo he'd probably gotten from the armory. The old man's tradecraft was strictly by the book.

The gun fired twice. The bullets struck Palumbo in the chest and knocked him to the ground. He lay there a moment, eyes wide, the wind knocked out of him. Lafever advanced a step and stood over him, shaking his head. Then Palumbo coughed and Lafever realized that he was wearing a vest. Hurriedly, the deputy director of operations of the Central Intelligence Agency brought his gun to bear. This time, he was too slow.

Palumbo's shot struck him in the forehead.

Admiral James Lafever was dead before he hit the ground.

61

Twenty-four hours had passed since the war council had convened on Balfour Street. In that time, phone calls had shot back and forth across the Atlantic with the savagery of a spring lightning storm. The Foreign Ministry to the U.S. State Department. Iran Command to the Centcom headquarters. The Mossad to the CIA.

At eleven p.m., the prime minister of Israel stood in his office, one hand behind his back, the other clutching the telephone to his ear. Like any other courtier seeking the emperor's company, he'd been told to wait his turn. The president of the United States would be with him momentarily.

Zvi Hirsch stood at the PM's side, seething with impatience. "Momentarily" had run out five minutes earlier. Every added second worsened the insult to his congenitally insecure heart.

Suddenly, a woman came on the line. "The President of the United States."

Before the prime minister could respond, a cold technocrat's voice filled the earpiece. "Hello, Avi, good to hear from you."

"Mr. President. I wish it were a happier occasion."

"I wanted to convey my thanks for consulting with us," the American president said. "These developments have caught us off guard. We didn't see this coming so soon."

"We were both caught off guard. I'm sure you can empathize with our position. We cannot tolerate the presence of nuclear weapons in the hands of a regime that has unequivocally stated their commitment to seeing Israel wiped from the map."

"Statements are one thing. Actions another."

"Iran's actions are a matter of record. For years they have been financing the terrorist activity of Hamas, Islamic Jihad, and Al-Aqsa Martyrs Brigade. Their participation isn't limited to Israel. I don't need to tell you about the havoc they've wreaked in Iraq. They have two goals: to gain de facto control over the Middle East and to destroy my country. They are well on their way to the first. I will not allow them to succeed at the second."

"The United States has always said that any act of violence against Israel will be viewed as an act of violence against us."

"This is not a situation where we can wait to be attacked. The first strike will be fatal."

"I understand, but I think it's too early to act. We have to take this to the United Nations."

"If you had known that the nineteen hijackers were planning to take over your jets and fly them into the World Trade Center, would you not have taken preventative actions?"

"Attacking a nation is different than taking out a band of terrorists," the president said in a carefully measured tone. Any mention of 9/11 left him wary. The hallowed date, and the immediate call-to-arms it inspired, had become this era's "Remember the Alamo!"

"And a nuclear weapon is different than an airplane," retorted the prime minister. "Any bomb will kill millions of Israelis."

The president drew a breath. "What can I do for you, Avi?"

"We require your permission to fly through Iraqi airspace," said the Israeli prime minister.

"If and when the State of Israel is attacked, you'll be granted that permission."

"With all due respect, Mr. President, by then it will be too late."

"The Iranians will retaliate."

"Perhaps. But some fights you cannot put off."

There was a pause and the prime minister could hear the U.S. president conferring with his aides. A minute later, the American spoke. "I understand you have a second request."

"We also require four of your B61-11 EPWs—earth penetrating weapons."

"That's a helluva request. We're talking about nuclear-tipped devices."

"Yes, it is."

The American president had been made aware of the request beforehand and had prepared his response with some precision. "Listen carefully to what I have to say. America will under no circumstance initiate the use of nuclear weapons. We do, however, believe in Israel's right to a strong and overwhelming defense. To this end, and in respect of our many years of friendship, I've ordered my men to immediately transfer four B61's to General Ganz. I will require your word, however, that you will not use these weapons unless you're directly provoked."

"I don't know if I can give you my word on that."

"This is nonnegotiable. I'll say it again. If that sonuvabitch in Iran lays so much as a finger on you or any of your interests, you have my permission to use those bombs as you see fit. You can fly back and forth across Iraq from dawn to dusk. But until then, I want your word that you'll keep them locked up."

Zvi Hirsch, who was listening on another line, shot the prime minister a shocked glance. Violently, he began to nod his head, indicating that the prime minister was to consent at once. The prime minister complied. "You have my word. On behalf of myself and the people of Israel, I thank you."

The call was concluded.

Zvi Hirsch set the phone in the cradle. "Did you hear him?"

"Of course," said the prime minister. "What are you so heated up about?"

"He said we can use the bombs if and when we are directly provoked."

"And so?"

Zvi Hirsch was so worked up that he had trouble getting the words out. "Don't you get it?" he asked. "They don't have to bomb us. It can be anything . . . any act at all . . . as long as we can tie it back to Teheran."

"They only have to lift a finger against us."

62

The Pilot held the stopwatch in his right hand. "Five minutes. Go."

The men moved quickly, but never hurriedly, from their positions at the foot of the garage. Breaking themselves up into three two-man teams, each group approached one of three man-sized stainless-steel packing cases called coffins standing against the wall. Two of the cases contained convex aircraft wings, each broken into two four-foot sections. The third case held the fuselage, which housed the aircraft's operational guts: the inertial navigation system, Ku-band satellite communications processor, fuel tank, primary control module, turbofan engine, and nose camera assembly.

Locking the landing gear into place, the first team set the fuselage on the ground. The men responsible for the wing assembly bolted the sections to one another, and then attached each to the fuselage by means of tungsten pinions. At the same time, the Pilot wheeled a low-slung gurney across the floor. Cradled in the gurney was a tear-shaped metallic nacelle, the size of a large watermelon, weighing thirty kilos, or some sixty-six pounds. The nacelle contained a powerful explosive charge.

The design was similar to the warhead used for Sidewinder missiles. In fact, the blueprint had come from Raytheon, the defense contractor responsible for the air-to-air missiles created over thirty years before. Little had changed in that time. Only the explosives had grown more powerful.

The nacelle consisted of a case assembly, twenty kilos of Semtex-H plastic explosive, an initiator device, and five hundred titanium fragmentation rods. When the proximity sensor detected the target—in this instance a passenger airliner—it would activate a fuse mechanism that ignited the explosive pellets surrounding the Semtex. The pellets would in turn ignite the twenty kilos of high explosive, causing it to release a huge amount of hot gas in a very short time. The explosive force from the expanding gas would blast the titanium rods outward, breaking them up into thousands of lethal flechettes that would effectively obliterate the aircraft's fuselage.

The goal was to destroy the drone as well as the plane. No trace of the delivery mechanism would ever be found.

As soon as the nacelle was attached and the wiring plugged into the main instrument panel, the Pilot rolled the gurney from beneath the aircraft and called, "Time."

He read the stopwatch. "Four minutes, twenty-seven seconds."

The men did not cheer or evince any satisfaction. As quickly as they had begun, they disassembled the drone. They couldn't take the chance that a random check might uncover the aircraft sitting in the garage assembled and ready for launch. In minutes, the three coffins were loaded and stored in locked cabinets inside the house.

Having supervised every aspect of the drill, the Pilot walked into the living room where a picture window looked down on the Zurich Airport. At eight o'clock, he spotted the landing lights of an incoming airliner approaching from the north. He was happy to note that it was precisely on time. But then, this particular flight had one of the best arrival records in the world.

He followed the lights until the Airbus A380 landed. The plane appeared oversized even from a distance of four kilometers. He knew its specifications by heart. Seventy-three meters in length. Twenty-four meters high. A wingspan of nearly eighty meters, nearly that of a football field. It was in every way the largest commercial jet aircraft in the world. It was configured to carry 555 passengers.

This evening the manifest put the total at a shade under five hundred. Tomorrow it was set to carry a maximum load.

The aircraft lumbered into its parking space. It was so large that even a special jetway had been built to accommodate it. It was then that he was finally able to make out the six-pointed star painted on the tail.

El Al Flight 863 from Tel Aviv had arrived.

63

Von Daniken arrived back at Tobi Tingeli's door precisely at nine o'clock. A maid led the way to the study. Tingeli sat behind a large mahogany desk, talking on the telephone. The jeans and turtleneck were gone. He was dressed in a black suit and pearl gray tie, his hair combed through with pomade. He greeted von Daniken with a glare, tossing a bound dossier across the table to him.

Von Daniken picked it up. Inside was documentation relating to the creation of one Excelsior Trust, based in Curaçao, the Netherlands Antilles. The holding company was formed with a capital investment of fifty thousand Swiss francs. Three directors were listed, two of whom were employees of the bank. The last name meant nothing to him. He was interested, however, to learn that the client had visited the Vaduz offices of the Tingeli Bank in August of the past year. The visit fit in neatly with Ransom's return from the Middle East.

More interesting were the documents that followed. Monthly account statements sent from the Bahamian bank kept by the Tingeli Bank on behalf of the Excelsior Trust. The statements detailed all activity in each of the numbered accounts that had sent money to Lammers and Blitz, as well as a third account that was used to purchase the Villa Principessa.

Still unanswered was the question of who had made the initial deposit into the Bahamian bank. Von Daniken shuffled through the papers. Both numbered accounts had been opened with cashier's checks. He found copies of the checks and read the name of the issuing bank printed on the upper right-hand corner. His heart jumped. It was one of the most venerable names in the American financial community.

"And so?" asked Tingeli. He had hung up the phone and come round the desk. "Not what you'd expected?"

Von Daniken recalled his conversation with Philip Palumbo. He wondered if he'd put his colleague at the CIA in danger. "Not a word of this, Tobi."

Tingeli took the dossier from von Daniken's hands. "I didn't like the way our meeting ended last night. I can't live my life the way I please with you looking over my shoulder, so I did a little extra work on my end. Peddle it to your superiors as a loyal Helvetic doing his patriotic duty. You want me to keep quiet? Sure. No problem. It's my job, right? But in return, I want you to stay off my ass, once and for all. I may be odd, but it's my choice. I'm not breaking any laws."

Von Daniken received the entreaty with skepticism. "So far, I don't see anything that merits a promise on my behalf. It was no skin off your nose to get me the information. It was right there in the files. In a week I could have had a subpoena on your desk and obtained exactly what you've given me."

"I figured you'd say as much." Tingeli handed back the dossier, his thumb marking a page. "Here's something that wasn't originally in the file. I had to make some calls to get this. It cost me dearly."

The dossier was opened to a confirmation of an outgoing wire transfer from the Bahamian bank in the amount of five hundred thousand francs. The money was sent from one of the numbered accounts in question to an account at one of Switzerland's largest banks. Below it was written the name of the account holder.

Von Daniken gasped. "You're sure about this?"

Tingeli nodded. "Do we have a deal?"

Von Daniken took the outstretched hand and shook it. "Yes."

Tingeli yanked him forward so that they were uncomfortably close to one another. "Then get out of here. And tell your buddies in Bern that the Tingeli family has done enough for its country."

Von Daniken descended the steps and walked to the sidewalk where his car was parked. All along he'd been aware of an unseen hand in the investigation. It wasn't anything he could put his finger on. It was just a feeling. Like most policemen, he knew better than to disobey his intuition. The information he now possessed was enough to shock the nation, let alone a middle-aged cop who still believed in the incorruptibility of his government. He stood for a moment, thinking of how he should proceed, reckoning whom he could trust and whom he couldn't.

As he unlocked his door, a dark, late-model Audi sedan roared up the street and braked beside his car. The window went down revealing Kurt Myer's flushed face. "We found Ransom."

"Do you have him in custody?"

"Not yet, but we have a line on his whereabouts."

"What happened?"

"Yesterday evening, two Bern police officers answered a call regarding an intruder gaining entry to an apartment. They knocked on the door and a man responded."

"Was it Ransom?"

"Looks like it. But before he opened the door, there was an explosion inside the apartment. The policemen broke down the door and found the kitchen and bedroom ablaze. Apparently, it was a gas explosion. A leak in the oven or range . . ."

A gas explosion. Von Daniken was reminded of

the ruptured gas main responsible for killing Drako, the Bosnian warlord.

Myer continued. "At first, the officers thought he'd been blown out of the building, but there was no blood and a search of the grounds failed to turn up anything. The woman who reported the intruder said that the man had identified himself as a doctor. Apparently, he had a wound on the neck and was bleeding. She thought it looked like he'd been cut with a knife. One of the officers thought it sounded like he might be a fugitive, so he ran his description through outstanding warrants. Ransom's name came back. They printed a picture and showed it to the woman. She recognized him, but said that his hair was black and very short."

"What was he doing in Bern?"

"He said he was there to see his sister-in-law. Her name is Eva Kruger."

"What do we know about her?"

"Not a thing. She's a ghost. No national ID. No work permit. The neighbor says she's hardly ever around."

"But the neighbor's seen her? In the flesh?"

"So she says. According to her, this Eva Kruger travels all the time."

Of course she does, thought von Daniken. No doubt to exotic destinations like Darfur and Beirut and Kosovo. Plainly, she was another member of Ransom's network. "I thought you said you had a line on Ransom."

"We ran Eva Kruger's name on the state and national level," said Myer. "We got a nibble from the chief of security for the World Economic Forum being held in Davos. He told me that he vetted the same Eva Kruger, domiciled in Bern, a week ago, and granted her a pass to the event. The pass was valid for one day."

"Today?"

Myer nodded grimly. "It's a VIP pass. She can get access to anyplace she wants, right down to the floor of the Kongresshaus."

"What's on today's schedule?"

"They have panels running all day long. Big shots from all over the world. The keynote speech this evening is to be given by Parvez Jinn, an Iranian."

"Have you alerted event security yet?"

"Not yet."

"Do so immediately. Tell them to invalidate her identification. Give them the latest description of Ransom. He may be armed."

"Is that all?"

"No," said von Daniken. "Tell them that we'll be there in an hour."

64

Jonathan observed the first trucks at the entry to the valley. Two army transports with a dozen soldiers loitering nearby. Five kilometers up the road, he spotted another pair of trucks. This time the soldiers weren't loitering. They were crack troops clad in crisp camouflage uniforms, submachine guns strapped to their chests. Every passing car merited a glowering inspection.

A single route accessed the alpine town of Davos. One entry led from the north. One from the south. The military presence increased as the highway wound deeper into the valley. Jeeps. Armored personnel carriers. Roadblocks set on the highway's shoulder, ready to be swung into place at a moment's notice. It was a trap waiting to be sprung. At any moment, Jonathan expected a soldier or policeman to dart into the road, wave his arms, and motion for him to pull over, but the Mercedes never drew a second look.

At eleven o'clock, he passed the town of Klosters. The snow had abated, and the sky had lightened a shade. Once or twice, he even caught a fleeting pennant of blue. As church bells pealed the hour, their melancholy timbre forced a shiver the length of his spine.

The road began a series of switchbacks up the mountainside, and he caught the whir of a helicopter overhead. He picked up the World Economic Forum identification and strung it around his neck. The name printed in black block letters no longer read "Eva Kruger." It had been altered by one letter to read "Evan Kruger." The picture, too, had been replaced with a passport photo taken earlier this morning at a copy shop in Ziegelbrücke. The work had taken him an hour to complete. The "n" came courtesy of a stencil set that he doctored to match the official font. Fixing the photo to the identification was harder to pull off and had required the use of a lamination press.

I've been in training and I never even knew it. I've been Emma's pawn all along.

A medical degree hadn't been the only requirement for a successful tenure at Doctors Without Borders. A taste for larceny and a bold imagination were equally helpful. He couldn't count the number of times he'd falsified import and export documents to facilitate the transfer of medicine across frontiers, or as importantly, to avoid paying bribes to corrupt government officials. If penicillin was forbidden, they altered the papers to read "ampicillin," which was stronger still but not as well known. When they discovered border guards ripping off shipments of morphine, they changed the bill of lading to read "morazine." Let them look it up in their Physicians' Desk Reference and discover there was no such thing.

The only part of the World Economic Forum identification he could not change was the memory chip. His solution was to run a magnet over it, effectively erasing its data. He was willing to wager that in the course of examining thousands of identification cards, security guards had come across one or two others with similar faults.

Eva Kruger's driver's license was easier to alter. The cardboard stock used by the Swiss authorities practically begged to be fooled with. An X-Acto knife and paint thinner combined to lift Emma's photo from the paper. A second passport photo replaced it. He'd made sure to subtly change his appearance. Instead of his suit and tie, he left his jacket off, his collar buttoned to the throat, his hair mussed. Though taken just minutes apart, the two seemed to be from different days.

Again, he changed Eva's name to "Evan." Emma's height was listed as one meter sixty-eight. He changed it to one meter eighty-eight. In fact, he was four centimeters shorter. The weight he likewise increased from fifty kilos to eighty.

He was all too aware that neither the driver's license nor the Forum ID would stand up to more than a cursory check. Subjected to rigorous examination, they would quickly give up their secrets and be exposed as bogus. But it was the Mercedes registration made out in the name of Parvez Jinn of Teheran that was his ace in the hole and lent him the legitimacy that a simple identification could not begin to match.

Until now, he reasoned, no one could know that he possessed the details of Eva Kruger's planned meeting with Parvez Jinn. Jonathan also knew that there would be no second Mercedes delivered to Jinn. Therefore, while Falcon might arrange for Emma's replacement to pick up his accreditation at Security Checkpoint 1, he most probably hadn't canceled the original pass meant for Eva Kruger.

Jonathan applied the same ruthless logic as before. The desire not to draw attention to oneself. If Eva Kruger's name was still in the system, he was certain that there would be a note attached stating that she was to deliver the Mercedes to the Iranian official. It would be the car itself, then, that would serve as his passport to entry. It was hard to argue with a two-hundred-thousand-dollar automobile.

The first blockade was set up two kilometers from Davos. It was a vehicle inspection point located on a level straightaway. Battered wooden farmhouses stood to either side. A barrier blocked the eastbound stretch of road. He slowed and waited in a line of four cars. He tightened his necktie and sat straighter. He had his driver's license ready, along with the registration slip. The Forum ID badge dangled from his neck. Even so, his mouth was dry as dirt, his heart hammering somewhere near his Adam's apple. He advanced toward the blockade. He noted the soldiers encircling every vehicle. His fingers tingled and he realized that he was hyperventilating.

Emma, how did you do this for eight years?

"Sir!" A police officer rapped on his window. "Move ahead."

Jonathan drove the car a few meters until the bumper nearly grazed the barrier. He was asked to step out of his car and produce his driver's license.

"Destination?"

"Davos. I'm attending the Forum."

"You're an official invitee?"

"I'm delivering this automobile to a guest at the Belvedere Hotel. Mr. Parvez Jinn."

"I'll have to take a look at your ID."

Jonathan freed the laminated badge from his neck. The policeman inserted the ID into a card reader similar to the one Jonathan had seen in the newspaper. From the corner of his eye, he watched as the policeman removed the card and thrust it into the reader a second time.

As he waited, a crew of soldiers ran mirrors beneath the chassis, checking for explosives. One gave a shout and the officer examining Jonathan's identification walked over to him. The men exchanged words and the senior officer hurried back. "This is an armored vehicle?"

"Yes," replied Jonathan. "As I said, I'm delivering it to Parvez Jinn, the Iranian minister of technology. He's exporting it to Iran." He forced a smile. "I've heard it can get a little violent over there."

"Wait here."

The senior officer moved a few steps away and radioed his controller. Jonathan overheard him give his name and inquire if there was anything that mentioned the delivery of the Mercedes. A minute passed. Finally, the officer nodded his head and returned to Jonathan. "All set. I'll have to ask you to allow us to inspect the interior of the automobile."

"Be my guest."

The officer barked instructions to his men. Five policemen swarmed over the car, examining the glove compartment, side compartment, yanking up the rear seat, demanding that Jonathan open the strongbox, running an explosives detector around the cabin.

"Roll up all the windows."

Jonathan slid into the driver's seat and closed the window. The officer pointed at the scars left by the assassin's bullets. "What happened? Someone shoot at you?"

"Rocks," said Jonathan. "Some punks in Zurich."

Just then, the senior policeman approached Jonathan, flapping the ID against his open palm.

"Where did you get this identification?" he demanded.

"What do you mean?" It was difficult for Jonathan to guard an even tone.

"Did you pick it up at police headquarters in Chur?"

"It was sent to me. Is there a problem?"

"The memory chip is faulty."

"I didn't even know there was a memory chip," he said contritely. "You can call my employer . . . please."

"You misunderstand me," continued the police officer. "I wanted to apologize for the malfunction. All your information checks out. They're expecting the car. I'm calling in your faulty ID to make sure you get another."

"Get me another?" Jonathan was smiling like an idiot. He couldn't help it. "Thank you. I appreciate it."

"Technical glitches still occur now and then. There was one discrepancy."

"Oh?"

"Your name isn't Eva, is it?"

Jonathan said it wasn't, and the officer handed him back the ID. "Go to the main checkpoint on Davosstrasse at the entry to town. They'll take a new photo of you there and issue you a replacement badge. Be sure to keep it visible at all times. **Alles klar?**" He banged lightly on the door, then stood taller and walked toward the next car. "Let's go! We haven't got all day!"

At the main checkpoint, Jonathan was issued a new ID badge and given a list of the day's events, along with a map of the town and passes to use the city's two cable cars, the Jakobshorn and the Parsenn. An officer escorted him back to the Mercedes and pointed the way to the Hotel Belvedere, which was visible on the hillside, three hundred meters down the road.

Jonathan kept his speed below ten kilometers an hour. The sidewalks were crowded to bursting. Soldiers manned every corner, randomly checking IDs. Policemen holding German shepherds on short leashes patrolled the streets. The road snaked through town, past jewelry boutiques and ski shops, quaint hotels and cafés. A steep driveway led to the porte cochere fronting the Belvedere. A pole barrier governed access. On either side was a temporary three-meter fence topped with curled razor wire. He saw that the fence ran up the hill and surrounded the hotel and its grounds.

Welcome to the red zone.

Jonathan braked to a halt. An armed guard approached and ran his badge through a handheld card reader. The barrier rose. He continued up the hill and stopped in front of the revolving doors. A brace of soldiers stood to either side, submachine guns strapped to their chests. In the rearview mirror, he caught sight of the barrier being lowered. To his ear, it closed with the finality of a bank vault.

He sat behind the wheel, wondering what his next move should be. Was the meeting supposed to be inside the hotel? Should he call Jinn, or just wait? It was exactly twelve o'clock. No Swiss banker was ever more punctual. He looked toward the broad flight of three carpeted steps that led to a grand revolving door. The guards on the landing bent to take a closer look at him. One started toward him. Jonathan swallowed, aware of the sweat beading on his forehead. He busied himself with a check of his fingernails, another look at his tie. He glanced back at the revolving doors. The guard had returned to his post and was scanning the approaches to the hotel as if his gaze alone, and not the three-meter barbed wire fence, would keep out all intruders.

The next moment, all hell broke loose. A storm tide of swarthy men in black suits surged out of the revolving doors. It was hard to count how many were in the group. Jonathan stopped at seven. By then, he had seen him. Tall, stately, trim, the hint of a beard. A man who strode on a higher terrain than the rest. At once among and apart from the others. But it was the expression of indignant anger stamped on the proud features that Jonathan seized upon and matched to the photograph he had seen the night before. **Parvez Jinn.**

Suddenly, there was a cry. Jonathan thought for a moment that someone had sounded the alarm. But it wasn't a cry of fear. No assassins or suicide bombers had been spotted on the radar. It was the opposite. A cry of joy. Parvez Jinn stood at the base of the stairs, neat hands pressed to his face, the percolating anger superseded by a look of beatific worship.

"My car," he said in American English. "The S600. It is a work of art."

"A V8?" someone voiced.

Jinn's voice slapped down the impudent dog. "A V12!"

At once, the assembled horde fell upon the car, circling it, eyes wide, hands hovering above the chassis, not daring to touch it. Jinn walked the length of the automobile. No customer possessed a more critical eye.

Jonathan lowered his window to ensure that no one spotted the three indentations caused by the killer's bullets. He'd banged out the dents on the fender himself. An attendant at the service station had found a matching black paint. It wasn't perfect, but you needed to be lying on your back beneath the chassis to see the contrasting hues. A wash and detail job had followed, with Jonathan applying a last coat of Armor All to the tires just before entering the Davos city limits. Except for the window, the automobile looked factory fresh.

Jonathan stepped out of the car.

The head of security approached him at once, but not with animosity. The security man bowed and made a show of shaking his hand and extolling the car's beauty. At six foot three inches in height, his newly black hair combed and parted just so, his suit in immaculate order, Jonathan was the picture of a German car salesman. The country of Mercedes-Benz was a longtime ally of the Islamic Republic of Iran. Jinn followed a step behind. If he was surprised to see a man in Eva Kruger's place, he showed no sign of it. He offered a limp hand to shake and addressed him in English. "Greetings, friend."

"Evan Kruger," said Jonathan, grasping the hand and feeling the jolt that passed through it as Jinn registered the name. The Iranian came closer, a fierce smile straining his handsome features, and Jonathan whispered, "Eva's had an accident. I've been sent in her place." Then louder: "I would enjoy taking you for a short demonstration drive of your new vehicle, Mr. Jinn."

At once, the head of security stepped up to Jinn's shoulder and uttered a string of warnings in Farsi. Jonathan understood only half of it, but he got the gist. The minister of technology was not to enter the automobile and go anywhere alone and unguarded. Parvez Jinn warned him off. No one told him what to do. With a dismissive wave, he circled the car and climbed into the passenger seat. "We go!"

Jonathan nodded and opened the driver's door. It all made sense. The meeting was to take place inside the car. Any exchange of information necessitated a private forum. The car was an ingenious device, at once a passport to allow Eva Kruger entry to Davos and a smokescreen behind which Jinn could hide to pass his traitor's information to the other side.

Sliding into the car, Jonathan spotted Hannes Hoffmann walking up the driveway. **Cormorant.** Hoffmann had a butterfly stitch above one eye and a hat pulled low on his brow to cover the bruise. Their eyes locked. Hoffmann began to run up the icy road. Jonathan shut the door. The engine revved to life and Jinn jumped in his seat, just as Jonathan had several days before.

"Automatic ignition," explained Jonathan, playing his role to the hilt. "You can program it for manual if you like."

"A marvel." Jinn gazed proudly around the well-appointed interior.

"I have the presents Eva promised you," said Jonathan as he put the car into drive and touched the accelerator. "The sweater and, of course, your fees in cash."

"Wait," said Jinn, motioning for him to keep the money hidden until they were clear of the hotel.

Jonathan rolled up the windows and the tinted glass shielded the car's interior. Hoffmann tried to force him to stop the car by moving into the center of the road, but Jonathan had no intention of slowing. Tapping the accelerator, he put on a burst of speed. Hoffmann jumped to the side and fell into the snowbank.

Parvez Jinn was too busy studying the onboard navigation to notice.

65

The Sikorsky helicopter traversed the narrow valley at maximum speed. In contrast to the trip of two days before, the weather was calm with barely a breeze to upset the aircraft. The sky was clearing by the minute. Patches of blue came and went. For a moment, the sun peeked out, its rays harsh and glaring after days of incessant shadow.

Squinting, Marcus von Daniken spoke into the radio. "The name is Kruger," he said to the watch officer at the WEF base security in Chur. "Anyone presenting themselves at a checkpoint using that name, or anything similar, is to be refused entry into the Forum grounds. You are to consider him armed and dangerous. Use any necessary force. I want him arrested at once. Do you copy?"

"Roger, sir. We copy."

Below him, he could see the two-lane highway

that bisected the valley floor as it passed the town of Klosters. The checkpoints were also clearly visible, clusters of men and materiel at set intervals on either side of the road. Ten kilometers up the valley, he caught his first sight of the town. Davos. Population: 5,500. Altitude: 1,800 meters. The alpine village cut a long and wide swath across the mountain's flank. A ray of sunlight reflected off the dome of the Protestant church. At the top of the mountain, he glimpsed the royal blue gondola of the Jakobshornbahn.

The radio crackled to life.

"Inspector von Daniken, this is base security."

"What is it?"

"A Kruger already arrived. First name: Evan. Passed through the valley checkpoint at eleven-oh-seven. A new identification was issued at eleven thirty-one at the Main Security Outpost."

"Did you say that you issued the man a new identification?"

"According to the report entered by the officer on the ground, Kruger's ID was defective. It lists the cause as a faulty chip. There was also an instance of erroneous data."

"What does that mean?"

"The name was originally Eva Kruger, but the guest was a male. He was slated to deliver a Mercedes-Benz sedan to Parvez Jinn, a member of the Iranian delegation."

Jinn, the Iranian firebrand. Von Daniken remembered the note that had been attached to the wire transfer of one hundred thousand Swiss francs to Gottfried Blitz, a.k.a. Mahmoud Quitab. "Gift for P.J." Now he knew beyond a reasonable doubt who the money was intended for, though the nature of the tie between the two men remained to be seen.

Von Daniken's mind fixed on the newspaper articles he'd read concerning the assassinations of the Bosnian warlord and the Lebanese police inspector. Did Ransom have another murder in mind? If so, why had he given the man one hundred thousand francs and a new automobile worth twice that amount?

"Where is Evan Kruger?"

"One second, sir. I need to check."

Waiting, von Daniken swore under his breath.

"He's inside the red zone. He passed through the Hotel Belvedere's grounds eight minutes ago."

"Get your men to the hotel," said von Daniken. "I want it surrounded as quickly as possible. Don't worry about making a fuss. You have my authority. I'll be landing at the southern helipad in four minutes. Have one of your men there to pick me up."

66

Formed in 1291, the nation of Switzerland considers itself the oldest continually functioning democracy in the world. The government is based on the bicameral parliamentary tradition and draws heavily from the American and British constitutions. The lower house, or National Council, is comprised of two hundred representatives, elected proportionally from the nation's twenty-six cantons. The upper house, called the Council of Cantons, counts two members from twenty of the cantons, and one each from the remaining six half-cantons. Instead of electing a prime minister from the majority ruling party to serve as head of the executive branch, members of both houses convene every four years to elect seven members to a governing federal council, the seats being split proportionally according to each political party's representation. Each councilor is assigned a department or ministry to run, with the president selected on a rotating basis for a one-year term.

Though at forty-five, Alphons Marti was the most junior member of the Federal Council, he had no intention of waiting six years until filling the president's seat. He'd made his name as a crusader, first in his home canton of Geneva, where he'd cleaned up whatever organized crime was there, and more recently, at the international level, where he'd campaigned against the Americans' practice of extraordinary rendition.

Sitting at his expansive desk that frigid Friday morning, he looked at the papers in his hand and knew beyond any doubt that the information they contained constituted his ticket to the presidency.

The papers had come from Swisscom ten minutes earlier and they held a list of all phone calls made to and from numbers belonging to Marcus von Daniken. There were a total of thirty-eight calls. Most of the numbers belonged to von Daniken's colleagues in the Federal Police. Marti spotted his own number on three occasions; at 8:50, when Onyx's intercept detailing the passenger manifest of the CIA charter was distributed; at 12:15, when the American jet requested permission to touch down on Swiss soil; and at 1:50, when von Daniken called to coordinate the drive to the airport.

Running a finger down the list of phone numbers, he stopped at a 001 country code. The United States. Area code 703—for Langley, Virginia. The number belonged to the United States Central Intelligence Agency.

Marti had his proof.

Setting the papers down, he called Hardenberg, the investigator he'd spoken with the night before. "Where's von Daniken? I need to speak to him."

"A helicopter picked him up in Zurich fifteen minutes ago," Hardenberg replied. "He's headed to Davos with Kurt Myer."

"Davos?" Marti's face fell. "What for?"

"We have a line on Jonathan Ransom. Apparently, he's delivering an automobile to Parvez Jinn, the Iranian minister of technology."

Marti pinched the bridge of his nose until it hurt. "Have you alerted security in Davos?"

"I believe so."

"If you learn anything else, call me immediately."

Marti hung up, then immediately dialed the number of the chief of the Federal Police across town. "Yes, Herr Direktor," he began. "We have a grave problem. A man high in your organization has been identified as acting on behalf of a foreign power. The man we're looking for is Marcus von Daniken. Yes, I was surprised, too. One never knows who one can trust."

He lifted his eyes from the incriminating list and stared out the window. He was gazing east toward the mountains.

"How quickly can you get your men to Davos?"

67

"Who are you?"

Parvez Jinn sat stiff-backed in the passenger seat, his eyes appraising Jonathan.

"A friend of Eva's."

"You work together?"

"For eight years."

"Ah," said Jinn, trying to play down his discomfort at the unannounced change of plans. "So you know her well?"

"You might say that." Jonathan could only offer so much without giving away his ignorance. Fifty meters farther on, a policeman stood in the center of the road, directing traffic.

"What happened to her? Why couldn't she come?"

Jonathan shifted his gaze to Jinn. "She's dead."

The news hit the man like a sledgehammer. "Dead? When? How? I can't believe it."

"Monday. She was climbing with her husband. It was an accident."

"Her husband? Of course. She was married. **Frau Kruger.**" He looked into his lap and Jonathan saw that he was pressing his lips tightly together.

"Are you alright?"

Jinn looked up sharply. "Of course. I don't know why I should feel sad after what she did to me."

The Iranian looked straight ahead. His lips moved for a moment, but no words came out. His hand had assumed a death grip on the armrest, his knuckles white as chalk. He was experiencing mild shock. Jonathan stared at the man, hating him. He had a strong urge to hit Jinn in the jaw and slam his shocked, undeserving face into the window. He had no right to mourn Emma.

Jonathan looked away, somehow gaining control over his emotions. It was crucial that he get Jinn's mind off Eva Kruger—**off Emma**—before he suffered a breakdown. He called to mind the information he'd discovered on Intelink. Invoices. Packing statements. Customs declarations. "You've received the last shipments, haven't you?" he asked.

Jinn nodded, but it took him a moment longer to find his voice. "The Chalus facility is up and running," he said weakly. "Four hundred cascades. Fifty-five thousand centrifuges. We shut down all our other facilities and moved everything there to reach our goal."

Cascades. Centrifuges. A fully operational facil-

ity. Jonathan's suspicions had proven true. ZIAG had been illegally exporting equipment used to complete the uranium enrichment cycle. But why would the company do that? And on whose behalf? If he knew that, he would be much closer to discovering the identity of Emma's employer. He recalled the articles he'd read over the last year about Iran's desire to become a nuclear power. "What's your output?" he asked.

"Four kilos a month enriched to ninety-six percent."

"Are you satisfied with that? Can't you get to one hundred percent?"

Jinn shot him a dismissive glance. "Ninety-six is already far above what's necessary. I thought you'd be impressed."

"I am . . . I mean . . . we are." Jonathan felt as if he were walking through an unfamiliar house in the dark, always a half step from banging into a piece of furniture or knocking a vase onto the floor. He had to be more careful. If Jinn suspected that he wasn't Eva Kruger's colleague, there was no telling what he might do. "And the other part?"

"What other part?" Jinn was growing anxious. His eyes no longer held Jonathan in the same esteem.

Instinct told Jonathan that the purpose of the meeting wasn't to review Iran's current status. It had been arranged for another reason. He guessed that it was a payoff. The money and the car in exchange for "Gold." And "Gold" had to be information. Jinn had nothing else to offer. "You know," Jonathan said, with an edge.

"If you're wondering whether I've got what you requested, you can rest easy. What choice did you give me?"

Jonathan shot him a sidelong glance. "We all have a job to do."

Jinn laughed mirthlessly. "Did you know that they make ministers attend the executions of spies? The French call it **pour encourager les autres.** To encourage the others." He didn't wait for an answer. He'd settled into a rhythm and Jonathan was careful not to disturb it. "If you are caught, they begin with your family. They take the youngest first. It's humane enough, if that's how you'd describe the firing squad. Pasha is eight. Yasmin will come next. She turned thirteen last week. According to the new law, she must start wearing a chador whenever she is in public. The rage is black silk scarves from Hermès in Paris. Be sure to pass that along to your analysts in Virginia or London or Tel Aviv, or wherever the hell it is you're from."

He rubbed his eyes, a gesture of fatigue that conveyed a weary ease with his situation. "Where did you find her, anyway?" he asked. "Is she the product of some sick school you've set up to take advantage of men like me? Is that it?" It was another rhetorical question. Jinn knew all the answers already. He had worked out his situation in excruciating detail and he appeared relieved to be able to share them with another man. "You know the funny part," he went on, with no smile in sight, "is that, to this day, part of me thinks she cares for me. In spite of it all. In spite of her threats. Do the photos count as blackmail or extortion? Or is it the banking records? All those bribes she insisted I take? Killed climbing, eh? I don't think anything less could have done the trick."

Jonathan had no response. He felt as if Jinn had been speaking for him. The light turned green and he continued along the town's main artery, called the Promenade, passing a turnoff to the railway station. Jinn appeared to have gotten himself under control. He pulled himself upright in his seat and sat with the posture of the zealot he made himself out to be.

"To matters at hand," he said. "The money, please, Mr. Kruger."

Jonathan handed over the envelope. He'd replaced the money he'd spent with funds from his private account. "One hundred thousand Swiss francs."

"Has the transfer been made to my account in Zurich?"

"Of course," said Jonathan, though he had no idea what transfer Jinn was talking about.

"The full twenty million?"

"Yes."

"It's for my children, you know," Jinn explained. "I can't touch it unless I leave the country."

The Iranian took a flash drive from his breast pocket and set it on the center console. "It's all there. Location of our rockets. Weaponization plants. Production facilities. A blueprint of our nuclear efforts from A to Z. I know what you're going to do with it. You made the mistake in Iraq. You won't repeat it. You have your smoking gun. This time no one can say that you didn't have a good reason."

"Our smoking gun?"

"Yes, whoever you are. Americans, French, the British, Israelis, it doesn't matter. You all want the same thing. War."

Jonathan had read enough about Jinn in the papers to piece together an idea of how his recruitment must have unfolded. It had started during one of Jinn's trips to the West. As a low-ranking official in the Ministry of Technology, it was his job to meet with businessmen eager to establish commercial relations with Iran. Had the first meeting been in Beirut or Geneva? Or somewhere else Jonathan had yet to learn about? It didn't matter. It must have been just a hint at first. A discreet remark passed along during the course of an encounter. For a price, ZIAG could arrange for the export of certain "controlled technologies." Of course, it was Eva who'd brought it up. The lure must have been irresistible to a man like Jinn. He would have seen the possibilities from the start. A chance to rise within the ranks. To become a patriot on the level of A.Q. Khan, the Pakistani engineer who had given his country the bomb. A national hero even. All combined with the attentions of a woman unlike any he'd ever met. He'd jumped at her offer.

At first, their relationship would have remained professional. Eva, Hoffmann, and Blitz made sure that the shipments arrived without incident. It was critical to establish Jinn's credentials with his superiors. By all accounts, it had been a meteoric rise. In six months, Parvez Jinn was minister of technology. As minister, he was able to travel more freely. No doubt he visited ZIAG's operations in Switzerland. Visits that coincided with Emma's "lightning safaris," her unannounced trips to points unknown to gather supplies. It was during one of these factory visits that Eva Kruger sank in her hooks. Perhaps she'd suggested an onward journey to Bern to continue their discussions in a more private setting. Discussions that involved a visit to her apartment, chilled glasses of Polish vodka, and whatever came next. It was the oldest trick in the book. Once they had pictures, they added bribes to the mix. Transfers to the account in Zurich. Even the ayatollahs might understand falling for a woman like Eva. They would not, however, countenance the taking of kickbacks.

Jinn was toast.

Jonathan looked at the Iranian official seated next to him, feverishly counting his cash. **You poor sonuvabitch,** he thought, with renewed hatred for the man. **You were no match for my wife.**

"Is that all?" Jonathan asked, fingering the flash drive.

"The blueprint of my country's nuclear program. I should think it's enough."

"You're not holding back? We can stop to check. I've got all the time in the world."

"There is one more thing," said Jinn. "A year ago we came into possession of four Russian-made Kh-55 cruise missiles. The missiles are being kept at Karshun Air Base on the gulf. Each has a ten-kiloton warhead. If our enrichment facilities are attacked, we will not hesitate to use them. The plan is to take out Jerusalem and the oil fields at Ghawar. Our president plans on making an announcement next week. I'm here to set the stage. Tell your masters to think twice before they act."

"I'll pass along the news."

"And so?" said Jinn. "Where are the pictures? Where's my passport? I need to know that I can get out. I'm done being your lackey. Eva promised to turn over everything."

Jonathan handed him the French passport. "You'll have to wait for the photographs. Eva had them. You don't have to worry. This is the end of the operation. No one's going to bother you anymore."

It was then that he noticed the commotion ahead of them. A squad of soldiers moved into the center of the road, setting down riot-control barriers to block both lanes of the traffic. Policemen swarmed the sidewalk, barking instructions to pedestrians. Some ran in the other direction. Others cowered against the wall in a pantomime of panic. A few even fell to the ground and covered their heads with their hands.

Jinn's phone rang. He answered with a grunt. His eyes swept to Jonathan. After ten agonizing seconds, he hung up.

"The police have surrounded the hotel," said Parvez Jinn. "They are looking for the man who delivered the Mercedes. It appears, my friend, that you have killed me."

68

Jonathan kept his eyes straight ahead. A squad of policemen advanced down the center of the road, guns drawn and aimed at the Mercedes. A glance in the rearview revealed more of the same, approaching from the rear. He heard the thrum of a helicopter's rotor overhead. A compact, determined man dressed in a suit and overcoat emerged from the pack in front of him. He had bags beneath his eyes, but there was no mistaking the energy in his step, or the barely veiled anger. It was the same policeman who'd led the charge up the Villa Principessa's drive two days earlier.

"Who do you work for?" asked Jinn. "CIA? MI6? Mossad? A man has a right to know who he's dying for."

"I don't work for any of them."

"What do you mean?"

"I'm her husband."

"Whose husband?"

Jonathan shot Jinn a sidelong glance. "Eva Kruger's."

"But . . ." A curtain fell over Jinn's features. "Give it to me," he demanded. "Give me the flash."

"Sorry," said Jonathan. "That's nonnegotiable."

"But the police will find it . . . everyone will know that I gave it to you. I must have it back."

"I'm afraid not."

Jonathan looked at the phalanx of police and soldiers converging on him. All along, he'd planned on turning himself in once he had proof. Now, though, he had the flash with a record of Iran's entire nuclear program, as well as the spy who could corroborate his every claim about the events of the past days, and he realized that he still didn't have enough. The police would confiscate the flash drive. Jinn would be returned to his delegation and whisked out of the country. And Jonathan? He'd be hung out to dry, doing twenty to life.

There was only one way clear. He had to get out of the city. He had to give the flash drive to the only people who would know what to do with it.

Shifting into reverse, he began backing up, swerving in and out of the line of cars. After twenty meters, he braked, threw the transmission into drive, spun the wheel, and accelerated up a side road. Moments later, sirens began to wail. He caught sight of several soldiers taking a knee on the road behind him, machine guns set against their shoulders. It was an easy shot: thirty meters, unobstructed, and straight as an arrow. But no one fired. There was no need. The city was a locked cage.

Jonathan punched the gas and the Mercedes devoured the steep slope. He turned left at the top of the hill. He was driving parallel to the Promenade, past chalets and apartments. It was only a matter of time until they stopped him. Still, time was what he needed. Time to think. To plan. To scheme. He was one of them now. A member of Emma's team. A professional.

"Stop!" cried Jinn. "You'll get us both killed!"

Jonathan looked at him from the corner of his eye. "It's not you I'm worried about."

A police car turned onto the road behind them. It kept its distance, content to hem in one side of the trap. Jonathan turned at the next corner. The road narrowed until it was hardly more than a single lane. Pines grew overhead. He was no longer in the official Forum area. Snow had not been cleared from this part of the village. Ice crusted the road as it curved uphill into a shady forest before ending abruptly. A wall of snow blocked the path. Jonathan slammed on the brakes and the car fishtailed before stopping.

Jinn fumbled with the door in an effort to escape. Jonathan punched the central lock and slammed the Iranian into his seat with his right arm. "Stay put!"

He reversed down the road in time to see a police car blocking his retreat. A pasture lay to his right. A hiking path on his left. Jonathan yanked the wheel to the left and accelerated onto the trail. Wooden fences lined either side. The path dipped, flattened, then plunged downhill. The car caromed left and right, battering the fences. Remarkably, his breath was calm, his heartbeat hardly elevated. The snow was his element. Instead of panicking, he gave in to a steely control. He held the steering wheel lightly, nudging the nose left and right, not daring to oversteer.

"Watch out!" shouted Jinn.

Directly ahead, a mother and father dragged their young children on a pair of sleds down the path. Jonathan touched the brakes, causing the car to slide left, but not to slow in the least. He slammed his palm against the horn. The couple stared back in horror and began to run. One of the children looked over her shoulder, smiled and waved.

Jonathan tapped the brakes again, which only amplified his lack of control. There was no way to slow the car.

The Mercedes rapidly ate up the distance between them. Twenty meters separated the car from the family. Fifteen. Ten. The mother slipped and fell. Her mouth opened in a silent scream.

A path opened to the right.

Jonathan spun the wheel. The Mercedes lost its tail. He nudged the accelerator and the car found its bearings. The tires asserted their grip, the nose lurching forward. But only for a moment. In front of them the walking path continued downhill, but now it was bathed in the shadows of a pine legion. Snow became ice. The tires lost all purchase. He was sliding, hopelessly out of control. The tail swung right, then left, continuing through forty-five degrees, as they careened backward down the hill, gathering speed.

Jinn sat wide-eyed, one hand pressed against the ceiling, screaming.

The car jumped as it crested the path's boundary. It hit a hard object and caromed away from it like a billiard ball from a bumper. Jonathan saw a hut flash by. Everything was moving too fast. He gripped the steering wheel and held on for life. The tail bounced violently, and suddenly, the ride grew smooth. The jarring noise disappeared, and there was silence. Jonathan realized that they were airborne. The rear of the car plummeted. The hood rose like a black wave before him, and he blinked as the sun flashed in his eyes. With a terrific thud, the car landed, tumbled onto its side, turned over once, twice, and then came to a rest on its roof.

Jinn was unconscious, his eyes closed. His teeth had dug into his lip and his mouth was bleeding, but otherwise he didn't look hurt. Jonathan forced open the door with his shoulder and rolled to the ground. His ears were ringing and his left arm was numb. Shakily, he rose to his knees. The Mercedes had plunged off a ledge, rolled down a short slope, and ended up in a small pasture. The air was alive with the seesaw whine of a dozen sirens, all of them coming his way. He could see blue lights flashing along the path in the forest above him. He blinked, and realized that he was seeing double. A sure sign of a concussion. He squinted and his vision cleared.

Looking down the hill, he caught glimpses of the Davosstrasse between the backs of stores and buildings. He pushed himself to his feet and stumbled toward the stores. Dazed and numb, he maintained enough presence of mind to feel for the flash drive.

Thank God, it was there.

A warm breath of wind touched his back, and suddenly he was airborne. The fury of the explosion engulfed him. He landed on his stomach, his face buried in the snow. He raised himself on an elbow and peered over his shoulder. The Mercedes was awash in flames, windows blown out, the hood bent into an A-frame.

Jonathan didn't know what had happened, whether the gas tank had exploded or if it had been something more sinister. Behind the burning car, on the hillside overlooking the meadow, a police car drew to a halt. A man jumped out.

"Dr. Ransom!" he yelled. "Stop. There's nowhere for you to go."

It was the officer from Ascona, the same grizzled cop he'd seen just a few minutes ago on the street.

Jonathan ran.

69

Von Daniken started down the hillside. The snow was knee-deep and wet, and it buried his leather brogues. He didn't care. He'd bill the department for a new pair. He put his hand on his pistol, then took it away. In thirty years of service, he'd never drawn his gun and he saw no reason to start now.

A second police car pulled up on the road behind him. Several plainclothes officers jumped out. Suits all around. He didn't recognize any of them. No doubt they hailed from the state police.

He turned to Myer. "Radio for a cordon to be set up on Davosstrasse to make sure Ransom doesn't get back to the main street."

"Chief Inspector von Daniken," someone called.

Von Daniken looked over his shoulder. The voice . . . **he knew it.** He studied the men closely. He'd never seen any of them before.

"Stay where you are," said the familiar voice. "We have a warrant for your arrest."

Von Daniken did a double take. Those are my words, he thought as he put a face to the voice. He saw the slight figure emerge from between the cars. The pale complexion. The red hair worn too long for a man his age.

"The charge is conspiring with a foreign intelligence service," Alphons Marti called from up on the hill. "Come back to the car, Marcus, so I don't have to tell my men to restrain you."

Von Daniken continued to trudge through the snow. **A warrant for my arrest. How ridiculous.** Yet, deep inside, he'd been waiting for the hammer to fall. It wasn't just what Tobi Tingeli had told him this morning, though that had sealed the deal. He'd known two nights earlier, when Marti had refused to let him call out the police to search for the drone.

He looked at Kurt Myer, but Myer was being led away, too, and forced into the back of the police cruiser.

"Are you accusing me of being a spy?" asked von Daniken.

"I let the law accuse. My job is simply to enforce it."

Von Daniken looked from Ransom to Marti. By now, several of his men were making their way down the slope. One of them had even drawn his gun. The American was jogging in the opposite direction, away from the car. "Aren't you going to stop him? He's the one we're after!"

"Not today, Marcus. Today, you're our number-one suspect."

By now, a crowd had gathered around the outskirts of the meadow. Several people ran toward the car, including one man with a fire extinguisher. Ransom threaded his way among them, slowing his pace to a walk, getting closer and closer to freedom.

Von Daniken began walking across the meadow, his pace quickening until he was jogging. "Ransom," he called. "Stop! Do you hear me?"

More soldiers and policemen were reaching the scene every second. No less than ten uniformed men were making their way up the western side of the meadow, fanning out to reach the burning car. Von Daniken waved at them. "He's over there," he shouted, motioning toward Ransom. "In the dark suit. The tall man with black hair."

The policemen's eyes flitted from von Daniken to Marti. Everyone knew the members of the Bundesrat by sight. As one of the seven-member Federal Council that ruled the country, he was a prominent national figure. They were not apt to disobey his orders.

Marti barked a command to one of his aides, who radioed a message via his walkie-talkie. The assembled soldiers ignored Ransom and converged on von Daniken. Dropping his hands to his knees, the chief of the Service for Analysis and Prevention, one of the nation's highest-ranking law enforcement officials, stopped in his tracks and waited like a common criminal for the officers to reach him. "It's alright," he said, out of breath. "Give me a minute."

Marcus von Daniken straightened up and looked across the snowy meadow. Caught in the glare was the outline of a black figure, dark as a rook's wing. Then it disappeared.

Ransom was gone.

70

Jonathan slid from shadow to shadow, concealing himself in dark corners and recessed doorways, in damp alleys and deserted passageways. His head ached from the blast and he was certain that he'd bruised a few ribs. Still, he was free, and liberty was a bracing tonic. He had just one goal: to get out of town.

He picked his way down a side street slick with black ice. He was anxious to distance himself from the town center. If possible, there were even more policemen patrolling the sidewalks than when he'd arrived in town. A minute didn't pass without a soldier or a policeman appearing out of nowhere and rushing past him up the hill. The column of black smoke acted like a beacon. The security teams were falling back on the red zone as if it were the Little Bighorn.

He passed several homes, an automobile garage, and an electrician's workshop. It was difficult to walk casually. Half of him wanted to run like hell, the other half wanted to crawl into a cellar, curl up, and hide. Worst was a nearly uncontrollable desire to look over his shoulder for pursuers. Several times he'd felt certain that someone was trailing him, but upon scanning the sidewalk behind him he hadn't been able to spot a tail.

He crossed the street and descended a steep walking path that passed between several chalets. At the bottom of the hill, the path widened. To his left rose an outdoor ice hockey stadium. To his right, a commercial road that led to the train station. A cluster of police cars were parked near the tracks. He wouldn't get out of Davos by train.

He considered where he should go. The busier the road, the more likely he was to run into the police. He needed quiet. He needed to think. He jumped a low fence that bordered a long, low-roofed wooden hut. The stink of manure seeped from its rough-hewn log walls. Listening to the low and rustle of the cows inside, he continued to the rear of the hut.

He pulled up abruptly.

There it was again. The scratching at the base of his neck. He was certain that someone was watching him.

Pressing his back against the wall, he poked his head around the corner and stared down the path. Again, he saw no one.

He leaned his head against the wood, telling himself to calm down. He took the flash drive from his pocket. It was his key to freedom. The question remained: who held the lock?

He gathered himself, mapping out his next steps. He would find somewhere to lay up, wait until dark, and then head up the mountain. Most of the speeches were being given after six p.m. With many visitors attending the Kongresshaus, the town would be calmer, and hopefully, the police presence reduced. Once he made it past the Promenade, the going would be safer. The outer fence surrounding the town was barely two meters tall. He could be over it in ten seconds. Keeping to the mountains, he'd walk out of the valley. By morning, he'd be in Landquart, where the whole thing had begun. From there, he'd find a train or hitch a ride to Zurich.

He froze, certain that he was being watched.

Turning toward the street, he found himself face to face with a compact man several inches shorter than himself. The man was dressed in dark ski attire, but Jonathan could tell that he was no skier. The black eyes bore into him quizzically, as if he were owed an explanation. Jonathan recognized the face immediately. He was the man from the train.

The assassin's arm shot forward, a stiletto in his hand. Jonathan dodged right, shoving the man viciously to one side. A knife. But of course, he thought. No one could penetrate security with a gun. The assassin slammed into the wall and fell to a knee.

Jonathan knew better than to fight. He'd tried his luck twice in the past days, and both times he'd come away injured. In his view, he had two strikes against him.

He ran.

He crossed the length of the livestock hut, cutting between the hut and the barn next to it. Soon he was back on a paved road, running for all he was worth. After one hundred meters, he came to a fork in the road. He chose to go in the direction that climbed the hill. Ahead, he could see cars and pedestrians crowding the Davosstrasse. He looked over his shoulder. The street was empty. The killer had vanished. Jonathan stopped running and settled into a walk.

Two police cars were parked at the end of the block. Beyond them rose a security fence topped with razor wire. It was a checkpoint governing access from the green zone to the red zone.

Jonathan slipped behind the garage of a beverage distribution company. Kegs of beer were stacked four high, row upon row. He ducked inside the maze of crates and barrels, snaking this way and that, until he reached a dead end. With nowhere to go, he freed a crate and sat down. For the moment, he was safe.

He pulled his coat around him and ran through his options. The list was depressingly short. He could no longer wait until dark. If the assassin had found him once, he'd find him again. Hiding was not an option. Bathed in shade, he began to shiver.

If only he could wait until dark . . . until the speeches . . .

Paul Noiret was scheduled to give his talk about Third World corruption this evening. If Paul was here, so was Simone.

Jolted out of his funk, he pulled out Blitz's phone and dialed.

"Allô."

"Simone," he said breathlessly. "It's Jonathan."

"My God, where are you?"

"I'm in Davos. I've gotten myself in trouble. Where are you?"

"I'm here, too, of course. With Paul. Are you safe?"

"For now. But I need to get out of here."

"Why? What's happened? You sound frightened."

"Do you see that plume of smoke not far from the Belvedere?"

"It's directly across the street from my hotel. Did you hear the explosion? Paul and I think it was a bomb. He won't let me leave the room."

"It might have been one."

Thinking back on the explosion, he realized that there was no reason for the gas tank to have ignited, and that the blast was several times bigger than what could have been fueled by a half tank of gasoline. Its force reminded him of an artillery burst. The car had been rigged to go off. He didn't know how it was set off, or why the police at the checkpoint hadn't detected the explosives. All he knew was that the explosion had blown an armored car's engine block off its mounts and left the hood bent like a ruined pup tent.

"You mean you know something about it?" Simone asked.

"I was in the car thirty seconds before it went up. Look, Simone, I need your help. Did Paul bring his car?"

"Yes, but—"

"Just listen. If you can't go through with what I'm asking, I'll understand." Jonathan forced himself to speak slowly. "I need you to get me out of town. I need a ride to Zurich. If you leave now, you can be back in time for Paul's speech."

"What would I tell him?"

"Tell him the truth."

"But I don't know what the truth is."

"I'll tell you everything in the car."

"Jon, you're putting me in a difficult spot. I told you to leave the country."

"I'll leave as soon as I get to the U.S. consulate."

"The U.S. consulate? But why? They'll only turn you over to the Swiss police."

"Maybe. Maybe not. I've got something that may buy me some time."

"What is it? Did you finally get your proof?"

"It doesn't matter," he snapped, losing his patience. "Will you do it?"

"I can't tell Paul. He won't allow it."

"Where is he now?"

"With his colleagues, preparing for his talk."

"Do this for Emma."

"Where are you?"

"Drive down Davosstrasse until you pass the tourist office. Turn left and go to the bottom of the hill. You'll see an old barn down the road to your left with a trough out front and a rusty tractor sitting out back. I'll be waiting there."

Simone hesitated. "Alright, then. Give me five minutes."

A silver Renault pulled up next to the barn on schedule. Simone rolled down her window. "Jonathan," she called. "Are you there?"

Jonathan waited for a few seconds, his eyes on the road behind her, waiting to see if she'd been followed. When no cars approached, he waited longer still. He was certain that the assassin was out there.

Finally, he ducked from behind the shed on the opposite side of the street and dashed to the car. "Open the trunk," he said, wrapping his knuckles against the passenger window.

Simone jumped in her seat.

"Hurry up," he said. "Someone's following me."

"Who is it? Where? Do you see them?"

"I don't know exactly, but he's close."

"They're saying an Iranian minister was inside the car when it exploded. Parvez Jinn. He was set to give the keynote address tonight."

Jonathan nodded. "The trunk," he said.

"Tell me what I'm getting myself into."

"I was in the wrong place at the wrong time. Come on. Hurry!"

Simone considered this, then motioned for him to get in. A moment later, she released the trunk.

"Stop in Landquart and let me out," he said. "I'll explain everything to you then."

With that, he hustled to the rear of the car, arranged himself inside the trunk, and pulled it closed.

71

"I have him," Simone Noiret said quietly into her cell phone. "I'll pick you up where we agreed."

She hung up, then lowered the car radio's volume. "How are you doing back there?" she called over her shoulder. "Can you hear me?"

A muffled voice and two thumps was her response. The trunk might be cramped, but there was more than enough oxygen for the short ride. After all, she was not planning on transporting Jonathan to Zurich.

For over two years, Simone Noiret had been working to infiltrate Division. It was odd to think of turning against your own country, but the world was a decidedly odd place these days. Rivalries were as fierce between organizations as between enemy nations.

Born Fatima Françoise Nasser in Queens, New

York, she was the daughter of a French-Algerian mother and an Egyptian father. Her earliest memories were of money, or more precisely, arguments about the lack of it. Her father was a congenital miser. When she thought of the cunning it had taken to wrest a lousy ten dollars from his tight fist, it made her sweat. She joined the army at eighteen because her brother had done so before her. Her language skills placed her in Intelligence. Besides French, Arabic, and English, she spoke Farsi. She was trained at Fort Huachuca, Arizona, and the Army Defense Language Institute in Monterrey before being stationed in Germany. She rose to E-5 before she got out. With the money she'd saved and the army helping to foot tuition, she attended Princeton University, graduating summa cum laude with a degree in Middle Eastern Studies.

Hardly a month later, she received a call asking her to come to a meeting in Manhattan with a representative of the CIA. He made his pitch straightaway. The operations directorate had been keeping an eye on her dating back to her time in the army. They offered her a slot overseas. It was spying pure and simple. Not like you saw in the movies, but the real thing. She would attend a course at the Farm, the CIA's training facility, near Williamsburg, Virginia. If she passed, she would go on for further training as a clandestine operative. He needed an answer in twenty-four hours. Simone said yes on the spot.

That was eleven years ago.

It was Admiral Lafever, the deputy director of operations, who had asked her to join his personal crusade against Division. It was not a request one could turn down, and in any event, she was eager for a new challenge. All records of her employment with the CIA were expunged. A simple legend was created, establishing her as a peripatetic teacher, one of the flock of displaced Europeans who travel from country to country filling vacant slots at one American school after another. Her husband's job at the World Bank provided a natural cover.

Simone arrived in Beirut a month ahead of Emma. To establish their friendship, she helped Emma secure working quarters for the Doctors Without Borders mission that served as her cover. Friendship came naturally. After all, the two had much in common. Birds of a feather, so to speak. It wasn't long before they were talking to one another daily.

All the while, Simone watched.

One by one, she uncovered the members of Emma's network, though not in time to prevent the hospital bombing that had taken the life of a Lebanese police inspector involved with the investigation into the former Lebanese prime minister's assassination.

In Geneva, Simone continued her work. It was only a month earlier that she'd identified Theo Lammers as a member of Emma's new network. She passed word to Lafever, and this time Lafever did not hesitate to take action. She'd always figured that somewhere along the line killing might come into things. In her past assignments, it usually did. Part of her wondered if he'd somehow killed Emma, too.

Simone passed through the two checkpoints without incident. At each, she stopped and showed her identification. At each, she was sure to look the inspector in the eye, though not quite respectfully. And at each, she was quickly waved on.

Instead of turning right when she hit the crossroads for the highway that led westward to Landquart, and on to Zurich, she guided the car in an easterly direction, heading deeper into the valley. There were enough twists and turns in the road to convince her that Jonathan couldn't possibly figure out in which direction they were traveling. Even if he did, it wouldn't matter. The trunk was locked.

He wasn't going anywhere.

Poor lamb.

72

Alphons Marti stood atop the hill overlooking the meadow, hands tucked at his side like a victorious general. "Did you think I wouldn't look into who tipped off the CIA? You know how badly I wanted to nail the Americans. They've been using our airspace to ferry suspects to their secret prisons for far too long. It makes me sick to think of the innocent men they've captured, the lives they've destroyed."

"Since when are they innocent?" asked von Daniken. "The Americans have stopped quite a few attacks. The system is working."

"That's what they'd have us believe. So high and mighty, yet always ready to step on a rule when it applies to them. We had them this time. Gassan was on that plane. It was a golden opportunity to show the world what Switzerland stands for."

"What's that? Getting in the way of the war on terror?"

" 'The war on terror'? You have no idea how much I despise that phrase. No, in fact I was referring to decency, honesty, and the rights of the common man. I think such things are the responsibilities of the world's oldest functioning democracy. Don't you?"

Von Daniken shuddered with disgust. "I don't pretend to believe that anyone cares what I think about those kinds of things. All I know is that it was Gassan who told the CIA about the planned attack on our soil."

"What about it? Are you any closer to finding the drone?"

"Considerably."

The answer surprised Marti. "Oh?"

"The van used to transport the UAV was photographed by one of our surveillance cameras driving through Zurich last night. Right now I have the Zurich police force combing all the communities surrounding the airport, looking for any sign of it."

"That's against my orders."

"Exactly," said von Daniken. "I should have told you to go screw yourself two nights ago. I knew you were up to something then. Of course, I didn't know what kind of traitor you really were."

"Traitor?" Marti reddened. "It wasn't me who contacted the CIA."

"No," said von Daniken. "You did worse."

"I think I've had just about enough. You're finished, Marcus. You purposely betrayed my trust. You gave secret information to a foreign government. Give your gun to my men." Officers of the Federal Security Service charged with Marti's protection stood to either side of him. Marti turned to one of his officers. "Cuff him. It's my opinion that he poses a flight risk." He looked back at von Daniken. "Why don't you call your friend Palumbo and see if he can get you out of this mess?"

"Just a moment." Something in von Daniken's voice gave the men pause. They held their ground, observers in the war between their superiors.

"Go on, cuff him," said Marti.

Von Daniken stepped forward and placed a controlling hand on Marti's forearm. "Come with me. We need to talk."

"What the hell do you think you're doing?"

Von Daniken tightened his grip. "Trust me. This is something you'll want to keep between us."

One of the security men made a move toward them, but Marti shook his head. Von Daniken led him down the hill away from the assembled officers.

"The van wasn't the only discovery we made," he said, after they'd covered twenty meters. "We were able to trace the money paid to Lammers and Blitz to a certain offshore trust opened by the Tingeli Bank. I believe you know Tobi, don't you? Weren't you at university together? Both law graduates, as I

recall. Tobi wasn't forthcoming at first. I had to remind him of his duties as a Swiss citizen."

"By stepping on more laws, no doubt," declared
Marti, yanking his arm free.

Von Daniken ignored the comment. "As you're
aware, it's standard practice for the bank where the
trust is domiciled to keep all account statements on
behalf of its clients. Tobi was good enough to give
me copies of the trust's monthly statements . . . for
'the public good.' We were both surprised to learn
that the money that funded the trust wasn't sent
from Teheran, but from Washington, D.C."

"D.C.? That's ridiculous!"

"An account belonging to the U.S. Department of
Defense."

"But Mahmoud Quitab was an Iranian officer.
You told me so yourself." When Marti saw that he
was making no headway, he changed tack. "Regardless, Tobi had no right to reveal that kind of information. It breaches every bank secrecy law on the
books."

"Maybe so," said von Daniken. "Still, I'm certain
that your fellow members on the Federal Council
will be keen to learn the identity of some of the other
individuals being financed by the trust. In fact, we
tracked some of the payments to a private account at
the Bern branch of the United Swiss Bank. You have
an account there, don't you? Number 517.62 . . .
um, help me out, will you?"

The color drained from Marti's cheeks.

Von Daniken continued. "For the past two years, you've been receiving five hundred thousand francs a month courtesy of the United States Department of Defense. Don't talk to me about being a traitor. You're a paid foreign agent."

"That's absurd!"

"All your talk about nailing the CIA and about showing up America was nonsense. You wanted to take Gassan off that plane in Bern so he wouldn't be interrogated by the CIA. You didn't want him to give up any information about the attack to Palumbo."

"I have no idea what you're talking about. What attack is it this time?" Marti turned toward his men and began to call out to them.

"Don't even think about it," said von Daniken, taking a sheaf of papers from his jacket. "It's all here. Account 517.623 AA. A numbered account, but even they're not anonymous anymore. Have a look, if you don't believe me."

Marti scanned the documents. "They won't hold up in court. Inadmissible. All of it."

"Who said anything about court? I've already e-mailed a copy to the president with a note explaining our ongoing investigation. I don't think she'll want to serve alongside a spy, do you?"

"But . . . but . . ." Crestfallen, Marti dropped his head.

Von Daniken took the papers from his hand.

"Now then, Alphons, what exactly is Jonathan Ransom doing?"

"I don't know."

"You don't know or you won't say?"

"All I know is that they wanted him out of the way. He's not a part of it."

"A part of what? Don't lie to me. There's a band of terrorists somewhere out there with a drone that they intend to crash into an airplane in the next forty-eight hours."

"I told you. I don't know anything about the drone."

"Well then, what **do** you know about? You're not earning five hundred thousand francs a month to twiddle your thumbs. I want to know everything. Who? Why? For how long? If you can tell me anything that might help stop the attack, now is the time. This is the only chance you're going to have to mitigate these charges."

"I'll tell you," said Marti after a long silence. "But if anyone asks, I'll deny all of it."

Von Daniken waited.

Marti sighed. "I don't know anything about the attack. It's export licenses they wanted. They're under my purview as justice minister."

"Who wanted them?"

"John Austen."

"Who's that?"

"A friend. A fellow believer."

"Don't give me that nonsense. Who is he?"

"A major general in the U.S. Air Force. His real job is running a top-secret outfit called Division. Two years ago, his organization arranged the purchase of a company in Zug called ZIAG that manufactures high-end engineering products. ZIAG was sending goods to Parvez Jinn in Iran. It was my job to sign off on them. But it's over now."

"What kind of goods?"

Marti looked at von Daniken as if the question were a personal insult. "What kind do you think?"

"I'm a policeman. I prefer that the crooks do the confessing."

"Centrifuges. Maraging steel. That kind of thing. I made sure that all the paperwork passed through the right channels and that no one at customs took too close of a look."

"You mean the machinery to process uranium for nuclear weapons?"

Marti nodded. "It's not my business what they care to do with it."

"What about the attack?"

"I told you. I don't know anything about an attack. I want to stop the drone as much as you."

Von Daniken took this in, squinting as he tried to make some sense of it all. Why would the United States circumvent its own efforts to prevent the Iranians from gaining nuclear weapons technology? He replayed the events of the past days—the murders of Blitz and Lammers, the discovery of the drone and the explosives, and now the revelation that a Swiss company secretly belonging to the Americans had been supplying Iran with state-of-the-art nuclear weapons technology.

Slowly, an idea dawned on him.

A monstrous idea.

He stared at Marti with a new and profound hatred. "Why?"

But Alphons Marti didn't respond. He'd clasped his hands and bowed his head, as if in prayer.

73

At one p.m., Sepp Steiner, chief of Davos Emergency Rescue, left his office on the summit of the Jakobshorn, elevation 2,950 meters above sea level, and walked outside. The forecast had called for a high-pressure system to move in from the south, but so far the sky was as woolly and threatening as ever. He strode to the far side of his office and checked the barometer. The needle was locked steady at 880 millibars. Temperature: −4° Celsius. He flicked the glass with his finger and the needle jumped all the way up to 950.

Turning his face to the sky, he studied the clouds. For the last three days, the ceiling had resembled a becalmed sea. This morning, there was a change. Instead of the gray panorama, he could discern individual clouds. The air was noticeably dryer. The breeze had picked up, but it had changed direction. It was coming from the south.

Steiner rushed back to his office and grabbed a pair of binoculars—Nikon 8x50's that his colleagues joked made him look like a tank commander. Putting them to his eyes, he scanned the mountains from east to west. For the first time in a week, he was able to make out the peaks above Frauenkirchen. He stopped at the Furga, his field glasses trained on Roman's, the near-vertical chute where his older brother had perished so long ago. The woman was still there, lying deep in the crevasse. Steiner would not want to leave his wife to sleep for eternity in the ice.

Just then, the breeze softened. A cleft opened in the clouds directly above his head and an azure sky gazed down. He jogged the few steps to the weather station. The temperature read minus two. The high-pressure front had arrived.

Hurrying indoors, Steiner fired up his radio and alerted his men.

It was time to go back to Roman's.

Three hours later, Steiner's team reached the knoll where Emma Ransom was last seen. They had come by a secondary route used only in fine weather that was favored by alpinists and ice climbers. It was a shorter trek but much steeper, presenting two separate vertical pitches of twenty meters each.

The last traces of the storm system that had sat over the entire country for the past five days had dissipated. Blue sky reigned and the afternoon sun shone fiercely. A vast field of snow glittered with the secrets of a thousand uncut diamonds.

Steiner gazed up the mountain. There was no sign of the life-and-death struggle that had taken place on this spot. Similarly, it was impossible to discern the location of the crevasse.

He ordered his men to spread out in a line. Each held a two-meter probing stick in front of him. Step by step they advanced, jabbing their poles into the snow to test for solid ground. It was Steiner who discovered the crevasse when he thrust his pole into the snow and it kept right on going until he was bent to the knee.

A quarter of an hour later, his men had cleared a ten-meter swath that permitted them a clear path to the fissure. Flags were set in the snow demarcating the crevasse's boundaries, as Steiner supervised the fixing of the ropes. He would be the one to descend into the chasm and retrieve the body. After a final check of his harness and knots, he turned on his miner's light and called, "On belay." Allowing the rope to play through his fingers, he walked backward into the earth.

Inside the crevasse, the air was cooler. As he descended, the ice walls gave way to striated granite. All light from above dimmed. Soon he was stranded in an obscure paradise, his eyes trained on the halo of light emitted by the halogen bulb.

After he'd rappelled one length of rope—exactly forty meters—he saw the body. The woman was lying on her stomach, one arm stretched out above her head as if she were calling for help. The walls fell away and he allowed himself to slide down the rope more quickly, a steady, unbroken descent like a stone dropping into a pond. As he approached the crevasse's floor, he was able to make out the patrolman's cross on her jacket and the fleece of auburn hair covering her face.

His feet touched the earth.

"I'm down," he radioed to his crew.

In the dim light, she looked fragile and at peace. Blood had congealed in pools around her legs and her head. Removing his pack, he took out a body harness, several carabiners, and a balaclava with which to cover her face to avoid any scratches or contusions on the ascent to the surface. He arranged the equipment in a row next to the body. Then, as was his custom, he knelt and offered a prayer for the departed.

Slipping both hands under the woman's torso, he lifted the corpse and flipped it onto its back. This way it would be easier to attach the harness. But immediately, he felt something odd. The long, tangled hair fell away. A load of rocks and snow spilled onto the ground. He stood up holding the empty parka in his hands, staring at the pants still lying on the ground.

A gasp fled Steiner's mouth.

There was no body at all.

74

They were heading in the wrong direction.

Ten minutes had passed since he'd been locked in the trunk. He'd felt the first hairpin leading out of the city, but was still waiting for the downhill chicane that prefaced rejoining the main highway. If he wasn't mistaken, the car was climbing, not descending. He was certain that Simone had a reason for disobeying his instructions. But what was it? Had she caught sight of a roadblock? Had the police closed the highway altogether?

Concerned, Jonathan ran through the functions on his wristwatch. The altimeter read 1,950 meters, then a minute later, 1,960. He was right. They were going uphill. He clicked over to the compass. The car was pointed due east. They were proceeding along the highway that led to Tiefencastel, and then on to St. Moritz. Instead of going toward Zurich and the U.S. consulate, they were heading away from it.

"Simone," he yelled, banging on the roof of the trunk. "Stop the car!"

A few moments later, the car pulled to the side of the road. Jonathan rose on an elbow, his head brushing against the chassis. He felt claustrophobic and increasingly frightened. Footsteps crunched in the snow outside the car. A male voice said a few words. The police? Had they come to a checkpoint? Jonathan held his breath, straining to pick up the conversation.

Just then, a door opened and the car swayed as a passenger climbed in. The door slammed and the car pulled back onto the highway.

"Simone! Who's in there with you?"

He banged harder.

"Simone! Answer me! Who is it?"

The radio began to play, the speakers positioned above his head thumping loudly in time to the bass. The car accelerated and he rolled onto his side.

Eyes open, Jonathan lay back and reviewed the past days' events: Simone's too-rapid arrival in Arosa, her pleas that he leave the country, her reluctance to track down the individual who'd sent Emma the bags, her frustration at his trying to save Blitz's life. All had been ruses to lure him off the scent. When he resisted her imprecations, she'd passed him down the line to the scalp hunters. He tore the Saint Christopher medal from his neck. It had to be some kind of homing beacon. There was no other way to explain how the assassin had been able to follow him to Davos. It did not, however, explain how he'd obtained a pass to enter the green zone. Like Emma, Simone had allies.

Sunlight seeped through the outline of the trunk. With the help of his wristwatch's Lumiglo dial, he found the trunk's lock, concealed behind a fiberboard veneer. Using Emma's keys, he dug at the fiberboard, fashioning a slot and then a hole. When the hole grew large enough, he rammed a finger through it and began to tear away at the veneer.

Finally, the hole grew big enough that he was able to touch the lock. He knew cars, and he was certain that there was a pushpin he could depress to free the catch. He wasn't as certain what he'd do once he opened the trunk. It wouldn't be any wiser to jump out of a car doing a hundred fifty kilometers an hour than to wait for a professional killer to fire a bullet into his skull at point-blank range.

He ran his fingers over the hook-shaped catch, wedged his thumb against it, and pressed for all he was worth. His fingers slipped off the metal. He tried again with the same result.

The car slowed and made a sharp turn to the right, leaving the pavement. They began a series of climbing switchbacks and he braced himself to keep from slamming into the chassis. The whine of the engine testified to the aggressive slope. The sharp turns and the constant speeding up and slowing down made him nauseous. Finally, the hairpin curves ended. He sucked down a deep breath, but it didn't make him feel any better.

Sliding to the rear of the trunk, he pulled back the carpetlike padding beneath him and freed the repair kit stuffed inside the spare tire. The best he could come up with was the tire iron meant to be used with the jack. He tried whacking the lock, hoping that it might break and pop open. No such luck.

The car came to a halt and the engine died. He grasped the tire iron in his right hand. It felt light and ridiculous. Still, he readied himself as best he could to spring from the trunk. He heard a key slip into the lock. The trunk opened and the afternoon sun hit him full in the face, blinding him. Reflexively, he closed his eyes and raised a hand to ward off the glare.

"Get out," said Simone.

Next to her stood a compact man with dark hair, a pale complexion, and dead eyes, holding a pistol at his side. Jonathan needed no introduction.

"If you please," the man said with a quick flick of his pistol. "And don't bother with whatever that is you're holding."

Jonathan dropped the tire iron and climbed out of the car. They had parked in a lay-by a few hundred feet from the top of the mountain. The vista was dramatic, a panorama of towering granite piers in every direction.

"I suppose it's too late to say that I want to leave

the country." Jonathan's throat was suddenly dry. He needed water.

"I tried to warn you off," said Simone.

"Why didn't you tell me you worked with Emma? That would have been enough."

"I don't. In fact, I'm as interested to learn what she was doing as you are."

"Then who are you with?"

Simone just stared at him.

He took a step toward the edge of the lay-by and glimpsed a sheer rock face. He judged it to be a thousand-meter fall to the valley floor.

Simone stretched out her hand. "I need all the information Parvez Jinn gave you."

"He didn't give me anything," said Jonathan.

"You came all this way to see Jinn and you didn't even ask him what he'd smuggled out of the country? I'd have thought he'd have practically pressed it on you."

"I went to see Jinn to ask him if he knew who Emma was working for, and possibly, if she'd told him her real name."

"No, you didn't. You came to Davos to get out of trouble. To get your proof."

Jonathan said nothing.

"Why are you making this so hard?" she asked.

"You don't have to do this, Simone."

"You're right. I don't. But Ricardo, here, does."

Ricardo, the assassin, sniffed the air. "Please, if you

have any information, now is the time to give it to Mrs. Noiret."

"What's your game?" asked Jonathan, ignoring the man who had tried to shoot him in the tunnel and later stab him. "Did you have this guy kill Blitz, too?"

"My game is the same as everyone else's in this business. This is not about playing doctor."

Jonathan took the flash drive out of his pocket and held it in his palm. "Iran's entire nuclear program is on this thing. Jinn thinks it's enough to start a war."

Simone glanced at the drive. "Does he? I don't concern myself with those issues."

"Tell me who you work for and why you wanted Emma so badly. Tell me that, and it's yours."

"I work for the Central Intelligence Agency. I'm your friend. Believe me."

"My friend?" Jonathan shook his head. Spinning, he cocked his arm and threw the flash drive over the cliff.

"Merde!" Simone jumped toward the cliff. Furious, she looked at Jonathan, then at the man named Ricardo. "He's yours."

Jonathan gazed into the sky and took a deep breath. The air was marvelously crisp.

Just then, there was a thudding noise, like a hand slapping a bare back. Jonathan flinched, expecting to feel something sharp and final. He drew a breath. Nothing had struck him.

The assassin collapsed to his knees. A red stain blossomed on his chest. He gasped, and as he fell forward onto the snow, blood poured from his mouth.

Simone spun to look behind her, searching the rugged terrain above them. A figure detached itself from a shelf of rock. A person dressed in black and gray, with a knit cap tight on their head and eyes hidden behind wraparound sunglasses. A hand pulled off the knit cap and a spray of amber hair tumbled free. When she was a few feet away, she took off her sunglasses.

"You," said Simone. "But how . . ."

Emma Ransom raised her pistol and fired a bullet into Simone Noiret's forehead. Simone tottered and retreated a step, stunned and uncomprehending. Emma kicked her savagely in the chest. Simone plummeted off the precipice.

Emma stepped to the edge and watched her fall.

75

She stood ten feet away cradling a strange-looking gun in her arms, some kind of pistol with a silencer and a folding stock. There was no sign of a broken leg. Nor were there any visible injuries sustained from a three-hundred-foot fall. She looked at him as if he were a stranger, offering no indication that she desired to hug or kiss him, or that she was happy to see him at all.

"But I saw you," he said. "In the crevasse."

"You thought you saw me."

"The blood . . . the trail in the snow . . . your leg was broken. I saw the fracture."

"It wasn't my bone. It was all incredibly sloppy. I had to work fast. When I found out—"

"Emma," he said.

"—that it was set for this weekend, I began to—"

"Emma!" he shouted. "Is that even your name?"

Without answering, she turned and began jogging down the hill. Rooted to the spot, Jonathan was filled with a flux of emotions: wonderment, anger, elation, and bitterness, all of them warring with one another. It took him a second or two to sort his feelings out. Still stunned, he followed her down the road to where she'd left her car two switchbacks below. It was a VW Golf that had seen a lot of wear. He made for the driver's side, but she was already there, opening the door and dipping her head inside the cabin. By the time he climbed into the passenger seat, the engine was running, the car in gear and beginning to move.

"I talked to the hospital," he said. "The nurse there told me that the Emma Everett Rose who was born there died in a car accident two weeks after her birth."

"Later," she said. "I'll tell you everything later."

"I don't want everything. I only want the truth."

"The truth, even," she said. "Right now, I need you to tell me something. Jinn's flash drive. You've still got it, right? I mean, you didn't really throw it over the cliff?"

Jonathan dug the second flash drive out of his pocket. "No," he said. "I tossed yours."

She snatched it out of his hand. "I'll forgive you," she said. "This time."

Emma attacked the hill as if it were a racetrack, punching it on the straights, braking into the turns, downshifting crisply. Emma who couldn't manage a stick to save her life.

Until now, he'd kept her identities separate. There was Emma Ransom, his wife, and there was Eva Kruger, the operative. He'd convinced himself that Emma was the true side of her—the authentic side— and that Eva was the cover. Watching her drive, he knew he'd been wrong. For the first time, he was seeing the real Emma, the woman she'd never allowed him to see. It came to him then that he didn't know this woman.

"I didn't expect you to be so good at this," she said, when they reached the valley floor and turned west toward Davos and Zurich.

"What did you expect?"

"I was afraid you might chuck it all and disappear into the mountains for a few years. Pull the lone explorer bit."

"I might have, if I hadn't gotten the baggage claims. Everything went haywire when I picked up the bags. After I killed the policemen, I had to keep going. It was the only way to clear myself. Simone tried to convince me to leave the country, but when I saw what was inside the bag, I couldn't run away. I had to know."

"Of all the days for the train not to deliver the mail," she said with a dismissive shake of the head. "I guess I was wrong about you going into the mountains."

"I'll forgive you," he said. "This time."

She laughed at this, but it was a concession and it rang hollow.

"And so," he said. "Your turn. I'll make it easy for you. Start with the mountain. What exactly did I see?"

A shadow fell across her features. Her change in mood was like a sharp drop in temperature. "Your patrolman's jacket, of course. A wig. Ski pants. Stage blood."

"How did you get down into the crevasse by yourself? It was way too dangerous to go solo."

"I didn't."

"What do you mean you didn't?" he snapped.

"I walked into it from below. You showed me the route once the summer after we were married."

Jonathan closed his eyes as it came back to him. They'd come to Davos for a weekend to do some hiking and had spent an afternoon exploring the warren of caves and couloirs that honeycombed the glacier. "But those caves are only accessible during the summer. You can't get in during winter, let alone during a blizzard."

Emma tilted her head, which was her way of saying he was mistaken. "I didn't go to that meeting in Amsterdam last Friday. I came here instead to see if my plan was actionable."

" 'Actionable'? Is that spyspeak or what?"

Emma ignored the remark. "It turns out that if you can find your way to the right spot at the base of the glacier, you can get into the caves. I programmed a handheld GPS unit, then route-marked the way up and back so I wouldn't get lost if it snowed."

"Which is why you insisted that we come to Arosa instead of Zermatt," he said, feeling somehow complicit.

"I had good reason. It was our anniversary. We made our first climb here eight years ago."

" 'Our anniversary.' Right." He knew then that she'd also lied about the weather report and sabotaged his two-way radio. "How did you know we wouldn't go down and get you?"

"I didn't really," she admitted. "I gambled on the fact that Steiner and his team would be coming up the mountain to rescue a woman with a broken leg, not haul her out of a one-hundred-meter crevasse. Rope is heavy. I didn't see them bringing more than was necessary. I was surprised they even had two lengths."

"Steiner . . . you know his name." He looked out the window. The hits just kept on coming.

"I had to hang around Davos to make sure things went as planned. I listened to his phone calls and radio transmissions. Don't look so surprised. It's a piece of cake to pull a cellular call out of the air."

"And then? Didn't you know that I would check on the baggage claims?"

"I hoped you wouldn't get them. I wanted to retrieve the bags in Landquart myself, but it was too much of a risk. Once I was dead, I had to stay dead."

Jonathan spun in his seat. "**You were there?** You

saw what happened at the train station with the police? You watched what they did to me?"

Emma nodded. "I'm sorry, Jonathan. I wanted to help."

He sank back, at a loss for words.

She went on. "Afterward, I trailed you back to the hotel, but I was too late. Some of our team had already been through the room. You arrived soon after they'd left. I didn't have time to get inside. Once, I thought you might have seen me. It was in the woods behind the hotel."

Jonathan recalled sensing the presence nearby and looking into the tree line, but he'd seen nothing.

Suddenly, he'd had enough. He wasn't interested in the who, what, and when. It was all just window dressing. He wanted to know why. "What's this about, Em?" he said quietly. "What are you involved in?"

"The usual," she replied, never taking her eyes from the road.

"You're supplying Parvez Jinn with restricted equipment to enrich uranium. That hardly qualifies as the usual."

"Nothing he wasn't going to get sooner or later."

"Don't act like that."

"Like what?"

"Cynical. Like you don't care."

"It's because I care that I'm doing what I'm doing."

"What **are** you doing? Who do you work for? The CIA? The Brits?"

"The CIA? God no. I'm at Defense. The Pentagon. Something called Division."

"But Simone said she was with the CIA."

Emma considered this, brushing her cheek with her fingers. "Really? Actually, I didn't know about her until today."

"Why would the CIA want to kill someone who works for the Pentagon? We're both on the same side, aren't we?"

"Power. They want it. We have it. The tug of war's been going on for a couple of years."

"But I thought you hated the American government."

A thin smile told him that he was way off base. Another illusion gone.

"So, you're American?" he asked.

"God, I wanted to wait to get into all of this. It's so bloody complicated." She ran a hand through her hair. "Yes, Jonathan, I'm American. If you're wondering about the accent, it's real. I grew up outside London. My father was with the U.S. Air Force stationed at Lakenheath."

"Did he steer you into this?"

"In the beginning, it was because of family, I suppose. Daddy being in the military and all. But I stayed because I'm good at it. Because I'm making a difference for something I believe in. Because I like it. I keep doing it for the same reason that you keep being a doctor. Because our job is who we are and nothing much else matters."

"Is that why you picked me?"

"At first, yes."

"You mean something changed?"

"You know what changed. We fell in love."

"I fell in love," said Jonathan. "I'm not sure you did."

Emma looked at him sharply. "I didn't have to stay with you. No one forced me to marry you."

"They didn't stop you, either. Who better to slide you into position for your assignments than a doctor who actually enjoyed serving in hardship posts? What exactly did you do in all those places? Did you kill people? Are you an assassin like that guy you shot back there?"

"Of course not." Emma dismissed the suggestion as if she'd never fired a gun, let alone shot and killed two human beings within the last thirty minutes.

"What then?"

"I can't tell you."

"You and Blitz and Hoffmann were selling uranium enrichment equipment to Iran. Jinn believed that you supplied the equipment in order to start a war. He said that we made a mistake going into Iraq without proof that they possessed WMD and that we weren't going to do it again."

"Did Parvez say all that? May he roast in hell forever."

"That's a nice way to talk about a man you screwed."

"Fuck you, Jonathan! That's not fair."

"Not fair? You lied to me for eight years. You pretended to be my wife. Don't tell me what's fair."

"I **am** your wife."

"How can you say that when I don't even know your name!"

Emma looked away. If he'd been expecting a tear, he was disappointed. Her expression was set in stone.

"Well?" he demanded. "Is it true? Are you trying to start a war?"

"We're trying to stop one."

"By handing out nukes?"

"We're only hastening matters along, so we can control how the situation develops. We supply Iran with the technology they so desperately want now, and then expose their work to the world. It's about being proactive. We can't afford to be caught unawares. Not this time. And besides, it won't be a war. It will strictly be an air campaign."

"Is that supposed to make me feel better?"

"Don't be so damned naïve. Some people can't be allowed to possess nuclear weapons. If Iran gets them, you can jolly well bet that the really bad boys will have them soon after. That's all there is to it."

"And what's going to happen when they retaliate?"

"With what?" Emma asked. "We gave them the equipment to make a little enriched uranium. Now we're going to take it away."

"Jinn said they have cruise missiles. If anyone

attacks their enrichment facilities, they won't hesitate to use them. The president of his country is planning to announce all this to the world next week."

"Jinn was lying," said Emma with the same unalloyed confidence, but her face had gone pale. "Iran doesn't have any cruise missiles."

"He called them Kh-55's. He said that they'd come into possession of four of them a year ago and that they're at their base in Karshun on the Persian Gulf."

"He was bullshitting you."

"Can you take that chance? If the United States or Israel bombs Iran, the mullahs in Teheran will turn right around and launch on Jerusalem and the Saudi oil fields. Then what do you think will happen?"

"Christ." Emma frowned, the muscles in her jaw working furiously. "Kh-55's? You're sure of it?"

"You know what they are?"

"The Russians called them the Granat, or pomegranate. They're long-range subsonic cruise missiles capable of carrying a nuclear warhead. They're old as sin and the guidance systems are out of date, but they work."

"Not good," said Jonathan.

"No, not good at all." Emma frowned. "He talked about having a surprise for me when I saw him in Davos. Double-dealer."

Jonathan saw that he'd struck a nerve. "If you're so sure of yourself, why did you have to disappear?"

"Sure of myself? God, do you really believe that?"

Emma looked over at him. "Do you know what a drone is?"

"More or less. One of those remote-controlled planes that fly around forever taking pictures. I know they can fire missiles, too."

"There's one in Switzerland now being readied for an attack. I wasn't supposed to know about it, but Blitz let it slip. He was my controller, the only one who was allowed to see the whole picture. He said it was going to be the most important thing we'd ever done. It was the boss's personal mission."

"You mean, it's you guys—it's **Division**—that's planning on taking someone out with it?"

"Not someone. Something. A passenger jet."

"They're going to shoot it down here? In Switzerland? My God, Emma, we've got to tell the police."

"They already know. At least, some of it. The man who tried to stop you back there in Davos is running the investigation. His name is Marcus von Daniken. He heads up the Service for Analysis and Prevention, the Swiss counterespionage service. He's convinced that you're masterminding the plot."

"Me?"

"Essentially, it boils down to the fact that von Daniken believes that you are me."

"Because I was at Blitz's house?"

"Among other things, yes. You were smart not to go to the police. You'd have spent the rest of your life in jail. Killing the policemen was the least of it. You knew too much about Thor . . . about **Division**. We have friends who would have seen to it. Anyway, that's why I had to disappear. I decided that I have to stop this whole thing. I have enough blood on my hands, but until now, it's never come from innocents."

"So you know when it's going to happen?"

"In a few hours, more or less."

"Then what are you doing here?"

For the first time, Emma met his gaze full-on. "I'm still your wife."

She reached out her hand and Jonathan slipped his fingers into hers.

"We have to tell von Daniken," he said.

Emma glanced at him, her eyes wet with tears. "I'm afraid it's not that simple."

76

The official in the Passport Control booth at Zurich Kloten Airport looked out at the long line of arrivals. The flight was just in from Washington Dulles. He checked his monitor for any passenger warnings. The screen was blank. He gazed out over the procession of well-fed faces and ample girths. Not a suspicious character in the lot.

"Next," he called.

A tall, portly gentleman approached and laid his passport on the counter. The official opened the passport and slid the data stripe through the scanner. Name: Leonard Blake. Home: Palm Beach. Date of birth: January 1, 1955.

"The purpose of your visit, Mr. Blake?"

"Business."

He checked the man against the photograph. Gray hair cropped close. Tan. A trim mustache. Expensive sunglasses. Gold Rolex. And a polyester tracksuit. **When would Americans learn how to dress?**

"How long will you be staying?"

"Just a day or two."

The official checked his monitor. Blake's name hadn't raised any flags. Just another rich American without a shred of taste. He brought the stamp down hard. "Enjoy your stay."

"Danke schön."

The passport official winced at the man's accent. He waved to the woman at the head of the line. "Next!"

Mr. Leonard Blake collected his bags, then proceeded to the car rental desk, where he had reserved a midsize sedan. After filling out the necessary paperwork, he walked into the parking garage and located the car. He put his bags in the backseat and climbed behind the wheel. He spent a moment adjusting the mirrors and the seat. All the while, he surveyed the lot. The place was still as a grave. He unzipped the tracksuit and peeled off the prosthetic padding that added twenty pounds to his weight and eight inches to his midsection. He set the padding in the backseat, then started the ignition and drove out of the garage.

He headed south on the highway. In twenty minutes, he was in the city center. He found a parking space on Talstrasse and strolled the two blocks to the

Bahnhofstrasse, the famed artery that ran from the Lake of Zurich to the main train station. Along the way, he passed several fashionable boutiques. Chanel. Cartier. Louis Vuitton. It was said that the two kilometers of Zurich's Bahnhofstrasse constituted the most expensive real estate on earth. Leonard Blake had not come to Zurich to shop, however.

He continued south, walking toward the lake, then turned up a narrow street. He made good use of the many shop windows, slowing long enough to use their reflections to observe the pedestrians behind him. Seeing nothing of worry, he quickened his pace.

He stopped at the third entrance on the right. The baroque wooden doors were unmarked, except for a discreet plate engraved with an intertwined "G" and "B." The letters stood for the Gessler Bank.

Inside, a porter in a frock coat greeted him. Blake wrote his name and account number on a slip of paper. The porter placed a hushed phone call. A minute passed, and a bank officer emerged from a long hallway. "Good morning, Mr. Blake," he said in impeccable English. "How may we be of service?"

"I'd like to access my safety deposit box."

"Please follow me."

The two men entered an elevator and descended three floors beneath street level. The elevator opened and the official led Blake into a floor-to-ceiling vault, whose open door was policed by two armed guards. Blake was shown into a private viewing room, where he offered the banker his key. A minute later, the banker returned, carrying a large safety deposit box. "Ring for me when you're ready."

Blake closed the door. Though there was no need, he locked it, then took off his sunglasses and sat down.

You could never be too safe, thought Philip Palumbo as he opened the safety deposit box. He removed a manila envelope containing valid Brazilian passports for himself and each member of his family, identified as the Perreras. Also in the box were packets of Swiss francs, U.S. dollars, and euros, amounting to one hundred thousand dollars. The money was legally earned and fully taxed. It was his runaway money. A man in his line of work made serious enemies. One day, he was certain, they would come for him. And when they did, he would be ready. He picked up a packet of ten thousand dollars. He could take the money and disappear. He had rabbit holes at five spots around the globe where he might hide. It would take years to find him.

He dropped the money back into the box.

He wasn't built to run.

By his calculations, he had thirty-six hours to accomplish his mission and return home. An hour from now, at approximately 0700 Eastern Standard Time, Admiral Lafever's body would be discovered by his driver. He would find the house burgled, the admiral dead in his study, shot while confronting the thief. The police would arrive soon after. Word would hit Langley by nine. News of the murder would be hushed up until the director could verify all the facts and put together a plausible story. Palumbo was well aware that, despite his best efforts, no one would buy the burglary story.

It would be another three hours before an official declaration was made. Noon in D.C., six p.m. in Zurich. Inquiries would begin in earnest, Lafever's agenda scoured, his closest associates questioned. At some point—probably not until late in the afternoon, or even tomorrow—Joe Leahy would come forward and mention the conversation he'd had with Palumbo in the cafeteria the day before. Palumbo's interest in Lafever and Operation Mourning Dove would be duly noted. Still, there would be many similar threads to trace. A man did not get to be the deputy director of operations—the nation's top spymaster, as it were—without having rivals, both inside the Agency and outside of it. In the event that the Agency phoned his home, Palumbo's wife knew what to say. She would contact her husband on his cell phone and he would call back promptly. An interview with Palumbo would not be a priority.

At some point, though, the Virginia police department's forensic squad would discover traces of Lafever's brains in the backyard and realize that the body had been moved. Then things would get seriously crazy.

Thirty-six hours was the max.

Palumbo picked up a second large envelope from

the box. This one was considerably heavier than the first. He opened it and slid the contents onto the table. The Walther PPK hadn't been touched in three years. He checked the magazine and the slide, and was pleased to find it in perfect condition. The envelope also contained a silencer, but he didn't think he'd need it today.

He closed the box, locked it, and rang for the banker.

Five minutes later, he was back on the street.

It was after two p.m. local time when he drove across the Limmatbrucke and headed into the bustling Seefeld district. His destination was a drab commercial building one block from the lakeside. Soldiers dressed in olive utilities and Kevlar vests, brandishing the regulation M16A1 machine gun of the United States Army, patrolled the street in front of Dufourstrasse 47, home to the American consulate. A pair of uniformed city police kept them company.

Three black Mercedes sedans crowded the sidewalk in front of the building. The cars all bore diplomatic plates with small American flags pasted to the upper right-hand corner. They were all the proof he needed to be certain that Major General John Austen, founder and director of the covert spy agency known as Division, was in the house.

Austen was a legend across all branches of the service. He had the record everyone aspired to. He was the hellraiser gone straight. Or, to use his own language, the Fallen Angel resurrected to stand at the right hand of the Lord; the Lord in this case being the president of the United States.

An honor graduate from the Air Force Academy class of 1967, Austen was trained as a jet pilot and sent to Vietnam, where he flew over 120 missions at the controls of an F-4 Phantom and shot down nine North Vietnamese MiGs. He came out of the war an ace, and a major before the age of thirty.

But there were chinks in his armor. When he wasn't flying, he was carousing. Night after night, he led his band of merry fliers through Saigon's depraved fleshpots, drinking to abandon and screwing everything in sight. They called themselves Austen's Rangers, in honor of the marauding World War II force of similar name. There were rumors of drug use, too, of rape, and on one occasion, of murder. But the rumors were hushed up. No one wanted to dent, tarnish, or in any way damage the halo of a bona fide hero.

Then came 1979 and the Iranian hostage crisis. Austen was a natural for the team put together by Colonel Charlie Beckwith. An instructor and test pilot after the war, he transitioned to the massive Hercules C-130 transports that would ferry the commandos into the Iranian desert. For once, his luck didn't hold. Horrifically burned in the accident that took eight servicemen's lives, he came out of the desert a changed man. He denied retirement and fought himself back to health and a position as director of the newly created Special Operations Command situated at MacDill Air Force Base in Tampa, Florida. He attributed his survival to a miracle and gave over his life to Jesus Christ.

Instead of carousing, Austen ran Bible study and prayer meetings out of his home. Every Tuesday and Friday night, the Austen house on Orange Lane was filled with sinners, soldiers, and any officer seeking a more rapid path to promotion and glory. Austen quickly built a loyal—some said slavish—cadre of officers who spread out through the four branches of the service. They, too, called themselves Austen's Rangers, but this time they preached the word of Christ and the ultra-hawkish political views of their founder and namesake. America was the city on the hill, the beacon of democracy for the entire world. And Israel was its closest ally, to be defended at all costs.

Austen's rise was nothing short of meteoric. Full colonel at forty, brigadier general at forty-three, a second star coming before his forty-sixth birthday. He appeared alongside the nation's most famous Evangelicals on Sunday morning television programs. He was called God's warrior and Jesus's pilot. He became the face of the religious right.

And then, his career seemed to stall. He never received a third star, or the divisional command that came with it. He stopped appearing on television. He took up residence in the Pentagon as head of a career morgue called the Defense Human Intelligence Agency, and all but fell off the face of the earth. But inside the armed forces, his presence was still felt. Hundreds of Austen's Rangers had reached flag rank and were generals in the army and admirals in the navy. All were still devoted to John Austen.

It was then, Palumbo realized, that Austen must have started Division. He hadn't fallen off the earth. To the contrary. He'd ascended to a more glorified place.

Palumbo drove another one hundred meters past the consulate. When he found an empty parking space, he told himself that fortune was smiling upon him. His fevered mind was anxious for any signs that he hadn't risked his career and dismissed the needs of his wife and family for nothing. He grabbed the spot, then pulled his workbag onto his lap. In it were two cell phones, a Taser gun, and a cellular GSM intercept device disguised as a laptop computer. He activated the intercept device and tuned it to search frequencies for numbers beginning with a 455 prefix—the prefix assigned to phones issued by the United States embassy to its staff, both permanent and visiting. Fitting the earpiece, he jumped from conversation to conversation.

It hadn't been difficult to track John Austen down. Like all good spies, Austen lived his cover. A major general and director of the Defense Human Intelligence Agency, his whereabouts were a matter of record at all times. A call from Palumbo's office at the CIA to Austen's office at the Pentagon had revealed

that Austen was on a tour of Western European cap-
itals in order to liaise with the military attachés
under his supervision. Earlier in the week, he'd visited the embassy in Bern and made day trips to Paris
and Rome. At two p.m. Friday afternoon, he was
scheduled to visit the American consulate in Zurich.
The fact that military attachés were not assigned to
consulates seemed to have been overlooked by everyone other than Palumbo. He knew that Austen had
come to Zurich for a specific reason, and that reason
was the drone. He also knew that Austen was scheduled to fly back to the States early the next morning.
It was what he planned to do with the intervening
hours that terrified Palumbo.

He listened in on a half-dozen conversations before picking up a snatch of English.

"We're just leaving. Everything ready?"

He recognized Austen's smoke-cured Texan twang
in an instant.

"Good to go, sir," came the reply. "We're sitting
tight and waiting."

"I'll be there in half an hour."

The call ended. Palumbo mapped the GPS coordinates of the intercepted transmission. A red dot su-
perimposed on a street map of Zurich showed the
location of the primary, or initiating, call to be Dufourstrasse 47, the address of the U.S. consulate. The
secondary, or receiving, party was sited in Glattbrugg, a town contiguous to Zurich. More interesting than the address was its location. The dot sat one

hundred meters from the southernmost boundary of Zurich Airport. Bingo.

He looked in the rearview mirror as a column of men filed out of the building and climbed into the waiting Mercedes. The visit from the director of the Defense Human Intelligence Agency had concluded. The cars pulled onto the street and sped past Palumbo. He knew better than to try to follow them through the congested traffic and one-way streets of an unfamiliar European city. Either he'd lose them or he'd be spotted. Setting the laptop on the passenger seat, he started the engine. He knew exactly where Austen was going. The problem wasn't strategy, but execution. Palumbo had to get there first.

He drove aggressively, dodging trams, beating yellow lights, taking the car up to a hundred and eighty kilometers an hour on the autobahn. All the while, he listened in on a constant stream of calls made from Austen's phone. Most were official and dealt with problems experienced by the attachés under his supervision. But several were more cryptic in nature. No names were spoken. The conversations ran to abbreviated bursts with mentions of "locking down the command center," "moving to the main house," and most frightening, "the guest's right on time."

Palumbo reached Glattbrugg in eighteen minutes. The address was located in a quiet residential district with plenty of trees and homes spaced twenty meters apart. He parked behind a line of modest automobiles. He'd hardly turned off the engine when he saw the black Mercedes with diplomatic plates approach in his rearview. As expected, it was alone. Austen had abandoned his cover. He was acting in his capacity as director of Division.

As the Mercedes passed, Palumbo got a glimpse of the man in the front seat. A wisp of graying hair, a noble profile, the skin of his face too tight, oddly shiny and furrowed.

The burn. Austen's badge of honor.

Palumbo started the car and pulled in behind the Mercedes. It turned into a driveway a hundred meters up the street. Palumbo brought his car to a halt behind it, blocking Austen's retreat. He was out in a flash, storming the driver's door, pressing his badge against the window. The badge was a fake, but it bought him a few seconds.

The driver opened the door, raising his hands to show that he meant no harm. Palumbo pulled him to his feet and jabbed the Taser into his neck. Ten thousand volts turned the driver's knees to Jell-O. He fell to the ground, unconscious. Palumbo slid into the driver's seat and slammed the door. "Hello, General," he said.

"Who the hell are you?" asked John Austen.

Palumbo had no time for explanations. "It's over," he said. "We're shutting down this op right now."

"What are you talking about?"

Palumbo dropped the Taser and pulled the Walther pistol from his jacket. "What plane are you targeting?" he demanded.

"Whoever the hell you are, you'd better have a damned good excuse for assaulting my aide."

"What flight are you going after?"

"Get out of my car!"

Palumbo jabbed his thumb into the crease between Austen's jaw and his ear and held the pressure point. The general's mouth froze in a silent, paralyzed scream, the sensation of the grip akin to having a sword rammed through the top of his skull. "What aircraft are you planning to shoot down?" Palumbo repeated. He released the pressure point and the general bent double.

"Who sent you?" Austen gasped. "Lafever? Are you the one who killed Lammers and Blitz?"

Palumbo pressed the pistol to Austen's cheek. Up close, his face had the sheen of day-old floor wax and was pulled as tight as a drum. "Where's the drone? I'm going to put a bullet in your skull if you don't tell me."

"You wouldn't dare."

"Are you sure about that?"

"Go ahead. It won't change a thing."

"Yes, it will. You'll be dead, and that drone won't be up there blowing a plane full of innocent people out of the sky."

"No one is innocent. We're all born in sin."

"Speak for yourself. Where's the main house? I heard you say that you were moving to the main house."

Austen closed his eyes. " 'Oh, the joy of having

nothing and being nothing,' " he recited. " 'Seeing nothing but a Living Christ in glory, and being careful for nothing but His interests down here.' "

Palumbo glanced out the window. The driver was still out cold. There was some motion behind the curtains of a picture window above the garage. He found the pressure point again and held it, longer this time. "Where's the drone? Is it here? Is this the main house?"

He released his grip.

Austen gazed at him. There were tears in his eyes, but whether they were from pain or some perverted sense of sacrifice, Palumbo couldn't tell.

"Thank you," said Austen.

"For what?"

"Christ had his test. He persevered and was delivered. Now, it's my turn."

"Christ was no murderer."

"Don't you see? All the conditions are as prophesied in Revelation. The Israelites hold Jerusalem. The Lord is ready to return. You can't do a thing to stop it. None of us can. We can only help it on its way."

He's raving, thought Palumbo. "What flight are you going after? I know it's tonight."

But Austen wasn't listening anymore, except to his own voice. "The Lord spoke to me. He told me that I am the vessel of His will. You can't stop me. He won't allow it."

"It's nobody's will but your own."

Outside, a door slammed. Two men appeared at

the top of the stairs leading to the house. Palumbo put his hand to the ignition, but the keys weren't there. He looked at Austen, and Austen stared back, as defiant as ever. Palumbo knew then that Austen was the one. He was the man who was going to pilot the drone.

Palumbo raised the gun to Austen's temple. "I can't allow you to kill all those people."

A shadow to his left blotted out the sun. The window shattered, spraying glass across the cabin. A hand reached in and grabbed him. Palumbo knocked it away. Austen was flailing at the gun. Palumbo elbowed him in the face, knocking him back into his seat. Then he raised his gun. As he did, someone took hold of his collar and yanked him backward. He fired the weapon. The bullet blew out the passenger window. A fist pounded his temple and he dropped the weapon. The door was flung open and he felt himself being dragged out of the car and onto the driveway. It couldn't end this way, he thought, kicking and struggling.

The plane . . . **someone** has to warn them.

And then a boot struck him in the head and the world turned dark.

77

El Al Flight 8851, nonstop service from Tel Aviv to Zurich, took off from Ben Gurion International Airport on schedule at 4:12 p.m. local time. The pilot, Captain Eli Zuckerman, a twenty-six-year veteran of the airline and former fighter pilot, with a combined seven thousand hours in command, announced that flying time aboard the Airbus A380 was scheduled to be three hours and fifty-five minutes. Weather en route was slated to be calm with little or no turbulence. The airliner would overfly Cyprus, Athens, Macedonia, and Vienna, before touching down in Zurich at 8:07 p.m. Central European Time. Zuckerman, an armchair historian in his spare time, might have added that these great locales were sites of battles waged by men with names like Alexander, Caesar, Tamerlane, and Napoleon. Battles that had determined the course of civilization for centuries to follow.

The flight that evening was full. Six hundred seventy-three names filled the manifest. Among them was Dahlia Borer of Jerusalem, director of the Israeli Red Cross; Abner Parker of Boca Raton, Florida, an American retiree who had lost both legs in Vietnam to friendly fire; Zane Cassidy of Edmond, Oklahoma, pastor of the Messiah Bible Church and leader of a tour group of seventy-seven Evangelical Christians; Meyer Cohen, leader of the National Religious Party, en route to Washington, D.C., to lobby the American Congress to favor expansion of settlements on the West Bank; and Yasser Mohammed, Arab Israeli member of the Knesset, also en route to Washington, D.C., to lobby the American Congress to forbid any further expansion of settlements on the West Bank.

These last two were seated next to each other. After an exploratory conversation and an exchange of political views, one took out a chessboard. The two men spent the rest of the flight in companionable silence, hunched over their knights and pawns.

Three hundred seventy men, three hundred women, including sixty-four children. Plus a crew of eighteen.

After the plane had reached its cruising altitude of 37,000 feet, Zuckerman addressed the passengers a second time, announcing that he was turning off the seat belt sign and that everyone was welcome to stroll about the two-story aircraft, the newest in the El Al fleet. He was pleased to add that they had picked up a considerable tailwind that would trim their flying time. The new arrival time was set at 7:50 p.m. Fifteen minutes ahead of schedule.

He wished all aboard a pleasant flight, and in closing, stated that he would speak with the passengers again shortly before landing.

78

"No," **said von Daniken** into the phone. "We don't have any details regarding a specific threat. All we know is that there's a terrorist cell operating in the country which has as its goal the destruction of an airliner on our soil. We don't know who they are, or where they are at this moment. But, I repeat: we do know that they're here, most probably in Zurich or Geneva. All our evidence points to an attempt on an aircraft, either airborne or at the terminal, within the next forty-eight hours."

He was speaking to the director of the Federal Office of Civil Aviation, the organization that had final say on all matters concerning flights originating or terminating at Swiss airports. The man was a friend, a former messmate in the army, but friendship didn't come into play with matters of such magnitude.

"Let me get this straight, Marcus. You want us to shut down all major airports in the country until further notice?"

"Yes."

"But that means canceling all outgoing flights and rerouting incoming aircraft to airports in France, Germany, and Italy."

"I'm aware of that," said von Daniken.

"You're talking about over one hundred flights tonight alone. Do you have any idea of the impact that would have on the entire European flight grid?"

"I wouldn't be making the request if it wasn't absolutely necessary."

There was a pause and von Daniken could sense the man's anguish. "I'll need the president's authority on this," said the director of civil aviation.

"Madam President is out of the country. She can't be reached at the moment."

"What about the vice president?"

"I spoke with him and he's unwilling to make a decision until he speaks with her."

"Have you talked to the Federal Security Service? All security aboard aircraft inside our borders is under their purview."

"I just got off the phone with them. It's a non-starter. The most they can do is to pass on a warning to all pilots. Advising them won't help. We believe the attack is to be conducted with an armed drone. Commercial airliners aren't built to take evasive maneuvers."

"No," agreed the chief of civil aviation. "They're not. What about the army?"

"The minister of defense has authorized them to position batteries of Stinger air-to-ground missiles around the airports in Zurich, Geneva, and Lugano. Unfortunately, they won't be in place until tomorrow morning."

Von Daniken didn't add what the general in charge of air defense had told him. **The problem is,** he'd said, **that the Stinger might just as easily shoot down the passenger plane as the drone.**

"I'm sorry, Marcus, but my hands are tied. The moment you hear something from the president, let me know. In the meantime, I'll issue a warning to air traffic control. Good luck."

"Thanks."

Von Daniken put down the phone.

Maps of Zurich and Geneva were spread across two of the desks. Myer stood beside the map of Zurich. With a pen, he was dividing the area around each airport into search grids.

Von Daniken approached and leaned over the maps. "How many officers do we have on this?"

"Fifty two-man teams are working the communities around Zurich Flughafen. In Geneva, just thirty-five. They're going door to door asking if anyone has seen a black or white van, or any suspicious activity."

Von Daniken bit back his anger. Combined, the

police forces of the country's two largest cities numbered more than ten thousand. One hundred seventy
was a paltry commitment.

"It's all the chiefs were willing to spare," explained
Myer. "Marti is a federal councilor and justice minister. They know his feelings about all this."

"Do they? Well, Marti's feelings have changed.
We'll have to call them up and let them know."

Von Daniken studied the map. Four communities,
or **Gemeindes,** surrounded Zurich Airport: Glattbrugg, Opfikon, Oerlikon, and Kloten. A total of
sixty thousand inhabitants in some eight thousand
homes and apartment buildings. Myer shaded in the
neighborhoods that had already been canvassed with
a pink pen. The pie-shaped sliver covered less than
ten percent of the total area.

"And so?" von Daniken asked. "What's the latest?"

"A dozen or so sightings of a black VW van, in-
variably belonging to a neighbor. Nothing suspicious to report except the usual. Someone peeking
in their windows at night, someone siphoning gas
from their car, a couple of drunk teenagers singing
too loudly. But no terrorists with a state-of-the-art
drone."

"Not one mention of a miniature aircraft with a
twenty-five-foot wingspan rolling down the street in
front of their house, eh?"

"Not a one," said Myer.

Von Daniken sat on the edge of the desk.

"What about Marti? Is he going down?" asked Myer.

Von Daniken shook his head. He explained that as it stood, Alphons Marti would never see the inside of a jail. Tobi Tingeli had violated Swiss bank statutes by showing von Daniken a client's correspondence. Evidence of the monthly transfers from the U.S. Defense Department's accounts to Marti's would never be admissible in a court of law. Likewise, von Daniken could not obtain a warrant to search ZIAG's premises unless Marti gave sworn testimony before an investigating magistrate about the company exporting contraband materials. Marti would be forced out of the government, but it would be done under the guise of a resignation for reasons of ill health, or some other ruse.

"So he gets off," said Myer.

Von Daniken shrugged. "I'm sure you and I might find some ways to make his life more interesting down the road."

"It will be a goddamned pleasure."

Von Daniken poured himself a cup of coffee and sat down at his desk. He couldn't stop thinking about Marti being on the Americans' payroll. Export licenses. Dual-use goods. It had all the smell of a setup. But to what end? Why equip your enemy with the devil's handiwork?

He finished the coffee, then called Philip Palumbo. He was anxious to see if his contact at the

CIA had dug up any information about the assassin who'd killed Lammers and, as the latest medical reports confirmed, Gottfried Blitz, a.k.a. Mahmoud Quitab. The call rolled over to voice mail. Von Daniken left his name and number, but no word of the reason for his call. Palumbo wouldn't need any prompting.

The Americans. Everywhere you looked, there they were. The key was Ransom. He'd met with Blitz and with Jinn. He was the sole figure to straddle both operations.

Just then, he spotted Hardenberg bustling across the floor. He wasn't wearing a jacket and his belly jostled back and forth like an unrestrained bowling ball.

"Sir," he called, not able to wait until he drew nearer. "I've got something."

"Get your breath first."

"It's about the Excelsior Trust, the one in Curaçao," Hardenberg continued, huffing. "I had the idea that if it held title to one house, it might hold title to another. I wasn't in the meeting with General Chabert, but I was told that he was certain that the drone had to have some kind of operations base that would grant the pilot a direct line of sight to the aircraft."

"That's correct."

"Based on that reasoning, I contacted the tax recorder and asked him to check the name of the trust against any recent property sales in all the communities surrounding the Zurich and Geneva airports."

"And?" Von Daniken locked his hands behind his back, hoping he wouldn't appear too anxious.

"So far, only two of seven communities have reported back, but it seems that the Excelsior Trust purchased a home in Glattbrugg."

Von Daniken swallowed, hope sparking like kindling in his belly. Glattbrugg was the community directly contiguous to the Zurich Airport. "Where in Glattbrugg, precisely?"

"The home is located less than a kilometer from the southernmost tip of the runway."

79

The assignment went to 69 Squadron of the Israeli Air Force, also known as the Hammers. Operating out of Tel Nof Air Force Base southeast of Tel
Aviv in the Negev Desert, 69 Squadron was comprised of twenty-seven McDonnell Douglas F-151
Thunder aircraft. Powered by two Pratt & Whitney
turbofan engines, the F-151 was capable of speeds up
to Mach 2.5 or some 1,875 miles per hour, and had
a range of two thousand nautical miles. It would be
able to strike seventy percent of the prescribed targets inside Iran without airborne refueling. More important, the F-151 was the only aircraft in the Israeli
Air Force capable of carrying the B61-11 EPW.

The nuclear-tipped bunker busters sat in their
cradles on the gleaming concrete floor. The bombs
were intimidating just to look at. Twenty-five feet in
length, they bore four fins behind a sharp nose and

four more on the tail. The B61-11 was slim as far as airborne munitions go. Its two-foot four-inch diameter corresponded exactly to the eight-inch artillery barrel of the deactivated M110 howitzer used in its manufacture. Equipped with a delayed-reaction fuse, it would strike the earth at a speed of two thousand feet per second and burrow through fifty feet of granite or reinforced concrete prior to detonation. Armed with a ten-kiloton warhead, the bomb and the seismic shock waves it would generate would destroy any structure up to two hundred fifty feet underground. It would also throw over sixty thousand tons of radioactive waste into the atmosphere.

"Just in time," said General Danny Ganz as he walked alongside Zvi Hirsch inside the large hangar.

"A miracle," Hirsch agreed.

Nearby, a team of airmen wheeled one of the bunker busters across the polished concrete floor. Positioning it beneath the plane's bay, they jacked up the gurney and fastened the projectile to the internal bomb rack. Hirsch and Ganz watched as the team attached a second bomb, and then a third. Ganz sighed inwardly at the sight. He was tired of the fighting. Tired of the constant vigilance. He wondered if Israel would ever have the luxury of peace.

"The first wave will concentrate on the newly discovered enrichment facility at Chalus," he said. "After that, we'll go after their missile launchers and warhead fabrication plants. Some Sayeret men are going in tonight to paint the targets in advance of our birds. We'll helo them in from our boats in the Gulf."

"Tonight?" asked Zvi Hirsch, more than a little confused. "Isn't that a bit rash? Remember what the president said: We can't go off half-cocked. We need a reason."

Ganz crossed his arms. "I received a phone call a few minutes ago from a friend in the Pentagon. A fellow pilot, actually."

"Who?"

"Major General John Austen."

"The evangelist?"

"I prefer to think of him as a friend of Israel." Ganz leaned closer to make sure that no one overheard their conversation. "He has intelligence pointing to an attack against our interests within the next twelve hours."

"Where?"

"Somewhere in Europe," said Ganz. He stared into Hirsch's bulging eyes. "I don't think we have long to wait."

"How will we find him?" Jonathan asked.

"Look in the backseat and get my laptop," said Emma.

Jonathan found the computer and turned it on. "Same password?"

"Same one. You know that you scared the hell out of everyone by cracking that code. They're going to have to redesign the entire Intelink system because of you."

"I don't know whether that's good or bad."

They were driving beside the Lake of Zurich. It was six o'clock. Lights sparkled along the hillside like a fairy-tale landscape. During the ride down the mountain, she'd finally opened up and began to talk. If she wouldn't tell him about everything she'd done in the past, she was more forthcoming about how she'd found him and about John Austen's plan to shoot down the plane. It was a first step in repairing the split between them.

Emma instructed him how to open the software program. The laptop's screen filled with a detailed map of Switzerland. She told him to enter the letters "VD."

A flashing red dot appeared near the outskirts of Zurich. The map zoomed in until it reached street level.

"What is it?" he asked.

"LoJack on steroids," said Emma. "I put a tracker on von Daniken's car three days ago. I needed to keep tabs on him. The signal from his car is sent to a satellite and bounced right back down to us."

"You've been busy."

Emma smiled cryptically. "Where is he?"

"Close."

"Glattbrugg?"

Jonathan studied the map. "How did you know?"

"Shit." Emma punched the accelerator.

81

"*Zurich Air Traffic*, this is El Al 8851 heavy commencing initial approach."

"Roger El Al 8851. You are cleared for approach. Proceed to vector one-seven-zero and descend to altitude ten thousand four hundred. You are number six in the grid."

"Copy."

The Pilot listened to the communications between Zurich air control and El Al Flight 8851 with anticipation.

Shutting his eyes, he whispered a last prayer. He asked for His guidance and a steady hand. He prayed for the courage to see the job done. He was not an evil man. Faced with taking more than six hundred lives, he trembled. He knew that Christ had felt the same as he bore the cross upon his shoulders. Their deaths would be as painful to him as the Crucifixion.

"It's time," said John Austen.

He walked into the garage. His men had removed the coffins from their storage lockers and rolled the steel containers to the center of the floor. With the precision of a pit crew, the team assembled the drone. The wheel struts came first, set down and locked onto the fuselage. The long, flexible wing sections were bolted to one another, then attached to the fuselage. Austen rolled the cradle holding the nacelle and its contents of twenty kilos of Semtex plastic explosive beneath the aircraft and fixed it to the UAV's belly.

"Fly well," he said, brushing his fingers against the drone's steel flesh.

He returned to the living room with its view of the airport. One wall of the living room was given over to his instruments. Monitors for the radar and nose camera. Flat-panel arrays broadcasting speed, altitude, position over ground. In the center of the array was a keyboard with a joystick positioned to either side. He climbed into the seat and spent a moment getting comfortable.

"Engines on," he called as he flipped on the ignition. A red light blinked five times, before burning steadily. Though he was not inside the drone, he could feel it shudder as it came to life. A thread of excitement ran along his spine. He'd waited twenty-eight years for this moment. The date was inscribed in his mind, no different than a plaque at a historic site. April 24, 1980.

Operation Eagle Claw.

He, John Austen, then a major in the United States Air Force, had been chosen to fly the lead Hercules C-130 into the Iranian desert on the first leg of a desperate, overly ambitious plan to rescue fifty-three hostages from the United States embassy in Teheran. Aboard were seventy-four members of the newly created Special Operations detachment trained by Colonel Charlie Beckwith and led by Lieutenant Colonel William "Jerry" Boykin.

The flight into the desert had gone according to plan, the only incident being a period of seven minutes when the plane had passed through a haboob, a blinding dust storm in the Dasht-e-Kariv, the Great Salt Desert, that spanned four hundred miles in the southwestern corner of the country. The plane negotiated the dust storm well enough, the turboprop engines holding up despite the onslaught of grit and sand. He landed without problem at a preordained spot christened Desert One. Eight Sea Stallion helicopters followed, inbound from the aircraft carrier USS **Nimitz** in the Arabian Sea. The choppers were to ferry the elite soldiers into Teheran, where they would free the diplomats and bring them back to Austen's aircraft for the return flight across the Persian Gulf to Saudi Arabia.

Disaster soon struck.

One of the helicopters landed disabled, its hydraulics severely damaged by the same dust storm that Austen had himself flown through. Another had turned back in mid-flight, lost and fearing a systems failure. With only six functioning helicopters instead of the eight planned, there would not be enough space to carry all of the rescued hostages out of Teheran. The mission was called off.

As one of the helicopters took off, its rotor wash stirred the fine desert sand into a maelstrom. Blinded, the pilot lost his bearings and flew into Austen's C-130, parked fifty meters away. The chopper's rotor blades sliced through the Hercules main stabilizer. Unbalanced, the helicopter toppled over the aircraft, gushing fuel and engulfing the plane beneath it in a fierce inferno.

Austen remembered the unexpected jolt to his plane, the burst of anger and confusion—**What the hell's the problem now?** he'd wondered—the thoughts seared by a blinding flash and cauterized by a wave of intense heat that in the blink of an eye had swallowed him entirely. Strapped into his seat, the flames licking at his flesh, he repeated the words, "I'm dead, I'm dead."

But he wasn't dead. Unstrapping himself from his seat, he clawed his way out of the inferno. He walked out of the wreckage, his flight suit, his hair, his entire being engulfed in flame. An apparition from hell.

Several troopers knocked him to the ground and rolled him in the hard desert sand, extinguishing the fire.

He woke up inside a helicopter taking him to the USS **Enterprise**. A navy corpsman was hunched over him. Austen reached up and grasped the cross dangling from the corpsman's neck. A jolt of salvation ran from his hand up his arm and through his body. Light surrounded him. Not flame, this time, but a healing light. In that moment, Austen saw Him. He saw the Lord, his Savior. He listened to His words and he promised to obey them. He knew that he would live. He had been given a mission to fulfill.

He, John Austen, who had not set foot inside a church since his confirmation at the age of thirteen, a user of alcohol, a womanizer who trampled on the sacred vows of marriage, a gambler who took the Lord's name in vain, a heathen in all senses of the word, had been chosen to usher in the Second Coming of his almighty Lord, Jesus Christ.

That was twenty-eight years ago.

Austen ran through his preflight check. Ailerons. Flaps. Oil. Antifreeze. The nose camera came to life. He was presented with a view of the street outside his home. A series of lights had been set down on either side of the runway to act as boundary markers.

He pressed the throttle and the drone edged forward.

The **Mahdi I** was ready to fly.

82

Inside the command center, von Daniken put the binoculars to his eyes and studied the residence from behind the protection of lace curtains. The home purchased by the Excelsior Trust was located at Holzwegstrasse 33. It was a sturdy two-story residence designed without the least imagination. An ivory stucco box with a gray slate roof. A garden surrounded the property. A balcony extended from one of the bedrooms on the second floor. But what interested von Daniken most was the road passing in front of it. Cleared of snow, it ran straight and level for five hundred meters. To his eye, it made the perfect runway.

He moved his binoculars to the left. A stand-alone shed occupied a corner of the property. It didn't appear large enough to house the drone, but then again, Brigadier General Chabert had told them that the drone could be assembled quickly. Otherwise, the house appeared quiet, giving no clue to any activity within.

The airport security fence began hardly ten meters away. In one direction, it climbed a mild rise then turned north and ran in a straight line for three kilometers bordering a lush evergreen forest. In the other direction, it cut through a broad meadow buried in snow. Farther on, the meadow yielded to a vast apron of concrete lit by tall, blinding lights. The southernmost edge of Zurich Airport.

Somewhere a plane was taking off. The noise grew in volume as the aircraft approached. Within seconds, the roar of the engines had drowned out every other sound.

He lowered the binoculars and returned to the dining room. "They chose well. No neighbors. A good view of the airport. Unobstructed line of sight."

"And not just of the airport," added a short, stocky man with curly black hair and a gambler's pencil-thin mustache. His name was Michael Berger. He was captain of the Zurich police department's special assault team. It would be Berger who would be first in the door to storm the house. "Whoever's inside will be able to see us coming for one hundred meters. How many do you reckon there are?"

"We don't know for certain, but we're estimating that there are at least five. There may be more."

"Armed?"

"Count on it. They're professionals. They took possession of twenty kilos of Semtex-H plastic explosives a few weeks ago that're almost certainly in the drone."

Berger nodded grimly, his eyes calculating his odds of success and survival. "We'll go in from the air. Two choppers. Rope down our team. We'll time it to coincide with the takeoff of a passenger jet. The helicopters are equipped with engine baffles that permit them to fly in near total silence. We'll send a second team up the main road and hit the house from the front. Your friends won't hear a peep until we break down the doors. The entire operation should take less than sixty seconds."

Von Daniken made a show of studying the drawings. "How many times have you done this?"

Berger squinted his eyes. "Never. But we do a very good job in practice."

Von Daniken could only nod.

"We'll be ready in forty minutes," said Berger. "Let's say seven-twenty."

The men synchronized their watches.

Von Daniken strode to the front window where Myer had taken up position with the binoculars. "Has anyone in the neighborhood seen or heard anything?"

"Apparently, there's been a lot of activity in the place the last few days. Men coming and going. Cars zooming up and down the street, parking in front of the house."

"Any sign of the van?"

"Everything except the van."

Captain Berger signaled from the back door that it was time to move out. Von Daniken joined him and they jogged to a waiting van and pulled the door closed behind them.

It was a two-minute drive to the local firehouse where Berger's men were staging. Two Aérospatiale Écureuil helicopters sat on a soccer field adjoining it, their rotors turning slowly.

Inside the firehouse, the tension was palpable as the policemen pulled on midnight blue jumpsuits and Kevlar body armor, followed by nylon harnesses to hold their equipment: radio, grenades, ammunition. This was not practice.

There were twenty-five assault troops in all. It was not as young a group as von Daniken might have hoped for, and he observed more than one officer struggling to secure his vest over a sizable paunch. The standard armament was a compact submachine gun, the Heckler & Koch MP-5. Two men hefted large, ungainly rifles called Wingmasters, used to blow doors off their hinges.

Von Daniken's two-way radio crackled. It was Myer. "Lights just went on inside the house."

"Lights on in the house," boomed Berger to his team.

The room reeked of sweat and anxiety.

"Any conversation?" asked von Daniken.

One of the tech teams had trained a laser microphone at the target's windows. The device was able to read vibrations in the glass caused by persons speaking inside the home and translate them back into something approximating the original sound.

"Television's on," responded Myer. "Let's hope they keep the volume nice and loud."

Berger divided his men into two squads, eight men each, with eight in reserve. "I need an official green light."

"You've got it." Von Daniken extended his hand and wished him good luck.

Berger turned and went back to his men. "We go in five minutes," he called out.

Von Daniken set off to the command post along a path that skirted the forest. He looked into the sky. It was a beautiful night, a velvet curtain punched through with stars, a crescent moon hanging low in the sky. The time was 7:16. Night had fallen. Behind him, he heard Berger ordering his men into the helicopters. He dug his hands into his pockets and quickened his pace.

"Von Daniken."

He halted, then turned in a circle, trying to locate the speaker. But nobody was there.

A tall, broad-shouldered man emerged from the shadows.

"My name is Jonathan Ransom. I believe you're looking for me."

83

Jonathan approached the policeman, holding his hands away from his body to show that he was unarmed, just as Emma had coached him to do. "You need to stop your men," he said. "The people you're looking for are not in that house."

"They're not?" said von Daniken warily.

"No. And neither is the drone."

"Why are you telling me this?"

"Because I want to stop them, too. You've made a mistake. It's not me you've been looking for."

"Who is it, then?"

"It's me," said Emma, stepping from an arc of shadow behind the policeman. "Mr. Blitz and Mr. Lammers were my colleagues, not Jonathan's."

"I'm not certain I understand, Miss . . ."

"Mrs. Ransom," she said.

Von Daniken considered this. His eyes jumped

back and forth between them, and for a moment, it appeared that he'd caught their sense of desperation. "You're Emma Ransom," he said, pointing a finger at her as if unconvinced. "The woman who died in a climbing accident last Monday?"

"There was no accident."

"Apparently not."

Emma met his eye. The unspoken shorthand of one professional to another passed between them. She allowed him a moment to figure things out, then said, "Jonathan is not involved in this plot in any way. The policemen he killed were acting on our orders. They attacked my husband in order to take possession of certain items that belonged to me. Jonathan responded in self-defense. I can't elaborate any further except to say again that I'm the person you were looking for. Not my husband. You need to listen to me. You're targeting the wrong house. You're mounting an assault on the decoy."

"The decoy?" von Daniken said skeptically.

"Yes."

"How can you be certain?"

"Because I know where the real house is."

"We have to hurry," said Jonathan. "Call them off."

Von Daniken had the stolid, immovable air of an exhausted fighter marshaling his energies for one last fight. His lips moved, and Jonathan guessed that he was sorting between the dozens of questions plaguing him. They were, Jonathan knew, the same questions that had beleaguered him.

"Where's the drone?" von Daniken asked.

"It's being kept at a house on top of the hill. Lenkstrasse 4." Emma pointed to the foothills that rose five kilometers behind them.

"And it's set for tonight?"

"The El Al flight due in from Tel Aviv," she said.

On a far runway, an aircraft was preparing to take off. The shrill whistle of the powerful engines pierced the sky. Then, from somewhere closer, came a different noise, a lower frequency. Their faces lifted to the sky as two dull gray shapes skidded low overhead.

"Stop them," said Emma.

"How do I know I can trust you?"

"Because I'm here."

Von Daniken pulled his walkie-talkie from his jacket and brought it to his mouth. Before he could utter a word, the night erupted in a blur of blinding explosions, shattering glass, and staccato machine-gun fire. A flare burst to life and burned magnificently. Illuminated in its glare were the silhouettes of men rushing into the rear of the house.

Von Daniken began to run down the path. Jonathan and Emma followed close behind. They reached the command post and went in through the back door. A dozen men stood congregated in the living room, staring out the front window as the police band radio blared crazily.

"Den. Clear."

"Kitchen. Clear."

"Bedroom. Clear."

The voices spoke in controlled telegraphese. And then another burst of machine-gun fire.

"Man down!"

The control was gone. Voices stepped over each other in a mad stampede.

"Who is it?"

"A bad guy."

"Hold it . . . what the hell?"

"He's tied up."

"But he had a gun."

"Get the boss in here. Now!"

Von Daniken glared at Emma, but she showed him nothing. Her eyes were fixed on the radio.

The melee stopped as quickly as it had begun. They stood enveloped in silence, waiting for further word. A minute passed. On the street, a dog began to bark.

Suddenly, Berger's voice came on the radio. "Marcus, get in here."

Von Daniken pointed at Emma and Jonathan. "Stay here."

He walked purposefully down the center of the road. He wanted to run, but he was a division head of the Federal Police and he knew that doing so would appear unprofessional. Procedure was all that remained for him to cling to.

He took the stairs leading to the front door two at a time, ducking past troopers making their way out. Cordite fouled the air, burning his eyes. He went inside. All power to the home had been cut prior to the assault. The hallways were dark and choked with smoke. Von Daniken turned on his flashlight. Berger appeared out of a side room, his face blackened. "They knew we were coming," he said, leading the way into the living room. "It was a setup."

"What was?"

"Take a look."

Von Daniken cast his flashlight's beam onto the mass heaped in the center of the floor. Toppled onto his side was a man tied to a low-backed chair. A length of duct tape covered his mouth. More tape strapped a pistol to his hand. Blood from his chest formed a pool that was still advancing over the wooden floor. In death, his eyes were wide.

"We're trained to fire if we see a gun," said Berger.

Von Daniken stepped closer, feeling his body go numb, his mind rejecting what his eyes were telling him.

The dead man was Philip Palumbo.

"What else do you know about the drone?" asked von Daniken when he returned to the command post.

"There will be a team of no less than six," said Emma. "Four to assemble the drone and keep watch. One to act as flight controller, and the other to fly the plane. They'll be heavily armed."

Von Daniken strode to the window and looked at the hilltop. He knew the area, a wooded hillside holding the ruins of the ancient walls that had once surrounded the citadel of Zurich. As his eyes adjusted to the dark, a plane took off from the airport. It rose into the sky and banked hard to the right, passing directly over the spot.

He looked down the road. Berger's men were filing out of the house. There was no time to have them reassemble.

"Get the car," he ordered Hardenberg. He turned to Myer. "Do you have the flight schedule I asked for?"

Myer produced a set of papers from his jacket. Von Daniken studied the list of arrivals and departures. Arriving at 8:05. El Al Flight 8851 from Tel Aviv. He checked his watch. It was seven-thirty. He looked at Emma. "What else can you tell me?"

"There are two routes to the house," she said. "One approaches along the road that will serve as a runway. The other comes from the rear. I suggest we split into two teams. I'll go in the front."

Von Daniken looked at this arrogant, self-assured woman issuing him orders in his own country. Gall rose hot in the back of his throat. It was a younger man's gall and was inappropriate for a chief inspector. "Very well. Do you need a weapon?"

Emma tilted her head toward Jonathan. "Just for him." She waited until von Daniken had given her husband a pistol and two clips of ammunition, then continued. "There will be men posted around the house. Get as close as you can, then hit them with the lights and the siren. That should spook them. After the attack on the decoy, they won't be expecting us."

"The man in charge of this? Is his name Austen?" Emma didn't answer.

"Can you speak with him?" von Daniken continued. "Will he listen to you if you tell him that we have his compound surrounded?"

"No," said Emma. "He only listens to one voice."

"What do you mean?"

"Only that he won't stop. Not now."

Von Daniken radioed the SWAT captain with instructions to bring his men to Lenkstrasse by the rear route as quickly as possible and to expect gunfire.

Just then, Hardenberg pulled up in a white Audi police cruiser. Von Daniken opened the door. "Do you have a car?" he asked Emma Ransom.

"It's up the road in back," she answered.

"Good luck, then."

Von Daniken climbed into the rear of the Audi. Kurt Myer, hefting a Heckler & Koch submachine gun, sat in the passenger seat. "To tell you the truth, I haven't fired one of these in a while," he said, looking over his shoulder.

"How long?" asked von Daniken.

"Not ever."

"Give it to me."

Myer handed von Daniken the machine gun and

he chambered a round and set it to full automatic. "Aim and pull the trigger. You're bound to hit something. Just make sure it isn't one of us."

Myer grabbed the machine gun and set it on his lap.

"Pull up Lenkstrasse on your navigation unit," von Daniken said as the car accelerated.

Hardenberg input the address. A map appeared on the screen. Lenkstrasse was a ruler-straight stretch of road bordering the city park. The home in question sat at its northern end, at the point where it ran around the far side of the park. "Go the back way," said von Daniken.

The car negotiated the streets of Glattbrugg, crossing under the freeway before commencing a steep, curving climb up the hillside. Von Daniken called the airport. It took four minutes until he was connected to the tower. He identified himself. "What's the status of El Al 8851?"

"Coming in twenty minutes early," responded the flight controller. "Posted for a seven forty-five arrival."

Von Daniken eyed the onboard clock: 7:36. "Contact the pilot and tell him to abort the landing. We have a verified threat against the aircraft."

"He's sixty kilometers out on initial approach. He hasn't reported any problems. Are you sure?"

"We have every reason to believe there will be a ground-based attack directed against El Al Flight 8851."

"But I haven't had any notification from the head office . . ."

"Do it," said von Daniken in a quiet voice that brooked no defiance.

"Yes, sir."

Von Daniken hung up. **Sixty kilometers.** If the smaller drone he'd seen in Lammers's office had a range of fifty kilometers, one this size could go ten times as far. If they didn't succeed in stopping the unmanned aerial vehicle before it took off, it would be too late.

"There's a roadblock ahead," said Hardenberg.

"Go around it. You've got room on the shoulder."

"Should I hit the siren?"

"Wait till we're closer."

Hardenberg eased the Audi off the road and onto the snow and hardscrabble alongside it. The car rocked gently. "Easy, easy."

"No problem," said Myer as the Audi regained the pavement. "I told—"

The windshield exploded, showering the cabin with glass. Bullets raked the car. A tire blew, and the Audi sagged to one side. The radiator exploded in a hiss of steam.

"Get down!" shouted von Daniken. A moment later, he was struck by something warm and wet. He wiped his face, and his hands came away coated with gore. Kurt Myer lay twisted between the seats, his face a pulp of bone and gristle.

Hardenberg threw open the door and commando-crawled to the rear of the vehicle. Von Daniken eased open the door, counted to three, then scrambled into the forest. He threw himself to the ground, his face buried in the snow.

The gunfire died down, an occasional shot flicking ice into the air.

"Call Captain Berger," he yelled to Hardenberg.

"My phone's in the car."

Von Daniken felt in his pockets. He'd dropped his own phone somewhere during his unceremonious exit. He drew his service pistol and fumbled with it until he'd managed to chamber a round and make sure that the safety was off. He swore under his breath. His watch read 7:42. He picked up a new noise coming from the top of the hill. It was the drone's jet engine coming to life.

He looked around him. The house was thirty meters directly uphill from him. It was a modern building, cantilevered over the hillside, supported by great steel pylons. The windows were dark, lending it an abandoned feel. He knew better.

He raised his head for a clearer view. A bullet struck a tree ten centimeters away. He dug his cheek into the snow. Night vision goggles. Of course. How else could they see him in this damned dark?

"Run down the hill," he said to Hardenberg. "You've got to warn the others."

Hardenberg sat with his back pressed to the rear bumper, his face bluer than ice. "Okay," he said, but he didn't budge.

"Stay behind the car and they won't be able to hit you," von Daniken went on.

Hardenberg stirred. He swallowed and his shoulders gave a giant shrug. He set off, crawling on all fours backwards down the road. Von Daniken watched him retreat. Five steps. Ten. **Stay down,** he urged silently. Hardenberg crawled a few more meters, then raised his head tentatively.

"Low," von Daniken whispered, patting the air, signaling for him to keep down.

Hardenberg misinterpreted the motion and began to stand.

"No," shouted von Daniken at the top of his lungs. "Get down!"

Hardenberg nodded hesitantly and continued to walk down the hill. A bullet struck him in the head and he collapsed onto the cement.

"Klaus!"

Von Daniken rolled onto his back, sick with himself.

84

Captain Eli Zuckerman adjusted the trim on his ailerons and eased back the throttle as a prelude to disengaging the autopilot. Flying a passenger jet had become so automated that once a plane's onboard computers were programmed with a particular flight's data—destination, cruising altitude, maximum allowable ground speed—the aircraft could literally fly itself. The only time Zuckerman felt himself in full control of the aircraft was during takeoff and landing, a total of thirty minutes per flight. The rest of the time, he was basically a technician monitoring all the instruments and making sure that his first officer kept up with ground communication. It wasn't exactly the job he'd dreamed of when he'd left the air force so many years ago as a red-hot fighter jock with twenty-one kills during three wars.

Zuckerman hit the disengage button. The plane

shuddered and dipped as he took manual control. Easing the yoke left, the A380 began a gentle turn to the south. It was a clear night, ideal flying weather. He could see the city's lights in the distance, and farther off behind it, a great black emptiness that was the Alps. He trimmed the flaps and the aircraft began its slow descent to Zurich Flughafen.

"Sixteen minutes to touchdown," said his copilot.

Zuckerman stifled a yawn. As expected, it had been an uneventful flight. He checked his watch—fifteen minutes to landing—then glanced at the first officer. "So, Benny," he said. "What are you thinking for dinner? Wiener schnitzel or fondue?"

"El Al 8851 heavy, this is Zurich Air Traffic. We have an emergency. Code 33. Divert to Basel-Mulhouse, vector two-seven-niner. Climb to thirty thousand feet. You are advised to use all possible haste."

Code 33. A ground-to-air attack.

"Roger. Code thirty-three. El Al 8851 heavy proceeding on vector two-seven-niner. Climbing to thirty thousand feet. Do you have radar contact of that bogey?"

"Negative, El Al 8851. No radar contact as yet."

"Thank you, Zurich."

Eli Zuckerman tightened his shoulder harness and shared a worried look with his first officer. Taking the yoke firmly in his hand, he banked the aircraft hard to port and pushed the throttle forward. The aircraft surged ahead.

It was time to see what this baby could do.

85

"*Mahdi I, all systems green.* You are cleared for takeoff. May God be with you."

Major General John Austen ran up the engine. The RPMs of the Williams turbofan jet rose smoothly. He released the brake and the drone began to roll down the runway.

Over the headset, he heard the crackle of fireworks. On the screen to his left, he saw sparks flying. No, not sparks. These were muzzle blasts from his men's weapons. A voice came over his headset. "Police."

"Keep them away."

As Austen powered the throttle and the drone began to roll down the runway, he felt a surge of pride and accomplishment. He had done it. He had fulfilled the mission entrusted to him. Israel, in rightful possession of the Holy Land, was gearing up for attack. Iran itself was properly armed. The Forces of Gog and Magog were set to do battle on the plains of Armageddon.

In brilliant detail, he envisioned how the conflict would unfold, all according to God's plan.

Israel's bombing offensive would fail.

Iran would retaliate with the Kh-55 cruise missiles in its arsenal, missiles whose sale he had personally brokered. The nuclear weapons armed with ten-kiloton warheads would fall upon Tel Aviv, but not upon Jerusalem itself. The Lord, in His power, would protect His holiest of cities. The Americans would, in turn, fall upon Iran. The Fundamentalist Islamic Republic would cease to exist.

All was in place for the Lord's return. And the Rapture that would follow.

Austen blocked out the noise of the escalating gunfight, focusing his eyes, his concentration on the screen in front of him. The trees passed by with increasing rapidity. The runway lights were flashes. The speedometer read one hundred knots . . . one hundred ten . . . he eased the joystick back. The nose began to rise . . .

It was then that he saw it. A pair of headlights barreling toward the drone. A car where no car should be.

He grasped the joystick in his fist and pulled it back while punching the throttle.

"Fly!"

86

"Did you hear that?" Jonathan asked, alarmed.

Emma glanced in his direction. "What?"

He rolled down the window and craned his neck out of the car. "I'm not sure, but . . ." A loud pop cracked the air, followed by another. The sounds were tinny, toyish, like the cap guns he used to play with as a kid. "Gunshots. Can you hear them?"

Emma pulled the car to the side of the road halfway up the hill. A medieval forest cloaked the slope. Remnants of an ancient wall were visible close to the road, clawed basalt blocks splashed with lichen. Deep amongst the trees, the shots burst like fireflies.

"Von Daniken. That will keep them occupied." She shifted in her seat and leveled her gaze at him. "Are you certain you're prepared to do this?"

Jonathan nodded. He'd made the decision days ago.

"Switch seats," said Emma. "You drive. Unless, that is, you know how to shoot a gun."

Jonathan paused halfway out the door. "I was going to say you hate guns."

"I do."

The two crossed round the front of the car, their shoulders brushing. Jonathan slid into the driver's seat and adjusted it for his height. Emma closed the door and told him to get going. He noticed that she no longer looked so much the professional. Her face had lost its confident veneer and her breath was coming fast and hard. She was every bit as scared as he was.

He put the car into gear and accelerated up the slope. They'd hardly covered ten meters when their headlights illuminated a riot barrier spanning the road.

"Whatever you do," said Emma. "Don't stop."

The car gained speed, hurtling toward the barrier.

"Cut the lights," she said.

Jonathan doused the headlights. Darkness cloaked the road. He pushed his face closer to the windscreen. The top of the barrier was barely visible, a white line cutting through the heart of darkness. He floored it. The car smashed the barrier, spraying shards of wood everywhere. The road flattened out. Lanterns placed at even intervals on either side of it lit his path.

The sound of gunfire picked up, frighteningly close. A salvo of bullets struck the car like hail pounding a tin shack. A bullet shattered the wind-screen, leaving a large hole and a sagging web of glass. Wind rushed in. He caught sight of several fig-ures kneeling in the snow, their silhouettes flickering in the wake of their weapons' muzzle blasts.

"Keep going!" Emma leaned out the window, fir-ing at the shadows.

Then he saw it. A silver beast with tremendous wings and a large pod hanging from its belly.

"Emma!"

The drone was coming at them, advancing from the far end of the road.

"Faster," she said. "Ram it."

"But . . ." He looked at Emma. It was suicide.

"Do it!"

Jonathan downshifted into third gear and pushed the accelerator to the floor. The engine screamed as the burst of torque hurled the car ahead. The drone showed no sign of taking off. It came at them relent-lessly, a malevolent metallic insect. Emma was firing at the aircraft. He had no idea if her bullets were going home. His eyes focused on the teardrop-shaped pod attached to the fuselage. It was the bomb. Twenty kilos of Semtex, she'd told him. The equivalent of a thousand pounds of TNT. A bomb large enough to obliterate an airliner.

"Faster," said Emma, ducking her head into the cabin.

The drone's nose lifted off the ground, then

touched back down. Jonathan braced himself for impact, squinting in anticipation of the collision, the exquisite burst of light . . .

The drone began to take off. The nose rose into the air. The front wheels left the asphalt. It was no good. They were going to collide with it. Every instinct told him to brake. He grasped the wheel harder and pressed his foot into the floorboard.

He screamed.

A gleam of silver whisked over their heads.

It was gone. The drone was airborne.

A second later, one of the car's front tires exploded. The car bounded to the left, abandoning the paved road. Jonathan spun the wheel in the opposite direction, but it did no good. The snow was too deep. The car plowed ahead, speed bleeding rapidly. It hit an underlying patch of ice, and slid sideways, coming to a halt in a hollow between several oaks some twenty meters from the house.

Emma slapped the pistol into his right hand. "The man you want is inside the house. Find the controls and he'll be there. Don't bother talking to him. He won't stop until he's accomplished what he set out to do. You have eight bullets."

"What about you?"

"I'll stay here," she said. "When I start firing, run into the forest and circle the house. You can reach the terrace by climbing on pylons built into the hillside. From there, you'll have to find a way in."

It was then that he saw that she'd been shot. Her shoulder drooped strangely and blood was spreading across her jacket. "You're hurt."

"Go," she said, her eyes deflecting his concern. "Before they spot you."

Jonathan hesitated for a split second, then took off. Behind him, Emma stood and began firing at the house.

87

The power.

Von Daniken lay in the snow, beyond cold, beyond feeling. During the briefing two days earlier, he'd learned that the control apparatus for a drone consumed an enormous amount of electricity. If he cut the power to the house, the drone would be incapacitated. It might fly, but it would be rudderless. Sooner or later, it would run out of gas. Odds were that it would fall to earth and explode harmlessly in the countryside. Regardless of where it fell, it would not take six hundred lives.

Rolling onto his belly, he raised his head and searched the hillside. Bullets struck the ground in front of him, spraying ice and dirt into his eyes. He ducked, eating a mouthful of snow, but not before seeing the rectangular metal casing that governed electricity to the neighborhood.

The junction box sat a few meters away on a flat plot carved into the slope. A section of the ancient citadel wall occupied the ground above it. The large stone blocks would provide a measure of protection.

He pulled himself up the hill, burrowing through the deep snow. He was shivering uncontrollably. He rested after a few meters and lifted his head, ready to throw himself back down at any moment. Gunfire was more or less constant, but the shots were no longer aimed at him. They were coming from the other side of the hill. A different caliber, too. It was Ransom and his wife.

The sound of a jet engine came to life. He thought it impossible that a small aircraft could generate such a deafening noise. The noise changed pitch, growing higher, straining. The drone was taking off. He turned onto his side and looked into sky. For a moment, he caught sight of a silver blade whisking over the treetops.

Pushing himself to a crouch, von Daniken scuttled up the hillside. He didn't give a damn about seeking any kind of protection. He knew that he made an easy target, but the absence of gunfire spurred an irrational confidence within him. The house loomed ahead, looking like a concrete bunker. And then, suddenly, he was there.

He fell against the side of the box, panting. A padlock held it closed. He distanced himself from it, took aim with his pistol, and fired. The lock was obliterated. The junction box opened like a clamshell. He looked inside. A sticker warned him not to touch anything for fear of electrocution. A skull-and-bones decal drove the point home. He was confronted with a maze of wires, some woven together in dense, multicolored braids, others bound by protective rubber housing. It all looked terribly complex. He had expected there to be some kind of master switch he might throw. He craned his neck to get a better view.

The bullet caught him in the shoulder and spun him around. Before he knew what had hit him, he was lying facedown in the snow. He turned over, stunned, breathless, robbed of purpose. He lay there for a few seconds, while the circuitry in his own mind got itself sorted out.

Forcing himself to a knee, he aimed his pistol at the house and got off a few wild shots. The pistol's kick made him feel powerful and optimistic. He aimed at the junction box and emptied the clip into it. Nothing happened.

He tottered, and in his fuzzy mind, decided that the situation was absurd. The first time he'd fired his weapon in thirty years, and it was at a giant metal box. He eased himself to the ground. The snow at his feet was red. He tried to move his left arm, but it was frozen and had no feeling whatsoever. Suddenly, he found himself fixated by the snow.

Water, he thought.

He didn't need a gun to do the job.

Reaching into the box with both hands, he grabbed a bundle of wires and yanked them free. A flurry of sparks drizzled to the ground. One wire in particular fired a steady blue pulse. He picked up a handful of snow with his good hand and lobbed it into the junction box. The wire sizzled, then continued to spark. He didn't know what to expect, but surely that wasn't it.

He felt around inside the box until his hand came to a larger bundle, a tube the size of a police baton. He pulled at it repeatedly. Finally, it tore loose, exposing a fountain of frayed copper wiring.

As he stared at the wires, he thought of the drone and the plane from Israel. He knew that the plane had no chance of escaping the drone, just as a man, however frightened, could not outswim a shark. Then he thought of Philip Palumbo, lying there in the dark, riddled with holes.

Von Daniken scooped up more snow. This time, however, he pushed it onto the exposed wires and packed it down. There was a smart, crackling noise, then silence.

For a moment, he was sure that he'd failed, but then a surge ran up his arms and into his chest. His back arched in spasm. He opened his mouth to scream, but his throat was paralyzed by the voltage coursing through his body. With a last effort, he yanked his hands clear of the snow. Something exploded in his chest and he was flung violently backward through the air.

Jonathan ran in a line perpendicular to the car, dodging through the trees. The snow was deep and uneven, making the going difficult. Twice he tumbled to his knees and had to struggle to pull himself clear. After fifty meters, he veered to his right along a track parallel to the road. He quickly found the remains of the Roman-era wall that had once protected the city. He hopped over it and, crouching, followed it to the rear of the house.

The home was cantilevered over the slope. Twin steel pylons anchored in the mountainside rose at a forty-five-degree angle to support the structure. Reaching the pylons, he stopped and cocked his head. The gunfire had ceased. The silence that took its place was just as ominous. From the crest of the hill, he heard several motors turning over, and at least one car leave some rubber behind.

The pylons were slick and wet and deadly cold. They were hard enough to hold on to, let alone climb. Wrapping his arms around one, he shimmied up the incline. By the time he reached the top, his hands burned with cold and his clothing was soaking wet. Wedging his knee into the gap between the foundation and the pylon, he stood and extended his hand onto the balcony. With a breath and a prayer, he swung clear and reached up with his other hand and pulled himself onto the terrace.

The sliding door was locked.

He stepped back and fired into the glass door. The window shattered and a shard landed on his ankle, embedding itself. Wincing, he pulled it clean. Blood welled up, filling his shoe.

The house was silent. No lights burned anywhere. If there had been any guards, they'd abandoned ship. He was aware only of a low-frequency thrum given off by an electrical current of some kind. He crossed the room and entered a corridor. A door at the far end barred his passage. A numeric keypad governed entrance. He fired at the lock. It did no good. The lock and door were both made of steel.

Putting his ear to the door, he made out a low hum and could feel a vibration against his cheek. Suddenly, the humming died. The vibration calmed. The entire structure went as still as if it had been unplugged.

Jonathan's eyes shot to the keypad. The pinlight was blinking green where before it had burned red.

The power had gone out.

He threw his hand to the door and turned the knob.

It opened.

Leading with the pistol, he walked into what could only be called an operations center. To his left, a picture window looked out over the Zurich Airport. Directly ahead, an array of instruments and monitors rose from the ground to the ceiling. A man sat in a chair, his back to him, his hand on a joystick. It would be John Austen.

A few feet away, another man was working feverishly at a bank of controls.

"Auxiliary power on," said the second man, who, Emma had told him, would be the flight engineer. "Satellite connection reestablished. We have picture." He looked up and saw Jonathan and aimed a pistol at him. Jonathan shot him twice. The man fell back against the wall.

Jonathan approached the pilot. "Step away from the controls."

The pilot didn't answer. The hand controlling the joystick moved to the right. The screen in front of him emitted an eerie green glow. At first, Jonathan wasn't able to make out anything. Looking closer, he observed a gray shape looming in the distance. The shape was gaining in definition. Now he could see a head and tail and a host of pinpricks that were the lights from passenger windows. It was the jet as seen by an infrared camera.

Jonathan's eyes moved to the radar screen. The two blips at its center were incredibly close to one another. The letters beneath one read, "El Al 8851H." The other blip had no designation.

"I said, step away from the controls."

"You're too late," said John Austen.

He won't stop until he's accomplished what he set out to do, Emma had said. **Believe me, I know him.**

Jonathan walked up to him, placed the gun to the nape of his neck, and pulled the trigger.

The pilot slumped forward.

Jonathan pushed his body out of the seat.

The image of the plane was closer now. He could make out a wing and the outline of the fuselage and the landing lights flashing. All impossibly close.

Jonathan shoved the joystick forward.

The image of the plane grew closer still. He was too late. The drone was going to strike the aircraft. A red light on the console was blinking. **Proximity fuse armed.** He looked at the radar. The two blips merged as one. Then back at the camera. The plane filled the entire screen.

Reflexively, he braced for impact.

Just then, the plane darted out of view. The screen went dark. Jonathan looked at the radar. The blip bearing the designation El Al 8851H was still there. Moments later, the second blip reappeared. The distance between the two aircraft had widened.

He kept the joystick pointed down, as the drone flew into the darkness.

He located the altimeter on the console and watched the numbers fall from twenty-seven thousand feet to twenty to ten, and then, to zero.

The picture dissolved in a blizzard of white noise.

Jonathan found Emma slumped in the passenger seat. She was conscious, but barely.

"I tried to stop him," he said. "But he wouldn't listen."

She nodded, and motioned for him to come closer. "He never listened to anyone," she whispered.

Jonathan peered into the abandoned woods. "Where did they go?"

"They're ghosts. They don't exist."

He took her hand. Her grip was weak and cold. "I need to get you to a hospital."

"The world thinks I'm dead. I can't go to a hospital."

"You need surgery to take out that bullet."

"You're a doctor. You can look after me."

Jonathan eased the seat back and examined her wound. The bullet had passed through her upper arm and lodged itself in the flesh below her shoulder blade. "You stopped the attack. You can come in now."

Emma shook her head, a forlorn smile tracing her lips. "I broke ranks. There's only one punishment for that."

"But Austen was acting on his own . . ."

"I'm not so sure." Emma shifted in the seat. "Anyway, it doesn't matter. Division's like the Hydra. Cut off its head and ten more grow in its place. They'll need to make an example."

Jonathan grasped her hand more tightly.

"They'll be watching you," she said, her voice stronger. She was an agent again. She'd been trained for this. "They'll suspect you had help. There's no way you could have found the drone on your own. Sooner or later, they'll find out what really happened. Someone will go into the mountains and discover that I didn't really have an accident. I made mistakes. I left tracks."

"I'll go with you."

"It doesn't work that way."

Jonathan stared at her, unable to bring himself to speak.

Emma reached up and touched his cheek. "We have a few days until they start looking."

The seesaw whine of sirens sounded from down the hill. Jonathan turned and saw the blue lights flashing in the forest as they neared the house. A police car pulled up in front of the driveway. Marcus von

Daniken climbed out, his right arm in a sling. He walked over to them. "Did you stop it?"

"Yes," said Jonathan.

"Thank God."

Jonathan gestured toward the house. "There are two men inside."

"Dead?"

Jonathan nodded. Von Daniken considered this. He looked at Emma. "Who are you?"

"You'll know soon enough," she said.

"I'll call an ambulance," said the policeman.

"I can take care of her," said Jonathan.

Von Daniken ran a hand over the bullet holes puncturing the hood. He tossed a set of car keys to Jonathan. "It's a blue VW. I left it in back of the command house. Take it and get out of here."

"Thank you," said Emma.

"You owe me." The Swiss turned and walked haltingly toward the house.

More police cars were arriving by the second. A helicopter swooped low and hovered overhead, its spotlight trained on the scene.

Jonathan reached into the car and lifted his wife into his arms.

"My name's Jonathan," he said.

"My name's Cary. Nice to meet you."

He turned and carried her down the hill.

EPILOGUE

The planes of Israel's 69 Squadron attacked at dawn. They came in low over the water beneath Iranian radar. The newly installed antiaircraft systems had only seconds to see them. By the time the first missiles were launched, it was too late. The bombs struck their target with deadly accuracy. In minutes, sixteen conventionally armed bunker busters had completed their job. The missile facility at Karshun on the Persian Gulf had been wiped from the map. Deep inside a fortified weapons magazine ten meters below ground, the four Kh-55 cruise missiles, each armed with a ten-kiloton nuclear warhead, were obliterated.

Operation Nightingale was a success.

Inside the prime minister's office, the relief was palpable, if temporary. The state of Israel no longer had to worry about being annihilated without warning. The threat to its existence had been quelled, its borders secured. For the moment.

In the wake of the attack, evidence about the true nature of Iran's nuclear enrichment program was made public. World leaders roundly condemned the Islamic Republic and called for an immediate cessation of its nuclear enrichment program. The United States went a step further and issued an ultimatum calling on Teheran to turn over all of its weapons-grade uranium within seventy-two hours or else risk a military reprisal. The government in Teheran waffled, but finally acceded to the demands rather than risk a repeated embarrassment.

Only Zvi Hirsch knew the identity of the person who had provided his country the detailed information about Iran's entire nuclear program and caused the raid to be diverted from Chalus to Karshun. And he wasn't telling.

As he crossed the street from the prime minister's residence, he tossed the small flash drive in his hand.

It was amazing what these computer wizards could do.

ACKNOWLEDGMENTS

A number of individuals gave generously of their time to help with the writing of this book. In particular, I would like to thank Dr. Doug Fischer, Special Agent with the California Department of Justice, Andreas Tobler and Andreas Janka of the Graubunden Kantonspolizei, Juerg Siegfried Buehler of the Swiss Federal Police, Hansueli Brunner, the finest mountain guide in Switzerland (and, I'm proud to say, my cousin), Gary Schroen, Nick Paumgarten, Jack Shaw, Arnaud de Borchgrave, and others in the intelligence community who because of their positions do not wish to be named.

At Doubleday, I would like to thank my editor, Stacy Creamer, for her enthusiasm, insight, and support. Also, my thanks go to Bill Thomas, John Pitts, Todd Doughty, Alison Rich, Suzanne Herz, and Janet Cooke. Finally, I want to give a special thank-you to Steve Rubin, who sets the standard for class in the publishing industry.

There are several persons who deserve a longer mention. Foremost is my agent, Richard Pine, who stood by me every step of the way during the writing of this book. I cannot begin to express my gratitude for his devotion to the manuscript, his criticism and suggestions, and, mostly, his tireless encouragement. It's not an exaggeration to say that an author is only as good as his agent, and I am blessed to be represented by the very best. Richard, thank you.

Elisa Petrini of InkWell Management was another key member of the Rules "team." Elisa is a fantastic reader and editor. I can't thank her enough for her many invaluable insights during the shaping of the manuscript.

Also at InkWell, I'd like to thank Susan Hobson, Libby O'Neill, and of course, Michael Carlisle and Kim Witherspoon.

In England, my thanks go to Peter Robinson.

Last, and most important, I want to thank my wife, Sue, and my daughters, Noelle and Katja, for their love and support. You make it all worthwhile. I have to point out that Sue is an early reader of all my work. I rely heavily on her judgment about whether a book works or not (and frankly on just about everything). If I don't say it enough at home, "Thank you, sweetheart, for showing the interest and taking the time."

ABOUT THE AUTHOR

CHRISTOPHER REICH is the **New York Times** best-selling author of **Numbered Account** and **The Patriots Club,** the latter of which won the International Thriller Writers Award for Best Novel in 2006. He lives in Southern California with his wife and children.